THE BATTLE FOR KORELIA

HORIZON OF WAR

BOOK 2

THE BATTLE FOR KORELIA

HANNE

THE BATTLE FOR KORELIA

Nom
Caladania
Tarraca
Kehldin
Cen
Elven Satrapy
Th
Hum
Sarmatia
Elearis
Halicia
Ekionia
Beastmen Con

PEOPLE
Province of Brigandia
Province of Arminia
Inglesia
Tiberia
Arvena
Rhomelia
MERCANTILE KINGDOM
ERIUM
Midlandia
Elandia
Korimor
Umberland
Ornietia
Edessa
Three Hills
White Lake
Korelia
Salceslia
South Hill
Galdia
Corinthia
Lowlandia Plains
NAVALNIA EMPIRE
ola
ATI
The Great Marshes

CHAPTER 1

THE GUILD REP

Korelia

The midday sun had just reached its zenith, casting a warm glow that bathed the land in golden light, and the air was alive with the sweet fragrance of freshly bloomed wildflowers. Lansius was just returning from a memorable visit with a nomadic family he met while riding, who welcomed him into their yurt.

Now, his black destrier carried him with power and speed through the verdant fields. The wind ruffled Lansius's black hair and fur coat as he allowed his horse to gallop to her heart's content on the final stretch toward Korelia Castle. From afar, the castle's walls and towering main keep beckoned them, its imposing structure visible from tens of miles away.

As he approached, the main gates came alive with the movement of guards and soon creaked open heavily. Lansius passed through the gatehouse and rode into the courtyard, where, unexpectedly, Calub was waiting for him.

"You're here? Will you be joining us for supper?" Lansius asked as he dismounted. A horse master immediately stepping forward to take care of his temperamental warhorse.

"The Mason Guild representative has arrived," Calub reported.

"Finally," Lansius remarked, now surrounded by page boys ready with drinks, clean boots, or a change of clothes. "Gratitude. I'm fine. Go help Sterling. He might need some assistance."

As if on cue, Sterling and the rest of the guards, riding horses less impressive than Lansius's destrier, arrived. The page boys hurried toward the dashing squire, eager to assist, even before Sterling had dismounted.

Lansius observed that Sterling was particularly popular among the younger staff, especially the female servants who seemed to fawn over him. The thought brought a chuckle to him as he walked with Calub. To avoid having to explain his amusement, he asked, "What do you think about the representative?"

"He seems capable. The Midlandia Mason Guild isn't known for doing things by halves," the reliable alchemist-turned-advisor responded.

"Now let's see just how well he can fix this castle," Lansius remarked.

"And whether our pockets will permit it," Calub said, much to the amusement of Lansius, as they bypassed the great hall and went straight to the inner part of the castle.

The reason for inviting the masons was Korelia's frigid winter and the castle's appalling heating. Despite having spent much on salt purchases, armor, weaponry, and delicate parts for crossbows, the castle was in dire need of repair. Several rooms had holes in the walls exposed to the elements, leaks in the roof, and inadequate fireplaces or nonexistent heating. Lansius felt the need to improve his staff's living conditions, believing that people were the most important assets or resources, not just the physical structures.

However, Lansius's enthusiasm was dashed a few minutes after their introduction.

Mason Caine, who looked more like an accountant, with neatly combed hair and a sharp nose, sat relaxed in his padded chair. He used a handkerchief to wipe his lips after taking a sip of ale. "The guild has records of this castle, and it's quite old," he said while looking at the ceiling. "I'm afraid our options are very limited, my lord."

"Couldn't you conduct a survey first before deciding?" Calub suggested, trying to persuade him.

"Certainly, Master Calub, but I prefer not to raise false hopes."

"Fair enough. I look forward to your assessment," Lansius replied warmly, seemingly concluding the conversation. Yet, he had more to discuss. "Maester Caine, if you will, could you tell me whether the guild also possesses a record of the layout of this castle?"

Caine shook his head. "The schematics with the layout were always made, kept, and destroyed on-site upon completion. Otherwise, the nobility could pressure us to reveal our work on their adversaries' defenses."

Lansius nodded. "What about the siege of Orniteia Castle? I heard the attackers breached it very quickly by attacking its weakest point. They didn't even need tunneling."

Caine smiled, making his sharp jaw even more prominent. "I assure you, we had no part in that matter."

"Aside from how Midlandia awarded your guild a contract to enlarge two castles?" pried Lansius.

"The timing was most unfortunate, but it had nothing to do with us," Caine replied, the same smile still on his lips.

Lansius smiled, looked around the chamber, sensing its archaic design, and asked, "I know a bit about design. May I ask what the main problem is in at least fixing the heating issue?"

"I may be able to apply the Centuria technique to install several pipes from the main fireplace to adjacent rooms, but that could take months and cause problems from all the chiseling on the stone structure."

"You don't have to chisel the stone. Just place the pipes hanging on the wall."

Caine was surprised by the answer and for a moment couldn't process what he heard.

Lansius continued. "Speak candidly. I won't be offended; otherwise, many details will be lost, and we'll be wasting time for nothing."

"My lord, the aesthetics would be ruined. The pipes, unfortunately, are unsightly, not to mention dangerous, due to the heat and potential leaks."

"I don't mind. Unburied pipes are easy to fix. I prefer an ugly, functional solution rather than freezing in a beautiful chamber."

Calub chuckled as he watched the mason's baffled reaction and added, "The Lord of Korelia is a man who values function over form."

Caine's usual smile returned to his lips. It seemed he was starting to like the new Lord of Korelia. "If that's what my lord wishes for, I think it can be arranged."

"Can it be done before this winter? I also need a similar system for the workshop in town," asked Lansius.

"Heaters for workshops?" Caine was uncertain. "It would be dangerous if they're made of wood."

"We'll quarry small stones for the flooring. Korelia's winter is far too long, and a lot of time will be spent doing nothing. I want a communal workshop where people can gather and work on their winter crafts."

Caine nodded in understanding. "It should be easy to install. But, my lord, are you sure about the cost?"

"Make an offer on paper, and we'll discuss it. I'm aware that metal pipes take a long time to produce and transport; can you install it before winter?"

"I'll try, my lord, but . . ."

"Speak openly," Lansius reassured him.

The mason sighed softly and explained, "Working in Lowlandia is inherently dangerous, especially in a fief that has just recently experienced a change of power. There are rumors that Korelia will soon be engulfed in a war. Because of that, it's difficult to convince skilled workers to come here."

Lansius nodded his head lightly and said, "It's not that big a deal. I'll win the war. In fact, I'm hoping they come so I can use their baggage train to fund more projects."

Caine seemed impressed by the bold answer and appeared to appreciate Lansius's straightforward manner, which was more akin to that of a tradesman than a noble. "Your words please me, my lord," Caine responded, a genuine respect in his voice. "I shall do my best to assist you and Korelia."

"One more thing," Lansius said, trying to find the right words. "Do you have a device to spin fleece with a wheel?"

"Spin fleece with a wheel, my lord?" Caine squinted.

Lansius nodded. "Yes, a device that can spin fleece into yarn almost effortlessly. I have those in my homeland. The device makes clothing so cheap that everyone can afford it."

Now, everyone was intrigued, even Calub.

He continued. "I can describe roughly how this device works if you can secure the rights and trade secrets."

"Leave it to me. I know just the master carpenter for this kind of work," Caine replied in a heartbeat.

"My lord, a word, please," Calub requested after the Mason Guild representative had retired to his guest room.

"Yes, speak freely," replied Lansius, as they were the only ones left in the Great Chamber. The only attendant they had was escorting the guest.

"Do you truly know about such a device?" Calub inquired.

"The spinning wheel?" asked Lansius. Seeing Calub nod, he explained, "Yes, the device does exist, and I plan to make many of them. The problem is I know what it looks like and have a general idea of how it works, but not the specific mechanism."

"H-how efficient is that thing? Is it faster than two women working together to spindle the yarn?"

"Probably much faster," Lansius ventured. "With that device, one person can produce as much as ten times the yarn."

Calub was left speechless. "My lord, Lans, why didn't you tell me you knew about such a thing? We could have started making one when we were in Midlandia."

Lansius hesitated, then scratched his head. "Well, today something just reminded me of it. You see, I rode south earlier and met a lovely shepherd family who gave me a remarkable shawl. I've never felt anything quite like it."

"And where is this shawl, my lord?"

"Sterling has the bag. Come, let's find him," Lansius said as he moved toward the corridor. "And, oh, you must join me for supper. Half the staff are on leave, and Audrey is eating in her room."

"Is there something happening?" Calub almost inquired further, but Lansius's expression was telling enough. "Alright, I shall accompany you."

Together, the two strolled down the corridor and arrived at the great hall.

Korelia Castle had limited living space, so most of the male retinues stored their gear in a series of cabinets in a small open room at the far end of the hall, hidden from guests behind a pillar. Sterling emerged from there, having put away his riding coat. "My lord, do you need anything?"

"The bag. I need to show the shawls to Master Calub."

Sterling quickly retrieved the two shawls he had stored in a separate compartment of his bag. As he pulled and waved them in the air, Calub was mesmerized by their lightness. They floated as if they were weightless, even lighter than the thinnest linen.

The presence of the lord and his interest in the unique shawl quickly attracted a crowd of curious staff members.

"Almost like silk," Calub commented as he reached out for the nomad's shawl.

"They're also good for warmth, don't soak easily, and like silk, they offer some protection against sharp edges, even arrowheads," Lansius explained.

"Arrows?" Calub couldn't believe what he just heard.

"Their legend has it that even if an arrow pierces the skin, the garment made from that material would often remain intact, making it easy to remove the arrowhead and lessening the risk of poisoning or infection."

"Fascinating . . . Even if only half of it is true, that's mighty impressive," Calub commented eagerly.

Lansius nodded.

"So, is this why, my lord, you asked for the spinning wheel?" asked Calub.

Lansius grinned. "I want to integrate them with Korelia. Alone, the town has a difficult future. We have no natural resources other than a sea of grass and a stone quarry to the east. However, if the two communities cooperate, we could start a better path."

Calub, Sterling, and the other retinues gathered around were intrigued, even though they didn't know what a spinning wheel was.

The lord continued. "I want a strong, mutually beneficial relationship between the townsfolk and the pastoral community. They can provide the fleece; the town provides them with sustenance and hospitality. Then, with the town's expertise, we could produce these shawls faster and with more intricate patterns for trade."

Calub was impressed. He never thought that Korelia had the potential to make a good product with its scarce resources.

Sterling asked, "My lord, I thought you wanted them as allies?"

"I don't want just an ally," Lansius explained passionately. "I want a true ally, not just scouts or light cavalry. I want one that is inseparable from us, sharing our front lines because they have a vested interest in our survival."

Calub couldn't help but grin, rubbing his chin and feeling honored to be part of Lansius's plan. Last winter, he had even considered advising Lansius to leave Korelia due to the impending war. He had heard from merchants, who were fond of Lansius's rule, that five neighboring lords were mustering armies. Of these five, four were likely only guarding their interests against the war, but one, in particular, the Lord of the Three Hills, was building siege engines.

Calub wished he could see Lansius's vision fulfilled and would gladly give his left hand to make it happen. However, he knew that Korelia's future was still held hostage by the neighboring lords. Blood feuds ran deep in these lands.

CHAPTER 2

BATU

The next day, Sir Justin and his small entourage arrived at Korelia Castle. Since the last season, like other low nobles, he had worked to manage his land to make it self-sufficient and profitable. As someone knowledgeable about horses and horse trade, the Arvenian-born knight tried his hand at horse breeding, thinking it might yield good results. However, progress was slow and required patience, just like everything else.

This season, after arranging for his estate to operate without him, Sir Justin was ready to resume his duties as Lord Lansius's marshal. His arrival at Korelia was also prompted by an urgent matter he had learned of through his contacts in the sometimes-shady horse trade. Unfortunately, the lord was away, so Sir Justin decided to meet with Calub instead.

He strolled along the corridors with a relaxed gait, whistling a carefree, wandering tune, until he encountered Calub in front of the Small Council chamber.

Calub greeted him. "Sir Justin, good to see you."

"The pleasure is all mine. Well then." Sir Justin politely gestured for them to enter. Despite being a knight and a mercenary, he was neither arrogant nor condescending, and was known for treating the castle staff with respect. Furthermore, he was outspoken about his profit-oriented motivations, yet that daring honesty earned him the trust of those around him.

Once seated inside, the marshal wasted no time, asking, "So, where's Hugo?"

"Oh, your deputy was stationed at the Eastern Mansion," replied Calub.

"Mansion, we have those?" asked Sir Justin.

"Turned out yes. A fifteen-room mansion. It's old, and only one wing is usable, but it's suitable for the retinues and guardsmen to winter."

"Splendid, that answered where should I sleep tonight," said Sir Justin excitedly.

Calub offered a sly smile. "I'm sure Hugo can arrange things for you."

Sir Justin grinned. "He won't like it, but that's his problem."

The two chuckled for a moment.

"So," Sir Justin said in a more serious tone, hinting at his growing horse smuggler dealings, "I have contacts in several places. They reported that the Three Hills are mustering their forces."

"Viscount Jorge," Calub muttered and added, "Three thousand infantry and one hundred cavalry."

Sir Justin's lips turned into a grin. "So, you've done your work, impressive, Maester Calub."

Calub chuckled. "Bad information nearly killed us last time, so, of course, I did my work."

Sir Justin drew a deep breath. His memory flew to the plains, where they had won their biggest victory against Lord Robert. "Has the lord said anything about this?"

"I saw him making plans, but nothing concrete at this moment," Calub remarked.

Sir Justin crossed his arms, disliking the odds. "We only got four hundred men and, at best, a hundred cavalry. About the same as the last time."

"Without Midlandia support, this is all we can get. Even this much is already an achievement," Calub remarked.

Sir Justin sighed and confessed, "I don't like this. Even with those new defensive works, I doubt the Lord of Three Hills will be stupid enough to repeat Lord Robert's mistake. Also, the report says they're stacking supplies already. I fear they're going to attack sooner rather than later."

Calub seemed surprised but glanced out the window at the dark clouds forming on the horizon. "There's still time to prepare. The rainy season will still last for two weeks."

The marshal rested his back against the hard wooden seat and pondered their options.

Suddenly, the door creaked open. "Oh, I didn't know we opened a council meeting today," said the Lord of Korelia as he entered.

The two rose from their seat. "My lord."

"At ease, gentlemen." He motioned for them to return to their seats. "So, what have you discussed?" Lansius asked as he took his seat.

Sir Justin gestured for Calub to speak, but Calub declined. "My lord, there's news that the Lord of Three Hills is preparing his troops and—"

"And siege engines, yes, I know that much."

The two were surprised. Sir Justin looked at Calub, who shook his head.

Lansius continued. "Let's not worry too much. We still have two months before the road is hard enough for anything."

"Two months . . . ?" The marshal found it hard to believe, leaving Lansius smiling in victory.

"I know you're relying on your *merchants*, and Calub is relying on his guild connection. But I just recently secured more reliable eyes and ears."

The marshal looked enthusiastic, while Calub furrowed his brow and finally asked, "My lord, who supplied you with this information?"

"Oh, you'll meet them soon."

Just after midday, hundreds of riders and horse-drawn carts appeared on the horizon, approaching the western plains of Korelia Castle. The nomads, invited by Lansius, had finally arrived. They were an impressive sight, with their vibrant garments and sturdy steeds.

Their carts carried their families, goods, and provisions, while a seemingly endless wave of white sheep and goats trailed behind them, grazing lazily on the recently green Korelian grass.

The Lord of Korelia and Sir Justin rode with a detachment of riders to welcome their new guests. Excitement filled the air as the two groups met, extending their arms in gestures of hospitality and friendship.

The people of Korelia watched in awe as the nomads, more numerous than they had ever imagined, set up their camps. In just a few hours, hundreds of white yurts stood against the lush green landscape, creating an impressive sight.

Before sunset, Lansius and his entourage were invited to join the elders in their largest tent for a feast. The air was filled with the aroma of horse wine, sweet honey-glazed snacks, and steamed dumplings. Laughter and music resonated throughout the camp.

Following custom, Lansius declined a wooden chair and sat on a cushion directly on the rugs, much to the hosts' delight. Despite his eagerness, he struggled to understand their dialect and mostly let Sir Justin, Calub, or even Sterling do the talking, while he nodded and smiled as required. Fulfilling his role and navigating the social intricacies was taxing, but he needed this alliance to work.

The proceedings went better than expected, with neither side demanding anything from the other. Lansius sought mutual respect and understanding, rather than their service. He treated the nomads not as subjects to bend the knee but as business partners working toward a mutually beneficial relationship.

As expected, the day concluded with only warm greetings and introductions, yielding nothing concrete. Lansius sensed that the elders would send someone important when they were ready to discuss further.

In the meantime, he welcomed the nomads to graze on Korelia's plains, just northwest of his castle. Using the nomads' presence as a pretext, he also ordered the Korelian shepherds to graze on the eastern side of town.

The next day, an envoy arrived at the castle bearing gifts, led by a man in his prime with sharp eyes and a commanding aura.

Lansius knew he had met the one he had been waiting for.

Lansius had invited the man, named Batu, and two other guests into the grand chamber for a discussion. Equally, Lansius had Calub and Sir Justin on his side. Both sides were seated and separated by a table. Drinks were poured, and they had introduced themselves earlier.

"I thank you for this invitation. It's an honor to enter the castle," Batu began.

Lansius noted with relief that Batu's accent was better than the rest. "The honor is also mine."

How educated is he?

"So, what does the lord wish to discuss by inviting humble shepherds like us to his pasture?"

Batu's eloquence awed Lansius, who replied, "As I stated yesterday, I wish for a trade relation."

"It seems our shawl is of great interest to you." Batu was pleased. "However, they are time intensive, and we hardly make more than we need."

"I understand the challenge. Let me explain. We wish to acquire just the raw material, the winter fleece to be exact."

The two guests murmured among themselves until Batu looked at them. He then replied to Lansius. "Only the raw material, not a finished shawl or garment?"

"Indeed, I want the pastoral community to produce the raw materials while the Korelians weave them into garments." Lansius clarified his concept as best he could. "I want Korelia to create something unique to sell to Midlandia and beyond. I believe these quality garments are the perfect choice. If this works, everyone can prosper."

Batu considered this for a moment. "What do the nomad people gain from this?"

"Supplies. We'll trade fairly for your winter fleece. We have grains, salt, fruits, iron, linen, and wood."

"Only our winter fleece?" Batu inquired with a sharp gaze.

Lansius smiled, having thought this through. "Aside from the winter fleece, I'm interested in horses. And as you know, there's no such thing as too many horses."

Lansius's answer elicited laughter from Batu. "My lord, you even understand our proverb. We're truly honored."

"So, have we reached an agreement?" Lansius asked.

"I would like to think so." Batu nodded. "I'll inform my elders and ask for our members to take oaths and honor this deal."

"That won't be necessary," Lansius interrupted. "I don't want to force anyone. Let the bartering process determine the outcome. If we offer too little, anyone is free not to sell their winter fleece."

Batu smiled but shook his head. "I appreciate your good intentions, but it'll be hard and could breed destruction upon my community. Some families may be tempted to trade too much and disrupt the bartering rate for anyone else."

This guy even understands the basics of supply and demand. Just how far does his knowledge stretch?

Batu continued. "Our offer is likely several hundred bags of fleece each spring to be traded for a fixed amount of supplies. I'll consult with the elders about their needs and what we can offer."

"What about this year?" Lansius asked, desperate for some raw materials.

"Most of the goats have shed their winter fleece, but we still have some in stock. I think there's enough to make a hundred shawls."

Lansius nodded, feeling the tension in his shoulders loosened. Noticing this, Batu decided it was time to address a more challenging issue.

"My lord, you've employed a few members of our community as scouts. While I don't speak for everyone, know that we don't want to take sides in Lowlandia's conflicts. Our wish is to simply live in the Great Plains in peace."

Lansius nodded vigorously in understanding. "I only want scouts and will pay accordingly—nothing more."

"Nothing more, my lord?" Batu asked, sounding skeptical.

"I don't desire your allegiance," Lansius asserted. "Your friendship alone is enough. Even if I am no longer the lord, I hope you will honor the agreement and maintain a relationship with the Korelians."

Lansius's statement sparked murmurs among those present. Even Sir Justin cast a questioning glance at Calub.

"It seems I've misjudged you, my lord," Batu said, glancing at Calub and Sir Justin. "You're a larger character than I anticipated."

Lansius turned wary, unsure whether the remark was complimentary or critical.

Batu exchanged glances with his fellow nomads, who nodded, and turned back to Lansius. "The working opportunities last year and the payments in salt have saved many families. No one perished last winter, and after witnessing your character today . . . I'm prepared to align my tribesmen to your side against our common enemy."

Our common enemy? Didn't he just say . . . ? Was that a trick question?

Lansius began to realize that in reality they shared the same feud against the western lords.

Upon Batu's words, the two other men proclaimed, "The Naimans agree. This is a gamble worth taking. We'll fight under your banner against the western lords' mercenaries."

"The Jadarans praise the agreement," the second man added coldly. "The mercenaries have enslaved enough of my brethren. I'll welcome any opportunity to collect the blood price."

They are but a few hundred men and women; where does this bravado come from?

Lansius was deeply moved. "I do not wish for your kinsmen to die for my cause."

"My lord, you misunderstand," Batu replied, eliciting chuckles from his men. "More than just sharing a common enemy. It's rare to find a leader worth fighting for. You've been ruling for barely a season, yet you've already saved many of our elders and children. Let it be known that as barbaric as the Imperium's painted us to be, we nomads know gratitude and will repay it in kind."

A tingling sensation ran down Lansius's spine. He had never anticipated that his salt payment scheme would reach to communities beyond Korelia. Glancing at Calub, he saw an encouraging nod. True, they had allowed outsiders to help with the work in the ditches, but he hadn't expected anything to come out of it.

It turned out that what seemed like a small act of kindness had, in fact, garnered Lansius the lasting gratitude of the nomadic tribes.

CHAPTER 3

FIRST COHORT

The dawn of a new day bathed the spring steppe in hues of gold and green. As the sun emerged, it cast long shadows across the undulating grasses, illuminating the beauty of the awakening landscape. However, the tranquility was soon disrupted as hundreds of men and horses took to the field.

Four hundred Korelians had marched out from the western town gate and quickly fell into a line formation facing west.

On the right wing, Sir Justin as the marshal led the first company, comprised of the most elite soldiers—battle-hardened Arvenians, Midlandians, and his small band of mercenaries.

In the center, Deputy Hugo directed the second company, consisting of a small group of Arvenians mixed with Midlandians. The center was reinforced by Roger, one of Lansius's squires, entrusted with leading the fourth company.

On the left wing, Lieutenant Sigmund, also known as the skald, was in charge of the third company, which was composed similarly to the second company.

This was Lansius's new formation. The traditional approach had a knight or man-at-arms leading four individuals to form a Lance. A hundred Lances constituted four hundred men, a mix of cavalry and crossbowmen. However, the traditional formation proved unwieldy in large-scale battles, leading Lansius to re-form them at least at the hundred-men level.

These troops of mixed origins called themselves Korelians, as they were now based in Korelia. Facing them in the field was the light nomadic cavalry, advancing from the west. Led by Batu and his brethren, the nomads halted, awaiting a signal from the Lord of Korelia.

From a hill, Lansius ordered his staff to wave two large red flags bordered in black atop two poles. This signal prompted Batu to unleash his nomadic cavalry against the Korelian line. In three waves of forty horsemen each, they rode against the morning wind, with the silhouette of Korelia blocking the sun from their eyes.

The pounding of horse hooves echoed across the plains like a distant thunder growing steadily louder, steadily closer.

The nomads, perched atop their lean, swift steeds, braced themselves for the charge. Their faces were resolute, eyes gleaming with the thrill of the imminent clash. Chanting in the ancient language of the Caladan Sea Grass from the Great North, their war song sent a chill down the spine.

Gradually, their cries grew more intense, adding to the wild energy that reverberated across the open field.

As Batu and his hundred brethren closed in on their target, the Korelian line formation reached a fever pitch. Half of them cursed their lord for this intense training, while the other half relished the excitement after months of winter monotony.

"Close formation, shields up!" the company leaders commanded, trying their best to organize their troops.

Despite being only a mock battle, there was undeniable fear in their eyes as they felt the ground shudder. The sight of hundreds of charging cavalry was nothing short of demoralizing.

"Brace your long spears, blunt end forward," Sir Justin ordered, echoed by the others. The four rows of Korelian men-at-arms, shoulder to shoulder, pointed their long spears at the enemy. For training purposes, they kept the lethal tips wrapped and staked into the ground. Within a few breaths, the Korelian front transformed into a wall of spears.

Then came the moment of truth. With a shout that echoed across the battlefield, the nomadic cavalry launched their attack. They hurled their training spears at a full gallop, then naturally slowed their horses to a trot and deftly maneuvered to avoid engagement.

The projectiles arced through the sky, briefly casting a shadow against the sunlight. There was hardly time to brace as the blunt missiles, tipped with sacks filled with pebbles and dirt, peppered the Korelian formation.

Despite their circular shields, armor, and helmets, ultimately it was the men who absorbed the brunt of the assault. Many recoiled in pain or shock upon impact.

"Hold your ground, keep your chins down!" Hugo shouted at his men. The veterans around him echoed his command. "Strong arms, firm shoulders, brace your necks!"

The soldiers reeled momentarily under the force of the attack, but they quickly regained their footing. Their shields rose once more, and just as quickly as they had arrived, the battle cries and thundering hooves receded. However, it was only a temporary reprieve, as a new wave of horsemen was already closing in for another attack.

In the face of suffering, rallying cries erupted from the Korelians' ranks. Their fear and doubt had evaporated. Through their pain, they discovered their valor.

* * *

The training continued with several variations for two weeks, pausing only for rest or when rain made the plains too muddy and risky for training. By then, Lansius had incorporated the militia from the Korelia populace.

Despite Lansius's low expectations, the townsfolk arrived in droves, eager and willing to participate. In total, six hundred volunteered for training, providing their own gear, while the lord supplied them with spears and shields.

The participation of the townsfolk boosted morale and intensified training. Lansius himself joined Sir Callahan to train in the newly formed heavy cavalry. Thirty of Lord Robert's former knights participated, along with the Midlandian riders from the previous year's campaign.

What Lansius drilled into his men during this training was unforgettable. Most memorable was the practice of orderly withdrawal, a basic but complex maneuver that the men-at-arms rehearsed almost daily. This training also forced the four commanders, Sir Justin, Hugo, Sigmund, and Roger, to coordinate effectively and maintain a good tempo within their ranks.

On the fourth week, Lansius stopped the training. While he still saw flaws and a lot of room for improvement, he understood this was the limit of what a non-standing army could achieve.

He and his advisors contemplated requesting additional training before summer, but they were cautious not to push them too hard. The training was, after all, demanding. It was also a drain on resources, as the army consumed more food and alcohol to keep morale high.

A significant number of bolts were expended during training. While many were retrieved and reusable, enough were broken or lost that the incurred a cost of a gold coin per day for bolts alone. However, this was an expense Lansius was willing to bear because, in Lowlandia, war was the sole currency of his survival.

After another week had passed, the time came for Lansius to bid farewell to the Korelian nomads. With so many nomadic communities in one place, the grazing grounds were depleting fast. Their horses, sheep, and goats had grazed almost the entire northern side of Korelia. They also yearned to return to their traditional grazing grounds, where they had left a portion of their tribes behind.

During a modest celebration, Lansius joined Batu, his brethren, and their elders in a feast. Knowing that Lansius had yet to take a wife, they offered several candidates as concubines, as per their tradition.

The proposal embarrassed Lansius tremendously, and he rejected it with considerable effort, striving to be as polite as possible. The nomads, delighted with the opportunity to tease the Lord of Korelia, took no offense. Lansius, in turn, offered them a generous supply of what he could spare as a parting gift.

* * *

Ten days after the nomads' departure, rain seemed like a distant memory in Korelia, as the sun shone ever brighter. The transition from spring to summer had begun.

Sensing this shift, Lansius poured more effort into his planning, often working late into the night at his worn oak desk. Accompanied by the warm glow of lanterns and the familiar scent of beeswax, Lansius patiently scribbled his strategies, occasionally glancing at a bird's-eye view map of Korelia.

Such a map was a rarity in this era, so Lansius had crudely drawn it himself from the highest vantage point in the castle's lone tower. Although the map lacked scale, it had proven invaluable in planning his defense.

Lansius had identified a small creek just west of the town that attackers from the west consistently used to supply their camp. It was so vital that he had considered fouling it with animal carcasses or tannery waste, but such a vile trick could be cleaned up by the opponent within a few days.

He could attempt to ruin or divert the water from its source, but the enemy could simply dig wells and establish their camp elsewhere. This would introduce an unpredictable element, a wild card he wished to avoid.

While he could trouble his opponent by ruining their water supply, he ultimately decided against it, preferring to know where the enemy would set up camp, rather than preparing his defense blindly.

With that issue settled, he returned to his central question.

What can I do? A bait-and-trap attack?

He began to sketch out a classic bait-and-trap plan on the map, but he quickly realized that it was highly unlikely the enemy would repeat the Lion's recent mistakes. Lansius suspected that the opposition would avoid his trenches and instead attempt a different strategy.

Moreover, news of the enemy building siege engines was concerning. Maester Caine, the representative of the Mason Guild, had warned before departing that Korelia's castle and walls were old and not designed to withstand the latest siege engines likely to be fielded by the Three Hills.

Feeling stumped, Lansius leaned back in his chair and ruminated on the situation.

He had secured the cooperation of the sturdy and brave Korelian nomads, but their numbers were few. The Korelian nomadic population numbered less than six hundred. They could muster two hundred cavalrymen, but even a mere fifty casualties could set the nomads back for generations.

Lansius estimated that there were fewer than two hundred male riders. Half of them were too young or too old to be combatants. Perhaps only a hundred could be relied upon.

Drawing a deep breath, a wave of emotion welled up within him. Lansius had witnessed so much death in just a few years, and now the last thing he wanted was to ask for more people to shed blood for him.

Although he was tempted to rely on his new allies, deep down Lansius didn't want them to get involved. However, he was short on options. Even with the help of the nomads and the militia, the enemy might still outnumber them.

What Lansius had at his disposal was:

- 400 men-at-arms, including crossbowmen
- 600 militia
- 100 cavalry, geared toward heavy cavalry
- 100 nomadic horse archers

It was a significant number, but Sir Callahan and Justin had advised him that he couldn't afford a high-casualty victory. A Pyrrhic victory would merely serve as an invitation for another of the Lowlandia lords to invade Korelia.

Lansius let out a deep sigh before jotting out his plan for tomorrow. The first was to reinforce the ditch, as the muddy season was over. He also wanted to make a small encampment in the forest up north, in case he needed a place to hide some of his men or supplies for reinforcement. Then, he also needed to allocate more time to train with his lance on horseback.

Ugh . . . more lance training.

Last year, at Toruna Manor, he discovered that physical training was not his forte. Although he enjoyed horse riding, the experience of doing so in armor and a helmet, with only small holes for ventilation, felt like a nightmare. Moreover, he had to practice fighting on foot while armored, in anticipation of the high probability of being unseated and needing to battle his way back to safety.

His retainers insisted on these rigorous exercises, to the extent that Sir Callahan was training him daily on horseback, and Sir Justin and Hugo engaged him in daily sparring sessions. Lansius understood their reasons, but his body was sore, and the armor he used was an uncomfortable fit. The custom-made armor he'd ordered had yet to arrive.

With a heavy sigh, Lansius gazed at his rudimentary map of Korelia and its surrounding area. He had made little blocks of wood to represent units, the infantry, and the cavalry. He just didn't know how many boxes would be on the enemy's side.

The Three Hills City and region was a viscountcy, similar to Robert's territory, but boasted a greater population and wealth. Although the Three Hills had suffered many losses, Viscount Jorge was young, ambitious, and aggressive. He'd also had a streak of recent wins, which made him a dangerous opponent to face head-on.

CHAPTER 4

IMPERFECTUM

Calub's House

"Master, you really should take a break and a bath," the page boy suggested.

Chuckling, the alchemist responded, "Do I truly smell that bad, Margo?"

"No, master, but the workshop does carry a strong odor," the youth said innocently.

Calub let out a faint smile. "In that case, would you kindly prepare a bath for me?"

With the decision made, Margo promptly retreated upstairs to arrange the bath.

Calub had resided next door to the workshop throughout the winter and continued to do so. Lord Lansius didn't mind him staying out of the castle, as it was relatively near, and there were guards present day and night at the workshop.

Originally, it was the workshop's occupants who suggested the place to him. The vacant house had been owned by a shepherd who had turned to trade. The man was more than willing to part with his old home in exchange for some additional capital.

While the house wasn't large, it featured two stories, an attic, and a cellar. Calub paid a substantial sum for the property, but he considered it money well spent. As was his habit, he established his alchemy lab in the basement.

Initially, he lived there with only his assistant, the pageboy Margo. However, as time passed, he became attached to a few of the orphaned youngsters from the workshop.

Calub welcomed the kids into his home, giving them the entire second floor and the attic. Among them was a bright lad named Timmy, who showed an uncanny knack for maintaining the house and had a meticulous way with tools.

Another who caught his eye was Tia. Despite her limp, she was adept at various chores and proved to be an exceptional cook. The two children, along with Margo, managed the household chores, and while there were occasional mishaps, they generally did well.

This arrangement allowed Calub the freedom to conduct his experiments to his heart's content.

A knock sounded at the door.

"Just a moment, Margo. I'll be right up," Calub called out.

As the door creaked open, a familiar female voice echoed down the stairs. "Really, in a basement again?"

Calub turned in surprise to see the speaker, exclaiming joyfully, "Hannei!"

"How are you, old buddy?" asked the blonde woman as she made her way down the stairs. She was wearing a blue tunic and a plain white surcoat.

"Why are you here? I'm doing quite well. I believe I've even put on a bit of weight," he replied, patting his stomach.

The girl giggled. "I'm here to visit, but honestly, I heard you're now a high-ranking official. Yet here you are . . ." She glanced around the basement with a smirk.

Laughing, Calub countered, "Then let me show you my office in the castle."

Hannei laughed heartily. "I'm just joking. You seem busy, Calub. I could always come back later."

"Nonsense. I'm merely tinkering with some small stuff. Just let me take a quick bath, and then I'll take you to the castle. I imagine you're eager to meet Lansius as well."

"Not particularly. Actually, forget the castle. Let's just enjoy some good food in town."

"That sounds delightful," Calub agreed.

As Calub went for his bath, Hannei made herself comfortable upstairs.

"So, you're Margo?" she asked as she was seated.

"Yes, my lady."

"No need for formalities, dear. I'm not of noble birth," Hannei replied with a warm smile that accentuated her brown eyes, which looked golden from an angle. It complemented her long, dull-blonde hair.

Margo blushed. From the moment he had opened the door and caught sight of the woman beneath the hood, she could tell he had been utterly smitten. "Yes, master. Might you like a drink while you wait?"

"Only if that doesn't bother you too much," Hannei replied.

Before Margo could respond, a young girl emerged from the kitchen area, carrying an earthen jug.

"I apologize for my limp, master," little Tia said.

"What happened to your leg? Please, sit," Hannei invited.

"It's not needed. I—"

"I insist."

Tia reluctantly sat next to Hannei who proceeded to examine the girl's leg.

"You weren't born with this, were you?"

"No, master. I was bitten by a wolf last year."

"I'm so sorry to hear that," Hannei said, her brow furrowing in concern.

At that moment, Calub emerged from his room, donning his characteristic milky-white leather coat adorned with numerous pockets. His hair was neatly combed, and he radiated a fresh aura.

Calub noticed the pair and asked, "Ah, Hannei, could you possibly help Tia?"

She looked at Calub and shook her head. "It's going to be very painful."

Master, could you really cure my limp?" Tia asked, her eyes filled with hope.

"It may still fail," Hannei explained gently.

"We could manage the pain with poppy milk, and I have some painkillers," Calub chimed in.

"Calub, those are expensive! Are you serious?"

"I am. Old medicine loses its potency over time, and I was planning to make some new batches, anyway."

Hannei was skeptical but decided not to pry further.

"If you're serious, then seek help from a physician. Depending on their assessment, I can decide whether to proceed or not. You'll also need to stock supplies for at least two nights," she said, mentally running through what would be required.

The news brought a wave of happiness to the household. Little Tia was loved by all. She cooked, knitted, and repaired items, making them look as good as new.

After some discussion, they decided to attempt the procedure the following day. Today, the two old friends had plans to enjoy a meal in town. They wanted to share stories and tidings, as well as gather necessary supplies.

During one of their chats, Calub remembered an important detail. "Hannei, I forgot to ask. Who did you travel with?"

Hannei seemed stunned for a moment before exhaling deeply. "With our dear friend, who is missing again."

"You're not saying . . . here in Korelia?" Calub asked in disbelief.

"Yes, despite precautions, it happened again," Hannei said, her face showing anger at her own incompetence.

"Don't blame yourself," Calub advised. "The way things work, it's often beyond our control. Let's just hope that nothing bad happens this time."

They both exhaled simultaneously.

Lansius, Council Chamber

Sir Justin's relocation to the Eastern Mansion had stirred up an issue that needed attention. Though he initially shelved it due to pressing matters with the nomads and spring training, he had now submitted a report detailing the scandalous activities that he uncovered upon his arrival.

The report, brimming with confessions from the women and girls interviewed at the mansion's gate, promised to be a delicious read. Sir Justin had sent it with the sole intention of teasing Hugo, confident that Lansius would revel in the juicy details.

"My lord, please. It's a misunderstanding. I didn't organize such a party," Hugo pleaded as he followed Lansius through the corridor.

"I already told you I believed you, Hugo," Lansius chuckled, folding the letter and keeping it in his pocket. Despite his assurance, Hugo was probably convinced that a judgment had already been passed.

"Mercy, my lord!" Hugo implored, his hands covering his face in a gesture of regret. "I only meant to cater to the men's *needs*. Last winter, they longed so much for their families, it was becoming utterly unbearable to witness."

"You should have arranged for them to be sent home," Lansius suggested nonchalantly as he opened the door to the council chamber and entered.

"B-but, my lord, please forgive us," Hugo pleaded strongly, a note of desperation in his voice.

Yet, Lansius's attention was elsewhere. He was surprised to see Audrey inside and only realized his mistake after catching Hugo's expression. "No, no, you misunderstood me. I meant that you should adjust their rotation schedule so they can return home."

"My lord, that's . . . an exceptionally generous and brilliant idea," Hugo responded, taken aback.

"Then do it," Lansius said as he sat in his chair, glancing at Audrey, who listened quietly. Turning back to Hugo, he clarified, "While I found nothing condemnable in your actions, try to prevent a potential spread of sexual diseases in the future."

"My lord, I assure you, they were all clean."

A chuckle echoed in the room. Audrey had heard enough and now, with a tone laced with mischief, she quipped, "I'm sure the deputy personally inspected each one of them."

"No, I didn't. Never," Hugo responded emotionally.

Lansius chuckled. They knew that the man's greatest fear was for this incident to reach his squire brother, Anci, who would relentlessly bully him for such a blunder.

"Anyway, I heard you're engaged." Audrey changed her angle of attack.

"A would-be fiancée," Hugo corrected her with newfound composure.

"So, when can I meet her?" Audrey asked, seeming overly excited at the prospect.

"Soon . . ." Hugo mulled.

"So, who's her father? I'm sure Lans—I mean, my lord would like to know?"

"Of course, I meant to ask for my lord's permission," Hugo remarked. Then, turning to face Lansius, he added, "Dame Lucielle is from a baronet family. She lost her father last year due to old age. Sir Callahan sent me a letter, suggesting I meet her, as he's the girl's uncle, albeit a few times removed."

A baronet family, huh? That's quite a catch. I must remember to thank Sir Callahan for his help.

"Is she attractive and well-formed?" Audrey probed before Lansius had a chance to respond.

This is rare, seeing her asking about other women this way.

Hugo glanced at Lansius, who simply shrugged in response. "Well . . . she's appealing enough," Hugo said. "Her family estate is quite substantial, and it would fall into ruin under inadequate management."

"Don't marry out of financial necessity or pity," Lansius advised. He knew that many lower nobility estates in the area boasted expansive manorial lands but lacked the capital to develop them. Thus, many had fallen into hardship after depleting their savings.

"I will take your words to heart, my lord," said the younger but more mature-looking squire.

"Good. But Hugo, keep in mind we're on the brink of war. Are you certain you wish to marry now?"

"I appreciate your insight. I'll give this matter more thought," Hugo answered readily.

"Best to discuss it with her. Adjust the rotation schedule for the billet, and then you can invite her here," Lansius said, concluding the discussion.

"My deepest gratitude, my lord," Hugo responded before exiting the room, head held high.

The door closed gently behind him.

"I didn't realize you were so considerate," Audrey remarked, standing behind her chair and leaning on it.

Now they were alone in the council chamber. "Oh really? And what exactly do you mean by that?"

"Nothing. Not much at all," Audrey replied with a playful smile. The chair she leaned against swayed gently.

"I haven't seen you much at training lately. What have you been up to these past few weeks?" Lansius inquired, noting that Audrey seldom sought his company unless others were present.

"Just practicing on my own," she replied casually.

Lansius could only nod in response. Their relationship had become somewhat strained, a situation complicated by recent events. "Would you like to go for a ride or do something together?" he suggested.

Audrey politely declined. "I have an appointment to attend to today. My apologies, my lord," she said, before leaving the chamber.

Her formal address, referring to him as "my lord," prompted a sigh from Lansius as he contemplated their complex relationship, one where duty, people's hopes, and personal wishes were all intertwined.

With nothing on his schedule, Lansius returned to his chamber. Yearning for a ride to clear his head, he gathered his riding gear and prepared to depart. As he emerged, he found his entourage, Cecile and Sterling, waiting for him.

"My lord, a messenger just arrived," Cecile reported, offering up an envelope of superior quality, bound and sealed. With the spring rains finally subsiding, the roads had become navigable again, and messengers began to arrive in Korelia.

Recognizing the signet on the wax seal, Lansius broke open the envelope. The letter was from Lord Robert, detailing the tax assessments from his realm after the previous year's harvest.

While primarily a formality, the missive intrigued Lansius due to its quality. The letter of that era weren't written on ordinary pulp paper, but on a thin, almost translucent animal hide known as vellum. They were typically penned with a sharp-tipped quill made from a large bird's feather.

The consistent black ink and elegant handwriting suggested the work of a highly skilled scribe. Despite its cursive style, the text was perfectly legible.

"Cecile, ensure that our staff treats the messenger well. I'll meet him tomorrow along with the council members," Lansius instructed. Turning to his squire, he added, "Sterling, let's go for a ride."

The two young attendants bowed in acknowledgment.

Suddenly, Lansius felt compelled to add, "Cecile, there's no need to inform your father about this."

Cecile smiled and nodded. "Yes, my lord, I understand."

Lansius had no desire for another impromptu training session.

As he was about to leave, Cecile motioned for a private word. Lansius nodded once in acknowledgment and turned to Sterling, "Prepare the horse for me. I'll be there shortly."

Sterling nodded without question and headed toward the stables.

"What is it?" Lansius asked gently.

"Pardon me, my lord, but I think you should know that Lady Audrey is trying her best to practice archery on her own," Cecile reported. As the cup-bearer, responsible for Lansius's drinks, she was his most trusted confidant.

"Archery? You mean with bows?" Lansius asked, showing great interest.

Cecile nodded. "Yes, my lord. She bought two from the tribesmen."

Lansius rubbed his chin. "She could have told me about this."

Cecile giggled. "No lady likes to be seen while she's fumbling. It's considered unsightly."

Lansius could only smile. "How good is she with the bow?"

"Right now . . ." She shook her head. "Especially not on horseback."

"She trained horseback archery on her own?" Lansius asked in disbelief. It was nothing short of an achievement.

"Indeed, my lord. She believes it's more practical to use bows on horseback than mini crossbows. She . . . Lady Audrey is trying hard to be useful in her own role."

Lansius nodded silently, well aware of Audrey's efforts behind the scenes. Acting as the matriarch, she held the female staff together and kept the younger staff in line. She had also become a figure that the rest of the army respected.

Cecile continued. "My lord, please don't mention this to anyone."

"Gratitude. I will heed my trusted cup-bearer's advice."

Cecile smiled and bowed slightly. Lansius then headed toward the stables in a much better mood.

Upon seeing Lansius, his destrier perked up eagerly, akin to a dog being offered a walk. With the day's fair weather, Lansius opted for a trip to the northern forest to inspect its outskirts.

Upon their departure from the castle, the destrier trotted excitedly. Over time, Lansius had grown accustomed to the horse's temperamental nature, learning to trust it to carry him safely.

Unlike a vehicle, a horse was more akin to a moody robot. The more robust the horses, the more unpredictable their behavior.

Accompanied by four others, Lansius and Sterling rode in a column formation. Sterling's riding skills had improved significantly, allowing him to keep pace with Lansius, despite riding a less powerful horse.

They had barely left Korelia when they encountered an unusual sight. Lansius reined in his destrier, who neighed and jerked in protest. He patted her to soothe her mood. The horse loved running, so halting her just short of the open plains made her irritable.

However, Lansius couldn't peel his eyes away from the strange spectacle before him. A woman was clinging to a large tree, precariously perched on a lofty branch.

The sight of her silhouette up so high was enough to induce dizziness.

A blonde girl? Is she nobility?

"Excuse me, my lady," Lansius called up to her.

"H-hang on, give me a moment, please . . ." came a melodious voice from above.

"My lady, that's dangerous!" Lansius warned. A fall from such a height would be fatal.

"I know," she responded.

Her actions left Lansius and his companions perplexed.

Sterling noticed a group of children hidden behind the bushes surrounding the tree, asked, "What's the lass doing up there?"

"Oh, please don't bother the kids. They're just helping me to—eh, ahh!" Her hand slipped.

"Look out!" shouted one of the guards, causing Lansius's heart to skip a beat.

CHAPTER 5

FORTUNA VIRGO

Look out!" A warning from one of the riders echoed through the air, making Lansius's heart pound in his chest.

Oh, shoot!

Lansius was closest, almost directly beneath her, so he swiftly urged his horse forward with a press of his thigh. But the lady tumbled headfirst, and he misjudged her trajectory. Their heads collided with a sickening thud.

"Kyaa—"

"Uwaa—" Lansius's vision turned pitch-black, yet his arms reached out instinctively, grappling in the air. Suddenly, a weight crashed into him. Blindly, he snatched at the flailing form, pulling it into a tight embrace.

The sharp jolts of pain from the flailing limbs hadn't yet registered when his mount surged forward in panic. Their cries of surprise merged as the destrier, startled by the unexpected burden, bolted.

"Easy, girl, easy!" Lansius fought to control the terrified horse, but she galloped a considerable distance before he could calm her down.

"I got her . . . My lord, is everyone alright?" Sterling gasped, his breath ragged.

"Well done, Sterling," Lansius praised, still clutching the woman tightly to him as she clung to him, her hands latched on to his coat and arm.

Clothes, frills? And what is this softness . . . ?

The woman beneath his hold was panting heavily. "My lady, are you hurt?" asked Lansius, still without his sight.

"Eh umm, no. I don't think so . . ." Despite their precarious fall, her answer was surprisingly coherent.

"My apologies, I couldn't catch you safely."

"No, no, it's my fault. I shouldn't have climbed that tree. Ouch." She whimpered, no doubt feeling the aftereffects of their collision.

Lansius suddenly became all-too aware of their awkward embrace. "Sterling, can you help . . . um . . . adjust the lady's riding position?"

"Of course . . . my lady, please excuse me," replied Sterling.

"Oh . . . Oh! Right . . . thank you," the lady responded, shifting in the saddle as Lansius carefully withdrew his hands.

After a bit of readjustment, she finally sat securely in the saddle. The destrier, capable of easily handling two unarmored riders, voiced its dislike openly. Lansius patted the horse's neck. Gradually, his sight began to return, and he attempted to focus on the beautiful golden blonde before him.

A golden blonde in Korelia?

"Earlier, did he refer to you as 'my lord'? Are you Lansius, by any chance?"

Eh, she knows me? Hang on, I'm the local lord, so that shouldn't be surprising.

"Indeed, I am," he replied, squinting to get a clearer look at the woman who was curiously peering back at him.

"Oh, it really is you!" Her voice was filled with excitement. "Lans, it's me, Felis!"

"Fe . . . Felicity?!" Lansius exclaimed, his voice echoing with surprise. "Why are you here? Am I hallucinating?"

"Haha. No, you're not. I'm really here." Her giggles floated back to him, as lighthearted as he remembered.

"But why—Wait, what were you doing up in that tree?" Lansius asked.

"Oh, I was searching for some fruit. But first, let me reassure the kids." Felis called out to the children gathered around the base of the tree, "Kids, it's alright. He's an acquaintance. Gratitude for your help."

The children waved their farewells enthusiastically. She was just as merry as Lansius remembered.

Meanwhile, Lansius's vision gradually cleared.

"I'm sorry about falling onto you. Are you alright?" Felis asked, her gaze filled with concern.

"No, it's fine. Just a bit tender." He touched his forehead, wincing at the slight sting.

"Just a bit of redness, but no bleeding." Her instinct from her days as a labyrinth explorer took over.

"And you? We hit pretty hard," Lansius asked, worry lining his voice.

"Ahaha, I'm fine. Calub always says my skull is pretty hard."

Her lighthearted response drew a chuckle from him.

"So, Lans, where were you headed?"

"Just out stretching the horse's legs. Oh, I can ride now," he said, beaming with a sense of accomplishment.

"Yeah, I noticed. Are you sure it's okay for me to share the ride?"

"No problem. I couldn't possibly leave you here alone; you have a knack for getting into trouble. So, where are you staying in Korelia, and who's accompanying you?"

"That can wait. Right now, I'm on a mission to find costard fruit," she declared passionately. "Do you know where it grows?"

"Costard? Can't say I do," Lansius mused, then turned to his squire. "Sterling, do you know anything about this fruit?"

Sterling, who was not a local, turned to the other riders. One of them rode forward. "The costard fruit is a local delicacy, my lord."

"Is it in season, and do you know where we might find it?" Lansius asked.

"Yes, my lord, it's currently in season. You should find some in the forest. Generally, the ones hanging low taste the sweetest. The ones on the high branches tend to be a bit sour."

"What?!" Felis squealed in surprise.

"So, your little tree-climbing adventure was for naught, huh?"

"Haha. There's no need to rub it in. You used to be so sweet, Lans."

Felis's dramatic complaint sent Lansius into a fit of laughter. "Well, you're lucky . . . I mean, you always are. As it turns out, I'm heading into the forest. Let's go find that elusive fruit of yours."

"Lucky," Felis sang out happily.

Guided by the Korelia-born rider, they set off toward the north.

Their destrier trotted energetically across the open plains, barely burdened by the extra weight. Despite not being bred for long-distance endurance, it had more than enough stamina to make the run to the forest, especially without her barding. Soon, they reached the edge of the forest. Due to the challenging terrain and tall vegetation, they moved carefully.

"So where are you staying?" Lansius asked as they slowly ventured into the forest.

"At the inn. I arrived just yesterday."

"Did you bring any guards? The journey to Lowlandia can be dangerous."

"Hey, I'm quite the explorer, you know!" she protested. It wasn't an empty claim.

Last year, during one of their marches to Lowlandia, Calub, slightly tipsy from wine, recounted tales from his days as an explorer on the old Progentia Continent. Lansius learned from him that Felis had spent her teens exploring ancient dwarven labyrinthine ruins in Progentia, the cradle of this world's civilization.

Each labyrinth teemed with deadly creatures. Despite her delicate appearance, Felis was formidable, even more so than Audrey. There was one particularly memorable story about young Felis, who once found herself trapped in a ruin.

She had run out of crossbow bolts, her dagger had broken, and she was forced to resort to wrestling, biting, and even using her hair as a garrote to fend off goblins.

When Calub and their comrades finally located her, her armor was in tatters, her nose and fingers broken, a few teeth missing, her jaw damaged, and her skin marred by bloody cuts. Yet, she didn't shed a tear. Her only requests were for bandages, a new dagger, fresh bolts for her crossbow, and a lion's share of the discovered treasure.

Thankfully, this world's humans, although similar in appearance, possessed some unique traits, one of which, as Lansius had discovered, was the ability to regrow teeth.

Despite her fearsome reputation, Lansius knew Felis enjoyed being treated like a normal girl. Thus, he teased, "So, where's your trusty crossbow now, expert explorer?"

"Ah, erm . . . I left it . . ." Felis admitted nonchalantly.

"Where?"

"In Midlandia," Felis answered innocently.

Lansius let out a chuckle.

"But I didn't travel alone. I don't know the way, either," she admitted innocently.

"So you joined a group of merchants?" he ventured.

"Bingo! We tagged along with one. They were happy to have us," she said proudly.

No wonder, she looked every bit a noble.

"So, who's the unfortunate guard leader?" Lansius asked.

"Guard leader . . . ? No, I only brought Hannei with me."

Lansius swallowed hard. "She's here?!"

"Lans, don't tell me you're still afraid of her even after spending two seasons in Toruna?"

"I am, she's volatile," he whispered in protest.

"Haha, you're overreacting. She's my adorable friend."

Lansius felt a shiver run down his spine, but the lack of guards raised an important question. "Why did you come to Korelia? Aren't you supposed to be preparing for your wedding? Don't tell me you ran away!"

Felis sighed before answering. "Archie isn't around, so I'm bored."

That was expected. Lansius had learned that Lord Arte, now confirmed as her fiancé, was visiting the capital along with Sir Peter, Anci, and Thomas to gather support for the occupied Arvena.

"Felis, you're the one who wanted to marry into nobility. I supported you before, and even more so now, knowing you're with Lord Arte. However, it's not all roses. There's a lot of boring stuff and little freedom." Lansius found himself repeating the words he had written in a letter last year.

"I know, I'm just bored . . . I don't mean to run away from it. After all, it's my dream." Felis smiled angelically.

"That's good to know. But seriously, traveling this far just because you're bored." Lansius sighed.

"Why not? Calub and you are here. Also, I heard that you got a castle," she said, her lips turning into a smirk.

"So that's your real intention . . ."

She's probably going to act like a princess. I must protect my staff from her . . . But then again, probably they're going head over heels for her.

"Eh, there's also another issue . . . I'm not sure, but I think there's a problem back home."

"What kind of problem?" Lansius asked anxiously. Felis had dropped an unexpected bombshell. He couldn't afford a crisis in Midlandia while Korelia was still under threat.

"I'm not sure. You'll have to ask Hannei about that."

"Let's invite you two to stay at the castle then."

"Ah." Felis turned to face him, her voice dripping with allure. Her deep blue eyes were truly mesmerizing.

"W-why are you looking at me like that? I'm innocent," Lansius protested in advance.

Being this close to her, sharing a ride, his heart pounded fiercely. Her hair's fragrance and her natural scent enveloped him.

"Sleeping under the same roof again, are we?" Felis teased.

"N-No, no, no! That's taken out of context—I wouldn't dare. I'm with Audrey now!"

"So you confessed already? Oh, I can't wait to see Audrey again." She had met Audrey last fall, and since then, she had been rooting for them to get married.

"Y-yeah, she'll be thrilled to see you." Lansius was grateful for the change in topic.

"She's not riding with you? Does this mean that she's pregnant?"

Pregnant . . .

"Eh! Don't start rumors like that!" he blurted out once he regained his senses.

This drew the other riders' attention, but luckily, Sterling was there to wave it off as nothing.

"Ah, not yet then . . . That's a shame," the audacious lady lamented.

She's actually serious about that?

"Felis, maybe you hit your head in the fall, let me check," Lansius's sarcasm was at its peak, but . . .

"Sure, sure," Felis agreed enthusiastically.

He ended up examining her head. There was no bruise. Her thick hair or her luck must have cushioned the impact.

"Find anything?"

"Sadly, no . . . It must be a birth defect that allows you to spout nonsense like that!" He tickled her waist, which sent her into fits of laughter.

"Ahaha! Stop it, ahaha, stop it! Or I'm going to tell Audrey," she gasped between laughs.

Then, out of nowhere, a small branch fell squarely on Lansius's head. "Gahh!"

Felis laughed at his misfortune. "See, even the forest is against you. No more tickling or something worse might happen," she warned playfully.

Lansius had nearly forgotten that Felis wasn't ordinary. Being an explorer on the old continent was already a feat in itself, but she was much more than that.

Felis carried with her an aura of peculiar fortune—be it a curse or a blessing.

Despite all the dangers she had faced in her exploring days, including the time when she was trapped, luck was always on her side. This led several individuals to rely on her.

Calub had relayed to Lansius the stories that circulated about Felis's previous group. They had depended on Felis as their scout, and she had discovered a new section of the labyrinth, which led them to unspoiled treasure. However, when the labyrinth collapsed, she was the only one fortunate enough to escape.

Such incidents seemed to trail in her wake, prompting other adventurers to approach her with a mix of awe and caution. The lesson was clear: Felis's presence was a serious matter.

It was only out of sheer desperation for wealth that Calub and Hannei welcomed her into their team.

Calub had once said that proximity to her could drastically change a person's fate, though not always favorably. He even jested that if Felis were to be involved in a war, it could lead to a crushing defeat, only for her to miraculously survive and capture the attention of the victorious leader, potentially her ideal partner.

Back then, Lansius had brushed off such stories as exaggerations. However, Felis had indeed captivated Lord Arte, using nothing more than her golden hair and blue eyes.

In a sense, Calub's words rang true, making everyone who knew her background nervous. Her luck could bring about the best or the worst of situations, as unpredictable as a roll of the dice.

Lansius suspected that her presence had significantly altered his destiny. After all, meeting Felis was the reason he went to the inn where he encountered Thomas, Anci, and Hugo. This led him to Sabina Rustica and the young Lord Arte.

Felis was also the one who directed him to Feodosia, where he received an invitation to Toruna and later met Audrey and Lord Bengrieve.

However, Lansius was also aware that this fortune was a double-edged sword. For example, in the aftermath of Sabina Rustica, the real winner wasn't

Lansius or the Arvenians, but Felicity, who secured a future with a high-ranking noble.

Now, she had appeared once more, unannounced, on the eve of a war. A wave of apprehension swept over Lansius. The arrival of Felis was like the raising of a curtain, a signal that the upcoming events would be monumental. The forthcoming summer held the promise of something grand and unavoidable.

CHAPTER 6

A WARLORD'S PERSONA

Lansius and his riders reached the dense part of the forest. Their pace slowed due to the narrow path here, a trail familiar to the riders who occasionally hunted deer, boar, and foxes.

The destrier neighed a few times, displaying curiosity about its surroundings. At one point, the horse even attempted to snap at a lizard hanging from a tree branch.

"Lans, I think even your horse is laughing at you," Felis teased, patting the horse's neck.

"No, the horse suggesting that I tickle this extra passenger some more." Lansius wiggled his fingers in the air to emphasize his point.

"Ha! No more, no more." Felis shielded her waist with her hands like a child.

Lansius chuckled at her response while silently pleading with the forest not to drop another branch on him.

"Ah! Now I understand why your hands were so naughty," Felis suddenly declared while they were avoiding low-hanging branches.

"What? My lady, my hands are on the reins," Lansius said, defending himself.

"Before, when I fell, I felt your hands touching me all over," she said in accusation.

He suddenly remembered feeling something soft in his hand.

Wait, that wasn't her waist?

"Erm . . . please don't say things like that," he pleaded, glancing nervously around. He had enough trouble with Audrey, and he couldn't afford a rumor.

Worse still, what if she tells Lord Arte or Bengrieve . . .

Shaming a lord's spouse or betrothed was a great offense. Enough to send a minor noble like him to the chopping block. Lansius gulped nervously.

His reaction was not lost to Felis, whose beautiful face regressed into wicked laughter. "I've got you now, Lans," she declared, a victorious smirk on her face.

He sighed and conceded. "Name your price."

* * *

As Lansius and Felis rode together and entered Korelia, the inhabitants respectfully slowed their pace and bowed their heads. Usually, Lansius's route took him directly to the castle, but today, in deference to his guest's wishes, they made a detour to an inn where Felis had stored her belongings.

Having served as a lord for several months, Lansius was familiar with the townspeople's customary greetings. However, the atmosphere was different this time. Their responses were closer to reverence than simple acknowledgment.

The difference, he realized, lay in his companion. Felis, with her cascading golden hair and bright blue eyes, riding a warhorse, perfectly embodied the image of a high-ranking noble.

In a land where most nobles sported varying shades of brown hair, her golden locks were a distinct anomaly. Her appearance was so striking that even Lansius understood the townspeople's reaction.

As they continued their journey, Felis sat comfortably, nonchalantly enjoying a costard fruit, which to Lansius resembled an apple. Three more of these fruits were neatly packed in a cloth resting on her lap, presenting an image reminiscent of a pampered princess.

Her interest in the fruit also made Lansius order one of the riders to take a young sapling to be planted in the Eastern Mansion.

Slightly embarrassed, Lansius guided the destrier carefully through the crowds toward the inn. All the while, the gazes of Korelia's residents were fixed on them. Whispers and comments followed their path, with some people even trailing behind for a closer look. In response, Sterling and the other riders grew vigilant, reinforcing their perimeter with any guards who happened to be nearby.

Above them, the sky was favorably clear, with only a smattering of clouds.

Upon their arrival at the castle, the guards and staff mirrored the townspeople's astonishment. The sight of a golden-haired woman was a rarity associated with the ancient northern dynasty. This dynasty was once known for its powerful great kings and lords before the era of the Third Imperium.

Although the dynasty's power had waned and blonde hair had become less uncommon, reverence for their lineage persisted. The irony was that there was nothing royal about Felis's heritage. She was merely fortunate to have been born with golden hair.

As they rode through the courtyard and into the entrance of the keep, Lansius spotted two familiar figures waiting. Felis, sharing his ride, noticed the presence of another blonde and exclaimed with joy, as if she had discovered another member of an endangered species.

What Felis saw was Lansius's cup-bearer, Cecile.

"Greetings, my lord, my lady," Cecile managed to say, concealing her surprise admirably. Lansius noted the grace with which she handled the unexpected situation.

As they halted, Carla, a female squire in training, swiftly moved to assist Felis to dismount. Lansius dismounted next, with Sterling, who had been shadowing him closely, lending a hand.

The powerful destrier snorted and whinnied as it was led away by the stable master, and all eyes were drawn to Lansius.

Seizing the moment, he introduced his companion. "This is Lady Felicity, fiancée to Earl Arte of Arvena."

While the revelation stirred shock among the onlookers, Cecile managed a solitary blink before bowing respectfully.

"Hello, you may call me Felis."

Cecile, choosing to maintain formal etiquette, replied, "Madam Countess."

Lansius interjected, "Her marriage hasn't been finalized yet, so you can still address her as lady."

Cecile nodded in understanding. "Yes, my lord."

Felis, ever cheerful, complimented Cecile with a great smile, "You have lovely hair. What's your name?"

Flattered, Cecile blushed. "This servant is named Cecile, my lord's cup-bearer."

Felis greeted her warmly. "Nice to meet you, Cecile. I look forward to your care today."

Lansius, observing the interaction, noted to himself that unlike most women who were drawn to the good-looking Sterling, Felis seemed more interested in his cup-bearer. "Cecile," he called, "find Lady Audrey, and inform her that a friend has arrived. But do not mention who it is."

Felis appeared delighted at the prospect of surprising Audrey.

Meanwhile, Cecile raised an eyebrow, but Lansius gave a confirming nod, and she proceeded to fulfill her task.

As Cecile led the way, Lansius escorted Felis to the Great Chamber. He chose a guarded corridor to avoid the great hall and any unnecessary attention. Lansius was showing Felis the Small Council chamber when Audrey found them.

"Felis!" Audrey screamed, rushing toward her, with Cecile trailing behind.

"Kyaa! Audrey!"

The two women hugged each other warmly. Despite being shorter, Audrey was surprisingly strong, and she twirled the taller Felis around like a younger sister. Their bond was special. They had only met briefly in Toruna, but something had clicked between them right away.

Both were daredevils in their own ways, not conforming to societal norms.

Each had been born a commoner, yet they were rising through the ranks and gaining status.

Lansius himself didn't know much of the details, as he had been in Cascasonne meeting with Lord Bengrieve when Felis visited Toruna. Thus, he hadn't witnessed their friendship developing. He only learned about it afterward, but it was a pleasant surprise, as he owed much to both of them.

As the two descended the stairs, they left Lansius behind. When he tried to follow, Audrey's gaze nearly made him trip.

Okay, understandable . . .

Deciding to return to his chamber, Lansius took the stairs but paused as he remembered a previous promise. He let out a resigned sigh and called, "Cecile."

"Yes, my lord," she responded, her voice void of any hint of annoyance.

Lansius was aware that his request might sound unusual. "Could you ask Sterling and a few others to move the guest bed from castle storage to this room? Our guests and Audrey will be using my room."

Cecile remained composed as she inquired, "Guests, my lord?"

"Yes, there's one more . . . She, too, is a friend of Audrey's. But I must caution you, Felis is a gentle person. The other guest, however, is . . . more challenging."

"I understand, my lord . . ." Cecil acknowledged. "But if they take over your quarters, where will—"

"Oh, I'll sleep in . . ." He wasn't sure either.

Hugo's room is in disrepair . . . Calub's? No, I don't want to bother his room. He's an alchemist and treasurer as well. He might have documents and I don't want to disturb . . . Guest room? No, there are a lot of important guest messengers. A lord can't be spotted using the room next to them.

Finally, he settled on an unconventional choice. ". . . the Small Council chamber. Would it be possible for the staff to prepare a bed there for me?"

"Of course." Cecile bowed her head a little.

"And don't forget bedding and a blanket," Lansius added, feeling a pang of guilt for imposing these tasks on the young girl.

She's not even seventeen. This is considered child labor, right?

"Anything else, my lord?"

"No, Cecile. You've been a tremendous help."

"I'm grateful for your praise." She graced him with a smile, bowed, and went to fulfill her duties.

As he watched her leave, Lansius couldn't help but marvel at how much his young staff had developed over the past few months. This was especially true for the squires, who had truly come into their own.

Under Audrey's rigorous training, Carla, Sterling, and Roger had matured noticeably. Either the training was responsible, or they all had sustained head concussions that somehow resulted in improved competence.

Roger's spear wound from their last encounter had completely healed. Carla had tempered her impulsive tendencies, and Sterling was now mastering Isolte's Elandia-style fencing technique.

Lansius dreamed of knighting them one day once he received his official title from the High Court. As of now, he was only an acting lord, a mere pretender.

Their swift advancement inspired Lansius, although his own progress on horseback felt slower in comparison.

I might need to spend more time with Callahan.

As he contemplated this, the blond knight appeared, trailing behind his daughter, who reported, "My lord, my father wishes to see you."

"Yes, Sir Callahan."

"My lord, Sir Justin has sent word that the East Lowlandia merchants are growing restless."

"Ah," Lansius mumbled. He had been delaying the meeting with the merchants, feeling he wasn't ready.

The older man sensed the tension and asked politely, "Do you still feel uncertain, my lord?"

"Indeed, sir," he admitted. "A lot is at stake, and I'm not confident enough."

The merchants were a part of the parties involved in last year's rising grain prices. Whether they were directly involved or not, they now came bearing gifts and honeyed words, proposing deals.

Lansius couldn't help but feel wary of their approaches.

"May I offer some advice, my lord?" asked Callahan, ever resourceful.

"Certainly," Lansius responded, his interest piqued by what his mentor might say.

"My lord, if I may be so bold, you often show too much gentleness toward those around you. While we, your retainers, appreciate this, it may lead to difficulties. Many might interpret your gentleness as a weakness, a soft spot to be exploited."

Sir Callahan's unexpected counsel struck a chord. Lansius nodded, murmuring in acknowledgment. "I'll keep that in mind."

"Don't show your gentleness to the world, my lord. Show it only to those you care about. For all others, let them see the face of a conqueror," Callahan advised.

Merchants from Eastern Lowlandia

As of the previous fall, three merchants from Galdia, Salceslia, and Edessa had been keen to engage with Lansius, smelling profits in the high grain prices.

While they were not the masterminds behind the price manipulation, they had spotted what the West Lowlandia merchants were doing and had played along, driving up the price even further.

They had hoped to exploit the vulnerability of the two lords, Lansius and Robert, but they began to worry when neither sought their assistance. Price manipulation was inherently risky. They had invested all their savings into buying grain to sell it at a higher rate.

As prices rose, the poorer individuals simply couldn't afford enough and bought less. However, this was expected. Their target wasn't the ragged poor, but the nobles who needed to prepare for the upcoming conflict.

Yet, Robert's passive response and Lansius's lukewarm reception cast doubt on their plans. The Lord of Korelia had deliberately left them in suspense for a week, during which they slowly became acquainted with the Korelian market and the city's situation.

Witnessing Korelia survive last year's crisis and transform into a budding salted meat industry was surprising, further eroding their confidence.

At last, today, a blond knight invited them to meet with Lord Lansius. They had thought this was the opportunity they had been waiting for, but instead of the castle, they were led into the trenches where the lord had set up a training shooting gallery, complete with an overhead field tent.

While they were uncertain about this unconventional setup, they followed the knight and observed as Lord Lansius and his garrison of heavy arbalesters were cranking their latest cranequins—heavy crossbows that were loaded using metal gears and a lever.

"My lord," Callahan greeted, and the three merchants echoed his salutation.

However, Lord Lansius appeared indifferent. He kept aiming casually at a thin barrel target. As he loosed his heavy bolt, the rest of the garrison followed suit, resulting in a deafening cacophony of bolts launching and crossbow limbs snapping back.

The barrage of heavy bolts landed like rain on the wooden barrels, causing some of them to explode on impact. This display of force affected the three, who were taken aback by the powerful weaponry they rarely encountered live.

Without a pause, Lansius commanded, "Crossbowmen!" Instantly, twenty crossbowmen advanced, unleashing a thunderous barrage of bolts at the already ravaged barrels.

Once the resounding echoes diminished, Sir Callahan reiterated his message, "My lord, the guests."

"I heard you . . ." Lansius replied with a hint of impatience, tossing his cranequin to Sterling. "Load it up for me." He then turned to the merchants. "What can I assist you with?"

The largest of the trio, dressed in crimson, stepped forward. "My lord, we appreciate this opportunity. We're here to discuss trade."

"Trade? Do you have plate armor or better-ranged weaponry?" asked Lansius.

The three merchants exchanged glances before the same man replied, "We have horses, medicine, and grains."

"Grains," Lansius echoed. "How much for the grain?"

The merchants' faces lit up at his question, their earlier worries seeming to evaporate instantly. They were well aware of the demand for grain—even a warlord like Lansius couldn't ignore the need to feed his troops. "We can offer you good wheat at twelve copper per bushel," they announced, brimming with newfound confidence.

CHAPTER 7

PAX IMPERAT

Lansius, the acting Lord of Korelia.

The traders from Eastern Lowlandia began to pressure Lansius about the grain price, proposing twelve copper coins for a bushel of quality wheat. The standard price was typically a mere four to five copper coins per bushel.

Regardless of the hefty asking price, Lansius was in dire need of the grain. He needed it as a safety net against the potential siege or a poor harvest. While Midlandia offered cheaper grain, the transportation cost was significant.

Moreover, the impending threat of war prevented him from committing his valuable cavalry for escort duties. Lansius sighed, recalling Sir Callahan's advice—to project the image of a conqueror.

"My lord, would you counter the merchants' proposal?" Sir Callahan asked politely.

This is it . . . Time to go crazy.

"Absolutely! That isn't a fair price. Raise it to fifteen, and then we have an agreement," Lansius countered wildly.

The traders were stunned, baffled as to why the lord would demand a higher price. "My lord, we are proposing twelve out of respect for you."

"Proposing? You're selling? But I'm not purchasing! I'm also selling." Lansius feigned a laugh. It wasn't convincing, but it was enough because the traders barely knew him.

The traders were perplexed, trying to question, but Lansius was faster.

"I've struck a deal with Midlandia to buy their grains. Now, I want to sell my grain while the price is high. Fifteen copper coins, a bushel. How does that sound?"

The traders were dumbfounded. They had heavily wagered on the assumption that the Lord of Korelia was desperate for grain, but now, their expectations crumbled before their eyes. Not only was Lord Robert uninterested in their grain, but Lord Lansius also had a surplus he intended to sell.

"Well?" Sir Callahan prodded, adding to their mounting panic.

The merchants seemed to realize they had lost their position in the negotiations. They recognized that they couldn't navigate this situation without a significant change of strategy. "My lord, it seems we have made a slight miscalculation. We apologize and will return shortly with a more suitable proposal."

"I hope so. Otherwise, I'll send this grain to Robert," Lansius retorted nonchalantly, retrieving his cranequin and instructing his arbalesters to release another volley.

As the merchants walked away. Lansius observed the traders' evident discomfort as they withdrew, whispering and arguing among themselves. Sir Callahan followed them with a confident stride.

He had entrusted Sir Callahan with the merchants. The knight understood Lansius's plan—he was a natural diplomat, intelligent, and respected.

Truthfully, Lansius was wary about not being able to negotiate directly. However, if he looked too bold and too direct, then his deceptions might be exposed. After all, traders are inherently suspicious by nature.

Once they were gone, Lansius let out a long, profound sigh. He had just executed his biggest bluff of the year. His grain for horse deal with Midlandia wasn't that lucrative, as the price they wanted was too low.

He had accepted Sir Justin's proposition to sell horses in the black market around Midlandia, but it would need time to fruition. He also didn't dare to ask about the buyers, who were likely brigands or slavers.

Regardless, his choices were limited. Korelia was undeniably poor. They barely had any grain to sell. What they did have in abundance was locally produced salted meat that needed to be offloaded. For this, he required the traders' assistance. However, he first had to weaken their resolve; otherwise, he would appear desperate for supplies.

"Your command, my lord?" a voice asked.

Lansius looked at Sterling and said, "Let's fire another round and then stop. Bolts are pricey."

"And so are those wooden barrels," the squire remarked.

"The cost of diplomacy," Lansius remarked with a nervous chuckle.

Calub's House

Morning dawned on Calub's residence. Unlike most days, which were quiet, today the place was bustling with activity as they prepared to operate on little Tia's ankle.

"Knocked out?" Hannei asked.

Calub gently lifted Tia's eyelid to check her response, then confirmed, "Yup, she's asleep."

Hannei continued. "Tourniquet and hourglass?"

"Ready," Margo, the page boy, responded.

"Maester, you may begin." At Hannei's command, the physician, a man in his forties with sharp eyes and a thin beard, nodded. He began by making an incision on little Tia's right ankle. Fresh blood flowed as the knife, the town barber's finest, cut into the little girl's skin.

At Hannei's insistence, the tools had been boiled to cleanse them of any taint.

Tia was laid face down on a makeshift bed. A bucket was positioned below for any bodily fluids. She had been given a small dose of poppy milk mixed with a quarter dose of Calub's powerful painkillers.

"Margo, watch for Tia's breathing. Notify us at once if there's any change," Hannei instructed.

"As suspected, the ankle bones are fused. We need to break them and return them to their proper place," the maester announced calmly, picking up a wooden mallet and a small bronze chisel, both of which had been disinfected with alcohol.

Hannei and Calub held Tia's leg and calf securely while the maester tapped the bone lightly several times. The sight and sound were unsettling. Margo and Timmy shuddered at each muffled noise.

Without hesitation, Hannei assisted with the dressing, using a clean linen cloth as gauze. Meanwhile, the physician diligently explained the deformations in the connecting sinew and muscle, likely resulting from the wolf attack.

As she listened, Hannei's golden-brown eyes flashed, betraying her nervousness, yet she nodded several times in affirmation.

Afterward, the physician, with precise movements, proceeded to stitch the skin back together. He used some linen to dress the ankle but left it without a bandage. "I'm done," he announced.

"Gratitude, maester," Calub said. "Margo, please assist the maester if—"

However, the man shook his head. "No, Master Calub. I must insist on staying here. You see, I'm curious."

Calub nodded gratefully. Timmy readily fetched another chair for the maester to sit on.

Now, Tia's care was in Hannei's hands. She observed that the ankle area started to swell.

"Start the hourglass," she instructed Margo, her right hand hovering above Tia's ankle. Then she began to chant in a language unknown to this world, *"Gloire au Père, au Fils et au Saint-Esprit. Comme il était au commencement, maintenant et toujours, pour les siècles des siècles."*

There was no dramatic burst of light, only the calm repetition of the short verses. At first, there was no discernible change. However, after several recitations, the blood around the stitches began to clot more rapidly.

Hourly, Hannei recited the verses four times. From morning to midday, scabs began to form on the stitches, and bluish bruises appeared.

By afternoon, the swelling had significantly decreased and new skin started to grow around the afflicted area. Calub, accustomed to the lengthy procedure, periodically provided Hannei with drinks and snacks.

The physician patiently observed the recovery with satisfaction. In between Hannei's sessions, he examined the bones gently with his fingers, ensuring they were properly positioned. He remained until sundown, when Timmy escorted him home.

Lanterns now bathed the room in their soft glow, yet Hannei's ritual remained unchanged. Every hour, she recited her verses, keeping her hand poised above the healing area, as if channeling energy into it.

By the time supper was served, more than twelve hours had elapsed since the process began. Exhaustion started to weigh on Hannei's body. After each session, she retreated to her bed in the adjacent room for a brief rest.

The flickering candlelight inside the lantern marked the passage of time, with wax melting and pooling as hours turned into evening and then night.

Calub, Margo, and Timmy took turns monitoring Tia's breathing, vigilantly watching for signs of the poppy milk's sedative effects wearing off.

Hannei's ritual continued throughout the night and into the early hours of the new day. As dawn broke, morning light gently filtered into the room, marking the start of another day.

They had breakfast early, during which Calub administered Hannei some of his potions to rejuvenate her strength. Margo also brought a spiced light ale that provided her some relief.

The physician arrived early, allowing Calub to catch some shut-eye. However, his rest was brief, as Tia soon woke up, prompting him to administer a dose of painkillers. Since Tia was too young for another dose of poppy milk, this was their only option.

Administering the dose proved challenging, as Tia vomited several times, leaving Calub concerned about whether she had ingested enough. Despite the effects of the poppy milk wearing off, she remained in a state of delirium.

Now Tia was resting on her back, making it easier for her to eat and drink. Nonetheless, she remained securely fastened to the bed as her leg wound was still fragile and could reopen accidentally.

Timmy attempted to coax Tia into eating, but she only managed a few spoonfuls and sips.

In the meantime, Hannei continued reciting her verses. Being the only woman present, she also helped with cleaning Tia as necessary. Thankfully, there was no trace of blood in Tia's urine, which Hannei declared a good sign.

Around midday, Margo brought meat pie from a well-known shop. Although it was delicious, Hannei managed only a few bites. The long, grueling day continued with its monotonous activity.

The physician stayed until supper time. By then, Calub had managed to catch a few hours of sleep, and Margo and Timmy also managed to rest a bit.

By evening, Tia had fully awakened. She spoke with Hannei during the breaks in treatments, and they even shared meals. Afterward, Calub administered another dose of painkillers as Tia was beginning to feel an excruciating pain in her leg.

Hannei observed that the wound was healing well, the swelling had subsided, and the skin around the wound had returned to a healthy color. Soon, Tia began to develop itchiness around her ankle and calf, which Hannei deemed another good sign.

Despite her exhaustion, Hannei continued her treatment. Dark circles had formed under her eyes from getting only a few moments of sleep since the night before.

Suddenly, a commotion outside the house startled everyone inside. The sound of several people entering the premises so late at night was alarming. Hannei was alert, her golden-brown eyes sharp with caution.

"My lord!" Calub greeted in recognition.

"That's not necessary, Calub. How is she?" another man's voice rang out, filled with concern.

"Hannei is upstairs, but she's tired," Calub answered.

"May I see her?" the man asked.

Hannei had recognized the voice. "You may. Come up, Lans," she called out from upstairs.

Ascending the ladder, Lansius emerged into the room. "You look like a panda," he blurted out without any finesse.

Unimpressed, Hannei immediately stepped on his foot. Meanwhile, Tia was puzzled and almost asked what a panda was.

"Okay, that's entirely my fault," Lansius conceded, his face contorted in pain.

Hannei remained stoic, too fatigued to indulge in jesting.

"I brought some medicine, a blanket, and . . ." Lansius pulled a parcel wrapped in clean cloth from his coat. This was a common way to package food items. Carefully, he unveiled a golden, crescent-shaped pastry.

"No way, a croissant," Hannei uttered in disbelief.

"It's a bit dry and crunchy, but here, have a bite," he offered.

A crunching sound resonated through the room as some flaky crust fell away.

"I know it won't be as good without *Frigo*—"

"No. Thank you, Lans. It's been ages."

The atmosphere between them softened.

Hannei approached Tia, offering her a piece of the croissant. Tia took a small bite and seemed unsure.

Seeing Tia contentedly munching away, Hannei subtly signaled Lansius. Recognizing her cue, he moved away with her, putting some distance between them and Tia.

With a glance toward the stairs, Hannei confirmed the absence of Calub, Margo, and Timmy. Taking a moment to gather her thoughts, she leaned in to Lansius. "Whispers are circulating."

"About Midlandia?" Lansius queried, his interest piqued.

"No, something even bigger."

His curiosity deepened. "Bigger than Midlandia's succession?"

Hannei hesitated. The words were treasonous, yet she felt that Lansius needed to know. "The Emperor, the Ageless and Immortal one . . . he's dead."

CHAPTER 8

HIC SUNT DRACONES

The Lore of this World

In the beginning, there were only the Ancients. The first sentients who roamed the boundless expanse of a world they later dubbed Aqua Terra. Birthed from the void, they maintained not one form but ever-changing ones as they devoured and consumed biomass.

As eras passed, they evolved in wisdom, and one among them was revered for her wisdom; she was called Mother.

Mother was the first to ascend into the boundless sky. Her form morphed into a creature resembling an incomplete, mutated, altered dragon. Towering as large as a small mountain, she bore multiple eyes, mouths, nostrils, wings, and tails. Her limbs morphed as necessary, as she was closer to a monstrous abomination than a living entity.

The rest of the Ancients followed, and they embarked on a journey across the vast verdant world. They were virtually ageless, their lives stretching across eons.

They wandered the primal world either alone or in small groups, resilient in the face of countless volcanic eruptions and ice ages, and adapting to a perpetually transforming world.

Despite their longevity, their number was small and finite, their presence leaving merely a faint imprint on their world. Their existence was a ceaseless odyssey of exploration, the hunt, challenges, and unending self-improvement.

Despite their intelligence and wisdom, the Ancients shied away from establishing a civilization. Given their staggering power and self-sustainability, they felt no need for such communal constructs.

Moreover, their inability to produce offspring inclined them toward solitude. This isolationist stance was also motivated by a desire to respect boundaries and avert conflicts, considering the immense power each wielded.

However, as time wore on, their numbers began to wane. After millions of years, the Ancients, in all their extraordinary vigor, were not truly immortal.

The death of the first Ancients marked the end of the First Age.

The Second Age began when Mother, the wisest, discovered a budding new race—the elves. Primitive woodland beings who were just beginning to use stone and sticks as tools.

So taken was she with these intelligent creatures that she shed her dragon form and adopted the refined shape of an elven goddess. In awe, the elves worshipped her, and to her surprise, she could bear offspring with them.

This joyful discovery led to the birth of a new lineage. From her womb, the high elves emerged, inheriting a fragment of her extraordinary longevity and achieving lifespans of up to twelve hundred years.

Under Mother's guidance, the elves transitioned from the Stone Age to the Bronze Age. Some among them even unlocked the secrets of magic and erected a sprawling metropolis—the world's first in the old **Progentia** Continent.

Several Ancients joined, dwelling in a grand city fittingly named the Everlasting Glade. It was the golden age of the elves' civilization, filled with wonder and magic. Yet, the shadow of mortality began to creep in.

Despite all the magic and wisdom they acquired, the first generation of high elves succumbed to death's inevitable call.

Their passing of her children reminded Mother of her own mortality, and her vigor started to fade in earnest. Her fall marked the end of the Second Age and the decline of the elves.

The dawn of the Third Age was heralded by an extraordinary discovery: nestled deep within the mountains, the elves uncovered a previously unseen race, the dwarves.

The Ancients found a new fascination and transformed themselves into perfect embodiments of dwarves. This new alliance stirred envy among the elves, who perceived it as a threat to their own standing.

With most surviving Ancients taking up residence under the mountains, a significant shift in power dynamics occurred.

Under the Ancients' patronage, the dwarves constructed grand citadels within the mountain range and forged the Gallery Road—a vast network of tunnels that spanned nearly the entire old continent of **Progentia**.

Unlike the elves, the dwarves were innate artisans, crafting wondrous tools, divine relics, and even sentient golems. With the magical prowess of the Ancients, coupled with the inherent skills of the dwarves, they ushered in an era of unprecedented innovation.

After hundreds of generations, they achieved the Ancients' greatest aspiration—a portal to another world.

Initially, only the shapeshifting Ancients could traverse this inter-dimensional gateway. But with time, they perfected the art, maintaining a portal that allowed all beings to pass through.

Almost all of the dwarves' population and a great number of elves accompanied the last of the Ancients in the Great Exodus to the new world.

For a quarter of a millennium, the remaining dwarves maintained the portal with the greatest of care until they were no longer able to do so. The portal eventually broke down, severing all contact with the new world.

Shortly after this, the dwarves met their inevitable extinction. No longer numbering in the millions, the current population, now only numbering in the thousands, was unable to maintain their advanced civilization. Their grand underground tunnels and vast citadels began to fall into decay, an invitation to fell beasts that thrived in the dark, subterranean world.

The conflict with these creatures greatly accelerated the dwarves' demise.

With the passing of the last dwarf, the Third Age drew to a close.

The Fourth, or current Age began amidst calamity. The amount of magic required to maintain the dwarves' ingenious creations and the high elves' lavish lifestyle ultimately drained the continent of its magic.

Even the forest encircling the Everlasting Glade languished in a pitiful state. With the subterranean realms overrun by fell beasts and the forests in decay, many were compelled to venture forth into the plains, and a new race was born.

They were the Grand Progenitors, the First Humans.

Historical accounts from this period are scant, clouded by the elves' unwillingness to share and the First Humans' penchant for self-aggrandizement.

They claimed lineage from the last Ancient's womb, but a millennium had passed since the last Ancients walked on Aqua Terra, casting doubt on the veracity of their claim.

Royal historians from the First and Third Imperiums dared to speculate that the Grand Progenitors might have been a hybrid of elves and Ancient-born dwarves, a plausible occurrence given their coexistence.

The Grand Progenitors exhibited remarkable martial prowess. Each was a hero in their own right, vanquishing numerous fell beasts to validate their might. They established multiple city-states and kingdoms on the **Progentia** plains, adjacent to its many rivers.

However, despite their formidable strength, they were helpless in the face of the continent's slow death.

Guided by tales handed down from the Ancients about a larger, more fertile continent to the west, the Grand Progenitors took to the sea, honing their skills as seafarers. Many perished while trying to tame the waves. Despite these adversities, they eventually learned to navigate the oceans and set sail westward.

As foretold by the Ancients, after enduring months on the endless sea, they chanced upon the land of promise: the continent of *Promissia*. The majority of the Grand Progenitors, along with the elves, embarked upon this verdant, pristine land.

This was the second Great Exodus, a singular epoch when elves and humans collaborated and journeyed in unison. These two races traversed the lush and vast continent from east to west.

As the years rolled by, more and more Grand Progenitors and their kin chose to settle, founding kingdoms in locations they deemed fertile. They domesticated the land and its beasts, populated the regions, and kindled civilization wherever their feet touched.

Finally, after centuries, only the elves reached the western shores, where they ceased their odyssey and erected their first city. This milestone marked the start of the Elven Calendar.

Four millennia, three Imperiums, or four generations of high elves later, a handful of the Grand Progenitors still draw breath. These first humans seemed unnaturally immune to the natural passage of time.

Renowned as warriors, their lives typically ended on battlefields, fighting against fell beasts or locked in conflicts among themselves. This immortality became a source of deep envy among the elves.

However, their kin and offspring did not inherit this trait. The current Emperor of the Third Imperium is the last of the Grand Progenitors. Legend has it that the Ageless One was already four-thousand years old when he ascended to the throne.

Calub's House, Lansius

Lansius was so taken aback when Hannei stated that the emperor was dead that he responded with a nervous smile, whispering, "You're jesting! The emperor is a Grand Progenitor. He's immortal."

Hannei cast a glance at Tia, who was quietly savoring a croissant before turning her sight back to Lansius. "You believe all that grand or great progenitor stuff?"

Lansius knitted his brows.

The pale blonde, garbed in a squire-like attire of a blue doublet and a white surcoat, gave a patronizing stare. "Back then in Toruna, you said you read about the Imperium's history—try to remember when the Ageless One took the throne?"

When the emperor took the throne?

"The Ageless One was the third one, right?" Lansius tried to recall the history of the Third Imperium.

Hannei nodded and spoke. "The current emperor was an advisor to the first emperor and a tutor to the second."

"And then he finally took the throne to avert a succession crisis because the second emperor has no child," Lansius recited. "That happened around 1300 years ago, or so I read . . . Why do you ask?"

Hannei glanced at the room and leaned in closer. "Remember, how old are the high elves supposed to live?"

Twelve hundred years . . .

A realization dawned in Lansius's eyes. He met her golden-brown eyes, shaking his head in disbelief. "No way . . ."

"Lans, it could be a lie. You of all people, should have suspected it."

Lansius had nothing to retort.

Hannei continued. "The last of the Grand Progenitors probably died before the Elven Calendar even began. Their legend and immortality was likely a myth perpetuated by the Ageless One himself so he could rule the Imperium."

Lansius shook his head. He had suspected something was amiss, but not to this degree.

For an elf to masquerade as a Grand Progenitor and rule humans as the emperor . . . What a devious scheme. But how could Hannei know about this? She can barely read the common text.

Hannei continued. "This is why Midlandia has been preparing to take action for three generations."

"You mean they suspected this?" asked Lansius.

"They're not stupid," she murmured. "This is also why Baldy Gottfried rallied the North, conquered four provinces, and invaded Arvena. Like Midlandia, he too must have suspected that the emperor is an elf and is finally dead."

Lansius had his doubts, but before he could voice them, a commotion from downstairs drew their attention. Two women's voices echoed, "We're here!"

Like a whirlwind of trouble, two women emerged from the stairs. "Rest assured, Felis is here! Everything is going to be all right," declared the newly arrived blonde, while Audrey, grinning behind her, waved at Hannei.

Hannei waved back at Audrey with a smile.

Lansius looked at the pair, still in disbelief that Audrey and Hannei had become fast friends despite starting on the wrong foot in Toruna. One was the captive, and the other was the captor's enabler. But their relationship transcended that.

It was Hannei who had suggested to Sir Stan to purchase Audrey during their incognito visit to the black market around Feodosia. Hannei was also the one who had tended to Audrey on her way back to Toruna until more treatment could be arranged.

Despite Audrey's obliviousness to the situation due to her severe head injury, her sharp instincts led her to trust Hannei. However, the same couldn't be said about the relationship between Lansius and Hannei.

Despite the one-in-a-million chance of them both sharing the same origins, Hannei was reluctant to help. Excluding today, she rarely divulged any information, and when she did, it seemed to be more out of pity than trust.

Among the secrets she held was the reason she and Sir Stan had chosen to purchase Audrey. Her tight lips constantly reminded Lansius that Hannei's loyalty lay firmly with Sir Stan and Lord Bengrieve.

Now, Hannei was eyeing Felis, anger flaring in her golden eyes. "Where have you been?"

"In the castle. I told you I was going to the castle," Felis replied innocently.

"No. You said you're going to get some fruit you just heard of from a peddler. Then you disappeared. I was worried, you know," Hannei said in frustration.

"Oh, that too, hehe. Sorry." Felis approached Hannei and tried to hug her. However, Hannei was still annoyed. This made Felis walk toward Tia instead.

The little girl's eyes were wide open.

"What's the matter, child?" Felis asked sweetly.

"Pardon, my lady, but am I in the afterlife?" Tia responded.

Felis erupted into giggles.

"Why do you ask that?" Hannei questioned as she approached with a concerned look crossing her face.

"Well, I'm surrounded by people with golden hair, and the Lord of Korelia is also present. Am I dreaming?"

Hannei snorted laughter, which seemed to break the ice. Afterward, the rest of the evening was filled with warmth and camaraderie. This was a rare reunion of the Toruna band, with Audrey, Lansius, Hannei, Calub, and now even Felis was onboard.

With Felis soon to be married into nobility, they all sensed this might be their last gathering. Perhaps it was this subconscious awareness that made them savor the evening, despite the ongoing healing process.

Felis readily helped Hannei, as Tia needed a change of clothes, while Calub busied himself with brewing herbal concoctions.

They kept Hannei company during the final stage of the treatment. With just one healer, it was hard, due to sleep deprivation. However, the grueling night was made lighter by friendly company. Conversation filled the air, and stories were exchanged, since Hannei couldn't afford to rest just yet.

At Lansius's suggestion, they dragged a bed up and put it next to Tia's, allowing Hannei to recite the healing verses while lying down. It was a measure to conserve her dwindling strength.

Upon Calub's insistence, Audrey and Sterling escorted a reluctant Lansius back to the castle after midnight while Felis stayed behind to assist Hannei.

At first light, Audrey returned. She had instructed the staff to let Lansius oversleep. Together with Calub and the rest of the household, she witnessed Tia's recovery.

Now unbound and attempting to move her once limp leg, Tia's first movement in bed was shaky, but gradually, her ankle began to display a full range of motion.

The little girl wept with joy.

Finally, Hannei could rest. In just two days, the ankle bones had healed, and the operation scar had mended.

After a light breakfast, she instructed Calub not to let Tia move from her bed. Then she retired to Calub's room, where she soon fell asleep. Her slender form curled up in the fetal position, appearing both beautiful and fragile.

Margo and Timmy vigilantly guarded the house that day, ensuring peace and quiet. The only sound they tolerated was the soft snoring coming from Felis in the next room. Meanwhile, Calub kept himself busy by reading some scrolls while periodically checking on Tia.

Feeling satisfied with what she had witnessed, Audrey returned to the castle. On her way back, she noticed that the wind was blowing harder than usual, sweeping from the south toward the north. The season was changing.

CHAPTER 9

SOUTHERN WIND

In the town of Korelia, whispers started to circulate overnight that a saint candidate was secretly visiting. The sight of blondes in the local inn and around town, combined with the lord's late-night visit and the local physician's tight-lipped demeanor, seemed to add weight to these rumors.

Despite initial doubts, curiosity won out, and a crowd gradually started to gather outside the alchemist's residence. In a world that lacked any form of religion, the closest thing to reverence was the respect shown toward the Ageless Emperor, followed closely by the saint candidates.

These extraordinary individuals, blessed with the innate ability to heal, were exceedingly rare. As a result, the saint candidates were usually kept cloistered, their abilities monopolized by the high nobility through the Healers Guild.

Among commoners, even a blessing from a saint candidate was considered to hold potent healing powers, although the truth was far more complicated. Upon hearing of the gathering crowds and to prevent unrest as well as possible property damage or injuries, the Lord of Korelia made the prudent decision to order the evacuation of the house.

As the lord's evacuation orders were carried peacefully, another change subtly started to manifest itself. The season was shifting, and with it, the wind's direction was changing. It began to blow eagerly from the south, sweeping warm, dry air into the Great Plains of Lowlandia. The locals called it the Southern Wind, the harbinger of change.

With this shift, Korelia had entered the height of summer.

Korelia Castle

"This is the Great Chamber. We can have meals or snacks here. It's probably the best place to hang out." Audrey was introducing the room to the recently arrived guest.

Hannei surveyed the room with visible awe. "I see. It's spacious and seems to have good ventilation."

The Great Chamber boasted a ceiling taller than most rooms in the castle. Despite being smaller than the great hall, it offered a less congested ambiance. The room's centerpiece was a solitary elongated table, surrounded by matching chairs.

Fully plastered walls, painted a serene shade of white, complemented the ceiling, which was of the same hue but adorned with an array of vibrant decorative plants and floral patterns.

The two of them walked across the chamber and proceeded toward the next place.

"And if you follow me, we'll reach the training hall," Audrey continued as tour guide.

As they approached the corridor connecting the two rooms, they heard the echoes of bowstrings being tensioned, released, and snapping back into place. Crossbow training for the castle's occupants was also held indoors.

This arrangement had been initiated last winter to prevent damage to the components from ice and moisture buildup. Despite the limited space, the place saw regular usage.

"Oh, you're here," Lansius called as they caught sight of each other.

"Hey, my lord, I'm just taking Hannei on a short tour!" Audrey replied.

"Ah, I see."

Ever since the guests arrived, Audrey's formalities had been somewhat relaxed. The lord didn't seem to mind, but the staff took notice.

"Are you doing crossbow training?" Hannei asked.

"Yeah, care to try?" Lansius offered his custom small pistol-gripped crossbow.

More than a dozen people were training with him. The strawman targets in the corner already resembled a pincushion.

"Nah, I'll pass. You should ask Felis; she's good with a bow," Hannei began, then quickly added, "my lord." She was aware she wasn't part of the nobility, unlike Felis, who was about to marry a high-ranking lord and thus was afforded some leniency. Here, she was required to adhere to the formalities.

"Uh, eh, yeah . . . How's the room. Is it too small?" Lansius asked, noting that it was the first time Hannei had addressed him as lord.

"No, it's spacious. I've been told that it's actually your room, my lord?" Her voice held a tinge of apology.

"Yeah . . . but Felis wanted it, so . . ." Lansius shrugged.

Hannei let out a sigh. "You shouldn't pamper that woman."

Lansius chuckled. "Well, I owe a lot to her."

"That's just your perception. For example, my lord won Korelia without her help."

"Gratitude for the kind words, Hannei."

"No, I should thank you for your hospitality, my lord."

Sharing a mutual smile, the two were closely observed by Audrey, who was grinning from ear to ear behind Hannei. She playfully remarked, "You two would make a great couple."

"What?!"

"No, we would not!" Taken aback, Lansius and Hannei retorted in unison, sending Audrey into a ripple of laughter.

Audrey was well aware of the shared background between Hannei and Lansius, despite not knowing all the details.

With a resolute tone, Hannei declared, "Come on, there are so many other places I'm eager to explore," as she gently pushed Audrey forward.

"See you. Oh, full armor training starts today, after midday," Audrey said as she was being shoved away.

Lansius could only offer a smile in response to their antics. Their armor purchase had arrived from Midlandia. He was excited to try it on but less so about sparring with Audrey, whom he knew would be brutal. He let out a sigh, hoping that things would remain this peaceful. However, knowing the trio's short tempers, he found it challenging to keep his expectations high.

"Fresh quiver, my lord," Sterling offered.

"Gratitude," Lansius replied, accepting the quiver and reloading his mini crossbow. His aim was unusually off today. Despite attempting to clear his mind, the notion of the emperor's death was difficult to dismiss.

Considering the thousand years of rule, the impact of his demise would undoubtedly be colossal. If Hannei's words were true, then it was clear that the Third Imperium would not stand. It would be a doomed entity.

Upon further reflection, Lansius felt that his preconception of elves as a wise and benevolent race was naive. The lore actually suggested they were prone to jealousy, and deviousness might not even be a stretch.

He realized that in a world filled with races that had much longer life expectancies than humans, it was almost absurd to think they wouldn't take advantage of or exploit the weaker races.

An ambitious elf could easily conceal his intentions, forge his way up, and through his talents, experience, and his gift of agelessness compared to humans, he could ascend the power ladder in a human kingdom, or in this case, the Imperium.

Over several generations, given that humans, including kings, naturally live to around a hundred years and heirs are not always guaranteed, an elf could merely wait for a succession crisis to arise. Whether natural or instigated by his intervention, such a crisis would present an opportunity to lure a faction to his side.

When such a situation occurred, the elf, as their elder, a face of stability, could easily convince them that he was the logical choice to settle their dispute as a stand-in for their monarch or emperor. After all, he would outlast everyone, even their great-grandchildren.

The more Lansius pondered, the clearer it became. Now, he understood how the Third Imperium had maintained a level of stability that would put even the Romans to shame.

Moreover, instead of organized religion, the Ageless taught to disregard superstitious aspects of life. Prayers for rain, good harvests, or the afterlife were forbidden, as was fear of weather phenomena, astrological events, or geological occurrences.

Without the clash of religion and its natural schisms, the Imperium proved to be more robust as an entity.

Lansius suppressed a sigh. The real question lingered: how long would the continent be haunted by strife before a new order could rise? This thought weighed heavily on Lansius's mind.

If only she would tell me more . . .

For Lansius, Hannei remained an enigma. He suspected that the problem might lie deeper than just her loyalty to Sir Stan and Lord Bengrieve. Probably, there was another reason that Lansius had yet to discover.

Hannei was eerily secretive about her background, even going so far as not revealing her real name. Lansius only learned that she was French, and unlike him, she had all her memories intact. However, frustratingly, she wouldn't divulge anything about her arrival in this world or how she could use magic.

She mostly kept her lips sealed and, when pressed, would resort to anger, much like Audrey. However, she did confide in him that her place was *here* and that she had no plans to return.

As usual, Lansius had tried to consult Calub, her compatriot. However, Calub himself explained that he didn't know much, out of respect for another professional. He only said that he had known Hannei for almost ten years and that he trusted her with his life.

Naturally, it never occurred to Calub to ask Hannei how or where she learned magic. In this world, a mage is a mage, and they were known to be a secretive bunch. The Mage Guild, like any other, kept their trade secrets. However, Calub had also said that Hannei wasn't part of any guild.

Lansius shook his head. The last thing on his mind was to pry about this issue. The last time he did so, they got into a heated argument and she ended up refusing to see him again. She didn't even appear when Lansius, Audrey, and Calub departed from Toruna to march against Lord Robert.

Cecile

Two weeks had passed since the lord first brought the guest into the castle, and unexpectedly it had brought a newfound vitality to the Great Chamber. Usually, this room was often quiet, as the lord had no family. Thus its grandeur was appreciated sparingly.

Lord Lansius and his closest confidants usually convened in the council chamber or the great hall for their affairs. Yet, the recent influx of guests, a charming assortment including a young girl from time to time, had infused the room with vibrant energy.

Today, however, the atmosphere was subtly different. The delightful presence of the little girl was missing, her usual spot vacant.

Similarly, the distinct personas of Marshal Sir Justin and Deputy Hugo were absent, their chairs empty. The two were currently engaged in an important assignment, their usual contributions to the room's discussions noticeably absent.

Lord Lansius, Captain Audrey, Calub, and the two guests were currently engrossed in a private lunch.

Although the lord and his retainers typically favored simple meals and weren't overly particular about the quality of food, the presence of distinguished guests sparked a change. These guests, with their blonde hair and an air of mystery, seemed to belong to a higher class.

Determined not to compromise Lord Lansius's reputation in front of such esteemed company, the castle staff went the extra mile to ensure the quality of the meal was exceptional.

In a significant departure from their norm, considering the pride they took in their craft, they even reached out to chefs from outside the castle for guidance.

Tap-tap-tap!

The rhythmic echo of footsteps broke the ambient noise as Carla entered the Great Chamber. She breezed past Sterling, halting near a column.

Cecile discerned from Carla's demeanor that she carried important news. Leaning over to the lord, she discreetly mentioned Carla's arrival.

"Ah, Carla, do you have something to share?" Lord Lansius paused, setting aside his plate.

"My lord, a messenger carrying a letter from the Lord of White Lake," Carla announced.

"From Lord Robert? Bring it here then."

Carla approached Lord Lansius and presented the sealed letter.

"Do you mind?" the lord inquired of his guests.

"Not at all. Please proceed as you wish, Lord Lans," Lady Felis responded, reaching for another slice of pudding from a silver plate.

Lady Felis was wearing a striking violet tunic dress, a truly captivating sight. Just a few days prior, she had fortuitously uncovered a cache of dresses in storage. Luckily, Lady Felis's stature suited the dresses perfectly, without the need for alterations.

She was indeed tall, matching the height of Lord Lansius and Calub. In contrast, Audrey and Hannei were of average height, and Cecile herself didn't anticipate growing past her current stature.

While Cecile contemplated their differing heights, Lord Lansius broke the purple wax seal of the letter and perused its contents. After nodding in affirmation a few times, he passed the letter to Master Calub.

"Is it important?" Hannei asked, her eyes on Calub as he read the letter.

"Well, almost every letter carries importance. But this one isn't urgent," the lord commented.

"Betrothal letters?" Hannei quipped.

The table erupted into a commotion. Audrey choked on her drink, Calub snorted with laughter, and the lord coughed. Felis, attempting to stifle her giggles, covered her mouth with an embroidered cloth.

"You really should consider getting married, my lord," Calub suggested after taking a sip of water.

"I plan to," the lord retorted dryly after clearing his throat.

All eyes turned to Audrey.

"No, guys, don't look at me like that . . ." Audrey's usually bright expression turned into a frown.

Cecile was aware that this conversation was typically off-limits. Only the lord's closest confidants were privy to this information.

"Well, there's no need to rush," the lord responded casually.

"Actually . . . it may become more challenging soon," Calub interjected.

"Why do you say that, Calub?" asked the lord.

"The letter mentioned a special envoy. I suspect this might be Lord Robert's daughter," Calub elaborated.

The chamber buzzed with conversation at the lord's expense.

"N-nonsense! Why would he do that?" The lord voiced his objection, snatching the scroll back from his advisor.

"He's being cautious," Felis said with an assuredness that drew everyone's attention. "Lord Robert is sending his daughter to meet you first, then gauging your reaction. If it goes well, he'll propose a betrothal. If it goes sour, he can cover it up. Even if rumors spread, there's no evidence to back them."

"That's surprisingly sensible. You've learned well, Felis," praised Hannei.

"Thank you. I gained much from my tutors in Midlandia." Lady Felis seemed pleased.

"But why would a special envoy necessarily mean his daughter? Couldn't it just be his advisor?" The lord expressed his lingering skepticism.

"My lord, the viscount went to great lengths to hint at 'someone,' not just a servant or follower. It would only make sense if it were a family member," Calub reasoned.

"Alright, no further comment. Let's just wait and see. It's probably just a misunderstanding." The lord did not share in the others' excitement.

Despite the joy in the air, Cecile wasn't entirely sure Lord Robert would risk such a play. Lord Lansius's standing in Korelia was still precarious.

If she were in Robert's position, she would wait for Lansius to solidify his victory against the western lords before taking such a step. However, Robert was known for his strategic prowess, and the thought processes of strategists could be deeply intricate and unpredictable.

Now, one of the supposedly fearsome strategists was engaged in pleasant banter, casually discussing potential schools for the young girl, Tia, and Calub's recently purchased house, which was now unusable due to the rumors about a saint candidate.

Cecile was more intrigued by Hannei's abilities, yet the conversation did not touch on this. Hannei was rumored to be a saint candidate. Still, she didn't fit the typical image of one.

Dressed in a doublet and surcoat similar to a squire, she projected a mixed impression. Her blonde hair, delicate beauty, and seemingly fragile demeanor suggested nobility. However, her lack of familiarity with formal etiquette and warlike attire contradicted this impression.

Just like Audrey's well-worn belt and scabbard, Hannei's gear hinted at her skills with a sword. This led Cecile to doubt the idea of Hannei being a saint candidate.

Saint candidates were known to lead a cloistered life, guarded and shielded from outside threats. It made no sense for them to become adept with swords.

Yet, Cecile couldn't completely ignore the whispers surrounding Hannei. One morning, a staff member reported that Hannei was in the courtyard when it started to drizzle. Oddly enough, Hannei's clothes remained dry while everyone else's got soaked.

Another mentioned that the main chamber where she resided remained cool as winter, even during the summer midday heat.

On reflection, Cecile acknowledged that sometimes she sensed something different when she was around Hannei. There was also Margo, Calub's page boy, who had become Hannei's assistant. His refusal to divulge what transpired in Calub's house only fueled further speculation and mystery.

The echo of heavy boots, pacing hurriedly against the stone floors, alerted Cecile. Sterling, the squire, instinctively moved to block the corridor but stepped aside respectfully when he recognized the unexpected guest.

Sir Justin burst into the room, his abrupt entrance startling everyone. Before anyone could ask, the marshal made a thunderous declaration: "War, war is coming!"

His proclamation, full of raw enthusiasm and unrestrained jubilation, crashed against the high vaulted ceilings. The usual calm and restrained ambiance of the chamber was gone in an instant.

"Permission to chant!" Sir Justin continued, his tone as resolute as the walls around them.

Triggered by the request, Lord Lansius exclaimed, "Granted!" and sprang from his seat.

To Cecile's surprise, Sir Justin proceeded to bellow a war cry that filled the chamber. It was a war song he had learned from nomads during their mock battles months ago.

Sir Justin was a unique personality; he viewed war as a competition or a way of life, and also a chance to make a profit. His infectious energy served as a vibrant counterpoint to Lansius's doom-and-gloom attitude.

Audrey unexpectedly joined in chanting, followed by Lansius, Sterling, and Carla. Their voices built in a crescendo of high-pitched tones and rhythmic chants, filling the chamber with an intensity that Cecile had never witnessed before.

This was Cecile's first experience with the news of impending war, but she was certain that nobles typically wouldn't react this way.

Lansius and his retainers were far from normal, she knew, but she was still taken aback. The usually gentle lord and his companions were now ablaze with a different kind of fervor in their eyes.

The Lord of Korelia, to whom she had pledged her loyalty, had revealed a new facet of his persona. He wasn't just a skilled administrator; he was also a warlord.

CHAPTER 10

DIRTY GAIN

The high spirits that had once filled Lansius and his retainers gradually waned, giving way to a growing sense of anxiety in the council chamber. First, there was concern over the safety of the guests. Second, the uncertainty surrounding the enemy's numbers and their anticipated time of arrival.

"Three Hills is a fifteen-day march away from Korelia," Sir Justin started. "The horseman who brought the news endured three days of riding, changing horses every half-day with minimal sleep at night. So, we likely have twelve days until they arrive."

Lansius responded with a nod while Calub stroked his chin, both of them bearing somber expressions.

"Is there anything we can do besides wait for Batu's messenger?" Audrey asked from her seat.

"Not much," replied Calub in a low voice. "Sir Justin and I have our informants, but they fall behind the tribal scouts in terms of speed."

Audrey frowned slightly but nodded her understanding.

The sudden knock at the door interrupted their deliberation.

"My lord, Tribesman Batu is here to see you," Sterling's muffled voice informed them from the other side of the door.

Batu is here by himself?

Calub saw Lansius's reaction and commanded, "Let him in."

As Batu entered, it was evident that he had indeed ridden a long way; his long hair was slick with sweat. "Forgive my intrusion."

"The honor is ours," Lansius responded, rising to his feet along with his entourage as Batu approached.

Given Batu's stature as a tribal leader, a seat was soon arranged next to Lansius.

"So, what's the tidings?" Lansius asked, pouring a pale ale into a silver goblet for Batu.

"A grim one. It seems you've managed to anger almost all the western lords."

The statement hung in the air, and the tension in the room grew thicker.

"What makes you say such a thing?" Sir Justin asked, his brow furrowed.

Batu drained his goblet in a single gulp before replying, "Our scouts report thirty groups, each numbering two hundred."

Thirty groups of two hundred? That's six thousand men . . . ? Fuck! That's equal to the entire population of Korelia.

Tribesman Batu

The tribesman noticed that Lansius was unflinching but stunned, while his companions exchanged uneasy glances.

"Thirty groups of two hundred . . . ? That's a considerable force. Are you certain your scouts reported accurately?" Sir Justin queried, his voice just shy of skeptical.

"Our shepherds are the best at what they do. Counting that high is second nature to them," Batu replied, not a hint of doubt in his tone.

"How many are we talking about, exactly?" Audrey pressed impatiently.

"Drey, we're looking at six thousand," Lansius replied, almost in a murmur.

The sheer enormity of the number left them dumbstruck. Audrey struggled to fathom such a figure. Only Calub and Sir Justin seemed to fully grasp the gravity of the situation.

"It's three times the size of Lord Robert's force last year," Lansius clarified.

"How can there possibly be that many?" Audrey exclaimed, baffled.

Batu simply shook his head. "That, I don't know."

"Did I inadvertently incite anyone's wrath?" Lansius wondered aloud, a frown creasing his brow.

Sir Justin shrugged his shoulders. "My understanding of the politics in West Lowlandia isn't comprehensive, but it seems unlikely to be hated by all. Should I get Sir Callahan? A local knight like him is best suited for this discussion."

Lansius shook his head. "Sir Callahan may hold deeper insights into this matter, but he's currently supervising our merchants. War or not, we're going to need grain supplies."

"I think these western lords are largely opportunists," Calub opined dismissively. "Like vultures circling an easy meal."

Lansius exhaled a weary sigh. "I have paid a lot to station four hundred men in Korelia, rallied the militia, even had crossbowmen drill in trenches in plain view of passing merchants, hoping to convey our might. But it doesn't seem to deter anyone."

Batu studied Lansius with respect, appreciating the Korelian lord's ingenuity. Although the ploy hadn't succeeded today, it was a commendable effort to prevent wars and unnecessary bloodshed.

"Not all took part, mind you," Batu informed Lansius. "The scouts only see the banners of the Three Hills, Korimor, and South Hill."

"Korimor's participation was expected, but South Hill's involvement is surprising," Calub noted.

Sir Justin nodded in agreement. No one had anticipated that South Hill, having rebelled against Lord Jorge of Three Hills, would participate. "There must be a reason," he mused.

"The reason doesn't matter right now; what matters is that we're facing six thousand," Lansius interjected, bringing the conversation back to the looming threat. "Do we stand a chance?"

"A slim one," admitted Sir Justin.

"Should we prepare to leave?" Calub asked.

"Oh, fun, all the work for nothing," Audrey commented bitterly.

Their frank responses in front of their lord surprised Batu, but he noticed that the trio was glancing at Lord Lansius as if expecting something. Despite their words, there was only urgency, not fear.

Lansius sighed deeply. "We have a mere thousand at best. I could perhaps withstand an army of three thousand, but six . . . That's a tall order."

"Perhaps, my lord miscalculated our odds like last year?" Calub remarked.

"I don't want to gamble with our lives again . . . Our victory last time was mostly due to luck, and I don't anticipate a repeat of such fortune," Lansius replied and then fixed his gaze on Calub. "There are times when things take a turn for the worse, and I fear this could be one of them."

While Calub nodded, Sir Justin voiced his concern. "What's our move then? Do we quit?"

Lansius's lips twitched into a faint smirk, a mysterious glimmer in his eyes. "Let's not rush into anything. First, let's send a messenger to Lord Robert. Then I need to address our men."

He rose up from his seat, followed by everyone. "You all should accompany me to the billets," declared Lansius, and then to his guest, "Brother Batu, I'll arrange for a guest room for you."

Considering the situation, the usually soft-spoken lord now exuded a level of confidence Batu had rarely witnessed before. "No need. My tribesmen have set up a yurt outside for the night."

"Then please join us in the great hall for supper. Let me know if you require anything or reach out to one of my men."

"It would be an honor, but I'd like to accompany you to the billets if you don't mind. There's a certain curiosity I wish to satisfy," explained Batu.

Lansius

The billets were a pet project of Lansius and his staff. Originally, whenever a lord wanted to station troops in a city or town, he would require the residents to provide shelter for his men and officers.

This arrangement had two advantages. First, it distributed the responsibility of housing and feeding the troops among the citizens. Second, it ensured the city's loyalty.

This was because, typically, only the wealthier citizens had extra room in their homes. As a result, having the lord's men stay with them turned a seemingly fair arrangement into a quasi-hostage situation.

Unsurprisingly, the populace never liked the idea. They felt as if the lord simply passed the bill to feed and house his troops onto them. Moreover, having their families live next to an armed officer or footman they had never met before was rarely comfortable, if not altogether dangerous.

Lansius saw the benefits but believed the traditional billets risked creating social problems between the Korelians and his primarily Midlandian troops. Thus, his first administrative breakthrough the previous autumn was to central- ize the billeting system by selecting sites with empty houses in the southern part of Korelia.

There, he established a permanent dormitory-style system, a field kitchen, a training hall, and an archery range. With the assistance of his staff, he laid the groundwork for a military police force, appointing senior guardsmen to main- tain order.

In doing this, he effectively created a barracks complex to manage and orga- nize his men. This also limited interactions between the troops and townsfolk, greatly coaxed discipline, and mitigated unnecessary risks.

Despite his attempts to instate a more rigid hierarchy, Lansius recognized that implementing a modern military structure or even a Roman-style system would cause too many problems. Thus, he relinquished any desire to microman- age, allowing them to govern themselves internally, to a degree.

After a short ride, Lansius and his entourage arrived at the billets complex. The guard on the post saluted him readily and opened the gates for them.

As Lansius and his entourage dismounted, the air vibrated with anticipation. His presence made his men gather around. His friendly gaze swept across their faces, absorbing the subtle shifts of emotion. "At ease," he said cheerfully, then said, "Take me to the training hall."

Hearing the lord's request, Sir Justin took over seamlessly, leading their party toward the heart of the complex. The men dutifully followed and created an escort for them.

The training hall, a brainchild of Lansius himself, was a hulking beast of a building. It could accommodate dozens of men, and was suffused with light and fresh air from meticulously placed windows and vents. The equipment within was rudimentary but effective.

As they stepped inside, the distinct smell of exertion and iron filled their nostrils. The men went alive, eyes turning toward their unexpected guests.

Sir Justin, ever the pragmatic commander, urged, "At ease, we're just looking. Carry on."

Lansius allowed his gaze to sweep over the battered surfaces of the grotesque iron dumbbells and wooden bench presses. Their scarred surface was a testament to their extensive use. But the true evidence of their usage was embodied in the men who stood before him.

As they lined up to greet him, Lansius couldn't help but grin at their transformed physiques. The once scrawny group from the previous year had metamorphosed into a team of muscular individuals.

The inclusion of meals in Lansius's contracts to his men-at-arms wasn't a mere act of generosity, but a calculated move. Unlike Lansius, the Midlandians and Lowlandians did not suffer from lactose intolerance. Plus, Korelia had a surplus of goat's milk, cheese, and meat. Thus, it was an easy plan to enact.

He had focused on bulking them up the previous winter. This served as a solution to several issues.

First, Lansius couldn't march his troops for more than forty days per year. Moreover, despite the all-year-round payments, they had only agreed to one week of armed training per month.

However, he had convinced them to commit to three days of personal training weekly. This commitment translated to three full days of weightlifting and stamina-building runs when weather permitted.

Coupled with the competitive games he had initiated, offering protein-rich food and alcohol as prizes, he ensured a high participation rate, driving his men toward continuous improvement.

By giving them a goal and rewards, he reduced their boredom and possibly prevented many issues usually faced in military facilities.

Now, his men had become warriors in spirit and form. Their presence radiated strength and confidence.

Catching Batu's impressed gaze, Lansius asked, "What do you think of them?"

"Only one way to find out," Batu replied, striding toward a table that was traditionally used for arm wrestling. "Come, I challenge your best."

"I'm up next after Batu," Sir Justin announced, encouraging his men as he took his place behind Batu.

Audrey, who had lined up behind the marshal, shed her traveling coat and was stretching.

The unexpected situation drew a chuckle from Lansius. As he warmed up his arms, he took his place in line behind Audrey.

Despite his unassuming appearance, the lord wasn't to be underestimated—his training on horseback, along with wielding hefty lances against wooden targets and engaging in hand-to-hand combat, had honed his physical abilities.

Their collective participation sparked a spontaneous competition. News of a competition against the lord and his entourage spread like wildfire, attracting hundreds of onlookers outside.

Sir Justin and Batu displayed formidable strength. Audrey performed remarkably well. Even Lansius held his own, besting seven out of a dozen plus competitors.

The contest was intense; these men were no pushovers. After a half hour of sweat-soaked, adrenaline-fueled excitement, the contest finally came to an end.

Their arms ached, but all were feeling satisfied as they shared drinks and laughter. The lord himself, despite losing a few silver coins, felt pride in his performance. His training had borne fruit. Now, noticing the crowd lingering outside the training hall, he decided it was time to execute his plan.

As he stood at the hall's entrance, he was met with a sea of eager faces. "Men, I'm here today to check on you because we've received news about our enemy."

Murmurs rippled through the crowd.

"Yes, the western lords are marching toward Korelia. And their numbers are big," Lansius announced, his tone casual and untroubled.

"My lord, how many of them are coming?" Sigmund, the skald, asked from the porchlike section of the training hall.

"Our scouts report thirty groups of two hundred," Lansius responded, still casually. All his pent-up worries had unexpectedly found release in the arm-wrestling bout.

His words triggered a wave of commotion. While many couldn't grasp just how large they were, they sensed it was more than ten times their size. They were numbered only four hundred.

Lansius glanced toward his nearest ally, who happened to be Audrey. Sensing his intention, she slammed her fist hard on the door, commanding attention. "Order," she demanded in a threatening voice.

The men, familiar with her reputation, respected her authority.

"Men, this is why I kept you in the dark last year." Lansius resumed his speech. "Last year, you were all innocent. You knew nothing about fighting and warfare. But now, you should have learned a thing or two. Our victory last year should teach you that it's entirely possible to win against an enemy more numerous and better armed than us."

His words had their full attention. Indeed, nobody could forget their miraculous victory last year against Lord Robert.

"I know how to battle against a bigger opponent, because I've trained for it. I mastered it since my youth," Lansius continued. "I understand it may be useless to try to convince you of my wisdom. But listen well to what I am about to say."

He paused for effect and declared, "Thirty groups of two hundred . . . Six thousand men is nothing! Don't be fooled by the number."

The crowd looked at him in disbelief.

A faint smirk formed on Lansius's lips. "Let me explain."

CHAPTER 11

THE BREATH BEFORE THE PLUNGE

Lansius's assertion that six thousand enemies were nothing captured everyone's attention. They were intrigued, excited, and relieved that the situation seemed salvageable.

From his pocket, Lansius produced several wooden blocks the size of a thumb and proceeded to sit on the wooden porch. "Imagine each of these is a thousand of the enemy's troops," he said, lining them up on the porch.

The hundreds of his men focused their gaze on the tiny objects, hanging on his every word.

"Now, the first one," Lansius began, lifting one of the wooden blocks and addressing his men like a teacher to his students.

"As you may know, a force of six thousand men marching through the Lowlandia Great Plains would require a massive amount of food and water. It's a fifteen-day journey for heavy ox-drawn carts. Thus, I believe it's reasonable to calculate that one-sixth of their number, or a thousand men, is dedicated solely to this task."

Based on their own marching experience, the men nodded in agreement.

Lansius continued. "So, you don't have to worry about this one." He put one block aside. "They're merely levies, transporters, men who take care of fodder, grass for their oxen, mules, horses. Not first-rate combatants."

From the blocks, the men could see that out of six, now there were only five left.

Lansius then picked up another block. "Next is the South Hill's barony . . . If you talk with the locals enough, any Korelians will tell you that the South Hill men despise the Three Hills. Enough that they rebelled multiple times throughout their history."

Almost all nodded. The last rebellion was considered recent, and people in Korelia still gossiped about it. The reason was, they were once a united entity. Korelia, Korimor, and South Hills were once a viscountcy under Three Hills.

Lansius continued. "Despite what their leaders are thinking, they are reluctant participants. They just need to show up, but they don't want to die in Korelia. They're likely a token army, unmotivated, and unlikely to put their lives in danger."

The men nodded again as Lansius put aside another wooden block. Out of six, only four were left, and the men were curious about what their lord would say next.

Lansius picked another block. "Now, this one is dangerous. This one is the Korimor barony. As you may know, they're mostly made of Nicopolan mercenaries. They're tough, brutal, and resilient. They're going to be our worst enemy on the battlefield."

Despite the warning, the men noticed how the lord said that with a faint smile.

"However . . . they're mercenaries. Everybody despises them, even men from their own Korimor-born regiment. The Lowlandians have no love for the Nicopolans. Because of this, I believe these mercenaries will be very cautious, not giving their all. They want money, not a tombstone. Thus, they represent only half of their strength, equal to five hundred."

The men nodded as they watched the lord place the wooden block on the right side.

Lansius then gathered all the remaining three blocks in his palm and asked, "These three represent the Three Hills troops. How many do you think are levied, and how many are men-at-arms?"

The men breathed a sigh of relief. They understood the intention behind the question. Some even chuckled, though none dared to answer.

"Sterling," Lansius called.

"Yes, my lord." The squire came to his side.

"Can you answer my question?"

"Out of three thousand, I think less than a thousand are cavalry and men-at-arms. The rest are levied troops," Sterling answered.

The men agreed and were eager to see Lansius's reaction.

As expected, Lansius removed two more blocks. "These are villagers who have seen so many terrors of wars. Unlike you, Midlandians who've only seen war a few times in your lives, here, even boys as young as ten have witnessed several."

He paused for a moment. "Now, these men, so far from home, waging wars they neither like nor agree with. I doubt they'll throw their lives away for nothing."

Lansius then moved the last block to his right side, joining the only sole block. "Now, as you can see, we only have to deal with a thousand Three Hills men-at-arms and knights, along with five hundred of Korimor's Nicopolan mercenaries." He gazed at his men and taunted, "It isn't so bad, is it?"

The men readily nodded, some even grinned, as they found no fault in the lord's reasoning.

"Our number at four hundred men-at-arms. We have crossbowmen with heavy arbalests and six hundred brave Korelian militia. Our defensive position is entrenched, and we also have the assistance of Batu's nomadic cavalry."

Lansius drew a deep breath. "We're not fighting a losing battle. We're going to give them a bloody nose and take everything from them! What do you say about this?"

His men started making some noise in agreement.

Lansius pressed on. "They're six thousand strong only in numbers, but the numbers lie. They're a hodgepodge of an army. Half don't even want to be in this war. Some just wanted to show up and do nothing more. Even in a siege, they won't coordinate well. Each faction distrusts the others. What kind of army is that?"

His men bought the idea Lansius was selling, and the idea caught on.

"This won't be easy, but give me a good fight. Don't you dare run! Don't you dare die on me! Believe in my plan, and you'll find yourselves victorious. And by the Ageless, I swear to employ you even when you're crippled, and I swear to send money to your family if you fall. Will you yield or will you fight?" Lansius repeated his question from the previous year to his men.

Some of his men answered with laughter, while others with serious faces declared, "We'll fight for you, my lord!"

"My brother and I will not shame you!"

"Let them come!" And then their voices coalesced into an excited war cry.

Those watching from behind Lansius—from Sir Justin, Audrey, to Batu—were impressed by Lansius's explanation. The lord might have omitted several aspects, but he had ingeniously steeled his men's hearts, dispelling their fear of the upcoming battle.

With just a simple speech, not only had the lord calmed his men and thwarted any potential desertion, but he had also rallied them. Now, they wouldn't shrink from war—they were clamoring for it.

Lansius returned to his castle and headed directly to the council room, which he had used as his personal quarters. He shut the door, shrugged off his coat, and took a seat on his bed, finally allowing his true emotions to surface.

His hands were slick with sweat from the summer heat, but the tremors coursing through his body were of his own making. The sheer number of lies he had spun was astonishing, even to himself.

Turning six thousand enemies into a mere fifteen hundred, that's some great bullshit . . .

He wore a manic grin, even as a wave of nausea threatened to overwhelm him.

The small window of the council room did little to mitigate the sweltering summer heat.

The door swung open, admitting Audrey, who promptly closed it behind her. "Are you okay?" she asked, concern evident in her approach.

"Yeah, I'm okay. Why do you ask?" Lansius responded, still seated on the bed.

"Because I know you." A rare warmth filled her eyes. She reached for Lansius's cup from the table as she advanced, drawing a small metallic flask from her pocket. "Mead," she announced.

"Gratitude," Lansius said.

"Do you need a bucket?"

"What? No, no, I'm fine, really."

Exhaling, Audrey poured him a cup of mead.

Lansius took a sip, appreciating the sweet taste of honey.

"Get some rest. You've done plenty today," she suggested as she started to unfasten her outer garment due to the heat.

He chuckled. "Will you let me off from full armor training tonight? The heat is unbearable," Lansius pleaded.

Audrey clicked her tongue, refraining from voicing a response.

Lansius exhaled again, this time with more gravity in his tone. "We only have twelve days left. I must finalize my plan."

"You don't have to wait until night to work your plan. Let me help you. Just tell me who you need to summon to carry out your orders. You're a lord, act like one."

Lansius nodded at her words. He contemplated summoning Batu, Sir Justin, and Sir Callahan, but they were likely dealing with their own issues. "Summon Calub and the guests. Also, ask Cecile for some cool water from the castle's cellar."

Audrey smiled. "We could certainly use that. Summer here is no joke."

Lansius nodded as Audrey exited the chamber.

Korelia's summer was quite harsh. The castle's defensive design, with its minimal windows, only heightened the discomfort.

The ache in his arms brought to mind the training from the previous day. All his muscles were still sore, and the arm wrestling had made it worse.

They had received their sets of full armor around the same time that Felis arrived in Korelia. Coincidentally, the merchant group that Felis had journeyed with was one of Korelia's suppliers.

The armor was also the reason Audrey was in a relatively better mood.

To think she's happy with armor of all things . . .

Lansius's stint in Midlandia last year had taught him that ordering a complete set of plate armor, aside from costing a fortune, also could take up to a year.

In order to navigate around this issue—since he needed armor for his men—Lansius opted for a radical half-armor design.

This style was not only cheaper but could also be sourced from old, incomplete designs or refurbished sets with minor adjustments. As a result, he had sufficient funds to acquire forty sets of plate armor for his best fighters.

Combined with the weapons, crossbow parts, and additional supplies, this expenditure consumed a significant amount of the money he had won from Robert the previous year, including the ransom Robert's knights had paid. But Lansius believed it was a wise investment.

The half-armor, protecting mainly the front side of the body, included a breastplate, gorget, pauldron, and some hip protection. It didn't offer all-around protection, but he needed quantity.

Though lacking in a few parts, they provided ample protection for vital areas. Ringmail and padded jacks would cover the rest.

For Lansius, Lord Bengrieve had commissioned his armorer to modify one of the unused collections that had a similar body size to him. While for Audrey, he commissioned a totally new piece.

Although Bengrieve called them unused, the style was avant-garde, the latest the Imperium could offer. This was high-tier plate armor.

Ever since the armor arrived two weeks ago and had been fitted for them, Audrey had subjected Lansius to rigorous training almost every day.

Whether in the midday summer heat, inside or outside the castle, mounted or on foot, Lansius was forced to master it all. Along with the other armor recipients, he weathered blow after blow from mock combat.

Occasionally, he felt as if she was simply venting her frustration on him. Now he understood how Sterling, Roger, and Carla must have felt.

So much dread . . .

His two-week-old suit of armor, stored at the castle's armory, was marred by dents and scratches all over its metallic surface. The visor joints even needed repairing once, as Audrey had bashed it too many times and too hard.

Every time Lansius protested after she had knocked him too hard, she would insist that his late start required crash courses for his survival on the battlefield.

Lansius had developed a persistent ringing in his ears.

Nevertheless, deep inside, he was grateful. He knew she wanted him to survive, but her method was close to madness.

As Lansius massaged his sore body, the upcoming battle weighed heavily on his mind. Instead of resting in bed, he rose and walked to his desk, drawing out his wooden blocks and attempting to arrange them on the chart he had prepared.

Six wooden blocks, three additional blocks inked with an *X* to indicate cavalry, and four half-blocks representing his significantly smaller force. This consisted of the men-at-arms, the militia, the cavalry, and Batu's tribesmen.

The idea of raiding their supplies was out of the question. Lowlandian armies, due to their geography, constantly placed their supply trains in the heart of their formations.

They wouldn't make such a beginner mistake to separate their supply convoy to be raided easily. Worse still, Batu had personally informed him that the enemy likely had three hundred cavalry at their disposal.

Even with their combined forces, Lansius and Batu's cavalry wouldn't be able to compete. The Three Hills, while possessing a large yet relatively weak group of levied troops, also boasted their elite Black Knights cavalry.

These knights posed a serious threat, even to the formidable Lion of Low-landia at the height of his power.

How could I possibly win this?

CHAPTER 12

WAR COUNCIL

The door to the council chamber swung open, and Lansius stepped inside. He immediately noticed the buzz of activity as Audrey, Calub, and Felis were already present. "At ease," he instructed nonchalantly.

"Where have you been?" Audrey inquired.

"Just relaying a message to Sterling," he replied.

"Your speech at the training hall was quite impressive, my lord," Calub complimented, setting Lansius's doubts aside for the moment.

"Gratitude, Calub," Lansius acknowledged, prompting a curious look from Felis.

"I'll explain later," Calub reassured Felis.

With only familiar faces in the room, Audrey shrugged off her black outer garment and hung it over the back of her chair. "Ahh . . ." she sighed, evidently affected by the oppressive heat. Her ivory-colored tunic clung to her skin, soaked with sweat.

"Isn't the Great Chamber cooler?" Calub questioned, removing his milky-white jacket in the process.

"Hannei mentioned she'd be willing to cool the room, but only if it's just us present," Felis remarked, settling into her chair.

Calub nodded in agreement, swiftly refocusing his attention on the scrolls spread out before him. On the surface, he maintained a calm demeanor, but internally, worry was gnawing at him.

The alchemist was among the few who hadn't accepted Lansius's explanation at face value in the billet's training hall. Yet, he chose not to challenge Lansius, especially when he had no better alternatives to offer.

Lansius retreated behind a thick canvas screen that served as a divider for his makeshift quarters. "Yesterday wasn't this hot," he mumbled as he sat on his bed, his skin glistening with sweat.

"In Lowlandia, they say the height of summer arrives as unexpectedly as a winter blizzard," said Calub.

"A blizzard sounds nice," Lansius murmured before snapping back to reality. "Calub, we're likely to face a siege soon. How are our food and grain supplies?"

"We're prepared for short sieges," Calub reported. "Korelians are hardy and experienced people. They've prepared for a siege and stockpiled what they could, mostly salted or smoked goods."

"And for long sieges?" Audrey asked, her voice laced with concern.

"We don't have to worry about long sieges," Lansius replied candidly. "The walls of Korelia aren't designed to withstand siege weapons, and our trenches don't cover the entire town. We'd stand no chance in such a scenario."

Feeling the need to balance the argument, Calub added, "Before the enemy arrives, reinforcements from Lord Robert should arrive with additional supplies."

"Let's not count on that aid," Lansius cautioned. "It'd be great if they came, but we can't rely on external help."

Reluctantly, Calub nodded and said, "Our food will last. The city will start rationing today."

Lansius acknowledged that with a nod and instructed, "Let's start the evacuation plan tomorrow."

Calub nodded again. They had agreed to evacuate non-combatants to several villages and knights' estates. Sir Callahan, Sir Justin, and several other knights had prepared for this eventuality.

"I apologize to burden you with this," Lansius said.

"Well, we're short on capable people," Calub sighed. "We have plenty of muscle, but not enough men trained with ink and papers."

Lansius chuckled. "You should ask Hannei for help."

Calub grinned. "She barely reads the common alphabet."

"Oh, right. She's only proficient in the old tongue," Lansius remarked.

Suddenly, the door swung open again.

"Thank you for accompanying me," said a woman before entering.

The people inside turned toward the door and saw Hannei enter. Outside, the page boy Margo gave a small bow before closing the door behind her.

"How's Tia?" Calub asked as Hannei entered.

"She's sleeping soundly after I cooled the room," Hannei replied while looking around, and then she looked at Lansius in his bed.

"Heya." Lansius waved his hand as their gazes met.

"Lans, do you really plan to sleep here continuously? It's been how many days already," said Hannei casually.

"Well, my study is too small. Besides, it's comfortable and spacious in here," he responded lightly.

"See, see! He likes it here," Felis chimed in.

So Hannei has spoken about her disapproval.

"That's okay, Hannei. I don't mind it at all," Lansius said with a gentle smile.

But that made Hannei let out a sigh. "Audrey, you should take better care of him. Otherwise, some girl will exploit him."

"Indeed. Sometimes he's so naive," Audrey replied so readily.

"Wha—" Lansius was surprised. Of all people, he was hearing it from Audrey. The room was chuckling at the lord's expense.

"This is so embarrassing . . ." Lansius conceded.

"This brings back memories of Toruna," Calub chuckled, setting aside his scrolls and quill pen.

After a moment of reminiscence, Felis clapped her hands. "I'm glad that our bond remains unchanged."

Lansius exhaled and offered a smile, believing the timing to be just right. "Felis," he called out warmly. "War is on the horizon for Korelia. Would you be willing to lead the refugees to Sir Callahan's baronet?"

"Why? Don't you need my help?" Felis asked, slightly offended.

Lansius gave a genuine smile, aware that she was referring to her marksman skills, not her uncanny luck. There was an unspoken agreement among their circle of friends to never discuss her mysterious power openly, fearing it might estrange Felis. "I want you to meet Cecile's little sister. I heard she's adorable, and blonde too."

Felis's interest was instantly piqued at the mention of a younger Cecile, stirring her motherly instincts. However, she shook her head. "No, I'll be staying here. You'll need my help."

Lansius glanced at Hannei and Calub. The pair shrugged but largely looked content.

"I'll stay with her." Hannei gave her words to ease Lansius's worry.

Lansius nodded.

At least I tried. If she wanted to stay then, who am I to go against Fortuna's favorite?

Afterward, Hannei seemed to notice the heat. Without being asked, she chanted a prayer in French. The air began to circulate faster, and then a whiff of fresh air breezed from the narrow window. There was no blinding light, just the sound of wind rustling inside.

The room gradually became cooler to the point where it almost felt like the top of a mountain. Everybody was looking much more relaxed.

"Gratitude." Calub and Audrey thanked Hannei almost at the same time.

"You're welcome," Hannei replied. Then she sat next to Felis.

Using magic like this was an extravagance, but a well-known practice. The Imperium's high nobles precisely employed their mages to do these things. As bodyguards and also walking air conditioners, even walking refrigerators, rarely did they put their precious mages into harm's way.

In retrospect, the mages in this world were fundamentally different from what Lansius expected. There was no casting fire or water out of nothing. No mana or magic circuits inside the body. And no hindrance to wearing heavy armor.

While mages couldn't control the elements, they could infuse the surrounding air with magical properties and manipulate it to a degree.

However, in combat, mages used their magical properties to empower their own body, making them more resilient and powerful, and giving them greater stamina. Meanwhile, healing followed a radically different mechanism. And it was a closely guarded secret of the Healers Guild.

"Anyway, Lans," Hannei called.

"Aye?"

"I heard about the war, but I still need to tell you about Midlandia."

Hannei's words jolted Lansius. "Eh . . . I totally forgot about it." He rose and reached out for a seat next to her.

"You look busy as the lord, so I don't want to put more trouble. But it doesn't seem like you'll have a break anytime soon."

"Well, a war is coming."

Hannei could only nod. Concern flashed across her face.

"So, what happened in Midlandia?" Lansius asked, not wanting to be distracted again.

Hannei took a deep breath before announcing, "The current Lord of Midlandia intends to vacate his position."

Lansius blanked when he heard those words. "What?"

The room immediately tensed. Even Calub appeared disturbed.

"It's not official yet, but the word is from Lord Bengrieve."

This is more than bad news . . .

"But why so suddenly? Is the Lord of Midlandia ill?" Calub asked, trying to comprehend the implications.

"I don't believe so. I heard he's relinquishing his claim. It appears to involve a saint candidate."

Lansius glanced at Calub, who shook his head in response, saying, "Large guilds are naturally secretive. I'm unaware of another guild's plans or design concerning Midlandia."

"Then who's the proposed new lord?" Lansius queried.

"That's the problem. Lord Bengrieve hasn't proposed a candidate yet."

Lansius let out a sigh.

Even if we're winning, we can expect no help or reinforcement from Midlandia. This is bad news.

"So, we're on our own?" Calub asked Hannei cautiously.

She shook her head. "No, Bengrieve said that Lansius should do his utmost. The success in Korelia would reflect well on Bengrieve and his potential candidate."

Lansius blinked, his mind racing with worries. "I'll try, but this is going to be the damnedest nearest-run thing."

His somber warning quieted the chamber. They all recognized the weight of the hopes pinned on Lansius, a man neither born nor prepared for such roles and responsibilities.

Hannei then turned to Felis and said, "Bengrieve also told me this: till the matter is settled, Felis should stay in Korelia. He fears someone might capture her as a bargaining chip."

A succession crisis is always a mess . . .

"Well, anyway, I'm surprised you got involved, considering your hermit life-style," Lansius remarked to Hannei.

"Felis is like a sister to me," Hannei responded, causing Felis to beam with delight.

Suddenly, there was a knock on the door.

"Who is it?" Audrey called, rising from her seat.

"The lord has instructed me to summon Batu and Sir Justin. They have arrived and are waiting in the Great Chamber," Sterling's voice came from the outside.

"Welp, that's my cue," Lansius announced, standing to change his clothes.

Lansius entered the Great Chamber with Audrey, Calub, and Sterling in tow.

Batu and Sir Justin rose from their seats as they arrived.

"Please remain seated," Lansius said, as he and his companions took their places.

"You summoned us, my lord?" inquired Sir Justin.

"Yes, I wish to discuss our war plan," Lansius responded.

Calub proceeded to unfurl a map of West Lowlandia on the long table. It lacked a bird's-eye perspective like Lansius's map, but it would serve its purpose.

"Now, there are twelve days left. They should be around here," Lansius indicated on the map.

"My brethren and I plan to raid their camp at night when they are exhausted or attempt an attack when they venture out to collect their water supply," Batu stated resolutely.

"That's a bold plan, but can you accomplish it without significant casualties to your clans?" Lansius questioned.

Batu offered a faint smile and shook his head. "Given their numbers and the size of their camp, my brethren and I are likely to be cut down after two attempts."

His sobering honesty cast a pall over the group. With only two hundred riders, Batu and his men would likely only have two chances. To pit them against a force of six thousand, plus three hundred cavalry, and expect a positive outcome was overly optimistic.

"The Nicopolan mercenaries are also renowned for their light cavalry. They are skilled trackers and hunters," Lansius warned.

Batu nodded. "Our brethren near Korimor have alerted us. They have vacated from the Korimor region due to such raids."

"Do they take hostages?" asked Sir Justin.

"No, they enslave immediately, given our nomadic origin," Batu replied, candid about the grim realities of war.

Lansius instinctively glanced at Audrey. She appeared composed, yet her eyes blazed with fury. Raising his hand to signal he was about to speak, he contemplated for a moment before finally announcing, "Batu, I want your people to steer clear of them."

Eyebrows knitted in confusion were directed at Lansius, who continued. "While harassing their water supply and attempting to burn their supplies will damage them, I doubt it will inflict enough to deplete their forces. I'm not willing to trade your nomadic horsemen for that result."

Batu gladly nodded. "Then what is your plan?"

"We'll confront them on our turf. They want a siege, so we'll give them one. Batu, you and your horsemen should only engage on my signal. Set up your camp farther south of town and stay well hidden."

"We're facing them head-on, my lord?" Sir Justin asked with excitement. His enthusiasm was contagious and lifted the mood of everyone present.

Lansius appeared less somber than usual. "Not quite, but let them think they've caught us off guard."

"What role do you expect us, the nomads, to play in this battle?" Batu inquired.

Lansius leaned forward toward Batu. "The role of the hunter. When the time comes, give me your hardest battle, and you will feast on their blood. Tell your brethren to stock up on their arrows, sharpen their blades, and steel their resolve. If need be, I will unleash something Lowlandia will never forget."

CHAPTER 13

MASTER OF THE MERCENARY

Three days after Lansius met with Batu, the nomadic tribesmen stealthily moved across the Great Plains, setting up camp far south of Korelia. There they waited for the inevitable battle, their numbers swelling as many heeded the call to avenge their enslaved brethren captured by the Nicopolan mercenaries.

As dawn arrived in Korelia, Sir Callahan continued training Lansius and Sterling in the art of jousting. This day was likely their last, as the enemy forces were closing in on Korelia.

As an experienced knight, Callahan would not risk injuring the riders or horses through over-training. The riders and the horses needed to recover for ideally a week before the battle.

Lansius, sitting astride his destrier, eagerly aimed his blunted lance at a wooden shield hanging on a rotating post firmly planted in the ground. Sometimes he struck a solid hit, but often he missed, failing to align his lance expertly. His arm muscles were sore, feeling as if they were burning, even with the lance resting on his breastplate.

Nothing came easy. Lansius had been practicing this skill since last year in Toruna, with only modest progress.

"Keep going! Mistakes happen; that's why we train," Sir Callahan encouraged Lansius after his last missed attempt. "Success is easy. How to survive from mistakes is what we trained for!"

Spurred by the encouragement, Lansius pressed on. Despite the aches, he tried again, spending the whole morning in training—practicing with lances and swords.

"That's enough, my lord." Sir Callahan finally called off the training, stopping before rider and horse were thoroughly depleted. He motioned to Sterling, who had been resting, as his horse lacked the stamina of a destrier.

Sterling helped Lansius dismount and escorted him to a nearby tent to seek shade. Lansius, with shaky hands, grabbed a jug of water and gulped it down.

As the squire, he removed Lansius's training armor, revealing new bruises on the lord's shoulder, arm, and wrist, despite a layer of arming jack beneath the armor. "My lord, you'll need some salves."

"Leave that for now," he said breathlessly, lying down on a canvas bed.

Sterling nodded and left the lord to recover.

After half an hour Lansius had changed his clothes and felt refreshed.

"My lord," Sir Callahan greeted as Lansius approached him.

"Any news from Sir Justin and Hugo?" Lansius asked.

The knight smiled. "Not yet. Even with fast horse messengers, it will take more time."

Lansius nodded, anxiety rising in his stomach. Three days ago, he had sent them as envoys. Imperium decorum dictated that a lord should extend courtesies if another lord was visiting their domain. It even suggested the types of gifts for the guest.

It was nothing but a political farce, considering most unannounced guests brought an invading force. But beyond the theatrics, what he desired most was an accurate assessment of the enemy's forces. He needed more information.

At the moment, however, he had no option but to wait. Taking in his surroundings, Lansius noted the war preparations around Korelia were well underway. Sir Callahan and the squires had been invaluable in preparing the men and the trenches.

Lansius glanced toward the blond knight, his mentor, the best support he could ask for. He had never received a harsh word from him; instead, he had been taught with a gentle hand, receiving daily doses of inspiration and motivation.

More than just a mentor, Sir Callahan was also their most able diplomat. The knight alone successfully negotiated the trade deal with the Eastern Lowlandia merchants, securing their grain for the rest of the year. For that, Lansius was truly grateful.

"Sir Callahan, you may take the rest of the day off. Take this time to be with your daughters. We might need to mobilize either tonight or tomorrow."

"Yes, my lord. Does this apply to the rest of the knights and cavalry?"

"Indeed. Please inform them. We'll feast in the great hall before sundown and await news from the marshal."

A week had passed. To the commoners of Korelia, the day started as any other—the sun slowly rising in the east under a blue, cloudless sky, heralding another sunny day.

Unlike the hectic planting season of mid-spring, summer was a relatively calm period. It was a time when farmers and peasants saw their work start to bear fruit. Even with minimal tending, the crops on the farms grew taller, and the livestock fattened.

Summer also marked the time when the roads hardened enough for travel by cart. After months of icy winter and muddy spring, merchants and peddlers resumed their travels and trade.

This should have been a good time of the year, but currently, things were looking bleak. To the west, typically nothing but empty plains, now stood more than a thousand tents. The invading army from West Lowlandia had arrived.

Hundreds of flags and banners announced large contingents of knights. Their vibrant coats of arms contrasted with the predominantly green and yellow landscape. Many of the Houses were hundreds of years old and had played their roles in Lowlandia's history.

Around a hundred horse-drawn carts were parked around the inner part of the camp, protecting fancy tents, some even lavishly adorned with bronze and gold embroidery, where the nobility resided.

Despite the early hour, the camp was already bustling with activity. Bonfires were lit for cooking throughout the camp, and hundreds of servants fetched water or did laundry at the small stream outside the camp.

Squires attended to their masters' horses and war gear, while patrols made their rounds to ensure security. The field was abundant with dried grass or hay, providing easy feed for the horses and bedding material.

After eleven grueling days of marching, the Coalition troops, as they named themselves, finally had some basic comfort.

Looking out past the eastern side of camp to Korelia, the scene was starkly different. The town and castle had barricaded themselves. No soul dared venture outside the surrounding ditches and gates.

This was the first morning of the invasion.

Coalition Side

Since the crack of dawn, Baron Omin had been engrossed in his duties. This campaign was his brainchild, and he had invested more than just resources into it.

He was the one who had incited Viscount Jorge to launch the attack, for unlike Omin, who was a relative nobody in Lowlandia, Jorge had a legitimate claim over Korelia.

Korelia was Jorge's birthright. He was born and raised there as part of a branch family. As fate would have it, Jorge was summoned back to Three Hills City to succeed his dying uncle. However, he proved to be an inadequate leader. His vassals seceded, and Jorge waged unsuccessful wars to retake the lost lands.

While Jorge struggled, individuals like Omin thrived. Ironically, times of war often presented great opportunities.

Omin, originally a migrant knight from Centuria, had risen through the ranks by outliving his counterparts in Korimor. Biding his time, Omin eventually orchestrated a coup in Korimor, then he astutely pledged his loyalty to Lord Jorge and became a trusted ally.

With Omin's assistance and the Nicopolans mercenaries under him, Viscount Jorge began to reclaim the lost territories. In exchange for his help, Jorge backed Omin's official nomination.

Last year, Omin finally received his royal patent and ascended to the status of baron—a rare feat in the Imperium. In a sense, he was a rising star. He had gained enough acclaim to make Jorge wary, and Omin was aware of this. As such, he designed this campaign to maintain his overlord's favor.

Goading Lord Jorge had been an easy task. The younger lord was known for his folly and thirst for glory. He also had a strong attachment to his birthplace, which fueled his desire to recapture Korelia.

With Jorge's authority, Omin managed to manipulate the grain prices last year, putting additional pressure on Korelia's troops and population, thus making them more vulnerable.

The invasion plan served to keep Omin close to Jorge, as the nascent baron still needed Jorge's protection until he could stand independently. After all, his domain, Korimor, was a small city, not even a tenth the size of Three Hills.

Despite its size, Omin's barony had established an effective bureaucracy, enabling him to maintain a considerable force. Of the six thousand troops brought for this campaign, a thousand were from Omin's ranks, including over a hundred cavalry.

Even though they were smaller in numbers, the Korimors were better equipped, with Nicopolan mercenaries at their core. Meanwhile, the troops from Three Hills were primarily levied peasants, second sons, and freemen—many of them no more than unemployed artisans or laborers.

The contingent from South Hill was not much better. They were only there to fulfill their sixty-day obligations. Most were seasonal farmers who were anxious about their upcoming harvest.

In this regard, the Korimors were more than triple their value in combat. Aside from them, only Jorge's Black Knights were superior in the field.

Now, Baron Omin and his entourage arrived at the section of the camp he sought. It was an open field workshop, cluttered with wooden structures, ropes, and pulleys.

"My lord," greeted the master smith.

"Let's hear your reports." Omin wasn't one for idle chit-chat.

"The construction of the mangonels is underway, my lord. As you can observe, the frames are now in place. We plan to stiffen and reinforce them today, and by tomorrow, we should have a solid base for installing the throwing arms," elaborated the master smith.

Observing the scene, Omin could see three catapults in the making. A team of carpenters, smiths, and specially selected men were engrossed in the task. The robust wooden frame was roughly as tall as three men standing atop each other.

"When will they be operational?"

"Provided the weather cooperates, two will be ready in five days."

Upon hearing this, Omin deliberated momentarily before deeming it unwise to accelerate the process further.

"I'll hold you to that promise, maester," Omin responded, admiring the progress before him.

Typically, it took several months to build a siege engine, but his were preassembled.

"Should you encounter any difficulties, come to me immediately. Your work is a top priority." He told the gray-haired man, who resembled a scholar more than a carpenter or blacksmith.

"My deepest gratitude, my lord." The master smith bowed in acknowledgment.

Omin departed from the workshop, observing the sprawling encampment. To the unacquainted, the site appeared chaotic, with tents haphazardly pitched and only narrow pathways in between.

As he walked, the early-morning activities of the camp came into view. Most of the infantry, still weary from their lengthy march, were slowly awakening as sunlight passed through their canvas dwellings. Some gathered near their tents, while others headed straight to the nearby stream. Portions of the camp now reeked of human and horse waste.

"Is breakfast prepared?" Omin asked, his appetite unfazed by the stench.

"It should be, my lord," his towering Nicopolan bodyguard replied.

The two, followed by a squire and a servant, navigated toward the heart of the encampment.

"My lord," a woman clad in a blue surcoat with bronze accents called out to Omin. She had been waiting by the secured entrance to the nobles' quarter.

Omin recognized her. Despite her youthfulness, she was the cavalry captain of the Nicopolans. "Lady Daniella, why are you here? You've already presented your report."

"Walk with me, my lord," Daniella urged.

Omin matched Daniella's stride. She was more than just a mercenary; as a daughter of a Nicopolan baron, albeit without inheritance, her background was notable. When she showed urgency, it was a clear indication that serious matters were at hand.

"What seems to be the issue?" Omin asked.

"The Korelians are mobilizing."

"Are you certain?" Omin looked taken aback.

"I have already readied your horse and my riders," she replied, guiding her employer toward the eastern edge of the camp.

Midway through the camp, a group of Korimors and Nicopolans brought forth their horses. Alongside twenty riders, they galloped eastward.

The terrain was flat, enabling them to spot distant silhouettes early on their journey. As they drew nearer, they could distinguish lines of soldiers standing between the castle and the town.

Omin pulled back on his horse's reins, bringing the animal to a standstill.

What is the meaning of this?

He studied the Korelian formation contemplatively.

"Tally their numbers, but keep your distance," Daniella directed her scout. Two scouts rode to estimate the size of the opposing force.

Meanwhile, Omin retreated into his thoughts. He hadn't anticipated any skirmishes today. In fact, no one had.

Yesterday, upon their arrival, Lansius had dispatched a delegation, requesting a parley. It wasn't a first-time occurrence either; several days prior, a group of horsemen had intercepted them en route to Korelia.

In both instances, Lord Jorge and Omin firmly declined any negotiation. They demanded that the delegation respect Lord Jorge's claim and forfeit Korelia.

Lansius had yet to respond to Jorge's invitation to battle. It was expected; strategically speaking, the Korelians lacked any incentive to venture into open battle. The Coalition's overwhelming numerical superiority effectively ruled out that option.

While Lansius's previous battle with Robert was shrouded in mystery, it was known that he favored mass crossbowmen tactics. This was why Omin had invested heavily in the construction of mangonels.

He anticipated that Lansius would adopt a defensive stance, waiting for the impending attack. After all, there was little a defending force, especially a smaller one, could do in such a predicament.

Omin surmised that the ditches encircling the town were meant to serve a similar function. Their purpose was likely to impede the Coalition's advance, much like how Lansius had thwarted Robert.

So, why is Lansius marching out today? Is he looking for a battle? Or is this bait?

"Seven hundred, possibly one thousand, my lord," his scouts reported.

That's almost all of Lansius's troops.

He wasn't sure what Lansius's intentions were, but he knew how to react. "Fine, I'll bring it to him."

In war, flexibility is paramount. When there's a change, there's also an opportunity!

Omin intended to thwart and exploit Lansius's tactics for his own gain. With his sights set, he rode back and prepared for battle.

CHAPTER 14

WARHORNS

The castle's curtain wall wasn't thick, and the overall construction was outdated. Against three fixed counterweight mangonels or early trebuchets, even the main keep was unlikely to survive more than a week of bombardment.

If the walls were targeted and breached, an uneven battle would ensue. Against six thousand invaders, there was zero chance to win. If the castle fell, the town of Korelia would inevitably surrender, despite its trenches.

Understanding this, Lansius played the only hand available to him: initiative.

Eight hundred men, consisting of three hundred men-at-arms and five hundred militia, had been readied since the previous night. They ate an early breakfast and marched out at first light.

Strategic positioning ensured the castle's garrison of crossbowmen protected their right flank while the town's nearby trenches covered the left. Sir Justin valiantly led the right wing, personally guarded by his band of hardened ex-mercenaries.

The center was under Hugo's command, bolstered by Roger and a group of arbalesters.

Lieutenant Sigmund, the skald, led the third company on the left wing. Despite their confident march, the troop strength wasn't full, as Lansius had assigned a hundred of them to a separate mission.

However, these troops, originally no more than troublemakers from Midlandia, had matured. They had developed discipline and loyalty, driven by Lansius's generous wages and fair treatment.

Lansius's decision to employ them year-round had transformed them mentally and physically. The previous year, the majority of Midlandian troops were distrustful, malnourished, and scrawny. They would only fight for their own lives.

Now, the same troops were well disciplined, followed orders, and were physically tough, a result of their work in the trenches, which provided even more income and physical training.

In addition, the lord provided meals and shelter, even in winter. With their basic needs covered, they could save money. Last year, thick, ragged clothes as the poor man's gambesons were their standard attire. Now, they wore proper gambesons, helmets, and even ringmail or brigandine.

Moreover, the vanguard as the crème de la crème had armor rivaling a knight. This small number of top performers, instead of gambling and drinking over the winter, had dedicated their time to training.

The billets, the training halls, and the training scheme provided sufficient motivation for them to hone their skills and physique.

To say that this year's Korelian troops were an improvement would be a serious understatement. They had become a fit, fully functional military unit, no longer a motley crew of poor peasants and vagabonds.

The price of their improvement was their quantity. Lansius recruited sparingly. He stood firm on his decision not to engage in large-scale or seasonal recruitment. For them, his approach was unconventional, but it seemed he was onto something innovative.

Well-fed and well-paid, the men of House Lansius had become a formidable force to reckon with. The same could be said with the militia. Driven by gratitude and hope for a better life under their lord, the Korelians were equally dedicated to fighting for him.

The summer sun didn't bother them; they were accustomed to laboring under it. They found standing in formation less taxing compared to digging the trenches.

Determinedly, the troops stood their ground while the vast Coalition army took to the field.

As the Coalition drew near, Sir Justin, clad in full plate armor, completed his preparations. "Men," he called out, drawing their attention.

Holding a piece of paper affixed to his gauntlet and with his adjutant standing beside him, halberd in hand, Sir Justin read aloud, "Lord Lansius wishes to share a few words with you. First, he wants you to know that he wished to stand with you, whom he regards as blood brothers."

He then commented, off-script, "Can you imagine that a lord thinks of you, the scum of Midlandia, as his blood brothers?"

His off-the-cuff remark prompted chuckles from the men, easing their tension.

The marshal returned to his script. "The lord feels disgraced that he cannot fight alongside you, but he is needed elsewhere to ensure our victory. On this matter, the lord has assured me that our victory today is as certain as death by old age."

As expected, this mention of death stirred strong emotions among the men. The marshal continued. "Men, do not fear death. It comes to us all equally. Some faster, some slower, but that doesn't matter." He then raised his voice and his tempo. "Embrace it! Let it strengthen your resolve and drive you to fight your hardest!"

His resolute words captured his men's attention.

"Yes, blood and guts will be shed, and sacrifices made. But none will be in vain. They will bring glory and riches to you, your family, and your descendants."

These words pumped up the men, fortifying their resolve. The promise of honor and wealth was always a good cause to die for.

Afterward, the marshal glanced at the final part of the letter. Finding it somewhat lacking, he improvised, asking solemnly, "Remember your upbringing and your life before today; it was wretched, wasn't it?"

The men collectively nodded in agreement.

Sir Justin chuckled, then rallied. "Men, now is your chance to change your fate. Aren't you tired of seeing them trample over your lives? Now, we stand on equal ground. Our armor and weapons are no less than theirs. I say let's take our lives back from these western nobles, from their knights, from anyone foolish enough to invade our lands. Be the master of our own destiny!"

Now, the men looked fierce but relaxed, almost meditative. There, in the field of Korelia with their sharpened polearms and swords in hand, they patiently waited for the enemy to come.

Tann-tann-taraaa! Taa-raaaa!

The Coalition's trumpets echoed across the plains of Korelia. Soon, waves of troops emerged from the encampment. There were no uniforms—each man donned a different style, pattern, or color of garment.

Ahead of the colorful troops, captains and lieutenants wasted no time in establishing formation. Slowly, the disorganized bunch began to coalesce into larger, orderly columns.

Meanwhile, the nobles on their horses took the lead, guiding the newly assembled columns. The nobles were flanked by two hundred mounted knights and the rest of the cavalry. In total, the Coalition brought more than three hundred cavalry.

Their brightly colored clothing, polished steel armor, and vibrant banners turned the scene into a spectacle. Indeed, for them, this was a necessary display of power. This was how they showcased their might on their subjects, peers, and, more importantly, adversaries.

Following the noblemen and cavalry was the main body of troops, consisting of six thousand men-at-arms and levied footmen. These were common men who had no part in political squabbles.

They were here to fulfill their contracts and obligations to their lord. Many were simple farmers, artisans, or tradesmen. Ironically, they were the ones who would bear the brunt of the fighting.

With another blast of the trumpet, the halt order was sounded. The entire army stopped while dispatchers on horses galloped to relay orders from the top.

Captains in each column received the commands and passed them on to the lieutenants. A flurry of activity ensued as the troops began to arrange themselves into a single formation.

Before long, the formation was complete. Four unbroken lines of men stretched out for more than a mile. It was an impressive and effective display of force.

The trumpets sounded again, and the formation advanced in unison. Hundreds of banners waved. Armor and helmets glistened under the bright summer sun.

As they neared the Korelians' line, the scale of their disparity became increasingly evident. The Coalition's six thousand dwarfed the defenders' eight hundred. It was akin to comparing a mighty river to a mere pond.

The breadth of the Coalition's formation covered such a wide swath of land that anyone observing from Korelia would see the plains teeming with invading troops.

The scale of the invasion was not lost on the observers. Korelia's population totaled slightly more than six thousand, including children and the elderly. The fact that the Coalition had brought this many troops was proof that they took Lansius's reputation seriously.

The mile-long formation continued their advance until another sound from the trumpets rang out. The formation promptly halted. Now, more than six thousand men stood, tall and menacing, all facing Korelia.

Coalition Side

"Mm . . . everything seems to be as expected, baron?" Lord Jorge, mounted on his horse but still clad in his arming jack, queried nonchalantly. He was kept under the shade by a large umbrella held diligently by a team of squires.

"Indeed, my lord. We shall proceed as planned," Omin responded and began to relay his orders.

Earlier, the two had ruled out a full-scale attack. Both understood the inherent risks of open battles. Even a stroke of bad luck could jeopardize superior forces. Thus, they opted to launch a smaller-scale attack in response to Lansius's invitation to battle.

A skirmish, not a pitched battle. This was to preserve the Coalition's numerical superiority. After all, they merely needed to exercise patience and wait for the siege engines to do their work. No one wanted to risk the entire army against a potential trap.

Their decision was also influenced by the landscape. With a hill on one side and the town's ditches on the other, there wasn't enough space for their mile-long formation.

Earlier, a scout had reported that only a few hundred could march side by side. They deduced this to be the reason Lansius had positioned his army there. The area essentially functioned as a natural bottleneck.

It acted as a barrier, preventing a larger army from deploying its full force against a smaller adversary. However, the two lords were confident that they could outmaneuver it. A trap was only a trap if they weren't aware of it.

As commanded by Lord Jorge and Omin, the Coalition force divided itself into three columns. Each contained two thousand men.

Sir Arius, one of Lord Jorge's cousins, had the honor of leading the attack. The young man was brave and experienced. His column stood in the center, preparing to attack eastward.

After Omin had concluded their planning with Lord Jorge, the baron and his entourage rejoined their column and began to march toward the south, facing the town of Korelia.

Omin positioned his troops to guard against a potential surprise attack from the town's direction or the south. This position also allowed him the opportunity to raid the town if the chance arose.

The Nicopolans under him were eager for action. The idea that the siege could be over before the end of the season was both thrilling and exciting to them.

However, Omin was cautious, not allowing himself to be swept up in the thought of an easy victory. He still couldn't fathom what the enemy was thinking by offering a battle.

Lady Daniella shared his concern. Her experience in minor skirmishes with the mercenaries informed her that something was amiss.

"The Korelians will try something. You'll do well to keep an eye on Lord Jorge," said Omin.

"Will do, my lord." Without a verbal command, Daniella led her Nicopolan cavalry to join Lord Jorge as a reserve.

Meanwhile, to the north, the last column, composed mostly of regiments from the South Hill, assumed formation. They positioned themselves against the hill and in the direction of the castle. They were there to counter any potential attack from the castle.

As planned, Lord Jorge and his knights remained with the cavalry, acting as a reserve and quick reaction force.

As the Coalition marched, the summer sun rose higher. Despite being far from midday, the heat was already unbearable. There were no tall trees for shelter, only plains of tall, yellowing grass.

In the vanguard, Sir Arius lined his fiercest warriors. His column formed into three hundred men wide and a solid six deep. Its width was strategically narrowed to counter the crossbowmen that lurked within the shadows of the castle and the ditches.

On the opposing side, the Korelians mirrored their formation. Two hundred men wide, four men deep, they stood ready for the onslaught.

Despite the looming shadow of Lansius's notorious reputation, Sir Arius and his brethren brimmed with confidence. Their numbers more than doubled their opponents, and their seasoned scars bore the testament of numerous battles.

As expected, the trumpets pierced the anticipatory silence. Sir Arius nodded toward his captain, who then bellowed the next command, his voice echoing across the battlefield. "Proud warriors of Three Hills, advance!"

At his command, the column began their march eastward.

"Shields at the ready!"

Heeding the command, soldiers hoisted shields of all sizes, their freshly painted surfaces reflecting the bright sunlight.

"Steady! Steady," the captain barked as the two armies advanced, each side wary of an imminent volley of bolts from the castle and ditches.

As predicted, the Korelians unleashed their rain of death. Bolts screeched through the air, embedding themselves in the Coalition's formation. Despite the forewarning, panic flickered in the eyes of the less experienced.

Only the nobility, encased in their suits of armor, remained fearless. Similarly, the few hundred clad in ringmail or brigandines, though fearful, maintained their confidence. However, for the majority, dressed in gambesons, this was a nightmare. With every breath, they clutched their wooden shields, praying these would protect them from the relentless barrage.

The sounds of deflected shots, near-misses, and shields punctured by crossbow bolts were a chilling symphony, disheartening even for the hardened veterans. The column stretched and contorted as the center was squeezed, taxing their strength and stamina as they advanced within the last hundred paces.

Fsszhhh! Clank!

Gasps, shrieks of agony, and desperation suddenly filled the air.

"F-fuck!" A bolt had found its mark, striking Sir Arius's neck gorget. It failed to penetrate the hardened iron and was cushioned by his padded linen arming jack, but the force was enough to choke him.

All around him, men were struck, their bodies crumpling as they succumbed to their wounds, even though encased in full plate. The advance wavered.

Then, a movement caught their eye. The Korelian front line had knelt, unveiling a hidden group of arbalesters. The morning sun, high in the east, had blinded Sir Arius's men from the incoming rain of bolts.

"Charge! Give the order to charge," Sir Arius wheezed, rallying his men through the slit of his visor. He knew the consequences of hesitation.

With crossbow bolts painting the air with a deadly rain, the Coalition charged headlong into the Korelian line, a tidal wave of steel and determination.

CHAPTER 15

BLOOD OF THE INNOCENT

Loose!" Hugo's command echoed, launching hundreds of bolts into the enemy ranks. The arbalesters and crossbowmen had just released their second volley.

The attack instantly caused mayhem, but the battle wouldn't be won by just sneaky attacks.

"No heroics, no captives until we've triumphed. We're outnumbered and there's no speck of noble in your blood—expect no quarter!" The deputy delivered his final reminder to his men.

The enemy was nearly upon them.

"Crossbowmen to the rear! Spearmen to the front!" Hugo's voice rang out.

There was no time for the crossbowmen to loose a third volley as they swiftly retreated. The spearmen quickly filled their positions. They stood steadfast, bracing for the incoming onslaught.

"Hold your line!" Hugo's voice thundered.

"Korelia is ours!" Roger, beside him, echoed bravely. Then the lines clashed. Iron met iron; spears were no longer merely brandished but thrust in fury.

Young Coalition men-at-arms, brimming with bravado yet lacking experience, surged forward recklessly. Their armor deflected numerous glancing blows, but the sheer force of some strikes was enough to stagger them.

As pain and disorientation took hold, they faltered against the onslaught of spears and swords, their legs buckling beneath them. For many, their first taste of battle turned to be their last.

Those who fell were remorselessly trampled as hundreds of men pushed forward. Locked in brutal combat, the battlefield offered no respite or room for evacuation. The fallen became mere obstacles under the trampling feet of their comrades.

Soldiers struggled to maintain their footing, fighting desperately to hold their ground against the onslaught of sharp-tipped steel. The cacophony of battle cries mingled with cries of pain, creating a deafening uproar.

In total, nearly three thousand men fought, seeking any means to push back, stall, or strike down their adversaries. The sickly scent of blood, urine, and vomit hung heavy in the air.

The Coalition crossbowmen repositioned, taking aim from the sidelines. Their volleys were met with swift retaliation from Korelian crossbowmen defending their vulnerable flanks.

Against all odds, the Korelians held firm. Many bore the scars of battle, but their resilience was unwavering. Despite their wounds, their ranks remained steady. As their line stabilized, they began to cycle out their wounded, maintaining their formation with commendable discipline.

As brutal as the battlefield might be, it wasn't all-out chaos. Most men were not suicidal and fought as trained in an orderly manner.

Among the sea of spears, shields, and polearms, specialized fighters armed with large two-handed swords carved out breaches in the enemy line. Every breach was an opportunity to exploit. One such breach erupted first on the Korelian left flank, with deadly consequences.

Korelian Left Wing

The Coalition's Doppelsoldner, expert men-at-arms wielding large two-handed swords, shattered the wall of spears of the Korelian left wing, forcefully creating a narrow gap in the enemy line. The nearest group of knights readily charged into the Korelian ranks.

Space was limited, but it was a fair three-on-three fight. A Coalition knight, clad in plate armor and a crimson red surcoat, held the center while his two comrades struggled to maintain the breach.

From the Korelian side, a tall man-at-arms accepted the challenge. The crimson knight squared off against the man, who hurled his broken bill hook at the knight, only to have it deflected by a gauntlet. Gambling on the knight's momentary distraction, the tall man drew his sword, leaped forward, and launched a powerful overhead strike.

The red knight countered, gripping his sword on both ends in a half-swording style. As the man attempted to retract his weapon, the knight guided his blade and interlocked their swords.

They wrestled for control, but the knight held the upper hand due to his advantageous grip. Unexpectedly, the knight redirected both blades to his left and, in a simultaneous motion, swung his sword's pommel into the adversary's helmet.

Ka-thunk!

Far from decorative pieces, the pommel caused as much damage as a mace, even against an armored person. The tall man's visor crumpled, and he fell to the ground.

The entire duel lasted only seconds, demonstrating the vast skill gap between a fully trained knight and a street swordsman, which couldn't be bridged by a short amount of training or a suit of armor.

Opting to leave the downed man alive for potential ransom, the knight in the crimson red surcoat faced the next challenger.

"Oo-rraahhh!" Another Korelian charged forward, trying to save his comrade.

The red knight parried, using the deflected momentum to slash at the opponent's arm. It wasn't a powerful blow, and the sword's blade wasn't razor-sharp, yet the speed and weight were enough to cause injury.

The Korelian recoiled from the clean hit, groaning as he realized his left arm hung limp. Behind him, another Korelian in plate armor, leading two men, rushed forward.

The red knight stepped back, allowing his comrade to take his place. Even without verbal commands, they cooperated seamlessly, the result of years of training and fighting together.

Knights, squires, and men-at-arms rarely fought alone; they operated in *lances fournies*. They had spent countless hours mastering the discipline of armed combat. Each blow sustained from mistakes and accidents had become invaluable experience, with every bruise representing a lesson learned, and each cut further honing their martial skills.

For them, their armor was akin to a second skin, and the limited visibility from their visors and restricted breath from small vent holes were part of their upbringing.

The knight in the crimson red surcoat and his comrades fought valiantly, eroding the Korelians' line.

Korelian Right Wing

In the right wing, after the initial contact, there was a second surge from the Coalition, and the fight devolved into a ruthless melee. Combat became so savage that men were shoved from behind, to the point where they couldn't wield their spears or swords.

Soon, there wasn't even enough room to draw their daggers. They were effectively squashed, resorting to brawling with just their fists and elbows.

Having lost his sword, which had become stuck in a previous opponent's armor gap, Sir Justin now resorted to wrestling. He landed a solid punch on his enemy's gorget with his iron gauntlet, followed by a blow to the jaw so strong that the opponent's bascinet was dislodged.

The lieutenant beside him fared no better, grappling with his foe and ultimately driving his thumbs into the unfortunate opponent's eye sockets as they both struggled to remain standing. The fight had devolved into a cruel, personal brawl.

Despite giving their best, the Korelian line began to unravel. Knowing this by instinct, they fought desperately to close the gap.

Barely catching his breath after his last opponent slid to the ground, Sir Justin, now armed with the fallen knight's sword, lunged at the next knight with a thrust. The knight blocked the attack with his armored wrist. Despite the recoil, he retaliated by swinging his mace at Sir Justin's hips.

Groaning in agony, Sir Justin slipped and fell to the ground. The blow from the mace, even through the plate armor, was excruciating. Several around him noticed his fall; some shouted, others cursed, but none were able to help. Their line was in disarray.

Quickly, the knight knelt on Sir Justin's chest, pinning him down, and tried to bash his helmet with his mace.

Sir Justin wrestled with the knight's arm while drawing his dagger. His left wrist, having endured two shallow blows, felt broken. Nevertheless, he managed to wield his dagger and drove it into the knight's visor.

The knight dropped his mace and frantically reached for his face as he gurgled out blood.

Hot blood rained into Sir Justin's helmet from above. His eyes stinging from the blood, the marshal managed to shove the knight aside. Enduring excruciating pain from his injured wrist, he forced himself to his feet. Staying on the ground would lead to him being mobbed or trampled.

The fallen knight beside him convulsed a few times. Leaving the man to his fate, Sir Justin picked up the discarded mace. His vision obscured by his visor, he tried to look around, attempting to aid his men still fighting for their lives.

Then, he felt a tap on his shoulder.

"Marshal," his lieutenant called in a hoarse voice. The man's gauntlets and lower arms were smeared with blood, yet he still held the banner high. Sir Justin grinned as more of his men rushed toward him, brandishing their weapons to close the gap.

He knew the Korelian side had almost lost it, but through sheer determination, his men managed to stabilize their right flank.

Korelian Center

In front of Hugo, one of his Arvenian fellows fought valiantly. Encased in plate armor, the man was nigh impenetrable. He delivered a feigned thrust followed by a swift foot sweep, and a powerful downward thrust, and just like that, his halberd claimed another enemy.

But glory was fleeting on the battlefield—advancing farther than his allies, he was blindsided and tackled by three opponents. These three skirmishers, clad in gambesons, traded protection for agility.

Despite the Arvenian's heroic struggle, he was soon overpowered and pinned down. One enemy slipped a dagger into the armor's armpit gap, stabbing repeatedly. Yet, the man's struggle continued; he gave the trio the fight of their lives.

In an effort to finish him off, one of the skirmishers picked up a discarded axe but was suddenly and violently thrown aside. He fell face-first, a spear protruding from his back. Red blood pooled around his punctured gambeson while his body convulsed in its final spasms.

Arriving late, Hugo and his men drove the two remaining skirmishers off. Roger took his spear back and dashed to the fallen warrior's side. He opened up the visor, only to discover a face as white as snow.

Looking at the youth, the man grinned, wanting to say something, but blood loss kicked in and then there was only silence.

"Leave him," Hugo instructed, gripping the fallen man's discarded halberd.

Before long, the Coalition side re-formed and headed into them.

"Korelians to me!" Hugo bellowed; his voice filled with anger and exhaustion. His brothers-in-arms rushed forward again, weapons gleaming. Inch by inch, they re-established their front line, and the two opposing lines at the center rejoined again.

Regardless of the blistering heat, accumulated injuries, and dwindling stamina, both sides plunged back into the fray yet again. They thrust, swung, and stabbed with savage desperation.

The faces of those without full-face helmets betrayed their exhaustion and thirst, yet also their defiance. Those with full-face helmets fared no better, their breaths laboring hard within the stifling confines of their heated metal headgear.

As casualties mounted, each side endeavored to funnel fresh troops to the front lines. This resulted in a grim spectacle as green, untested men faced battle-hardened fighters.

Pushed to their limits, the Korelians deployed their last reserves—the militia, who eagerly rushed to aid their beleaguered lines. Despite their enthusiasm, they stood little chance; many fell as swiftly as they entered the fray.

Inexperienced combatants futilely swung their weapons at torsos or heads while seasoned fighters targeted easier to hit limbs with maces and axes, content to take their enemies out of action.

The grassy battlefield turned into a grimy, slick mess of blood and human insides. Fallen men were soon trampled, their cries lost in the chaos.

Hugo saw desperation etched in his men's eyes. Nobody to his left and right was without injury, despite their armor. They were past their limits. Brave as they were, they were outclassed. His gaze frantically swept across the chaotic scene, searching for the familiar sight of Sir Justin's banner.

On the far right, amid the fiercest clash of steel and the roar of men, Sir Justin finally realized how his left flank and center were on the brink of crumbling under pressure. Even the militia's brave sacrifice had failed to blunt the opponent's momentum. Trying to salvage what remained of his force, he gave a commanding cry. "Fall back! Fall back!"

With a heavy heart, the Korelians began to give ground.

CHAPTER 16

MOVING PIECES

Lansius

The dense forest canopy sheltered everything beneath it, allowing only small rays of sunlight to filter through. The scent of the earth was robust, arising from layers of dry leaves on the ground. Flanked by his command staff, Lansius sat upon a tree root, a large tree at his back.

They were already partially armored, eagerly waiting for developments from the battlefield outside the forest. The air was humid, but the lingering chill from the previous night kept them cool.

The knights with their custom-made armor had good weight distribution over their bodies and limbs, minimizing discomfort.

For the past four nights, nearly two hundred of them had hidden in borrowed yurts on the far side of the forest. To ensure secrecy, they restricted movement and even only allowed fires inside the yurts for cooking and night heating.

Speaking of cooking, Lansius realized that Audrey was eyeing his bowl.

"Umm, aren't you going to finish that?" Audrey, clad in avant-garde black plate armor, finally asked.

"I'm feeling full. You can have it," Lansius offered the bowl.

Audrey accepted it readily, fishing out the half-eaten bread that had sunk into the soup, and took a bite.

They heard someone approaching, and then a figure clad in a brown cloak appeared. They recognized the man as the scout, who quickly knelt. "My lord, one Coalition column is marching toward Marshal Hugo's position."

The staff burst into lively discussions, while Sir Callahan calmly updated the earthen map on the ground.

Audrey shot Lansius a sharp glance, but Lansius merely noticed crumbs around her mouth and carefully wiped them away with his hand.

Afterward, Lansius spoke with unusual calmness. "It's time. The diversion won't hold for long. Return to Korelia and ride south."

Audrey placed the unfinished bowl on the ground and stood up. Her movement drew the attention of the staff.

"Sir Callahan," Audrey addressed the older knight, who stood in response.

"Captain," the blond knight replied.

"I entrust my lord to you. Keep him safe."

"I shall put my life on the line," Sir Callahan pledged.

Their exchange was brief. Next, Lansius rose, and all eyes were on him. "Ready the men," he commanded.

The staff, in turn, relayed the order to the entire camp.

Stealing a moment for himself, Lansius called to Audrey in a softer tone. "Come, let me walk you to your horse."

Preparations for battle were well underway as they walked through their forest hideout.

Finally, they reached a quiet spot. "Audrey," he called.

She slowed down. "I figured you wanted to talk."

"Yes, I still have great doubts about this," he admitted.

Her expression hardened. Other people would be deterred by this, but Lansius knew that this was just her natural demeanor. Confirming his thoughts, she let out a sigh.

"I sort of understand your feelings. Sending men into harm's way is never easy. But it's your duty as lord. I have mine, they have theirs, you have yours."

"Men are going to die . . . for what reason?" Lansius calmly argued. "Half our men aren't even Korelians, they have little reason to fight. If we just retreat to Midlandia, then even the townsfolk wouldn't need to take up arms."

Audrey clicked her tongue. "Retreat . . . ? My oath is to protect you, but I'll strike you if you utter such nonsense again."

Lansius wasn't surprised by her reaction. He knew he shouldn't utter nonsense like that on the eve of battle, but his conscience begged him to. "Apologies, I've got so many things on my mind—"

"Lans, you're overthinking this," she cut in. "The men under you, me, and even the people in town are fighting, not because you told us to. It's because we want to."

Lansius was perplexed. "But why? I may have done some small good deeds here and there, some small help, but nothing worthy—"

"To us, you are worthy," Audrey declared, exhaling deeply. "Look, I can't put this into words. How can I explain this? You're the smart one, ugh, why give me a headache . . ." she complained, scratching her head in frustration.

Her expression stirred something deep within him. A whirlwind of worries and doubts suddenly passed over him, and something within snapped. A chuckle, his first in days, escaped him unexpectedly.

Despite Audrey giving him a funny look, Lansius couldn't suppress it. The laughter felt too good, too freeing. He was gasping for air afterward.

"Feel better now?" she asked.

"No, I'm not okay. I'm sending my men and my loved ones into battle," he replied, but something within felt lighter. The brooding was gone.

Audrey suddenly came closer until their breastplates bumped with a dull thud.

"Wha—?"

"Just be still." Her hands were on the sides of his head and their lips met in a brief, heated kiss, just like their first beside the stream. Not wanting to let go, Lansius wrapped his arms around her and pulled her close. This time, he kissed her.

All that lance training paid off, as she couldn't resist as easily. Her breath, her lips, and her tongue overwhelmed his senses.

She finally pushed him off and wiped her lips with her palm. "That should do it," she said with a mischievous gleam in her eye.

"Do what?" he asked with a slightly reddened face.

"Grow you a pair." She smirked.

"You rascal," he retorted, but that failed to erase the grin on her face.

"Don't die," Lansius said as she turned away from him.

"You too, Lans. I'll see you after the battle." Audrey waved her hand casually and headed alone to where they had left the horses.

Later, through the forest, Lansius caught a glimpse of three riders. They must have been her and her escorts. They detoured eastward before returning to the town of Korelia via the east side. In town, twenty cavalrymen were waiting for her.

The vivid recollections still rang in Lansius's mind as he walked back. He instinctively licked his lips as if savoring the aftertaste.

I should propose when this is over.

Lansius made a mental note before clearing his head as he returned to the command site. There, he noticed the scout who had remained behind.

"My lord," he greeted him.

"Good report. Go get something to drink." Lansius handed a silver coin to the scout. Informants were paid well in his troops.

The scout bowed and then walked proudly to his hideout. The stump on his left arm dangled freely.

Lansius employed men who had lost their limbs as scouts. They often joked that losing a limb made them faster and stealthier. It was heartening to see them take pride in their work. As for Lansius, he was just glad that he could provide a source of income for his veterans.

As Lansius sat back, the map they drew on the ground was getting updated. Now, one of the Coalition rectangle drawings that represented the A column was moving closer toward the Korelians' only rectangle.

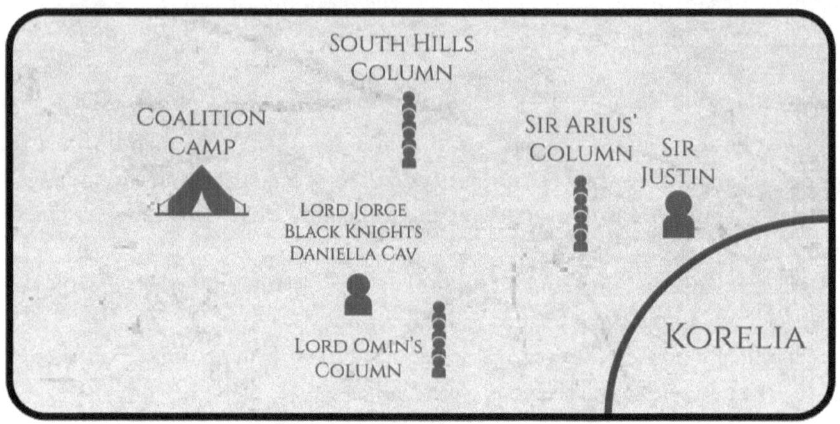

Lansius recalled that no matter how many times he had simulated this battle, Korelia didn't have any chance to stop the Coalition's gargantuan force.

If he waited, the Coalition would complete their siege engines, and it would be over once the castle sustained severe damage. If he chose to sally out, the Coalition's six-thousand-strong force would counterattack, targeting both Korelia's town and castle.

When that happened, even with the aid of trenches, they could hold out for no more than a few days at best. Victory seemed a distant hope. Engaging the Coalition in a conventional way would certainly be a losing battle. Thus, Lansius had opted for a more radical approach.

He planned to hit the Coalition's weak spot. That in itself wasn't new or radical. What was radical was just how far he would go to make certain that he could hit his mark.

More than just a halfhearted distraction, Lansius needed substantial bait. This required a column of men, so he had pulled his force, even leaving the castle practically undefended.

Now, only two guards remained in the castle, both crippled and serving as lookouts. If not for Cecile, the castle staff, the cooks, and the page boys, the castle would have appeared abandoned.

They manned the walls, creating the illusion of a well-defended castle. Many of them were competent with crossbows, enough for well-aimed shots, lending credibility to the castle's defenses, at least from a distance.

For the same reasons, Lansius had pulled most of his men out of town. Apart from Sir Justin's column, the town and its trenches were only lightly defended by a mixture of crossbowmen, militia, and Audrey's twenty cavalrymen.

Given the length of the trenches, Lansius earnestly hoped that the presence of the militia was enough to maintain the illusion of being properly manned. If the other Coalition column were to attack the trenches, his weakness would be exposed.

With the castle nearly empty and only a token defense in the town, the situation was daunting. The Coalition could potentially steamroll their defenses purely by chance. Yet, deep down, Lansius was prepared to sacrifice the town if it meant securing a victory.

He was resolved, however, to make the enemy pay a high price. He had instructed his defenders to switch to urban, door-to-door fighting once the enemy column breached the trenches.

What Lansius needed was time and a diversion to keep the enemy preoccupied. This was the role that Sir Justin's column had taken. They acted as bait, effectively keeping the Coalition forces locked in place.

Now, the plan was in motion, which heightened Lansius's anxiety. He personally disliked this plan, but he couldn't devise a viable alternative. Strategically, he was cornered. His opponents were simply too well prepared.

Crackling sounds of crushed dry leaves alerted them. Two scouts appeared under escort. "My lord, the Coalition column has engaged Marshal Justin's forces—"

Murmurs and comments cut the report short.

"Not yet. The man still has things to say." Sir Callahan rebuked the rest and motioned for the scout to continue his report.

The scout resumed. "We saw the Coalition cavalry moving more southward than before. My lord, we think that the Lord of Three Hills is trying to get a better view of the battle."

"Well done," Lansius exclaimed while clenching his fist. It was better than expected. Sir Justin's column not only had baited and locked a Coalition column but also drew their reserve away.

Everybody was looking at Lansius tensely. They could feel that the time had come.

"Bring out the horses," Lansius ordered.

His command moved the men to scramble from their spots.

"How's the other columns' position?" Lansius asked the scout as his men were preparing to battle.

"There are no changes, my lord."

"Good. What else do we know about his column?" Lansius pointed to the column nearest to them on the ground map.

"My lord, I recognize their sigils. They're men from South Hills," the scout replied with confidence.

The second scout chimed in, "They look weak, my lord. Not many are wearing armor. Mostly peasants with only a shield, spear, and thick clothing."

"Levied troops. My lord, they can be bypassed," Sir Callahan advised.

"How about the wind?" Lansius asked the two scouts.

"The wind still blows from the south, my lord."

The board is set, and the pieces are in motion . . .

CHAPTER 17

BLUE AND BRONZE

With the battle situation unfolding before them, Lord Lansius finally made his decision. He pointed at the nearest column on the drawn map on the ground. "Sir Callahan, let's hit this column."

"The South Hill column? My lord, may we learn the reason?" Callahan inquired. Even though the lord had a victory against Lord Robert last year, his inexperience remained a concern among the knights.

Although the Marshal had assisted the lord in proofing the plans and their variations, there were still lingering doubts. Thus, Callahan had made it his mission to guard against any potential problem.

"We don't need to inflict a crippling blow, just enough to cause a rupture in their seams," Lord Lansius explained.

"But even if we successfully charge this weak column, the Black Knights will arrive quickly," warned Callahan, noting that despite the surprise factor, they were just eighty cavalry against two thousand. Such a disparity meant it was unlikely for them to damage, break, or rout the column.

"If we do enough damage. When the time comes, they'll break on their own," Lord Lansius assured him.

Callahan looked at Lansius for a second or two before nodding in response. He wasn't wholly buying what Lansius had said, but it was good enough of a reason. Back in his youth, he had charged a column for worse reasons.

The blond knight glanced at his fellow knights, his eyes brimming with determination. His brothers-in-arms nodded and voiced no complaints. Their trust stemmed largely from the fact that Callahan vouched for this, and that the lord was joining them in person.

More than thirty knights and dozens of horsemen among them were formerly Lord Robert's vassals. Against such a large opponent, there were risks that they could become disheartened and flee. Thus, the lord felt compelled to lead them personally.

Without any objections from the cavalry, Lord Lansius turned his attention to his trusted ally. "Calub," he called.

The alchemist, who had been waiting patiently in a corner, perked up.

"Yes, my lord." Calub stepped forward. As a high-ranking but non-noble among the knights, Calub wisely downplayed his importance to avoid potential friction.

"Take command of the hundred men as planned. Spread them between the glade and the opening near the entrance. If things go as planned, we might bring a large prey, and you'll be the snare. If not, then you'll be our shield."

"Understood, my lord," Calub responded firmly.

"Sir Callahan," the lord called.

The blond knight stood. Even nearing fifty, he retained a captivating presence.

"Let's ride," the lord commanded.

Sir Callahan rallied the cavalry with vigor. "The lord is riding with us!" His declaration set things into motion. One man wiped the map from the ground, while the rest readily mounted their horses.

Sterling had Lord Lansius's horse ready. He helped him mount and handed him the gauntlets.

"Sterling, last chance. Forget about courage and honor. This is war. You could be crippled for life," the lord warned from atop his destrier. Many knew that the lord hadn't asked Sterling to join, but the young squire insisted on coming.

The squire's face remained adamant. "My lord, I shall not be a burden."

Lansius drew a deep breath and just rode after Sir Callahan.

Behind him, Sterling in half-armor dutifully carried their lances. Carrying a lance was burdensome and an unnecessary hazard within the forest, so he wouldn't let the lord have it until they reached the open field.

Only knights were in plate armor, the rest were either in half-armor, brigandines, or ringmail. The horses were also protected by barding or horse armor. The head part and some of the horses' bodies were covered by metal plates or hardened leather. There was no uniformity. Each owner had acquired and equipped their steed on their own. The result made them look like a circus with plenty of colors and unique designs.

Before long, the column of cavalry reached the forest outskirts and quickly fell into formation.

"My lord, with your permission, Sir Harold and I will ride in front," Callahan requested.

Lord Lansius looked at the tall man who saluted with an open visor. His polished plate armor was impeccable. Sir Harold and his small band of brothers were the unofficial Midlandian reinforcements. Despite the small number, they were highly enthusiastic warriors and war aficionados who volunteered for the sheer thrill of combat.

Lansius let out a grin, finding some similarities with Anci. "It would be an honor to ride with you, Sir Harold."

"The pleasure is mutual, my lord," the tall knight replied with an honest smile.

Without time to lose and with the cavalry ready, the lord gazed at Sir Callahan. In the direct sunlight, the blond knight's armor displayed its intricate details. The black decorative gilding and ornaments gave it the appearance of ancient ceremonial armor. However, the buffed-out scrapes and dents betrayed its use in battles.

"Sir Callahan, lead the way," Lansius instructed as he latched his own tried-and-tested helmet and gazed upon the plains that would become their battlefield.

Coalition Side

Beneath the shade of an umbrella, Viscount Jorge witnessed the battle unfold in front of him. His heart beat faster as the Coalition column slammed into the Korelian line. "Morton, you see that? You see that?" Jorge jumped from his folded chair as he remarked excitedly.

The lord was so proud of Sir Arius, his most trusted cousin who personally led the attack. Meanwhile, Sir Morton, the Black Knights' captain, merely nodded his head. He wasn't the type to talk much.

Somehow, this seemingly mismatched master and retainer actually had good chemistry. Both men deeply respected their differences. This was quite uncommon. In the Imperium, a servant who wouldn't lick the master's boots was usually discarded early.

But then again, Jorge was hardly normal. So abnormal that his peers mocked him as the "big fool of One Hill" behind his back. Originally, Jorge's viscountcies held four regions: Korimor, South Hill, Korelia, and the capital in the center.

Each castle was built on a hill, thus the capital was aptly named Three Hills. Under Jorge's nascent rule, a branch family and another old follower had seceded.

In response, Jorge launched wars multiple times without a victory. Each time he won, he installed an ambitious knight who eventually rebelled. In the end, he gained nothing and lost even more.

The young lord was not entirely to blame. His only fault was being naive and idealistic. Jorge idolized the school of meritocracy, an ideal governing system where people were promoted based on their ability, not by blood relation.

However, not even the best of the Imperium lords was able to implement such a radical system. After all, family ties and nepotism ran deep and were central to feudalism.

Traditionally, a House placed family members in powerful positions to secure their grip on power. Thus, when a lord promoted non-family members into high positions, envy and political intrigue often followed. This led to distrust and contempt among the various factions. Ultimately, it usually ended in a purge, assassination, or open conflict.

That same issue still haunted Jorge, whose only hope now lay with Sir Arius. The younger cousin was respected by various factions and might be the solution to the instability. Jorge didn't mind sharing some of his power with Arius if that would resolve the crisis.

Contrary to the myths circulating about him, Jorge wasn't overly ambitious; he merely sought to keep the legacy of his forefather intact. All he truly desired for himself was Korelia, his birthplace.

"We've beaten them! They're pushed back," Jorge clamored excitedly as he watched Arius's column gaining ground.

The staff cheerfully congratulated Jorge. Only Morton kept silent.

Far to their right, in another cavalry column, the Nicopolan cavalry captain was also silent. Daniella had learned that the Lord of Korelia had a keen eye for battle. However, today's battle was too brash even for an overconfident nobleman.

"Something bothering you, my lady?" one of her mercenary lieutenants asked.

"It's too quiet and too stupid," Daniella replied, and then she felt the urge to act. "Tell the scout to move farther. Leave no blind spot."

"Will do." The rider quickly relayed the order.

Her rider barely left when cheering erupted from Jorge's position. Daniella felt the cheering was so contrasted with what happened on the battlefield. As she could clearly see, there was no glory in the mangled and beaten bodies that littered the field.

Many of the wounded, drenched in their blood, limped and even crawled for help.

However, as a part of the nobility, she understood that for the ruling class, this brutal sight was no different from a sporting event.

Tara-taraaa!

A different trumpet signal from the South Hill column on the north side caught everybody off guard. Everybody who heard it looked northward in confusion.

Daniella was quick to action and rode north with a few riders to get a better look. Meanwhile, Jorge stood and squinted his eyes. "What's going on? It's one of ours, right?"

One of his staff promptly sent a scout to ascertain the situation, but it would take time, and Jorge was impatient.

"It's likely a cavalry attack. My lord, please let me have a hundred," Morton calmly requested. By now, they could see an unknown cavalry heading toward the northern column.

"No, we'll move as one," Jorge declared, clenching his fist.

Jorge's declaration drew the attention of his entire command staff.

"My lord, do you wish to attack?" Morton asked on behalf of the staff.

"Certainly. Now that we know what Lansius's intention really is, let's not hesitate. The chance has presented itself. Let's move out," the young lord commanded.

The staff readily relayed the order, and everyone mounted their horses. The squires strapped Jorge's cuirass back on and helped him mount his horse. Spurred by the lord's urgency, a hundred knights rode north at full gallop.

Daniella hastily rallied her Nicopolan cavalry and gave the command to follow. She still found it suspicious, but the Lord of Korelia had shown his hand, and now she could play hers.

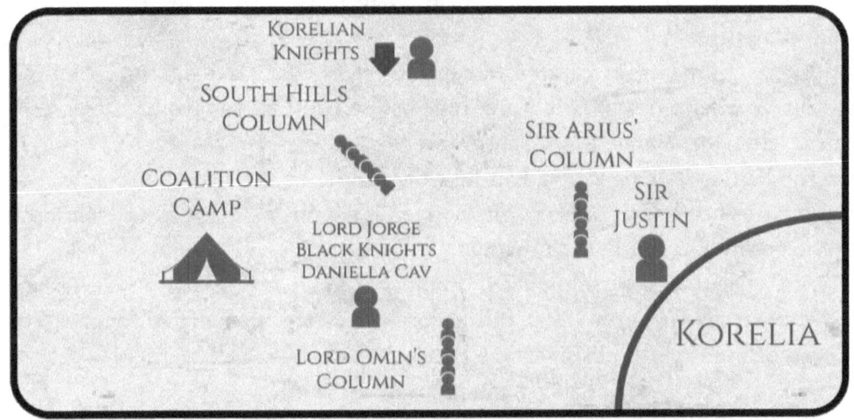

Korelian Knights

Lansius clenched his right arm against his side, feeling the weight of the lance under his armpit. Even when kept at an angle, it remained heavy. The breastplate's lance rest helped reduce the burden on his right arm and hand, and stabilize the shaft while the horse trotted.

After almost two years of training, Lansius was still very much struggling not to kill himself by dropping and plunging the lance into the ground. His arm and muscles felt on fire as he wrestled against the rocking motion. Minuscule adjustments were made to keep the lance at an angle, far off the ground.

Meanwhile, his destrier continued to run like a charging buffalo. The rocking motion was anything but gentle. Weighted by the armor, on every up and down, the saddle's hard leather punished Lansius's loins and battered his breath.

He wanted to say he was used to this, that he was trained for this, but he couldn't. This wasn't something someone could get used to in a mere year and a half.

Suddenly, the horse leaped.

Oof!

They landed gracefully. It wasn't a big jump, but the saddle smacked his butt and gut from beneath. In a trained reflex, Lansius exerted all his might to control the lance as it wobbled.

He realized that to survive this would be one of the crowning achievements of his life. Yet, he held no regrets. This was a necessity—he simply couldn't afford to sit this one out.

Understanding Lansius's inexperience, Sir Callahan and Harold, who rode in front, made small adjustments here and there to ease their lord's burden. Instead of having Lansius follow them, they centered the whole formation around him.

The rest of the eighty cavalry were spread evenly on his left and right. Sterling and the experienced standard bearer rode beside Lansius. The banner depicted a blue shield with a single bronze chevron.

The banner was new, and Lansius's own. Felis had designed and sewn the coat of arms just a few days ago. She boasted it would bring good luck, and now Lansius prayed fervently that it would.

Sir Callahan and Harold picked up more speed. Lansius kept up with them and soon realized they were at full gallop. The wind screamed through every open vent in his visor. His sight was a blur.

"Close ranks!" Sir Callahan shouted from the front.

"Close ranks!" The standard bearer beside Lansius relayed the order.

They rushed the last stretch of land between them and the opponent in an arrow-like formation. The standard bearer moved in front of Lansius, while Sterling remained at his side.

Sir Callahan had told them that he was expecting crossbow attacks, but only a few materialized. At this range, Lansius saw that the Coalition line now looked jagged and uneven. More importantly, there was no wall of spears or pikes.

This column was supposedly two thousand strong, but what Lansius saw was just a group of men, scared and frightened.

By the holy, I'm going to trample them . . .

His conscience screamed, but his trained instinct kept him going.

This is my plan, and I'm responsible for this. Go haunt me if you must, but judge me fairly against your lords who led you here in the first place!

He steadied his mind as the distance closed in at a frightening speed.

Sir Callahan in front lowered his lance and the rest followed. Lansius felt the numbness in his arms as he lowered his lance into position.

By now, the opposing men were in full view. Lansius saw their faces and reactions as Callahan and Harold, along with the front riders, dove into their ranks.

The screams and the horses' beastly noises immediately filled his ears. There was no time to observe; gripping his lance tightly, Lansius made his charge.

CHAPTER 18

CHARGE OF THE KORELIAN KNIGHTS

C*RACKKK!*

The sharp crack of a wooden lance shattering battled with the screams of men. The air was punched painfully and abruptly from Lansius's lungs, overwhelming his senses. Dazed, he barely registered that this was nothing like mere exercise.

His right arm and shoulder recoiled from the lance's impact. Through the slit in his helmet, deafening chaos was unfolding before him.

The men from South Hill, clustered to Lansius's left and right, cowered as they frantically tried to escape the horror of being trampled.

The destrier's loud neighing alerted him. Without hesitation, Lansius tightened his lower body to signal the destrier to continue the charge.

Amid all that chaos, Lansius barely kept up with the forward element, who was doing the heavy lifting. Sir Callahan and Harold, along with the frontline knights, cleared a path and bore the brunt of the enemy's resistance, facing spears, swords, and thrown stones.

However, despite their successful charge, the enemy formation was simply too large to be routed this easily.

Behind Lansius, the rest of the Korelian knights charged into the poorly defended South Hill column. The column's front line had buckled, taking flight at the cavalry's entry.

As for Lansius, the adrenaline masked the lightness of his right arm. He found himself still clutching the lance, the shaft of which was gone. He dropped it and was about to draw his blade when a spear struck his left arm.

Instinct kicked in, and Lansius clenched his left arm into his chest, creating multiple layers of steel, just in time as the same spear slammed again. It was uncomfortable, and panic-inducing, but nothing more.

Sensing danger, the destrier broke into a short gallop, and more screams erupted as the beast barreled forward through the disarrayed formation.

Screams could also be heard from behind, as the Korelian cavalry followed Lansius's lead. One of them, Sterling, was desperately closing in on his lord. Despite being in only half-armor, he was fearless, even managing to strike down the spearman who had attacked Lansius.

The ground was littered with discarded weapons, shields, and bodies. Suddenly, an open field enveloped Lansius's view.

His horse snorted in delight while Lansius was dazzled by the sudden change of scenery.

I actually survived that shit?!

The serene grassy plains felt surreal in the aftermath of what he had just witnessed. A smirk formed on his lips as he clenched his fist, slamming it into his breastplate in a primal expression of victory, a release after surviving tremendous physical exertion.

The knights in front began to slow down, making a wide turn. Sir Hugo and Callahan formed up on Lansius, followed by Sterling from behind.

"Are you injured, my lord?" Sir Harold asked after opening his visor. The man had barely broken a sweat.

Lansius's right hand was still clutching the sword since he was too shaky to sheathe it. Using his left hand, he tapped the side of his helmet and found the small latch. It was hard with the gauntlet on, but he managed to open the visor.

Regaining full peripheral vision and the ability to breathe freely was an immense joy. "I'm good," he declared after swallowing a breath of fresh air.

Then, situational awareness kicked in. "Are we clear for another pass?"

Sir Harold and Callahan looked at the horizon and both noticed that the Coalition's entire reserve of two hundred cavalry was bearing down on them. Lansius noticed it too.

"One pass only, my lord," Sir Callahan answered.

"How many did we lose?" Lansius asked the knights while glancing at Sterling. The squire nodded in response.

"A few or none," Sir Harold responded, after taking a quick look at their forces, which seemed intact.

"Give the signal, we're going for another," Lansius ordered.

Callahan grabbed his silver hornlike apparatus and blew it. Unlike Anci's loud and clear buccina, Callahan's was richer and deeper.

Buuu-buuuuu!

As they re-formed, the standard bearer returned to Lansius's side and proudly hoisted the blue and bronze chevron high.

Once again, the Korelians trotted into the enemy. Nobody retained their lance, so they were at a disadvantage. But the enemy had it worse.

The South Hill column was demoralized, and many were dead or injured. Worse, a large portion was distraught. Now, they noticed that the cavalry had wheeled around toward their rear. The South Hill command rushed their strongest troops to the rear, trying to re-form, but it was utter chaos.

The levied element refused to cooperate. Only at the last minute did they manage to re-form into thicker ranks, seven or possibly eight men deep, trying to counter the cavalry charge without risking their exposed flanks.

The Korelian knights did nothing. Sir Callahan refused to lose time or momentum. Like an arrow loosened by the bow, they flew straight.

Lansius drew a deep breath and latched back his visor. The sound of his breath echoing inside the helmet was triggering something.

Is this PTSD?

Tens of hours of full armor combat against Audrey had made him into either a fighter or a patient eligible for disability benefits.

Fuck it!

He cleared his mind and braced for impact. The destrier neighed as she understood by instinct what was going to happen. Following Sir Callahan's lead, Lansius allowed his warhorse to gallop as he was without lance.

His limited vision slowly turned into a blur. He breathed deeply as the knights in front gallantly dove right into the enemy line. Despite more spears being directed at them, it wasn't a unified wall of spears.

The South Hill's front line broke for the second time, and mayhem ensued.

"EYAAH!" Lansius yelled, ready to swing his sword, but he entered the fray without any resistance.

The opposing men scattered to the left and right. Some even stood still as if frozen, their teeth chattering while their eyes locked on to the incoming knights. Their wills had been broken.

But then, men surged from the left side as they formation contracted. Their faces were drained of blood as their panicked column squeezed them into harm's way.

Lansius swung his sword to deter the nearest group of men. He was preoccupied with them when a poleaxe landed on his greaves. It was no more than a glancing blow, but it startled him. Before he could react, a short, frightful shriek caught his attention.

His horse had mercilessly trampled a man who stood in her way. However, Lansius barely had time to react as another man was abruptly shoved into him.

The unfortunate man came so close that Lansius ended up whacking the man's helmet with his pommel as the space was too tight for a blade swing. The person collapsed where he stood, narrowly dodging the horse's deadly hooves.

There was no time to breathe—a bigger threat loomed ahead. A group of well-armed men had made their way to the rear of their formation, attempting to reach the Korelian knights. Seizing their opportunity, they brandished their polearms against the cavalry, who, now without their lances, had limited means to counter.

Sir Harold and Sir Callahan swiftly maneuvered to confront the new threat, fighting off the brandished polearms and carving a broader path for their lord.

Behind them, Lansius, on his way out, parried attacks with his sword and jostled the rest away with his gauntlets.

Three times the sharp edges landed on his armor. Each time, the steel's smooth contour deflected the thrust that grazed without biting. Lansius kept squeezing his knee on his horse, signaling her to keep going while planting his feet in the stirrups to avoid falling.

Now, he noticed that the destrier ran wilder than usual, as if it were injured. Being only partially armored, a wound was always a possibility. However, the beast remained aggressive and didn't seem to falter.

Just a little bit more . . .

As Lansius parried the last polearm brandished against him, the rest of his knights followed behind and tore through the South Hill column.

The green grassy field was within their sight.

"GAAHH!" Lansius gasped. Something had struck his back. The hard blow rattled his gut and made his head feel light. He coughed, narrowly avoiding vomiting, all the while searching for his assailant.

He craned his neck and spotted a man with a bardiche, a big axe-like blade mounted on a pole.

The bardiche wielder charged, ready for another blow, but was impeded by his own frightened comrades. With a face full of scorn, he taunted Lansius, just as his helmet flew off and fresh blood spurted from the side of his head.

Sterling had swooped in from behind, delivering a fatal blow after the standard bearer had driven off two men to clear a path.

Meanwhile, Lansius had reached the open field and savored the change of scenery. Even the destrier's breathing had calmed.

Sir Harold and Sir Callahan formed up around him as they slowed their trot. Fresh blood coated their armors and mounts. Suddenly, Lansius felt unwell.

"My lord, are you hurt?" Callahan asked, his visor already up.

Frantically, Lansius opened his visor. He took a deep breath, as if he were drowning.

This spurred the two knights into action. Sir Harold quickly moved to Lansius's side and tried to find the problem. "My lord, try to take a deep breath."

"I-it's hard," Lansius gasped. "My back!"

"There's a dent. You've been hit, my lord," shouted Sterling from behind.

"Get the backplate off," Harold urged Callahan, as he took the destrier's rein to steady the pace.

"Do it, do it," Lansius said.

Sterling could only watch as Callahan managed to undo the latches and remove the backplate after several tries. Instantly, Lansius felt better as he breathed freely again.

Unintentionally, the absence of the backplate provided a remarkably refreshing coolness, in spite of the drenched arming doublet underneath the armor.

"The dent looked shallow, but it bent the waist part inward," Callahan reported as they rode further.

Only then, Lansius realized he had lost his sword. Likely, when the bardiche man had hit him.

Soon, they reached a safe distance and slowed their pace. Lansius noticed several streaks and marks on Callahan's armor, including a bolt head embedded near his shoulder that had failed to penetrate. Red smears also coated Callahan's legs and saddle.

Seeing Lansius's gaze on the stains, Callahan quickly reassured him, "It's not my blood."

"Sir Harold, how about you?" Lansius inquired.

"Lost an axe, and my left arm is a bit numb, but I still have my sword. I can do another pass."

Sir Harold's bravado sent Lansius into a chuckle. "How many did we lose?"

"Five, maybe fewer," Callahan replied flatly.

Lansius couldn't suppress a smile at that result, especially when Sterling looked unharmed.

Unbelievable . . . This is better than my wildest prediction.

"My lord, the Black Knights," the standard bearer called out from the rear.

At his warning, they turned to see riders clad in black armor galloping toward them. The South Hill column had split in two, providing the Black Knights with a clear path to approach.

Although Lansius's charge had inflicted significant damage, it clearly wasn't enough to rout the South Hill column. With the arrival of Lord Jorge and his Black Knights, the column quickly recovered.

As Sir Callahan had predicted, this minor charge had only a small impact on the overall battle.

"Sir Harold, want to have a go at them?" Lansius jested.

"For you, my lord, I'll do it," the tall knight replied with a wide smirk.

Lansius chuckled and gently signaled his destrier to pick up the pace.

Just then, Sterling called out, "My lord, smoke!" He pointed to the east, toward where Sir Justin's column was fighting.

Lansius glanced in that direction, then turned to Callahan. "Aim for the forest. Get us out of here!"

CHAPTER 19

NICOPOLAN PURSUIT

Coalition Side

The morning sun blazed upon the battlefield. North of the Korelia plains, two cavalry units charged into the forest. The Coalition was in close pursuit of the Korelians, ready to punish them for their daring surprise attack. Every move made by the Korelian cavalry was quickly mirrored by the Coalition forces.

With their lords present, both sides gave their all in this chase. Even as they entered the outskirts of the forest, dense vegetation did little to slow them down. The sunny scenery of the open plains rapidly gave way to the brown and dark green foliage of the woods, with both sides navigating the increasingly narrow paths in single file.

The Korelians began to slow down as the terrain became harder to traverse. Their horses, already tired and some injured, struggled to maintain pace. It was then that the foremost riders of the Coalition finally caught up with the Korelians' rear guard.

They weren't the famed Black Knights, but the Nicopolan mercenaries. With their lighter cavalry, they began their attack.

The Korelian horsemen tried to fend them off, but it was simply too hard. One rider, unable to keep his balance, tumbled from his horse and was quickly taken hostage. Another, already wounded, was grabbed from behind and captured without much resistance.

At this point, the Korelian cavalry seemed destined to be overrun. However, the mercenaries' hunger for ransom proved to be a double-edged sword. Each Korelian they captured slowed down the entire pursuit.

This occurred with such impunity because their commanding officer and the Black Knights, burdened by heavier armor, lagged behind. Ironically, the mercenaries' success was inadvertently aiding the Korelians. After five of their riders were captured, the Korelians managed to gain a considerable distance from their pursuers.

In the narrowness of the forest path, the pursuit became bogged down, until Daniella arrived on the scene. Taking control, she ordered her most loyal group to continue the chase. Despite being a mercenary herself, Daniella often found herself frustrated with the lack of discipline among her ranks and their penchant for taking hostages or looting at any opportunity.

With Daniella at the helm, the Nicopolans returned to the chase. They were on the verge of catching up with the Korelians' rear guard when the Korelians suddenly led them into a large glade in the middle of the forest.

Daniella initially thought little of the clearing, but then the Korelians abruptly split in two directions. Tens of her riders blindly pursued them, but Daniella's instincts sensed a trap. "Halt, halt!" she commanded, her eyes darting between the glade and the two narrow paths.

Despite her command, several riders stubbornly chased after their targets. Many more would have followed if Sir Morton hadn't arrived and blocked the path. He, too, had sensed that something was amiss.

Riding up to Sir Morton, Daniella said, "I don't trust these narrow paths, not on horses. We should send men on foot."

The knight captain silently agreed, though for a different reason: they were venturing too far from the battlefield, thereby putting their allies behind at risk.

Following Daniella, the rest of the ranking officers gathered around Sir Morton, deliberating whether to pursue or not. Meanwhile, behind them, the sudden halt of their advance caused a bottleneck in the clearing.

Though the glade was quite large, space quickly became limited. With barely enough room for thirty horses, the area soon became overcrowded as more cavalry flooded in. Friction ensued as the horsemen jostled against each other, struggling to turn or find a spot to stop.

The mercenaries, feeling deprived of ransom and loot—their main sources of income—started to grow increasingly agitated. "Why aren't we giving chase?" they grumbled.

"Are the men from Three Hills afraid of the woods?" another taunted.

"You dare to mock us, sellsword?" the Three Hills knights shouted back angrily. And just like that, curses filled the air. Several men needed to be restrained before drawing blood.

Despite having been allies for several years, there was little love lost between the Three Hills knights and Korimor's Nicopolan mercenaries.

"What's the meaning of this?" demanded Lord Jorge, addressing the situation as he arrived, flanked by his retinue. He unlatched his visor to fully reveal his handsome face.

Nobody dared utter a word. They all knew too well that a viscount could throw anyone into a dungeon on a whim and forget about them indefinitely.

"Morton, why are we stopping—"

Fssshh!

Jorge's question was cut short by the sudden sound of crossbow bolts. They rained down on them with deadly accuracy.

"Crossbowmen!" several cried in panic.

"Ambush!" others shouted as a warning.

Horses collided as their riders scrambled to hide or evade the attack. Crossbow bolts landed indiscriminately, often shattering upon impact against plate armor. Each near miss drove the riders into a greater panic.

With no place to run, the riders frantically dismounted and scrambled for cover. Those attempting to ride back found themselves trapped in a bottleneck. The return path was still clogged with the incoming cavalry, who were also under attack.

Caught in a dire situation, unable to advance or retreat, they became easy targets. Each successive salvo injured more horses, sparking a deadly rampage. More and more wounded warhorses galloped wildly, without care for their riders.

These once-proud mounts had become a menace, stampeding everything in their path. Under their mighty hooves, unlucky men were trampled into bloody pulp.

One large steed, with a bolt embedded in its neck, trampled a knight and then slipped on the fallen man's cuirass. The warhorse tumbled onto two other men, crushing them to death.

Despite the carnage, the crossbow attack did not ebb. The dry leaves on the forest floor were stained red, and the smell of blood, along with other fouler stenches, permeated the air.

All those who stubbornly clung to their horses eventually met their deaths. The last one to persist was now being dragged deeper into the forest by his maddened horse. What remained of him was the dull, muffled sound of his plate armor being thrashed around.

Amid this madness, only Morton stood unfazed, with Daniella at his side holding a kite shield to protect them both. Another Black Knight had raised a shield in defense as well, but despite their efforts, a few bolts struck Morton.

Fortunately, Lord Jorge had equipped Morton with high-tier plate armor. The Centuria steel deflected the bolts, resulting in only superficial scratches on the armor.

Behind them, a dozen frightened men huddled, using trees for cover. Meanwhile, Morton continued to recite a verse corresponding to the wind barrier that surrounded Lord Jorge. However, the barrier, due to their distance, did not extend to protect Morton himself.

The forest finally turned quiet, as all who still drew breath had successfully hidden or found cover. The pause prompted everyone to look around, trying to make sense of the situation.

Morton ceased his recitation and withdrew the barrier over his lord. He then turned to the Coalition men who had lost their nerve. "Where're your balls? Cowards!" he roared.

"Regroup!" he commanded, before adding, "You're wearing plate armor. Act like it!"

A few bolts stormed toward Morton's location, but his scathing rebuke had reached its intended recipients. The Black Knights began to regroup on foot, with the other knights clustering behind them.

Morton grabbed Daniella by the arm and guided her to a safer spot. "You lead them out. I'll hold the rear."

"We can fight them back on foot," protested Daniella.

"Not against an ambush like this."

Daniella sighed, her face glistening with sweat, and her long, brown hair disheveled. "What's your plan?"

"Wait for my signal," Morton replied, then hurried off to his lord's hideout. Daniella whistled to call her lieutenant and signaled for them to approach.

As the Coalition forces began to reorganize, the Korelians unleashed their ranged attack again. Yet, this time, the Coalition knights remained resolute. They were not fearless, but they drew confidence from their experience and trust in their gear.

As trained knights, they knew that at such a distance, potshots were unlikely to penetrate their plate armor. While some areas were vulnerable, these were small and well hidden.

After Morton reached Lord Jorge, they, with concerted effort, successfully escorted him to the safety of a large pile of fallen trees.

Just as things were nearly under control, two mercenary groups suddenly launched a sortie, determined to flank the attackers' position.

Daniella and her lieutenant dashed to Morton and Lord Jorge's side. "Those fools wanted to die, but they'll buy us some time. I suggest we make our move."

Morton glanced at his lord, who appeared still shocked by the turn of events. "My lord, you need to return to the open field. The best of my Black Knights and Lady Daniella's finest will escort you."

Lord Jorge remained silent, his face etched with sourness from the failure.

Morton continued. "I'll keep twenty men with me to act as your rear guard."

"Do as you wish," Jorge responded harshly.

Unperturbed by his lord's tone, Morton chose his lieutenant to spearhead the escort duty.

Daniella then stood, raising her shield above her head. "Korimors, Nicopolans!" she shouted with authority. "Listen to me: follow my lead and fight your way back, or face death. There is no other way!" Her voice echoed throughout the woods.

Her urging ignited a spark in the broken-willed mercenaries, stirring them into action.

Under Morton's watchful eye, the column, led by his lieutenant and Daniella, began to carefully navigate their way out.

Contrary to the Coalition's expectations, the returning column faced heavy opposition on its way out. As fate would have it, the Korelians had repositioned themselves. Morton, at the rear, was preoccupied with only light attacks; meanwhile the newly formed vanguard was braving a hailstorm of bolts.

Daniella led the Coalition men as they trudged through the dense underbrush, no one daring to venture onto the open and exposed path they had used on their way in.

The bushes surrounding them provided almost no protection from steel bolt heads. Just moments ago, a knight had been struck in the backplate. The bolt hadn't penetrated but was deflected into the man behind him. With their visors raised due to exhaustion and heat, the unfortunate man's upper lip and everything behind it was torn.

A similar fate loomed over everyone as they made their slow escape through the forest.

After enduring a series of relentless attacks, the mercenaries became blinded by anger. Recognizing the futility of holding them back, Daniella directed their fury toward the emerging silhouettes of the crossbowmen. Just like that, the Nicopolans launched another daring assault.

The initial stages of the Nicopolans' counterattack seemed promising, with the mercenaries' rallying cries echoing through the forest. Some of the Three Hills knights and their squires even joined in.

However, the counterattack was soon bogged down, lasting only a few moments before it was brutally crushed. What remained were only cries of agony, as the mercenaries lay writhing with bolts embedded deeply in their limbs and bodies.

For the Korelians, their heavy crossbow, the windlass, and cranequin proved to be worth their weight in gold. In combination with spears and polearms, they were a lethal force.

The devastating defeat finally emptied the mercenaries' appetite for battle, causing them to shy away from danger. The dwindling number of Three Hills knights also had lost their courage.

In a desperate move, the remaining nobles used their squires, clad only in ringmail, as body shields. Many of these young squires fell, struck by direct hits or stray shots, their tight groups providing an ideal target for the crossbowmen.

It was only through sheer tenacity that the Black Knights, together with Daniella's elite, were finally able to lead the survivors through the thickest of the attacks. Eventually, they reached larger openings in the woods.

They had passed this spot before while chasing the Korelian cavalry. It was previously empty, but now the place had been barricaded. Dozens of wooden frames bristling with spikes were aimed toward the approaching Coalition forces.

The Korelian crossbowmen who had haunted the Coalition now revealed themselves. Scores of them poured from the forest, reinforcing their footmen. They were completely protected by the barricade. Blue and bronze chevron banners marked their allegiance.

The blockade wasn't just on the road. Men with polearms and swords were also spotted waiting in the woods.

Now, it was obvious to everyone there that the Korelians were well prepared. This wasn't an amateur trap.

Fear was in everyone's mind. Without knowing the opponent's numbers, dismounted and exhausted, the once mighty Coalition knights hesitated. Their situation was dire. Many simply hid away, waiting for someone to take action.

Even the Black Knights' lieutenant was having second thoughts. Only Daniella had a stiff smile. Silently, she conceded defeat to the opponent's strategy.

Defeating this many knights and cavalry . . . Turning the famed Black Knights into target practice, how ridiculous . . .

Daniella watched as the mercenaries, lost all confidence and wanted no further part in the chaos. They dispersed, each seeking a different escape route. Unconcerned with their desertion, she remained behind with only her trusted retinue, biding her time to make her escape.

The battle in the forest came to a standstill. Defeated as they were, the Black Knights and Three Hills nobles still had their numbers. If forced into a showdown, in a fight to the death, every man would readily show their mettle. Lord Jorge understood this.

Outwitted but unafraid, the head of the Coalition stood with a sword in hand. Once known as the Big Fool of One Hill, he now embraced his fate with calm grace, awaiting the slow coming of death.

CHAPTER 20

MAGE KNIGHT

Coalition Side

When the expected attack never materialized, the remaining Coalition knights trapped in the forest turned their eyes to Lord Jorge, who, in response, summoned Morton for counsel. A messenger was sent to hurriedly call back the Black Knight captain from the rear.

Sir Morton and his rear guard quickly rejoined his master. As he knelt, one of the staff members briefed him on the situation: "The enemy crossbowmen are positioned to our right, and their men-at-arms are in front of us. That leaves only the route to our left open."

Morton nodded in acknowledgment, remaining silent as he calmly surveyed the enemy's barricade from behind the cover of the trees.

"I know a route exists. I used to hunt here," Lord Jorge said. "Alas, the path is narrow and treacherous. We can't possibly proceed in armor."

Nobody gave an answer. To escape without their horses and armor wasn't even an option. First, they would be hard-pressed to escape Lansius's cavalry when they reached the plains. But more importantly, to do so would get them ridiculed and shamed for the rest of their lives.

Jorge was shivering, not from fear, but from rage. His earlier composure had gone. He couldn't believe that he had been tricked this badly.

In less than an hour, more than one hundred knights and a similar number of cavalrymen had been reduced to a mere mob. The reputation of anyone involved in this was in ruins.

With a forced smile, Jorge turned to his captain and suggested, "Morton, why don't we just storm the blockade?"

Morton pretended he didn't hear it. Despite the jovial tone, he knew that the young lord was looking for a heroic death at this point. The Black Knight captain wanted to distract his lord, but he was too preoccupied with looking for a way out.

Just as he was assessing the situation, a sudden warning echoed through the forest. Almost instantly, several spots were engulfed in blasts of green fog.

"A green fog," one of the squires on the lookout warned.

And then screams began to echo inside the forest. Droves of men emerged from their hiding places in complete agony.

"Alchemist! They employed an alchemist," one of the knights cried out as they abandoned their positions in panic.

"It's just a fog. It's a trick, it can't harm you," someone attempted to reassure, to no avail, in between intense coughing and sneezing.

Several knights and mercenaries panicked, running out of fear of the unknown. The rest stayed put, either unable to make a decision or just adamant to stand their ground.

The green fog spread out, its hue fading as it covered more ground, but the hope of it being less lethal proved to be wrong. The fog seeped into armor and helmets, then caused excruciating pain almost instantly.

The eyes and nostrils felt burning, but the real agony was in the throat and lungs, which felt as if filled with molten metal upon breathing.

Everyone in the area of effect either collapsed from choking or was left shriveling and writhing uncontrollably. The forest was now filled with screams and wailing.

Morton had chanted his barrier, creating a blast of wind centered around Lord Jorge. He had tried to enlarge it to cover more people, but he could only protect no larger than the size of a small hut. Before long, everyone outside of Morton's barrier was engulfed by the green miasma.

The Black Knights knew they were being flushed out from their hiding position. In desperation, fueled by the insane pain, the best of Jorge's knights charged through the green mist. As expected, many were greeted by a hail of bolts.

Several stumbled in their advance, with a few falling to the ground, but some reached the Korelian lines and exacted vengeance upon their adversaries. Led by their lieutenant, they swung their weapons with relentless ferocity against the Korelians' wall of spears.

The Korelians' formation held firm initially, but more and more Black Knights arrived and went berserk. They attacked left and right without regard for themselves. The Korelians managed to take down three more knights, yet more knights quickly surged into the gaps their comrades had created with their blood.

Another two knights, followed by ten more, joined the fight. Despite injuries and losses, they pushed the Korelians hard, forcing their opponent to withdraw behind their barricades. The knights fought on and stormed the barricades, only to suddenly burst into flames.

"The alchemist!" the lieutenant warned his comrades.

Even from a distance, Morton took notice. The green fog had dissipated, and his lord was safe. "With me, with me!" he roared, rallying the rest of his knights.

The last of his men gathered alongside Morton and launched a fresh assault on the Korelian barricade. Bolts rained down on them from the side, but this time those were deflected away by an unseen barrier.

The barrier lasted but a few seconds, as Morton needed to strengthen his muscles. Yet that brief moment of protection was enough. With a wide, sweeping swing, Morton deflected a wave of brandished pikes aimed at him and then leaped over the barricade. Every knight had been trained in this maneuver since their days as squires, but the way Morton executed it was so effortless as if he wasn't weighted down by his armor and weapon at all.

Without missing a beat, the knight captain swung his sword vertically into a man's shoulder. The shocked victim could only kneel, his shoulder gushing blood like a fountain. Just like that, the knight captain created a foothold beyond the barricade.

With hearts full of pride, the Black Knights closest to Morton leaped over and fought savagely. More and more Korelians fell under the relentless slash and thrust of their weapons.

As the center of attention, Morton deftly blocked attacks from several opponents. When unable to block or parry, he confidently took the sharp edges with his gauntlet and pauldron. Yet, he wasn't rendered on the defensive. He stole an opening and swung his broadsword with both hands against two men.

The large broadsword flashed through the air, and red blood sprayed as one opponent screamed, losing an arm. The other was thrown back, his ringmail severed and ribs cracked.

Fearful but enraged, four Korelians thrust their polearms in unison at Morton, but he blocked and parried with strength and stamina that was beyond belief.

Out of the blue, an object flew toward Morton. With quick reflexes, he swatted it away using the flat edge of his sword. A distinct cracking sound echoed as it burst into flames in the air. The searing heat from the airborne fireball was palpable even through the visor, halting the fighting as many cowered from the sudden inferno.

The alchemist stared at Morton in disbelief. The Mage Knight was as terrifying as the ancient dwarven golem he once had encountered.

The remaining Coalition poured at the barricade with renewed fervor, despite heavy resistance from the Korelian crossbowmen. With the famed Sir Morton on the offensive and the effect of the green miasma wearing off without a trace, they were riding the wave.

The Korelian line was quickly turning into shambles.

Calub

The small clearing inside the forest had turned into a battlefield. The Korelians desperately relied on their wooden barricade for defense. Their crossbowmen now fired from point-blank range, and many resorted to hatchets to defend themselves.

But as hard as they tried, it was impossible to plug the breach.

I've made a mistake . . .

Calub clutched the composite cords of his slinger. The green miasma he had launched to break the enemy's spirit had unintentionally galvanized their resolve instead. Now, the Coalition was out for blood.

Faced with the relentless advance of the Black Knights, the Korelian line had stretched, straining to contain the enemy.

"Maester, the men won't hold!" his lieutenant warned.

Calub didn't need anyone to tell him what he could see for himself. The bloodied Mage Knight was advancing straight toward them. "Get the windlass guys," he commanded.

The lieutenant immediately ran to fetch the arbalesters, but the situation was deteriorating too quickly.

The situation wouldn't have been this dire if Calub had knights at his command. However, due to their elevated status, these knights might not have heeded Calub's orders. Consequently, Lansius had assigned only men-at-arms to him. Now, despite their best efforts, these men-at-arms were no match for the Black Knights, especially not against the Mage Knight.

Calub himself had prepared well and even expected a Mage Knight or two to make an appearance. But the one in black armor was unstoppable. Not even a fire grenade was effective.

"Maester," his men warned as the Mage Knight roared and battled his way into their position.

Clad in only his brigandine and jacket, Calub clenched his poleaxe. "No retreat!" he said sternly to his men, who nodded nervously.

His redeployed arbalesters finally had a clear line of sight and sniped at the Mage Knight from two locations. One shot narrowly missed, while the other glanced off and struck another Black Knight.

The Mage Knight remained unharmed, but the attack provided some breathing room for Calub's men. As the Mage Knight redeployed his barrier, Calub reached into his jacket.

Fire grenades wouldn't work against that barrier, but this . . .

Calub's gloved fingers could feel the coldness from the special alloy.

Suddenly, a commotion was heard from the Coalition's side.

"The enemy cavalry—" a Coalition squire shouted. He was clearly out of breath from running. "Their cavalry is on our rear!"

His high-pitched warning was heard by everyone. Both sides paused as the situation became uncertain. Suddenly, the rhythmic sound of hooves echoed through the woods, confirming what the squire had said: the Korelians' cavalry had returned.

Calub drew his hand back from the metal object and shouted, "The lord has returned. Steadfast, men! Give it everything you've got!"

The Korelians clamored. "For Korelia! Blood for blood!"

The barricade held.

The Coalition

Morton was out of time. His small contingent couldn't afford to get flanked, especially by heavy cavalry. Any advantage they had would be undone. "Fall back," he commanded bitterly, stepping back while maintaining his barrier.

"Fall back, I said," he bellowed, frustrated as his men disregarded the command.

His knights grumbled but started to disengage. At this range, without their captain's barrier, the enemy bolts would surely be lethal. However, they were too late.

The sound of splintering wood heralded the arrival of the Korelian cavalry. Two mercenaries, stragglers who had split from the main force, were unceremoniously hurled aside, never to see daylight again. The surviving Nicopolans dashed toward the forest, desperately trying to avoid the cavalry's lances.

More than fifty Coalition knights were locked in combat. For some, the sudden appearance of the cavalry and their failure to break through proved too much. They began to drop their weapons and bitterly surrender.

Yet, the rest fought on, haunted by the fear that the new Lord of Korelia would slaughter them instead of taking them hostage, as the outcome of the battle was yet to be decided.

Morton's lieutenant had caught up and asked in a ragged breath, "What should we do now?"

"There's no other way. Gather everyone with polearms and try to block the cavalry," ordered Morton, picking a spot to make a stand.

"There's little chance we can hold out," the lieutenant argued.

"If the cavalry cuts us off, then everything is doomed," Morton remarked. They needed time for the rest of their forces to disengage and flee.

The lieutenant turned from Morton and rallied everyone within sight. Only eleven answered. Thirsty and exhausted, only honor kept them going.

Suddenly, Jorge's squire appeared and handed Morton his crossbow.

"You shouldn't be here, boy," Morton warned him.

"Eh, nobody should be here, sir," the squire retorted wittily. The answer drew nervous chuckles from the ranks as they assumed a wall of spear formation against the incoming cavalry. Due to their inadequate size, it looked more like a hedgehog in the middle of a dirt road.

Morton loaded his bolt, took several steps forward, and picked a target with the best-looking armor. He fired at the incoming cavalry from sixty paces away.

His bolt deflected off the foremost rider's pauldron, but now Morton had the rider's attention. With enhanced strength, he calmly pulled his crossbow string with just one hand as if it was a small bow.

The cavalry advanced toward their small formation. Now, it was clear that the entire Korelian cavalry was present. The sight demoralized the Coalition's side. On foot, exhausted, and greatly outnumbered, one by one, they abandoned the spot and fled toward the forest.

Not everyone had come prepared to die that day, and Morton's wall of spears crumbled. Yet, Morton had expected this to happen. Now, only he and a few of the bravest stood unperturbed. The ground shook from thundering hooves of the incoming warhorses.

It was less than twenty paces when Morton fired his second bolt.

Thuck!

A dull sound resonated from his crossbow, which Morton quickly discarded as he leaped to the side to avoid the incoming cavalry. Behind him, his small line of defenders either engaged in combat or ducked away as the first wave of four warhorses charged through. It was unnerving, even for a seasoned knight like Morton.

Coughing from the dust, he looked back and saw that the Korelian first wave, which had just surged past, seemed unharmed. He assumed the bolt hadn't penetrated deep enough. However, one rider, adorned in gorgeous-looking armor, started to wobble and eventually fell from his horse.

There was no time for celebration as the rest of the cavalry bore down on them. Unfazed, Morton drew his broadsword.

A quick glance to his right showed Morton his lieutenant, bloodied and limping, retreating from the fray. The man had bravely intercepted a rider and emerged worse. Nearby, another lay mangled on the ground, likely having been trampled.

Morton counted only five who remained standing. "Their sacrifice will not be in vain!" he rallied them.

"To the bitter end!" his comrades, both old and young, responded with fervor as the cavalry closed in on them. The horses' nostrils flared menacingly, their hooves thundering against the ground.

Morton gripped his broadsword tightly. Magic had enhanced his lungs, heart, and muscles, staving off exhaustion, but he knew even that had a limit. With a defiant war cry, he surged forward, aiming to intercept another rider clad in impressive-looking armor. His objective from the outset was to strike down one of the Korelian leaders, perhaps even the lord himself.

A moment later, his sword and the rider's lance clashed.

CHAPTER 21

LAYING A TRAP

Morton shouted defiantly and dashed forward to intercept the charging horseman. The lance aimed straight at him, and he parried it with all his strength. The Mage Knight's amplified strength enabled him to deflect the force of the lance thrust, but he almost lost his footing.

He recoiled as his momentum wasn't enough to counter the combined weight of the warhorse and its rider. The mounted knight, lance still unbroken, passed by just inches away. Their gaze met.

Morton had created an opening. He regained his stance, advanced one step forward, planted his foot firmly, and swung his broadsword. The rider was perched too high on the warhorse, so Morton directed his attack at the horse's neck instead.

The horse's barding protected the beast's neck, but the impact was more than it could handle. The horse reared, panicking wildly, and luckily veered off instead of trampling Morton. He knew he had won this gamble and stepped away.

His arms and shoulder felt like they were about to burst, but that was only to be expected. Such an impact would've ripped muscle from bone and dislocated joints in a normal man. But the Mage Knight survived with only a nasty cramp.

A second pair of warhorse and rider rushed toward Morton. He readied himself once more. Behind him, his previous opponent had already crashed to the ground.

The incoming rider was without a lance but brandished a sword. Anticipating the rider's move, Morton crouched low at the last moment and dashed forward, aiming his broadsword at the horse's front leg.

Seeing Morton went low, the rider instinctively swung his sword toward Morton's head. The blow landed squarely, causing the top of Morton's helmet to cave in.

Reeling from the impact, Morton lost his balance and narrowly avoided the panicked horse. Dazed, he discarded his helmet and the padding within. Blood trickled down his face.

He glanced toward the rider who had struck him, only to find the person had crashed to the ground, his leg trapped beneath his own bloodied horse.

The Mage Knight took a step back and surveyed his surroundings. With blood streaming down his face, he observed the last of his comrades either falling or retreating. The situation was hopeless. He couldn't hold off ten cavalrymen alone, let alone several dozen.

The next horseman had spotted him. Initially, they approached cautiously, having seen several riders fall, but now they were out for blood.

Morton knew he could do no more but to retreat. As the next riders charged and tried to trample him, Morton jumped and rolled in the dirt. His hair became disheveled and covered in dirt and leaves.

Clutching his sword tightly, he ran toward the trees.

"You're not going anywhere!" a cold voice came from behind.

Morton glanced back and immediately raised both of his arms to block the stones thrown at him. His gauntlets protected his hands, but dirt got into his eyes. A moment of carelessness had blinded him.

A knight charged at Morton and lashed out with a blindingly fast horizontal slash.

The Mage Knight used magic to force his eyes open. He reacted just in time to block the sword aimed at him, but the force was so great that even with his enhanced strength, the blade slammed into his left elbow.

"Guh," Morton groaned as he was thrown to the side. The tall knight gave him no time to breathe, relentlessly lashing out with consecutive slashes and thrusts.

The Mage Knight was hard-pressed; the man fought like a wounded bear and could almost match his strength. Almost. After parrying the last attack, Morton blasted a concentrated jet of wind into the knight's helmet. As if anticipating the attack, the knight protected his face with his left hand while swinging his broadsword with the other.

"Hrrah!" Morton slammed his opponent's blade hard, trying to create an opening, but the knight reacted by taking several steps back. Afterward, like a whirlwind, the knight charged again with a thrust.

Morton blocked the thrust, but the knight followed up with a left punch that grazed the Mage Knight's cheek. Instead of keeping their distance, Morton used his enhanced physique and head-butted the knight's helmet with his bare forehead.

The knight staggered but managed to let out a chuckle. "What a fun fight. Against a freak, that is."

"You're not doing too badly yourself, for a nameless Midlandian amateur," Morton retorted viciously.

"It's Harold, you piece of elven shit!" And just like that, the two ramped up their tempo. They traded blows, grappled, and landed heavy smashes on each other.

Harold landed a solid left-handed hammer fist against Morton's jaw. But the Mage Knight smashed his pommel hard on Harold's hip.

The knight staggered back. There was no penetration through the plate, but his entire left leg was numb.

For the first time, Morton could look at his surroundings, saw more Korelians closing in, and decided to flee.

"Oi, woman, I'm not finished!" Harold taunted.

"You're too drunk. Amateurs should drink in moderation," Morton quipped as he trekked south. Soon, the dense trees shielded him from sight. He regretted pulling out his head's padding, as he could have used the linen to bandage the wound on his head.

Watching the Mage Knight disappear from sight, Harold just dropped to the mossy ground, opened his visor, and took in a big breath of fresh air. He had just fought toe to toe with a Mage Knight, and his entire body was exhausted. However, his heart was full of pride.

To fight against a Mage Knight and survive was such a rare feat, and he had just added that accomplishment to his repertoire. All the mock training and the theories on how to fight against a Mage Knight had paid off.

As for the Mage Knight. he continued south and started to find some of his wounded comrades, including his lieutenant and the squire. Without saying a word, he helped carry the lieutenant, and they retreated deeper into the forest.

Lansius

The clash of steel and the cries of combat had ceased, replaced by the heavy silence of the aftermath. The forest around Lansius seemed to close in, the leaves whispering secrets of the skirmish's brutal end. He sat on the mossy ground, his helmet beside him, his back against the rough bark of an ancient tree, stunned and lost for words.

Several of his men had helped him up from the fall and escorted him to this spot. His armor felt uncomfortable, pressing against his chest as he struggled to draw breath in the hot and humid air, sweat pouring down his face.

His destrier lay a few feet away, whinnying softly as a rider calmed her down and examined what was likely a bruised neck or flank beneath the barding.

Lansius looked down at his left wrist, encased in metal, as pain shot through his arm with every heartbeat. Yet, the physical agony paled in comparison to the torment in his mind. His plan—what he had envisioned progressing smoothly—had faced a harsh reality.

The black knights, or more specifically, a lone Mage Knight, had become the bane of his plan. The charge, intended to be swift and a clean sweep, had targeted the enemy's ranks that dared to attack Calub's column but faced unexpectedly strong resistance. It failed, resulting in many losses and injuries.

As the dust settled, the groans of the wounded filled the air. Lansius turned in the direction of the sound and noticed numerous injured men from Calub's column, indicating another miscalculation in taking the knights from there. He hadn't expected the Coalition to be able to rally and counterattack a strongly prepared defensive position.

Guilt gnawed at his heart as he watched his men suffer, a mark of his failed leadership. His gaze slowly drifted away from the painful scene.

The nature of war is unpredictable, he lamented. Instead of hardening his heart, Lansius turned off his emotions, a mechanism he had subconsciously learned. Yet, that didn't numb the throbbing pain in his left wrist from the fall.

"The men are ready," Sir Harold reported, kneeling in front of Lansius.

His words brought Lansius out of his daze. He noticed his cavalry had come to a halt as the last of the Coalition forces around the barricade surrendered. Unwilling to allow the enemy time to regroup, he summoned his courage and ordered in a hoarse voice, "Get our cavalry to dismount and quickly form a hunting net."

Sir Harold nodded, then turned to his men behind him and said, "Fan out, form a hunting net!"

"But don't spread too thin. Approach carefully," Lansius emphasized. Although he had started the day with a brilliant charge, his meticulously planned ambush was costing him dearly, leaving him deeply rattled.

"Understood," the tall knight responded, then added in a lower voice, "But what do you plan to do with the Lord of the Three Hills?"

"I'll accompany you. We'll play this by ear," Lansius replied as a squire brought him a piece of cloth for an arm sling.

Harold nodded while watching his lord struggle with the arm sling.

"Do I really need to wear this?" Lansius asked.

"You'll have to, my lord." Harold responded, unable to suppress a smile. "The gauntlet will hold the bones, but it'll get painful once you start moving around and riding."

Lansius, intrigued by Harold's smile, asked bluntly, "Have I done well as a leader?"

"You've fought bravely, my lord. For someone with little experience, you've made us proud. Just a little unfortunate to stumble into a Mage Knight."

Lansius nodded, trying to decipher whether the praise was genuine or simply flattery.

"You asked for me, my lord?" The standard bearer had arrived.

"Indeed, I need a herald," said Lansius.

"Certainly, what will be your message?" the standard bearer asked.

The Coalition

Quietly, the remaining Coalition knights and squires watched and waited from afar as the Korelians fanned out and moved inside the forest.

Fate seemed to conspire against the Coalition, as their scouts couldn't find any alternative route out. After all, it had been many years since Lord Jorge last hunted in this forest. His loyal retinue from that era had all perished in the ensuing power struggle.

At this moment, Lord Jorge was taking shelter deep within the forest, with Morton at his side, attempting to organize a final stand. Their numbers had dwindled to less than thirty as the rest of their forces had scattered. Meanwhile, the Korelians probably had a hundred.

They could see the Korelians drawing near, but oddly, there was no longer any hesitation. The Coalition patiently awaited their finale.

The upcoming fight was destined to be brutal, and everyone was determined to give their best. For many, their determination stemmed from a lack of trust in the new Lord of Korelia, an unknown foreigner. No knight would gamble on this man's benevolence or mercy.

For others, it was a matter of logic. The Coalition still had six thousand men just outside the forest. If they survived this forest ambush, then the war was still within their grasp. Even without the cavalry, the Coalition only needed to wait for the catapults to be completed. This thought kept them spirited.

Time passed as the rustling noise approached. Everyone crouched to lower their silhouettes. The smell of decomposing leaves filled the air. Their clothing stuck to their skin as heat and humidity pervaded the environment.

By now, many knights clung to their daggers, having lost their primary and secondary weapons. Yet, fear was absent from their faces. As the old saying goes: a cornered beast is the most dangerous.

This time, the Coalition was prepared. Many even covered their noses and mouths with cloth, anticipating another green fog attack. However, just as they steeled their resolve, a shout came from the Korelians' side.

"We've come to parley," the Korelian herald repeated twice as their advance halted.

Immediately, the faces of the Coalition men softened. Even full of suspicion, the word "parley" had its intended effect.

Morton looked at his lord, whose brown eyes were lost in thought. Catching Morton's glance, Jorge nodded approvingly.

The Black Knight captain donned a helmet his squire had found for him. It wasn't a fit, but it would cover his bandaged head. He then stood up and shouted, "We will neither yield nor be taken hostage!"

Morton's voice was clear and powerful, surprising both friends and foes.

"We do not intend to take anyone hostage, unless forced," came the reply.

"What's your offer?" Morton asked.

"Cease fighting. My lord declares that he has no quarrel with the Lord of Three Hills. He believes that Lord Jorge was provoked to attack Korelia. The two Houses can still make amends."

Several nervous glances were exchanged on the Coalition side. "There will be amends if you let us return to our camp unharmed," Morton responded without consulting anyone. Politics be damned, he thought. This was a good opportunity to save his lord's skin.

"Swear an oath," the herald responded after a brief hesitation.

Morton glanced at his lord, who took a deep breath. Without needing a signal, Morton chanted his verses, and a barrier of air and water vapor took shape. It was transparent, akin to looking through solid glass.

Lord Jorge finally stepped forward, his squire ready with a shield in front, Morton by his side.

"I, Viscount Jorge of Three Hills, Protector of Korimor and South Hills, hereby pledge my neutrality in this conflict," he announced formally with a voice amplified by magic. "Let there be amends between our Houses."

Jorge had wanted to say more, but his staff was whispering to him that fewer promises were better, to minimize political fallout.

A pause followed before the Korelians blew their horns. Slowly, the Korelians withdrew from the surrounding area.

Witnessing this, the remaining Coalition could finally breathe freely. They knew they almost had it. Although they didn't like it, they owed their skin to the opponent's mercy, or stupidity. For some reason, the Lord of Korelia had given them a free pass.

Despite the oath, Lord Jorge's words could easily be disowned. Even if Lord Jorge wanted to honor it, he could simply sit in his tent and let Lord Omin win the siege for him. While the recapitulation would be messy, that was preferable than losing the campaign.

With that on their mind, the survivors regrouped and began their trek through the forest. Some still had their horses, while others managed to secure abandoned steeds. Still even with horses, they dared not use the main path, deeming the Lord of Korelia untrustworthy.

After a thorough search, someone stumbled upon an old dried-up stream. The rocky path was slippery and treacherous, but it was open, with fewer trees in the way.

The Three Hills knights and their remaining allies moved slowly in their heavy armor. Those with horses took extra care, guiding their mounts cautiously.

Moss quickly became a problem. Unperturbed for decades, if not centuries, the thick layers of green carpets were tricky to traverse.

Tired men were bound to slip, and many fell unceremoniously. Thankfully, the thick padding under their armor provided good cushion against impact.

As they navigated the terrain, the forest began to thin. For the first time, they could see the plains. The few horses they still possessed also seemed excited, their nostrils flaring at the sight of the open land.

Renewed in spirit, they traversed the final leg of their escape. However, as the first group exited the forest, their hope quickly vanished.

Gasps rang out as they saw what had happened outside the forest.

"This, this cannot be!" one of the knights exclaimed.

Nobody had an answer. They only exchanged looks of disbelief.

CHAPTER 22

WANING BLOOD

Korelia Plains

The skirmish between Sir Arius's column and Korelia had ended. The fight only lasted less than an hour, but it was hard fought. However, it ended inconclusively after the Korelia side resorted to fire tactics to disengage.

Against the dried summer grass, fire grenades worked wonders to create a fire barrier between them. With fire roaring, both columns withdrew to lick their wounds.

The inconclusive result didn't prevent the Coalition from claiming it as their victory. Sir Arius was paraded by his knights in celebration as they returned to their main formation.

Sir Arius's victory stabilized the South Hills column in the north, which had endured casualties from Lansius's surprise cavalry attack. Now they stood in formation with renewed spirit.

They had beaten back the Korelian column and survived the surprise attack. There was nothing else their opponent could do.

Things had very much turned in the Coalition's favor once again. Even the blaze that the Korelians had started didn't last. The fires smoldered once the strong southern wind blew them against the foot of the hill.

With the fire settled, if they wanted, the Coalition could launch another assault, but that was probably what the enemy had wanted. So, Arius calmed his staff and simply waited for the enemy to make a wrong move.

The young leader knew he had won enough to boost their morale, and it was risky to ask for more.

Out here in the field, the result of Korelia's ambush in the forest remained unknown. While it was decisive, the Korelian side had committed almost all their forces. What remained at their disposal was only Audrey's twenty light cavalry and a questionable number of nomadic cavalry.

Meanwhile, the strength of the Coalition was still at five thousand, eight hundred men. The Korelian charge had only dented their numbers.

On paper, with such a big disparity in numbers, Korelia's light cavalry wouldn't stand a chance. Especially against Korimor's troops, which were still fresh, ready, and willing.

After circling in the sky for a while, the steppe's native birds of prey finally landed in droves, drawn by the scent of meat on the battlefield. They busied themselves gorging on the abundance of carrion.

Propelled by this sorry sight, volunteers from both sides stepped forward to retrieve their dead. Yet, with both sides still armed with crossbows, the task was fraught with real danger.

Midday was yet to arrive, but already hundreds had paid the ultimate price. Once again, the southern wind blew fiercely across the Korelia plains.

Lansius

Several men, including Sir Harold, helped Lansius mount his horse. The destrier was lucky to only be bruised and not injured. Her mood seemed to improve once Lansius was back in the saddle. "Easy, girl, easy . . ."

She had thrown Lansius in panic, but could hardly be blamed.

Who would've thought that a Mage Knight would be blocking our way? Some bad luck.

Stinging pain still lingered in Lansius's nose and lips as the adrenaline wore off. Despite the thick padding on his helmet, both were bloodied from the fall. But they were considered cosmetic damage. The real pain came from his left wrist. Even secured in a sling, it throbbed relentlessly.

Using his hips, Lansius gently spurred the destrier forward. His cavalry followed. They planned to return to the open fields.

There was no hurry in their movement. Lansius was using the sun to his advantage, keeping the enemy waiting in the open field under the harsh summer sun in full armor, a tactic that was beneficial to his side.

Their slow pace also allowed time for information to reach them; his scouts had provided reports on the conditions outside the forest.

"How's the battle between Sir Justin and the Coalition?" Lansius asked.

"The battle has ended, my lord. We saw fire, and then both sides retreated," the scout replied.

Lansius nodded thoughtfully. "Any changes in the Coalition's formation in the field?"

"Nothing has changed, my lord."

"They're quite stubborn," Sir Harold, Lansius's temporary cavalry commander, remarked.

Lansius gathered his thoughts for a moment before saying to the scout, "Get some rest, but tell your men to keep watch around Calub's position and the hostages. I want no surprises."

"Understood, my lord." The scout then ran toward the forest to inform his men.

The cavalry continued their march. After the Mage Knight debacle, Harold had put more men around their lord to protect him.

"My lord, not to be nosy, but may I ask you a question?" Sir Harold asked as they had time to discuss.

Lansius nodded, so the knight continued. "Why don't you just capture Lord Jorge?"

Lansius drew a deep breath. Since Harold wasn't a member of the council, he hadn't been briefed on the full plan. "There are several reasons, but mainly, if we captured Lord Jorge, then the rest of the Coalition would fall under Lord Omin. And I don't want them to be united."

"Could such things happen? Won't the Three Hills and South Hill simply back down?"

"Normally, that would be the expected outcome," said Lansius. "However, Lord Jorge's reputation is so bad that their own nobles might use this opportunity to replace him. I don't want to give them the pretext to do just that."

Sir Harold nodded, his expression revealing a hint of surprise.

"There's also another reason," Lansius continued. "Whether we capture Lord Jorge or not, it won't affect our victory. It's just a secondary long-term goal."

Harold's sharp eyes squinted after hearing such an absurd claim. "The Lord of Three Hills is a secondary goal?"

Lansius nodded without hesitation. "For Korelia, the perfect victory is not about just defeating the enemy, but also forging a new alliance. For that to happen, I need Lord Jorge's trust. That's why I let him go, for now."

"For now?"

Lansius looked at Harold and said, "Before this day is over, I reckon we'll meet with Lord Jorge again."

"That's a bold statement, my lord."

Lansius nodded but didn't comment.

The sunlight on the far end signaled that they were getting closer to the open plains. With a wave of his hand, Harold signaled two knights to move ahead as vanguard.

Calub

The alchemist winced as he tended his wounded right arm. Despite his riveted ringmail sleeves, the axe attack had left a painful laceration. He was loath to admit it, but his insistence on joining the fight almost got him killed.

Although he was still in his prime, the days spent working as a treasurer had dulled his combat skills. He no longer possessed the sharp reactions and instincts of his days as an explorer. Worse, his proficiency in sword and spear play had rusted.

However, in retrospect, nobody was in the wrong. As planned, they had subjected the Coalition to a barrage of continuous crossbow attacks from the glade and into the barricade.

Thus, everybody expected the opponent to be weary and disorganized. Instead, the Black Knights fought like possessed monsters.

Calub let out a sigh.

Just like in the dwarven catacombs, things in battles are nigh unpredictable.

Despite serious setbacks, the fact that they could still complete the ambush proved just how solid Lansius's plan truly was. For that, Calub was grateful.

Right now, he was leading a small detachment to act as rear guard. Meanwhile, the rest of his men, all with wounds of varying degrees, were preparing to return to their hideouts and yurts.

With their original mission completed, the men were tasked with picking up the wounded and carrying them to their camp. There were also hostages to be attended to.

Earlier, Calub had met with Lord Lansius, who, despite his injuries, insisted on riding with the cavalry. During their exchange, Calub had kept his wound hidden. He didn't want to add to Lansius's worries—the lord was already burdened with concerns, and the battle was far from over.

"Erggh . . ." Calub grimaced as he tightened the cloth he used as a makeshift bandage.

Nearby, his men were busy preparing makeshift stretchers for Sterling, whose leg had been crushed when his horse fell on him. Sterling had fallen unconscious not long after they freed him from the dying horse. The poor beast, in pain and shock, was mercifully put down by the standard bearer, who did so as painlessly as possible.

As Lansius had wished, Calub had done everything in his power to treat the squire. Now, it was up to Sterling's own body.

"Remember, no bloodletting under any circumstances," Calub instructed his men, who would carry the stretchers.

The men dutifully nodded and continued to work.

"Master Calub," someone called urgently from behind him.

"Yes, what do you need?" Calub turned to face the speaker. It was one of his lieutenants.

"Master, it's Sir Callahan. He's . . ."

From the lieutenant's tone, Calub understood the situation. He patted the man's shoulder and spoke. "Show me the way."

Calub followed the lieutenant to a place not far from the barricade. There, Sir Callahan was lying on the ground, his head resting upon a tree root. His discarded helmet was by his side. There were spots of red on the mossy ground. It was clear that the man had vomited blood.

Callahan's eyes were bloodshot, but his face was as pale as snow. The cause was easy to find: a crossbow bolt was embedded deeply into his breastplate.

"Don't worry, Sir Callahan. The alchemist is here. I'll patch you up," Calub knelt and said in an upbeat tone, but they both knew the situation was grave. There was no red health potion or instant healing. Even magic would take hours, if not days, to regenerate injured tissue. A burst artery or punctured organ was a death sentence.

"Don't give me false hope, Maester Calub," Callahan answered in between pained grimaces. Each breath was a painful struggle. His face strained, and his hands began to tremble.

Calub removed his gloves and then Callahan's gauntlets, holding his hands with a firm yet gentle grip. As an ex-explorer who had parted with numerous colleagues, the act of holding his hands felt natural to him.

As soon as their hands touched, Callahan's strained expression quickly softened. "Maester, I can feel it. It's near . . ."

"Is there anything I can do? Perhaps a painkiller potion?" Calub asked gently.

"Save it for the wounded, maester. It's useless for the dead." Callahan managed a jest despite his pain. The joke must have strained him, as he vomited blood afterward.

Calub quickly assisted him, turning him to the side so as not to obstruct his airway. Afterward, the weakened Callahan half-whispered to Calub. "My daughters, Cecile and Claire, are the last of my House . . . Promise me you'll look after them."

Those words shocked Calub. "Sir Callahan, what are you saying? I can't do that. I'll promise to help—"

"Maester . . . you must . . . I cannot trust anyone else—" Callahan's voice was growing fainter.

Calub could only listen with mixed feelings.

"I had hoped . . . Lord Lansius, but . . . with so many noble ladies around . . . I fear even as a concubine, Cecile won't—" He restrained a cough, but some blood escaped. "Calub, you're my last hope."

"Please, Callahan. There must be a better candidate. Can't you see my dark skin? I'm of Tarracan descent," Calub pleaded.

Callahan smiled. He understood that Calub was worried about bloodline and all. "Blond is just a color . . . It doesn't make me a better husband." Callahan's breath was getting shorter, and he involuntarily tightened his grip on Calub's hand.

Calub's heart was in turmoil. He had barely known Callahan. Despite his friendship with Lord Lansius, he was a non-noble and an outsider. He felt he was just a tool, an instrument to be used and then shipped back home when not needed.

But now Callahan wanted to entrust his daughter to him. The girl was so bright, so unique, that Calub felt unworthy.

"Take Cecile as a concubine if you wish . . . As the lord's confidant, you'll ascend high." Callahan paused as he gasped for air. ". . . just promise me you'll never cast her aside."

Calub couldn't react but tried his best to comfort Callahan. But the man's eyes lost focus and wandered into the distance.

". . . even if she's not to your liking." Callahan's body jerked slightly. "Claire . . ." he whispered, uttering the name of his youngest daughter, but his strength was quickly fading.

". . . do . . . not . . ." His words trailed off, unfinished.

"I promise, Callahan, I promise," Calub said, tears welling in his eyes.

Under the shade of the tall costard tree, Callahan's breathing finally ceased. There was no longer strength in his grip. Pain no longer troubled him, whose eyes were now fixed on the sky. A faint smile touched his lips.

The lieutenant and others in the vicinity wiped tears from their faces. All who passed the place knelt and touched the fallen knight's armor in a final gesture of respect.

As the knight who had successfully led the merchant caravan from Midlandia and organized a refugee in his estate, Sir Callahan was respected and well-liked.

Calub gently closed the knight's eyes. With this act, the long lineage of House Callahan, which stretched back into the second millennium, came to an end. The knight's great-great-grandfather had been a king in the north. Now, the unbroken line from father to son finally ended.

Just as foretold, the northern blood would wane in the south.

Lansius

An abrupt, cool wind blew over Lansius, causing the surrounding trees to whisper soothingly. It was pleasant enough that for a moment, he forgot about his troubles and his pained wrist.

"If I may, another question, my lord?" Sir Harold asked again.

Since conversation put Lansius's mind at ease, he quickly agreed. "Speak."

"Many are curious. Why haven't you deployed Batu and his brethren?" asked Harold.

Lansius mulled for a moment. "Just how far can I trust you, Sir?"

The knight tapped his breastplate twice proudly and said, "I may not look the part, but I never spill anyone's secret. Not even when I'm drunk, because, after a bottle, it's all gibberish."

Despite his throbbing pain, Lansius chuckled at Harold's answer. "You'll be the only one to hear about this. So, if this leaks out, then it's on your head."

The knight grinned. "I feel a bit threatened, my lord, but also honored."

Lansius motioned him to get closer, so Harold leaned closer as they rode side by side.

"Since you wished to know," he began, "I don't want the nomads to contribute greatly to this war."

Harold knitted his brows. "Knowing you, my lord, I doubt this is about honor or glory. So why?"

"If the nomads were to contribute significantly, everyone in Lowlandia would crave their assistance," Lansius explained. "I trust Batu as our ally this year, but what about in several years' time? Can we guarantee their loyalty?"

Harold began to comprehend his lord's line of thought.

Lansius continued. "Sadly, anyone, even tribesmen, are easy to be manipulated. Meanwhile, Korelia is naturally poor . . . Do you think the nomads would turn down offers of supplies and riches from the other lords?"

Harold sighed. "No, my lord, that would be naive."

Lansius nodded slightly. He recalled how the great Jin dynasty's poor handling of the Mongol issue eventually led to the rise of Genghis Khan.

He had planned a role for the nomads, but nothing that would thrust them into the limelight.

Harold still had lingering doubts. "But, my lord, we're at war with an uncertain outcome. Is it wise to hold back?"

"Hold back?" Lansius smiled as if amused.

The knight clarified, "Many have even expected you to unleash the nomads to raid the western army on their march."

"That's foolish." Lansius shook his head. "Tell me, Sir Harold, do you show your cards before the showdown at the gambling table?"

The knight unconsciously rubbed his chin. "Are you implying that the nomads are your ace card, my lord?"

"Indeed. They're our reserve, and I can't afford to employ them recklessly. They're also the only hand unknown to the enemy."

"But, wouldn't a raid be beneficial to us?"

"Such a strategy would gain us little. It might delay the Coalition's arrival by two or three days, or make them tired. But a full day's rest would easily remedy that. Moreover, it would make them more cautious, which could jeopardize our ambush."

Sir Harold nodded deeply. Only now did he truly grasp the reasoning behind his lord's actions.

"Only an overconfident man rushes toward a trap," Lansius asserted. "That's what we need. And to achieve that, Korelia needs to appear weak, insignificant, and non-threatening. Deploying the nomads would shatter the western lords' illusion."

Intrigued, the knight asked, "So, can we win without deploying the nomads?"

"They'll have their roles, but right now, I am certain that we can achieve decisive victory without relying on them."

The revelation sent Sir Harold into a grin. "Now, I got to see just how Captain Audrey can win against six thousand with just twenty cavalrymen."

"You'll see. Unless the Ancients hate me or something . . . The conditions are all in place," said Lansius, as they rode toward the open plains.

"But why go to this length for the nomads, my lord?"

Lansius momentarily pondered before admitting, "I want more . . . I want Batu and his tribe as my strength. I refuse to let them become Lowlandia's newest mercenaries for hire."

Harold's eyes narrowed in thought. The answer reminded him of his masters, who had taught him sword and fencing styles. They, too, often approached things differently, finding unexpected solutions from new perspectives.

He felt the same way about Lord Lansius. The manner in which he not only foresaw a future problem but turned it into opportunities to empower himself was a clear reminder that he was more than just an ordinary noble.

Harold was deeply impressed by Lansius's responses. While to Lansius they might have seemed like mere answers, to Harold, they were insights that satisfied his hunger for perfection. Serving under such a lord, he felt he would have the opportunity to refine his skills as both a knight and a fighter.

As they left the forest area behind, the summer sun shone warmly upon them.

The knights and the standard bearer quickly rode up to Lord Lansius and Harold's side, in a cohesive formation.

"Carry on," Lansius ordered. "Let's show them some of our magic tricks."

CHAPTER 23

COUP DE GRÂCE

Drunken with Sir Arius's recent victory on the fields of Korelia, the Coalition gave little thought to Viscount Jorge's and the cavalry's whereabouts. Many were optimistic, assuming another victory was just around the corner. Things were looking promising, and discipline was relaxed.

When dozens of cavalrymen emerged from the forest, the South Hill column cheered for them, believing it to be Lord Jorge's triumphant return. But their hearts quickly fell when they saw the dreaded blue and bronze chevron heraldry on the battle standard.

Panic ensued as the captains flocked to their commander, seeking instructions. Meanwhile, riders were dispatched to the other columns, warning them of the unsettling development.

As for the South Hill column, still shaken by the previous Korelian charge, they could hardly stomach another round. In a flash of inspiration, one of the captains shouted that the Korelian cavalry was simply evading pursuit, and the Black Knights were hot on their tails.

This gave their men a semblance of hope and allowed the column to function. However, that illusion was shattered when the Korelians paraded black helmets and pieces of black armor atop their lances.

This was the Lord of Korelia's magic trick: making two hundred Coalition cavalrymen disappear in the forest.

Now, the parading Korelians threw fresh taunts and mockery at their opponents, further demoralizing the South Hill column.

Yet, the South Hill men persisted. Another charge was probably needed to break them, yet Lansius didn't see the need to do so. A parade was all he had instructed his knights to do.

After all, what Lansius wanted now was the Coalition's undivided attention to him. That way, Audrey, in the south, could roam free.

For Lansius, after the ambush and the elimination of the Coalition's cavalry, the war was largely over. What was left was simply cleanup and tying up loose ends.

While close to six thousand men were still standing in the field, to him, the best they could do was make noise before their eventual defeat.

Audrey, Town of Korelia, Southern Gate

Lady Felis knotted three strands of her golden hair into Audrey's headband. "I wish you the greatest of luck," said the lady as she completed the knot.

"Gratitude, Lady Felis," Audrey replied with a smile. She then donned her helmet, looked at her men, and gave her command. "Open the gates!"

"OPEN THE GATES!" the men echoed her order and swung the sturdy southern gate open.

The two friends exchanged a glance, conveying much without words. They had only met several times before Korelia but had quickly become fast friends.

Felis's naturally bubbly, happy-go-lucky, and largely carefree personality matched well with Audrey's daredevil style. More than that, Audrey's sharp instincts told her subconsciously that Felis was someone she could trust, even more so than Hannei, who had saved her life.

"Be safe," the blonde said.

"I'll see you soon," the brunette replied, and then gallantly rode her horse toward the southern gate.

Cheering erupted from the townsfolk as the twenty cavalrymen rode out.

Once outside the city, Audrey led her cavalry westward. This late in the fight, their presence and intentions were hidden from the enemy, and they aimed to capitalize on that aspect.

Even if someone spotted them, there was little risk at this point. The lord was holding a parade to the north to draw the attention of the western lords. It was also Audrey's cue to sortie.

With only twenty riders, they certainly weren't going to charge into a column of two thousand men. Clad in only their brigandines or ringmail, they couldn't even come close to replicating what Lansius had done with the knights.

Among them, only Audrey was furnished in her black, gothic plate armor. However, this arrangement wasn't accidental. Speed was commanded to them.

Lord Lansius had purposely instructed them to ride light. Only two riders carried lances. Everyone else carried torches.

Led by an experienced scout with a dog in his lap, these twenty riders weren't interested in charging a column.

Audrey and her riders slowed down as they reached the first spot, confirmed by the scout's dog.

The lady in black smiled at the cute little creature before turning to her men, her expression turning serious. "Burn all the caches. Let's make a big pyre for the wretched western lords' army!"

She recalled Lansius's words. *Every battle is won before it is ever fought.*

Lansius had confided in her that even if his cavalry charge had failed, or if he hadn't succeeded in baiting Lord Jorge, he was still confident of winning the battle through fire tactics alone. His preparation had been immaculate.

His failure would have only resulted in more Coalition casualties, which, in his eyes, would mean not a complete victory for Korelia.

Baron Omin

Facing the city to the south, Baron Omin commanded a fresh column of two thousand men. Because of the distances, he was unaware of Lansius's parade to the north and thus content to play his part in the siege.

A veteran of several battles, Omin held command under a large umbrella that protected him from the summer heat. From there, he periodically sent out scouts, rotated his troops, and listened to reports.

Nothing had piqued his interest until a scout reported movement to the south.

"Cavalry to the south, you say?" Baron Omin craned his neck in that direction, frowning when he saw nothing from his seat.

"Yes, my lord. A small group, galloping without a banner or colors."

"How the hell—" one of his staff cursed, grimacing. No one had anticipated that Lansius still had another cavalry at his disposal.

"Get the captains and form a square formation," Omin ordered his staff, who sprang into action.

Omin, too, was surprised but concealed it well.

What are these Korelians thinking? They have launched two charges against the northern column. Surely, they put all their cavalry to even have a chance of success . . .

Despite moments of pondering, Omin couldn't fathom why the Korelians had split their cavalry. He put that thought aside as he watched his troops assume a square formation.

Though this formation was naturally slower to move and lacked concentrated strength, it offered protection on all flanks.

"So, where are they?" Omin asked the returning scout from atop his horse.

"My lord, the Korelian cavalry doesn't seem to be heading here," the scout reported, doubt evident on his face.

Omin sensed something was wrong. In a spur of the moment, he pulled on his horse's reins and rode southward, willing to take more risks to learn the Korelians' intentions.

Eleven riders followed Omin. They had no more horsemen available. They had barely traversed two hundred meters through the yellowing wild grass when Omin noticed something.

Smoke. White puffs billowed from multiple spots on the southern horizon.

Unsure if he was seeing things correctly, Omin reined in his horse and came to a stop.

His accompanying riders noticed it too and reported, "My lord, look. Fires. The Korelians are burning the wild grass again."

Something bothered him, so Omin dismounted. Once on the ground, he found himself surrounded by grass taller than his knee, almost reaching his waist. He drew his knife and cut the closest bunch of grass.

The husks in his palm were yellowing from the summer sun. As he ripped it out, he found it was sturdier and thicker than usual, but not old enough to be harvested for hay. He discarded the grass and started looking around, noticing an odd uniformity in the grass.

"Scouts," Omin suddenly yelled.

A man quickly dismounted and approached him.

"Haven't the Korelians been grazing their livestock here? Why is all this grass full-grown?" His shock was apparent.

The scout looked perplexed but quickly knelt to inspect the roots of the grass. His wide eyes confirmed Omin's suspicions.

"My lord, the fire is spreading," one of the riders reported with some urgency.

With haste, Omin mounted his horse again. His gaze swept across the plains, now filled with smoke. A gust of dry wind swept past his face. The heavy scent of burning grass filled his nostrils, and in that moment, he realized something: The Southern Wind, the wind that blew from the south to the north.

"Lansius, Lansius, Lansius!" he cursed, full of rage, slamming his fist into his armored thigh three times. He had just realized that the opponent had outmaneuvered him, trapping him in a precarious position.

Perplexed by the baron's behavior, his captain queried, "My lord, why does this small fire disturb you so much? They tried the same tactic before against Sir Arius with little effect."

Omin had no time to explain. Biting his lips, he calculated his next move.

"Should we move the column to the south and try to put out the flame?" his captain suggested.

"There's no time," Omin snapped. "Don't you fools get it? The Korelians are trying to burn the whole plains!"

Omin's outburst failed to sway his staff. The thought of someone attempting to burn the vast Korelia plains was easily dismissed as a joke. Even at the height of summer, it wasn't easy to burn wild grasses. If it were, their attempt at cooking the previous night would've burned down their entire campsite.

"Go now! Ride to the column and get them back to the encampment immediately. Sound a retreat if you have to," Omin ordered.

His staff nodded, albeit with skepticism. They probably thought the fire was a distraction at best. However, they welcomed the chance for an early rest. Standing in armor under the summer sun was far from comfortable.

"My lord, where are you going?" asked one of his staff as Omin steered his horse away from them.

"I'll head to the encampment and alert them. We need to start packing before the fire reaches them," Omin said as he rode away.

Accompanied by only his Nicopolan bodyguard and four horsemen, he raced westward toward the encampment.

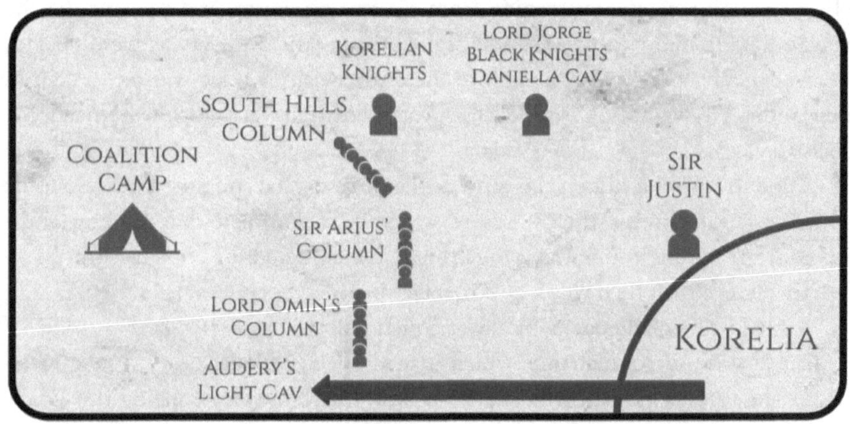

Last winter, Lansius had consulted various records and eyewitnesses in Korelia. He learned that in summer, the wind consistently blew to the north. At the time, he gave it little thought, as nature was unpredictable.

Still, as early as spring, out of caution, Lansius began to stockpile flammable materials of mostly locally available animal fat, thinking they might prove useful. Furthermore, he persuaded local shepherds to graze only on the eastern side of town.

Even when he wasn't certain that the plan would ever see the light of day, Lansius went so far as to prevent Batu's tribesmen from grazing on the west side of the town of Korelia. Because of his orders, the western plains were left wild and untouched.

When news of the western lords' invasion reached him, bringing with them a massive number of troops, Lansius knew his fire strategy was the only way out. However, he disliked the idea. Scorched earth was generally frowned upon by anyone, so he tried his best to mitigate the effects.

After all, his aim was not to create more enemies, but to strike a favorable deal. War isn't just a matter of killing and spilling enough blood but also, ironically, a means to resolve issues. Thus, the plan underwent several changes and revisions.

When Lansius revealed the draft for his final plan to the Small Council, many were surprised. Despite the lord's remarkably open and chatty attitude with his closest peers, he had managed to maintain a secretive side. Only Audrey and Calub suspected something.

The reason Lansius had visited the forest many times since spring was to study its layout, memorize paths, and familiarize himself with the details. His seemingly casual forest excursions were, in fact, careful preparations for the upcoming ambush. Finding the costard fruit tree was just a bonus.

Despite Lansius's clumsiness and unassuming looks, he was ready for war. His hesitation was merely coming from his fear of failure, and the fear that he may inflict too many casualties, practically burning the bridge to a favorable end.

As capable as he was as a warlord, he didn't wish to wage war on the entire Lowlandia. Above all, he yearned for peace. For that very reason, he needed a decisive victory.

Aside from bloodline, the Lowlandians respected might. Thus, Lansius aimed for a knockout punch so severe, a victory so complete that the Lowlandians couldn't ignore it, one that would be be remembered for years to come.

To achieve this, he devised a four-stage plan:

1. Sir Justin's challenge, which was a distraction.

2. Lansius's surprise charge, which turned out to be bait.

3. The forest ambush, which was his crippling blow, neutralizing the Coalition cavalry and securing Lord Jorge's neutrality.

4. The final strike: setting the plains ablaze, to rout the entire Coalition army.

Right now, the plan had reached the final stage.

This final strike part was kept hidden from everyone except his most trusted retainers. For this reason, Lansius trusted Audrey to carry it out.

Knowing this, Audrey and her twenty horsemen rode with pride. This was their hour of glory. The sea of yellowing grass greeted them with open arms while the dry wind clamored for their success.

Accompanied by the scout and the dog, they dashed across the western plains, seeking and burning every cache of flammable materials they had hidden—mats of hay soaked in animal fat and covered with dried grass.

On their own, the cache wouldn't be able to cause a significant fire. The real threat lay in the untouched, full-grown, ungrazed pastures of the western plains. The wild yellowing grass, almost completely dried from the summer heat, was perfect for a wildfire.

Lansius's strategy required them to do more than just start a series of fires. They needed to turn the entire western plains into an inferno.

Audrey and her men set fire to every cache they found. The dried hay and animal fat flared up, blazing hot and brightly. Propelled by the dry wind, it grew so hot that the wild grass caught fire almost instantly. What started as hundreds of isolated fires rapidly transformed into an uncontrollable wildfire.

Like riders of hell, Audrey's cavalry raced across the plains, leaving a blazing trail in their wake. They had no one to challenge them, as the Coalition cavalry was neutralized and Lansius's parade in the north kept them in check. Even if they realized the intention, it was far too late by now.

Fanned by the strong southern wind, the fire spread across the entire western plains. The once serene fields of Korelia had transformed into a roiling inferno. The Coalition could only watch helplessly as the inferno advanced northward toward their formation and encampment.

CHAPTER 24

FLEETING

Upon Baron Omin's orders, the Korimor column began its march back to camp. This movement alerted the other two columns, but the reason behind it soon became apparent: the plains were ablaze, with the fire rapidly intensifying.

As the column nearest to the fire, the Korimor's men were heavily subjected to billowing smoke and the steadily encroaching flames. Before long, there was no semblance of an organized march. Everyone rushed toward their encampments in a desperate attempt to save their lives and belongings.

Those who had most of their possessions with them, or who quickly realized that the battle was lost, bolted westward with all their might. They understood the consequences and had no desire to be taken captive.

Thus, the retreat of the two thousand Korimors and Nicopolans devolved into a full-blown rout.

On the north side, watching this development with great interest, the Lord of Korelia stopped his parade, spread out his cavalry formation, and ordered his knights to lower their lances.

The billowing smoke from afar had created chaos within the South Hill ranks, and now the sight of the incoming charge finally broke their morale. Without an ounce of bravery left, the remaining men fled in total panic, with total disregard for order or formation.

As the vast plains burned red and churned out thick black smoke, every footman ran, and the commanders were helpless to stop them. They had good reason to desert. For levied troops like them, to be captured meant servitude.

Ironically, their best chance to escape from slavery was to outrun their comrades. A trail of body armor, weapons, and helmets littered the plains. Everyone lightened their load as much as possible to outrun anyone in front of them.

The last column that remained on the field was Sir Arius's. The encroaching fire, along with the sudden collapse of the southern and northern columns, demoralized his men.

While Sir Arius had wanted to march into the forest to regroup with Lord Jorge's cavalry, his knights were against it.

Even the crimson knight, his most trusted champion, told him not to. Sir Arius eventually relented as the fire threatened to cut off their retreat.

Sir Arius's retreat finally reduced the might of the Coalition to a shambling mess of an army. Just as he had feared, like the other two columns, his Three Hills column also suffered massive desertions.

Amid the chaos, Lansius's cavalry made their presence felt, taking hostages, capturing knights, and terrorizing the fleeing Coalition. They goaded their opponent to escape far west or into the fire.

The western Korelia plains had turned into a spectacular show of wildfire, while the tragedy of the once mighty Coalition army was just beginning.

Things were only marginally better inside the encampment. In the vast, sprawling city of tents, guarded by the most loyal retainers, servants, and a small number of camp followers, there was still a semblance of order, despite the panic.

Baron Omin rode to the heart of the encampment and tried to organize a retreat. His quick reaction to abandoning his column had paid off. The smoke and fire hadn't yet reached the encampment, and he had enough time to prepare.

"Find your lieutenants. Tell them Baron Omin of Korimor has summoned them!" He rode around the inner encampment to establish a working chain of command.

With great effort under the heavy smoke, he organized a convoy of baggage trains. Each cart was full of war funds and valuables. He knew he could rebuild the army if he could secure the supplies. Through honeyed words and bribes, he also convinced Jorge's baggage guards to join his ranks.

Without the sighting of Lord Jorge's banner or the rest of the nobles, even the most loyal were compelled to flee. Lastly, Omin gathered as many horsemen as he could find, and then, leading sixty carts, he fled westward.

His escort consisted of just ten cavalrymen. However, behind his convoy followed many nobles, some even traveling in horse-drawn carts accompanied by their servants and baggage. Among the chaos, their only consolation was that the spare and draft horses they managed to acquire were fresh and eager to run.

In total, close to one hundred carts were fleeing west, leaving the rest of the Coalition army behind.

Earlier, the baron had traded his horse for a fresh one. His Nicopolan bodyguard rode calmly beside him, giving Omin some necessary mental support.

Time passed and the great Lowlandia plains loomed on the horizon.

"Split up! Split up," Omin commanded.

The convoy split in three directions. This was his masterstroke to foil capture. With Jorge's baggage train in his hand, even if he could only secure one of the three convoys, he would still come out far richer.

The Battle of Korelia had ended in disaster. However, Omin could still turn this into a great opportunity.

Audrey

The front riders slowed to a stop, and the rest of the cavalry followed suit. Several spread out as lookouts. Audrey had led her cavalry to the far west, where the Korelia plains and the great Lowlandia plains connected seamlessly.

After ensuring the area was safe, Audrey dismounted. Their horses, having endured a sprint from the town and through a field of billowing smoke, were in need of some rest.

As they were resting, the lookout informed them of a sighting from the west.

"Allies?" Audrey asked.

"It's ours, Captain."

Soon, Audrey saw a group of thirty civilians arrive on their small horses or mules. They were either too old, too young, or unfit to join the militia and were certainly not part of the plan.

The leader of this group shared a horse, stopping next to Audrey. Margo, the page boy, dismounted first, then helped the rider with whom he had been sharing the horse.

"Are we sticking to the plan?" the second rider, a woman wearing a traveling cloak, asked.

"My plan," Audrey replied, patting the head of her prized warhorse.

"Yeah, I meant that," Hannei said, lowering her cloak to reveal sweat trickling down her forehead. "You knew I could proceed alone."

"Nah, it's too dangerous for you to go alone. You need at least four," Audrey advised, glancing at the group of boys, elderly men, and a few individuals with missing limbs.

"Okay, so where are the men who'll follow me?" Hannei asked, rummaging through the saddlebag for a water flask.

"Sigmund, Dietrich," Audrey called out, turning to her men.

There was a ruckus, and then two men showed up with smiles on their faces. One even offered a handful of wildflowers and said, "For the good captain!"

"You know damn well that I can't eat them, Dietrich," Audrey responded, sparking laughter from the men. Dietrich, one of their best horse riders, retracted the flowers, feigning heartbreak.

Meanwhile, Sigmund, the soldier-bard, showed a wide smile, already thinking about making a lyric.

"Sigmund, I appreciate your willingness to come. I need someone to look after them," said Audrey, motioning to the group of thirty.

"Please, I'm always happy to help. This Sigmund is at your service, my ladies," he replied, bowing graciously toward Audrey and Hannei.

Hannei smiled, while Audrey could only shrug.

"And I am also at your service, captain," said Dietrich, not to be outdone. He then turned serious. "But are you sure you can manage the chase on your own?"

Audrey nodded. "I think I can manage against slow-moving carts. Your part is even more demanding. Try to keep them safe, especially Hannei."

"Understood," said Dietrich.

"Let the men rest a little more before you reorganize them," Audrey instructed.

Sigmund and Dietrich nodded before returning to their group.

"They're either the bravest I've got or the stupidest," Audrey commented about their antics, prompting giggles from Hannei.

With no trees in sight, they sat in the shadows of their horses, quenching their thirst, discarding their helmets, and wiping off sweat.

"That Sigmund, shouldn't he be responsible for some tens of men?" asked Hannei.

"Yup, he's the leader of the third group," confirmed Audrey.

"So, is taking him with us okay?"

"Heh, it should be," said Audrey, with a hint of nervousness. Despite her closeness with Lansius and the fact that she had bashed him so many times in training, she didn't want to overstep Lansius's authority. He was the lord, while she was barely a captain.

Hannei noted her concern and said confidently, "Look, I'll help cover for you when this is over. I think I can manage that much."

"I'll be counting on you then," Audrey replied with a grin. Last year, they had a cordial but professional relationship. But now, after living together in a small castle and sharing a room, they were closer than ever.

Since spring, the two, along with Felis, had become as close as sisters and were the prime troublemakers in Korelia Castle. They dabbled in food experiments and even attempted to make uniforms for the castle staff.

Now, two of the "rascals," as Lansius referred to them behind their backs, had planned something risky. Lansius would never approve, but they knew it was within their ability.

As they waited, only the breeze offered some respite against the scorching summer sun. To their east, they saw black smoke billowing into the sky.

A shout attracted their attention. They watched as the scout with the dog in his lap came galloping toward them.

"Carts on the horizon," the scout reported as he reined in his horse.

"That is faster than predicted . . . No matter, I'll give chase," Audrey declared, and then to her friend, she said, "I'll depart first then."

"Bon courage!" Hannei wished her.

"I hope it's a good wish," Audrey commented, drawing a giggle from Hannei.

Audrey then mounted her horse and quickly departed with sixteen horsemen.

"What should we do then, my lady?" Margo asked. Behind him, Sigmund and Dietrich, along with two other riders, were ready with their horses.

"It's time for us to leave as well," Hannei replied.

Led by Sigmund and Dietrich, along with two other horsemen, Hannei, and thirty civilians, rode eastward.

Chase on the Plains

The vast Lowlandia plains were predominantly flat terrain, which made traversing them relatively easy, even without a road. While there was no place to hide, avoiding detection was possible, as there was no road to follow.

At this moment, Baron Omin's convoy had built up a substantial distance, moving as fast as their carts and horses could manage. However, they were slowing down as the heat and exhaustion began to take their toll on the animals.

The convoy had just split up when things started to go awry. Hidden by the trail of dust kicked up in the wake of the carts, Korelian riders had caught up and were subjugating the carts in the convoy one by one.

"My lord, the Korelians," warned the Nicopolan bodyguard.

Omin was furious. The pursuers were so efficient that by the time they noticed, one of the split-up convoys had been completely captured.

"Damn it! Why are their horses so resilient?" Omin watched in dismay as the Korelians easily transitioned from the last convoy to his own. Their horses seemed as fresh as ever.

His lieutenant raced to Omin's side and asked, "What should we do, my lord? The convoy can't keep up much longer."

"You know what to do. Lead our escort to intercept! The Korelian horses should be as tired as ours," Omin urged.

The lieutenant felt disheartened but obeyed the order as instructed. Soon, ten horsemen detached from the convoy. They turned around and awaited the arrival of the opponents. They were mostly officers, not expert cavalrymen.

Omin and the convoy pushed forward, but many carts lagged as their horses' stamina was nearly spent. From afar, they witnessed their ten horsemen engaging in a brief but one-sided fight. Only five fought; the rest yielded.

The convoy's morale plummeted. Their escort had barely bought them time to run.

"We must escape," urged the bodyguard gravely.

Accepting the inevitable, Omin gave up. Riding only their horses, they veered wide and abandoned their allies.

Watching their lord escape, leaving them behind, served as the final straw for the coachmen. They slowed their carts and accepted capture. However, a stubborn few continued to flee. They fired their crossbows haphazardly and split up further to dissuade their pursuers.

Some put up a fierce fight before being subjugated, as their horses refused to run any farther. Ironically, their frantic struggle to escape inadvertently bought precious time for their lord to evade capture unnoticed.

Audrey's cavalry remained unaware of Omin and the third convoy's existence until it was too late. It was only after they began rounding up and questioning people that the Korelians realized a third convoy even existed.

They had mistakenly assumed that there were only two convoys, believing Omin would likely be in one of them. However, it was a mistake.

Audrey's force was now exhausted, having engaged in numerous individual chases to capture each fleeing cart. Additionally, a few riders were wounded, and their horses were spent from the relentless pursuit and skirmishes with each cart. On top of that, they still had to secure the captured baggage train.

Simply put, they were in no condition to search for Baron Omin or the third convoy.

Furious, Audrey slammed her fist against one of the carts. "Erryaahh!" she vented, acknowledging her failure.

In her mind, she cursed the name that had twice crossed her. Like a bad joke from the past that continued to haunt her, another Omin, this time a baron, the instigator of this war, had escaped.

If only Audrey hadn't split her forces, if only she had another rider as capable and cautious as Dietrich, all of this might have been prevented.

CHAPTER 25

THE BLUNT STICK

The Encampment

The camp for the six thousand was swallowed by thick black smoke. Fire encroached from the southern side, growing stronger by the minute. Suddenly, thirty-four horsemen appeared. They had crossed a small stream, dousing their horses and attire in an effort to shield themselves from the intense heat.

Many donned wet scarves to protect their nostrils and mouths as they navigated the path of blackened, burnt grass. Despite the surrounding sea of fire and smoke, they were kept safe by a transparent barrier that warded off the heat, smoke, and fire.

No one fully understood what was happening, but they knew that Hannei was responsible. She was chanting the same verse slowly in an unknown language, almost like singing.

She had created a large spherical barrier by controlling the wind to blow from above, causing it to swirl around them in a protective cyclone. Not just a gentle breeze but a strong current, enough to snuff out the flames trapped inside the sphere.

It was as if they had a dome of invisible walls for protection. While the raging winds couldn't extinguish the flames completely, they kept the heavy smoke at bay and made it safe for them to press on.

Witnessing this, everyone in the group regarded Lady Hannei with profound reverence. They mistook her for a saint candidate and felt blessed to see one in action.

Sigmund, Dietrich, and the others had moved beyond their initial skepticism about her plan. At first, they believed they would have plenty of time to loot, but their hearts sank when they saw the encampment already surrounded by fire. Nevertheless, Hannei had shown the way.

As she advanced, the smoke cleared, and the flames died out. The men used sticks, other tools, and even their boots to stamp out the fire, ensuring that Hannei's horse could proceed unhindered.

The blonde mage rode alone, while Margo guided her horse on foot, striving to make her as comfortable as possible. Under her protection, the group reached the outer layers of the encampment and increased their pace upon crossing the blackened, fiery terrain.

The Coalition had allowed their horses to graze and their footmen to collect hay for bedding, so the inner parts of the camp were yet to be burnt. However, the thick smoke had rendered it deserted, with no signs of life. Evidence of panic was everywhere, with gear and supplies littered about.

There were carts ready to be used, but many more were still neatly tied.

"There's no more fire. I will enlarge the barrier, but you must work quickly," Hannei said to Sigmund at her side.

"You heard her! Split up and ready the carts," Sigmund commanded the group.

"Disregard the carts with water barrels! We don't need them. Get the carts with the grain, the armor, and the weapons," Dietrich added.

"What about salted meat, boss?" one of the riders jested.

"Fuck them!" answered Dietrich, sparking laughter among the group. Last winter, Korelia had produced a record amount of salted meat, such that it was no longer a luxury.

The enlarged barrier was sending more air downward, but it was far from perfect. Smoke and soot got mixed in, and everyone started to look blackened. Two riders braved the smoke to ensure the exit route was passable.

Despite their reddened eyes and coughs from the smoke, the men hastily prepared the carts and their horses. One by one, even with just a single horse, the supply carts were set in motion.

Western Plains

Lansius had led his cavalry to capture and terrorize the remnants of the Coalition. His priority was to prevent them from regrouping, while simultaneously allowing his knights to collect ransoms and trophies—and they were raking it in.

Laden with spoils and captured nobles, the cavalry moved slowly. The once mighty western nobility were now bound by ropes, the other ends of which were tied to their captors' horses. Forced to walk on foot, they were filled with shame and fear for their lives.

Fortunately, their fear of Lansius made them easy to control.

Far to the south, the fire was still raging, and thick, blackened smoke billowed high into the sky, enough to obscure even the mighty summer sun.

The area in which they rode would soon be engulfed in flames, too. Only the most northern plains near the outskirts of the forest would be spared, thanks to the time when Lansius had welcomed nomads to graze their livestock there in the spring.

Now, there was only one more thing to do. Following their scouts, Lansius's cavalry easily met up with Lord Jorge's remnants. Their situation looked pitiful; many were injured and without steeds. Only about fifty remained, including some Nicopolan mercenaries.

The situation immediately grew tense, but Lansius raised his right palm to indicate parley. "I wish to talk. Tell them I guarantee no harm will befall them," he told Harold, who flanked him closely.

Nodding at his lord's command, Sir Harold rode farther and heralded, "My lord wishes for a parley. He guarantees that no harm will befall the Lord of Three Hills and his retinue."

While waiting for a response, Lansius instructed his knights not to surround or show aggression. Instead, they were to fan out and present themselves with discipline. His aim was for a visible show of force.

"Speak softly and carry a big stick," he mumbled. Then, he gritted his teeth and slowly removed his arm sling. The throbbing was getting worse. It was possibly more than just a fracture.

A pair of horsemen approached. One of them looked regal with black and bronze-accented armor. Lansius spurred his destrier forward until he was next to Harold.

He finally met Lord Jorge in person. Despite all that had happened, Lansius oddly didn't harbor hatred but pitied the man's foolishness.

"That's close enough," Sir Harold said openly to both parties. The sight of Morton, who remained steadfast despite their overwhelming odds, put Harold on high alert.

"Lord Lansius," Jorge began from atop his horse, his voice as alluring as he was charming. "Earlier you promised me a safe passage to return to my encampment, yet it's all gone in flames. Now, I pray that you'll allow us to return to Three Hills unharmed."

"My lord," Lansius addressed humbly, the fate of many lives in Lowlandia depending on his words. "The situation is unfortunate, but you're my guest. I urge you to stay for a few nights. Your men and horses are exhausted and without provisions. If you insist on returning today, more disaster will befall the men from Three Hills."

Jorge looked alarmed and likely mistook Lansius's warning for a threat. "Lord Lansius, for what it's worth, we have made amends. I have pledged neutrality."

"My lord, please understand my predicament. You brought a great host from Three Hills, Korimor, and South Hill to attack Korelia. As such, it was impossible for me to stand alone." With these words, Lansius skillfully redirected the blame back to Jorge, also giving hints to leverage his position.

He paused to let his words sink in before continuing. "I had to rely on Lord Robert and the nomadic tribes. In return for their aid, I promised they could freely hunt the remnants of this war."

Morton took a deep breath, gazed at his lord, who had been waiting, and nodded once. He knew his lord wasn't going to win a contest of wits. He also feared for his lord's well-being if they forced their way to Three Hills. It was twelve to fifteen days on foot, with nothing but grass on the horizon.

Meanwhile, Jorge found Lansius to be very different from what he had envisioned. Riding with part of his armor exposed, likely from a battle wound, the foreigner looked gallant. "It seems you have placed me in a situation most dire."

"I wish to rectify that. That is why I beseech you to stay, so many of your men will be spared. Your banner will gather men from Three Hills to return, saving them from the nomads' wrath."

Jorge looked amused and boldly questioned, "Lord Lansius, I can't help but wonder why you are so concerned for the welfare of my men, who, until this morning, were attempting to invade your land."

Lansius held back a chuckle, realizing that his motives must seem suspicious, and also admired Jorge's honesty. "I need Three Hills to survive as intact as possible in order to maintain peace."

"What do you mean by that?" Jorge asked, discarding any pretense.

"I wish to end the conflict in this land. If my lord, and Lord Robert, through my intervention, could reconcile, then a new power balance could be established between East and West Lowlandia. Perhaps, that way, peace, and a beneficial relationship can be achieved."

Jorge nodded thoughtfully, absorbing Lansius's points. "I always wondered why you kept Lord Robert in power . . . Will you also allow my House to continue ruling Three Hills then?"

"That is not even a question, my lord. I have no claim over Three Hills."

Lord Jorge seemed to regain some color in his pale cheeks at this reassurance. "Very well, as long as my House can continue to rule Three Hills, I shall heed your words. Then, what are your suggestions?"

Jorge's positive answer calmed Lansius. Winning at diplomacy was as crucial as winning the battle. While as the victor, he could force his demands, if the other party was deeply unsatisfied then it was just a prelude for another war. What Lansius needed was a mutual understanding.

Thus, with all the charisma he could muster, Lansius suggested, "I would like to offer you the best lodgings in Korelia, but it may seem like I'm holding you hostage. I think it's best for my lord to establish a new encampment. There's an abandoned village north of here. It has wells with clear spring water."

Without being asked, Morton looked at his lord and nodded to show that he wasn't against the idea.

"I recall such a place," said Jorge. "Then we shall set camp there. Will you permit me to search for my men?"

"I'll allow it, as long as they're *your subjects*," Lansius emphasized the last part.

Jorge seemed to catch the meaning.

Watching them, Morton coughed, and Jorge readily motioned his captain to speak.

"My lord, I hope you'll forgive my blunt language," the Mage Knight addressed Lansius. "You're showing us significant leniency, for which we are grateful, but you haven't stated your demands. This concerns us."

Lansius chuckled. This Mage Knight had caused him so much pain, yet somehow he had to keep his emotions aside. "Sir Knight, my demands remain the same. Uphold your oath of neutrality, respect my claim over Korelia, and allow my men's rights to the spoils of war. In return, we'll guarantee a safe haven. If you wish, I'll also arrange a carriage so Lord Jorge can march home with the dignity befitting his station."

Satisfied with the offer, Morton and Lord Jorge agreed to the terms. With this, the two Houses ceased all hostilities. The Lord of Korelia would assist with basic supplies, tents, and other materials. In return, Lord Jorge forfeited all gear and supplies left behind, to be seized as war reparations.

They exchanged liaisons and parted ways peacefully. Lord Jorge and his remnants marched northwest and started to gather the wounded and stragglers.

Midday had passed, but the summer sun was obscured by thick smoke from the burning plains, providing the men in armor with some much-needed shade.

"My lord, won't it be dangerous if they regroup and rally?" Harold asked as they prepared to ride again.

"It might seem unnecessarily risky, but an army marches on its belly," answered Lansius as a squire helped him with the arm sling. "Without daily supplies or weapons, what can they do? Now, they're depending on us like children to their parents. If they bite the hand that feeds them, then it'll be a slow and agonizing death for them."

"I see . . ." Harold remarked, his expression clearing.

"Besides, they fear Lord Robert's cavalry and the nomads," added Lansius.

"It's funny that my lord mentioned Lord Robert. I heard nothing about reinforcements from White Lake."

"They're going to be late, probably by a few days. I mentioned their name because Three Hills respects and fears Lord Robert's cavalry more than the nameless nomads."

"Indeed, that makes sense." The knight rubbed his chin in satisfaction.

Continuing his earlier plan, Lansius sent two unburdened squires to inform Calub and Korelia of their newest agreement and situation. He also instructed his burdened main cavalry to head east to Korelia Castle, where Sir Justin would be ready to assist.

Meanwhile, Lansius, his scout, and twenty knights rode west. While the battlefield was still filled with stragglers, he needed to connect with and reinforce Audrey's cavalry.

As they rode, the Korelia plains smoldered. Nearly a third of the plains was blackened, the ashes carried by the wind painting the landscape a ghostly gray.

CHAPTER 26

SETTLED

The scent of smoke and charred vegetation filled the air, while ash rained down like grim snowflakes, blanketing the ground with a layer of gray dust. The once verdant steppe had transformed into a smoldering wasteland.

Lansius and his knights had been searching for Audrey for quite some time. They had crossed paths with straggling groups several times, but nobody was in the mood to start a fight.

After riding across the western plains, the scout finally found traces of carts that led them to a small creek.

"They've crossed, my lord," reported the scout confidently.

Just as planned.

"Let's give chase," ordered Lansius. He was relieved to find no signs of fighting at the crossing, suggesting that Audrey's cavalry were able to subdue the retreating convoy without resistance. And they were fast enough to evade the retreating forces.

Lansius and his knights crossed the small stream and headed south, following the cart tracks.

"My lord, I see something," one of the knights reported.

"Guide us in," Lansius ordered. Things were going as planned, and he hoped everything would end well.

"Vanguard, ride ahead!" Sir Harold shouted, and two knights sortied ahead.

As Lansius saw the outlines of the unmoving caravans and horses, he asked, "They're stopping?"

"It seems that way, my lord," Sir Harold answered.

They rode straight, showing their banner high.

"Unbelievable . . . So many carts, there must be more than fifty!" Harold commented, his eyes wide with astonishment.

Indeed, the result exceeded even Lansius's expectations. As they rode closer, Audrey's men noticed their approach. They stood tall and straight as their lord arrived.

"My lord, the victory is yours!" The men began to clamor as they caught sight of Lansius.

Lansius wasn't accustomed to such treatment. They hailed him as the great victor and showered him with praises. Using all his strength to maintain a stoic expression, a smile nonetheless formed on his lips. As he slowly rode past them, the men reached out, touching his gauntlet and greaves as if they were charms or amulets.

Their devotion had Sir Harold grinning from ear to ear.

Among the cheering crowd, Lansius spotted Audrey standing near a laden cart, her face slightly blackened with soot.

"What's happened to your arm, and your backplate?" she blurted out as she approached, taking the destrier's rein as if it was nothing more than a docile dog.

"Well, things happened, probably a fracture, but no blood," Lansius commented about his left wrist, which was in an arm sling.

"You shouldn't be here. You should ride straight to Korelia—"

"I know, but"—Lansius gazed around the group—"I need to make sure that we're winning."

At the mention of winning, faces around them broke into smiles, eyes welled up with tears of joy and relief; their gratitude for the outcome of the war was showing. Nobody had expected Korelia to win the siege in just half a day. This victory was nothing short of a miracle.

"Umm, my lord, may I speak to you about *something*?" Audrey fidgeted.

Lansius sensed something was amiss. "Are you injured?"

But then somebody even more blackened than Audrey came forward. "My lord, I can explain."

A female voice. Her face and attire were blackened, but her blonde hair still stood out.

Lansius furrowed his brows and asked with suspicion, "Hannei?"

"Yes, my lord, I asked Captain Audrey to allow me to ride with her—"

"But you can't ride," Lansius retorted, interrupting her words.

"Ermm . . . Margo helped me a bit on that matter," Hannei admitted.

"Oh, please no," Lansius groaned. He never allowed the young pages into war.

"My lord, please listen . . ." Hannei's tone was polite, but her eyes were sharp as knives.

Lansius sighed. He might be a lord, but the mage was wrathful and well connected. Thus, he motioned for her to continue.

"We split our forces, and I went to the encampment. Using my *tricks*, there's little danger from the fire. And we successfully captured a few dozen supply carts." Hannei ended her story briefly, clearly omitting the dangerous part.

She seemed pleased, and indeed it was a great achievement. However, they had broken military rule by disregarding Lansius's command, which could set a bad precedent.

Lansius took a sharp breath. He didn't like to censure, but men would die and battles would be lost if they acted on their own just to fill their pockets. "Lady Hannei, I applaud your courage. However, military law and discipline are not to be trifled with," he said sternly.

As expected, the one responsible, Audrey, put herself on the line, shielding Hannei. She stood with her back straight, helmet carried in hand at breast level. She silently waited for the punishment, as Hannei was her charge.

Hannei gave Lansius a look, hinting at him to let this slide, but he couldn't. Military law was where he drew the line. "Captain, were you able to capture Lord Omin?"

The crowd went silent.

"I was unable to find him, my lord," Audrey replied.

Lansius closed his eyes for a moment. "Capturing Lord Omin, while vital, isn't the primary objective. So, I don't blame you. Especially when you only have so few horsemen. It's only natural to lose him in the chaos of war."

"However," Lansius continued ominously, "you violated a direct order, endangered my guest, and put your men in unnecessary danger. Do you have anything to say?"

Audrey knelt. Her face was downcast as she spoke. "No, my lord, I . . . humbly ask for your pardon."

The men's faces around them looked sour. Nobody was satisfied with this development.

"In deference to our victory and this bountiful result, I shall sentence a lighter punishment. Half pay for a year," Lansius announced the punishment.

"My lord, please, we beg your forgiveness! Have mercy," the men cried out, pleading for leniency on behalf of their beloved captain. Receiving half pay would barely cover rent and food, let alone allow for any indulgences like spare clothes or alcohol.

Outwardly, Hannei looked composed, but Lansius knew she was seething.

"Order, order!" Sir Harold rode forward to assist. The knights behind him also assumed formation to show support. But it was unnecessary; there was never a threat to begin with, just discontent.

"Military laws are strict for a purpose," Lansius shouted, using the pain in his left wrist to fuel his anger. His voice commanded attention and caused surprise. "Failure to follow a command may ruin an army. If that happens, we would all pay the blood price."

He paused to gauge their attention before continuing. "You may have succeeded this time, but can you guarantee the same result in the future? Are you willing to gamble all of our lives against death or, worse . . . servitude?"

His words eventually pacified the men. Even though they were uneducated and only understood a fraction of military law, they feared its consequences.

"Pageboy," Lansius called.

"Y-yes, my lord." As he had expected, a blackened Margo appeared.

"Write the punishment for Captain Audrey. Half pay for the rest of this year."

"At once, my lord," Margo replied, albeit weakly.

With the punishment dealt with, it was time for the reward. "Margo, while you're here, let's distribute the loot. How many carts are there?"

The words "loot" and "distribution" gathered everyone's attention. The previous emotion and bad taste immediately cooled down.

"There are a total of seventy-three carts, my lord. Composed of—"

"Let's do the ones that Lady Hannei specifically captured," he told the squire.

Margo checked the piece of wood he used as notes as he was without parchment or ink. "There are thirty-three carts captured, my lord. They are filled with grains, clothing, and weapons."

Lansius pondered for a moment. "Eight carts should go to Sir Justin's column for their sacrifices. Four for Calub's men as they bled as much. Another four for the knights as they have lost horses and gear. That's sixteen, correct?"

"Indeed, my lord," Margo replied while jotting down on the wooden board with his knife.

"Another four should go for future military expenses to capture Baron Omin. And four should go to the city's militia," stated Lansius.

The men around Lansius grew weary. They had worked hard to secure the baggage train and hadn't been mentioned. Furthermore, the lord had yet to say how many he wanted. As was the rule, the lord always took the lion's share.

"Twenty-four recorded. There's . . . nine carts left, my lord," Margo informed him after counting furiously with his fingers.

"Three should go to Lady Hannei for her invaluable support. Three for the men who participated in this, and the rest should go to Captain Audrey," Lansius concluded.

"Oooh, three carts!" the men shouted in pure joy. Each imagined getting three pieces of clothing and a bagful of expensive trinkets. For them, it was as good as a laborer's pay for three harvests.

In front of Lansius, Audrey poked at Margo. "Hey, how many are my share?" she asked curiously. Mental math was uncommon in this world.

"Please, a moment," Margo replied to Audrey, then facing Lansius and spoke. "My lord, there seems to be a slight mistake. You haven't taken your share?"

The crowd went silent.

Lansius let out a faint smile. "No, this is purely the men's hard work. They took the risk and endured my wrath. Besides, Captain Audrey has taken full responsibility. So, I shall claim none from the thirty-three carts."

This evoked something primal among the men who shouted even harder, grateful for their lord's generosity.

Undisturbed by this, Audrey pressed Margo for an answer. "Well?"

"Three carts, Captain. You got three." The page grinned as he said it.

Audrey punched a fist into the air while the men rushed to congratulate her. She was well-loved.

Nearby, Hannei let out a smirk and nodded approvingly at Lansius, and he nodded back. They let Audrey and her men bask in the limelight.

When the commotion was over, Lansius rode closer. "Audrey."

"Yes," she replied with a wide smile.

"Apologies for the harsh words."

"That's okay. You also gave me three carts." She grinned.

"I think it's only fair," Lansius replied.

And then Audrey smiled at him so innocently that it made his heart race.

I have to tell her . . .

His heart pounded hard as if he was about to charge the enemy's line again. Worse, he only had cheap corny lines in his head. He had tried to collect some good lines, but this was a different era. Here, if a man liked a woman, he would send his uncle to meet the woman's father to discuss lineage and dowry.

"Audrey . . ." he called with a slight nervousness. Her eyes met his, and Lansius continued. "Ever since I met you three years ago, I've met many ladies, but none as capable or as interesting as you. Lady Audrey, would you marry me?"

The lord's unorthodox and sudden declaration hushed the entire crowd. Eyes widened, and many faces broke into wide grins. Even the usually stoic knights were smirking.

Suddenly, the blackened Dietrich appeared out of nowhere. He approached Lansius, surprising him with a bouquet of colorful wildflowers. Meanwhile, the equally blackened Sigmund strummed a looted lyre, providing a melodious backdrop to the scene.

Amid all the chaos, Audrey, the center of everyone's attention, stood her ground but blushed red. Her lips parted, as if to speak, then closed again as she gathered her thoughts.

The crowd hung on every word, their faces showed a myriad of emotions. Smiles and anticipation were in the air.

Audrey finally smiled. Her answer was almost certain, but the words that came out from her lips were, "No, I can't."

A pang shot through Lansius's heart at the rejection, reopening an old wound that could be felt despite his amnesia. His face remained stoic, but his mind went into overdrive to control the emotional turmoil.

Of course, she rejects it, dumbass! You just cut her pay and rebuked her openly!

Cold logic pounded reason into his senses. The chaos still whirled around him. Dietrich politely took back the wildflowers, while Sir Harold approached with an opened wineskin to ease the pain.

Before Lansius could take a drink, Audrey approached, and the knight wisely gave them some space. She stepped on the destrier's stirrup, grabbed the horse's saddle with her hand, and pulled herself up.

Suddenly their faces were so close that Lansius could see the faint freckles on her skin despite the smudges of soot. He could see the beautiful hazelnut color of her eyes and feel the heat radiating from her blushing cheeks.

"Wha—" Lansius's word was left unfinished as their lips met. He was completely taken aback by the sweet surprise and instinctively wrapped his right arm around her.

Meanwhile, the crowds went berserk with loud wolf-whistling, clapping, and shouts of approval. Everybody went mad, their pent-up frustration from the war and their victory combined into one.

"But you said no?" Lansius said, still dazzled.

"Lans, I can't marry you, but maybe a concubine is more fitting," Audrey replied with a reddened face while avoiding direct eye contact.

Her explanation baffled Lansius. "W-who gave you the idea?"

"Mm, Hannei, but mostly Felis . . ." she answered.

"Well, can't have you as that . . . How about as a baron's consort?" Lansius proposed a more honorable status with all the recognition and standing, just shy of a noble wife who enjoyed the full privilege and rights, including the priority for her children to become heirs apparent.

Audrey shyly nodded her head.

"Then it's settled," the lord exclaimed as he pulled her closer to share the saddle.

With hoarse voices from so many successive rounds of cheering, the crowd gave their loudest support for them. Sir Harold, Dietrich, and Margo readily removed the destrier's barding and the saddlebag to lighten the horse's load.

Lansius and Audrey also helped each other to remove parts of their armor to make their ride more comfortable. She was particularly careful with Lansius's arm sling.

"Hail to the lord and the captain consort," Dietrich yelled, and a burst of laughter followed. Lansius had to admit that was quite funny, while Audrey just took it in stride, looking embarrassed but happy.

"Lans, are you sure this is okay?" his soon-to-be consort asked.

Braving the cheering and merry laughter, Lansius cuddled her from behind, reassuring her. He gently pulled the destrier's reins to the side. "Come, let's head home. Korelia is waiting."

Observing the lord's reaction, the men cheerfully obliged and promptly readied themselves. The cavalry group finally set off for home along with the captured convoy. For them, the Battle of Korelia was finally over. But for others, it was only just beginning.

"Mm, Lans," Audrey whispered as they rode home. "What about the Lord of Korimor?"

"Baron Omin? Don't worry about him." Lansius tightened his grip on her hands. "Remember when I told Batu to act once he sees a signal?" He gestured toward the smoldering western plains, a clear signal of their victory. "I doubt he'll miss that."

"Ah, the hunt?!" she exclaimed, her eyes sparkling with anticipation.

"Yup, I won't allow anyone to escape. They have to pay the price," Lansius stated firmly as they approached Korelia from the southern side, flanked by the knights and the slowly moving caravans trailing behind them.

CHAPTER 27

FIVE FATES

The room inside the guardhouse was bathed in the soft glow from a small chandelier. There Hugo sat in silence. He had emerged from the battle relatively unscathed, save for some minor lacerations that had since dried. He was alone, his only companions a humble jug of water and a smaller jug of wine that sat on the wooden table.

Despite the near-miraculous victory they had achieved, he was surprisingly restless. As a squire, Hugo had always compared himself to Lord Lansius, believing they were equals at least in skill if not in status. But now, it was clear just how wide the gulf between them was.

As if in an attempt to lift his spirits, bright stars twinkled in the night sky, visible through a small window. The sight was not lost on Hugo, who softly quoted, "Shine brightly like the stars in the night."

His lord's achievements were indeed bright, like the stars. Suddenly, a smirk appeared on his lips. He was envious, yet also proud. There was no malice in his feelings, only disappointment in himself as he lamented, "Why don't I possess even a quarter of his talent?"

Despite his mood, Hugo resisted the wine. He had volunteered for watch duty, as the lord was worried about a possible night attack. More than just good faith, he wanted to think clearly. Today's battle had been hard fought, and he would be a fool if he didn't try to learn from it.

There were many rising stars in Lansius's household, and he felt that even his rank as deputy marshal wasn't guaranteed. He sighed heavily and kept watch patiently, his gaze fixed on the darkened landscape below.

Outside, it was all quiet. Only the occasional wind carrying fine dust and the scent of burnt grass.

The door creaked open, and Sir Justin entered. The marshal was wearing a half-open, stained-white padded jack. What was interesting about his appearance was the wooden splint bandaged over his left hip. He had been experiencing pain in his hip and had worn them as a precaution against a possible fracture.

Hugo rose. "Do you need help, sir?"

"Nah, the pain lessened after I bandaged it tightly." Sir Justin limped toward the chair, carefully lowering himself into it, mindful of his bandaged hip.

"Are you sure you want to be here? I'll allow you to celebrate in town. You've earned it," the marshal said jovially.

"Gratitude, sir, but I think the men deserve it more than me," Hugo replied. He felt honored by the offer, knowing the marshal was the type who meant what he said.

The older knight grinned as he reached into his pocket and placed several trinkets on the table: gold rings, a silver medallion, and a rectangular golden belt buckle. "Say, here's Korelia, and this is the Coalition's encampment."

He was explaining his makeshift map when someone knocked. "I'm looking for the marshal."

"Enter," Sir Justin invited.

A tall figure with a well-defined jawline and flamboyant hair entered, dressed in a comfortable tunic. "You asked for me, sir?" there was an alluring confidence in his voice.

"Sir Harold, welcome to the Small Council," greeted Sir Justin.

Harold remained at the door. "But I'm not a member, just a temporary cavalry commander."

Sir Justin casually motioned for the tall knight to enter. Sir Harold closed the door behind him and approached the two. The rectangular wooden table was positioned so that one of its long sides was flush against the wall, leaving just enough space for three people to sit around the remaining sides.

The tall knight rested his sword's scabbard against the chair. As he sat down, his interest was piqued by the trinkets scattered about on the table's surface.

Sir Justin motioned to his deputy, who spoke. "Sir Harold, you might not know this, but Sir Callahan has passed away."

The knight's face turned stoic momentarily before looking downcast. "So the bolt penetrated deeply." He sighed and closed his eyes as he recalled, "I was riding next to him. That could've happened to me."

Sir Justin readily poured wine for the younger knight, who took a sip just for the sake of it.

"I only knew him for a season, but he seemed like a great man," Harold lamented. "He had the patience of a good mentor. And as a knight, he had the looks and skills to back it up. May he meet the Ancients and hunt for all eternity."

The other two bowed their heads slightly as a sign of respect.

"So now, what do you need of me?" Harold asked, certain that they hadn't called him in just to inform him of Callahan's passing.

"We want to bring you up to speed," explained Sir Justin. "House Lansius requires . . . delicate hands."

"Lord Lansius may be strong for his size, but his health isn't as robust as we'd like," Hugo added. "There have been instances where he fell ill for weeks following a battle, even without sustaining any injuries."

Sir Harold seemed unfazed. "Well, he has his strengths and weaknesses. Do you have any plan about it?"

"The idea is to keep the lord well-rested," replied Hugo. "We want him to stay in the Eastern Mansion. Hopefully, he can recover without worrying too much about the aftermath."

Harold rubbed his chin in understanding. It was a good suggestion. Right now, the castle was akin to a large hospice, with the injured and dying weeping, groaning, and even wailing until they either got well or died.

The same sad scene happened in other makeshift hospices throughout Korelia. Despite the concerted efforts of the town's physicians, castle staff, and volunteers, many wouldn't see the light of day again.

"I'm all ears," Sir Harold said in a clear tone, indicating his readiness.

Sir Justin smiled. "Since the lord trusts you in command, I think he'll be comfortable if you and your most trusted men bolster the Eastern Mansion's security. While they have fences, it's not a castle."

"I can do that. I'll arrange a garrison and patrols."

"Then, I'll put Lord Lansius in your care," Sir Justin said conclusively. "Now, with that out of the way. Care to tell us how the war unfolded on the cavalry side?"

The tall knight perked up. "Of course. Where should I begin?"

"Well, if this is Korelia . . ." Sir Justin pointed at the rectangular belt buckle first and then to the silver medallion. "And this is the western lords' encampment . . ."

For the next half hour, Korelia's military commanders discussed the day's battle, examining Lord Lansius's strategy and contrasting it with their own approaches. Although Lord Lansius had discussed the plan at length with Sir Justin—indeed, the marshal had even finalized many parts of it— he was not aware of the variations the lord had ultimately chosen.

Battle tactics weren't fixed; they evolved depending on the circumstances. There were several contingencies, including one where Sir Justin's column would need to leave town and assist with the fire strategy. However, Lord Lansius ultimately deemed this unnecessary.

This decision didn't come as a surprise. What did come as a surprise was his decision not to employ the nomadic cavalry in the main battle. There had been multiple opportunities to include them, but in the end, Lord Lansius used them only for the cleanup operation.

* * *

"Did the battle proceed so smoothly that the lord didn't even feel compelled to use his reserve?" Sir Justin queried as he returned the cavalry piece to its original spot on the table, concluding their simulation of the battle.

"It's as if he hesitated to call them," Hugo suspected.

In contemplative silence, the marshal took a sip of water and reclined in his sturdy wooden chair, groaning slightly from his injured hip. It was easy for anyone to see that he would need bed rest by tomorrow. "The audacity to envision victory without the aid of Batu's tribesmen is remarkable," he commented wearily.

Sir Harold massaged the back of his neck. He knew the answer, but couldn't reveal it. "The lord may not want the nomads to get too much attention," he finally said, careful to keep his statement vague enough to not breach his oath.

Hugo furrowed his brow. "The lord said that?"

"Something to that effect, yes. He didn't want to show the nomadic tribes as potential mercenaries," Sir Harold confirmed.

Sir Justin's expression brightened. "True . . . Why didn't I think of that? If I were still in the mercenary business, after that training last spring, I'd consider recruiting some of them."

Hugo could only grin. The thought that the lord had also fooled the two knights satisfied him.

Sir Justin pondered hard. "It's wise to hide them, but don't you think we could win the battle more easily by employing them?"

"Let's simulate another one," Hugo suggested, as he reset the pieces on the table.

"How about, after we've drawn out the column, the nomads simply attack the encampment with fire?" Sir Justin proposed, moving a gold ring with a black gemstone.

Harold looked at the silver medallion on the table and quickly pointed out, "The scouts reported that the encampment was fortified with a ring of carts and had only two well-guarded exits. Even when they marched out onto the plains, they likely still had enough men for a garrison."

Sir Justin mulled over it. "Given their numbers and ferocity, I think they could cause havoc . . ."

"Well, if they use fire, it would certainly cause some damage, but would it be significant? The cavalry of the western lords is nearby." Harold picked up a gold ring and placed it near the silver medallion. "The Black Knights and the Nicopolans. Once they react, the nomads' attack would amount to nothing."

The marshal crossed his arms. "I guess it would alert them of our use of fire . . . our only ace."

Harold furrowed his brow. "Pardon my language, but I think that's the problem with a halfhearted attack like this. The nomads would cause damage, but they wouldn't deliver a knockout blow. Worse, they would also reveal our hand."

The other two refrained from commenting, allowing Harold to continue.

"I believe the lord made the right call by drawing the cavalry into an ambush. After that, he didn't need a large number of nomads. Even our small light cavalry could do it," he asserted.

Hugo nodded deeply, suggesting, "Perhaps, we're too focused on attacking the encampment."

"Indeed. After Lord Jorge was gone with the cavalry, the northern column was routed, and the fire started to burn. Without even setting the encampment alight, the western men would be forced to flee."

Sir Justin said nothing, allowing Hugo to ask, "Sir, what about the fire tactics? If it's a secret, then why did the lord instruct us to use fire grenades?"

Sir Harold was equally piqued and eyed Sir Justin, whose expression suggested he was amused by the question.

"Well, it's because it would fail," the marshal, more familiar with the original battle plan, revealed. "The grass around the battleground and castle hill is shorter than on the plains. After all, we use it for training, horse grazing, and marching. A fire wouldn't spread there."

"To use, but expect it to fail. Is there a particular reason for this?" asked Sir Harold.

The marshal shrugged. "The lord only said that it would create a false sense of security. He feared Lord Omin might read that far, so he wanted to lure him into thinking he's safe from fire tactics."

The two nodded despite not fully grasping the idea.

Amid the silence, Hugo tried his best to think of something to prove that he still held a candle against the lord, but he came up empty. "So, this is the only tactic to win? We don't have any other solutions?"

Sir Justin exhaled deeply. "Someone in the past era did this kind of thing, digging trenches, and burning the field. But I always thought it was just a story. Most of the time, it's simply unreasonable or even impossible to do such a thing."

"Indeed . . ." Sir Harold looked at the chandelier and said, "I imagine burning the whole western plains requires a lot of preparation. Since when has the lord been planning for this?"

The marshal shook his head but wore a sly smile. "I didn't ask, but I knew he forbade anyone—even the tribesmen—from grazing the western plains since early spring."

"The wind." Hugo realized something. "Before winter, the lord asked for things like weather reports. He even met with several old people. I thought it was just his hobby or something."

Sir Harold grinned and drew a deep breath. "So he learned about the summer wind and planned all this? To think anyone was thinking that far ahead of time."

Sir Justin chuckled happily. "This is why I'm following him. Besides making a profit, I'm curious just how high he can climb. He's the most interesting fellow I have encountered in my life."

He drank his cup of water and added, "Now, this is a good time to ask, are you guys with me, or do you have another plan?"

The tall knight chuckled and without hesitation said, "I'm thinking of leaving after the war. Korelia is too far out. Surprisingly big population, but the town has little to offer."

There was silence after the knight's revelation until Hugo cleared his throat. "You might want to reconsider. The lord . . . has quite an ambition. I doubt he'll stay in Korelia."

His words piqued the interest of the two knights. Sir Justin stared and remarked, "Interesting. He never revealed as much."

"When Lord Arte made Lord Lansius his squire . . . the young lord questioned Lansius so hard that he revealed a different side of himself." Hugo suddenly felt a thirst for wine, so he poured a little into his cup of water and drank it down.

"What kind of a man is he?" Sir Harold asked while readily helping Hugo with another pour of wine.

A squire like Hugo couldn't refuse a knight, so he gratefully took the offer. "Lord Lansius, he cunningly fooled everyone . . . I was a fool to try to take his contribution after a battle. I was talking big, trying to boost my importance in battle and get Lord Arte to bestow a title upon me, and then he appeared like a hero, bearing grand gifts."

"What kind of gifts?" Sir Justin asked with a heartfelt chuckle, surprised at his deputy's honesty.

"Tens of highly educated freed slaves. Freed slaves! They even volunteered," Hugo exclaimed, complaining about the absurdity of it.

The ludicrousness of the story made the two knights burst into laughter. Even Hugo couldn't resist a dry chuckle and added, "I was there with just bruises and honeyed words, and he appeared with gifts fit for a king."

"But how?" Sir Harold asked with tears in his eyes. The sharp and stern line on his face melted away.

Hugo shook his head and groaned, "To this day, I have no idea how he did that. Why the slaves didn't just bolt home after being freed remains a mystery."

"Drink up," said Sir Justin, but Hugo shook his head with a sheepish smile. "I volunteered for the night watch, sir."

Sir Harold patted Hugo on the back. "Drink! The lord did you dirty. I'll do the night watch for you. You should have some merriment."

Hugo sheepishly accepted the offer and drank some more. This was the first time he had revealed his greatest shame to anyone else, and apparently, nobody judged him harshly.

The night watch ended peacefully without incident, and a bright new day dawned in Korelia. Dew and morning air erased yesterday's scent of smoke. The siege had ended in a day, an unprecedented event that everyone saw as nothing short of a miracle.

Despite the activity in the hospice and the graveyard, the mood in town was uplifting. The Lord of Korelia had prevailed against an army of six thousand men in just a single day. Such an achievement was beyond anyone's dreams.

Naturally, everywhere in town, over meals or drinks, people, militia, and men-at-arms praised their lord, embellishing their deeds and elevating Korelia's victory to greater heights. The heroic fights, the cavalry charge, the ambush, the burning plains, and even rumors about the saint candidate's involvement all contributed to the fervor.

Rumors of the lord's impending marriage only added to the excitement. The town was alive with anticipation, yet the victory celebration was yet to be held, due to the ongoing risk of another battle.

Even now, the cavalry was preparing for another sortie to guard against regrouping. Before they could sortie, however, a group of twelve riders, accompanied by a band of men, marched toward Korelia Castle, crossing the scorched western plains.

The uninvited group bore a white flag but moved with composure. A woman in a white traveling cloak led them, her stature upright and her gaze steady, hinting at her uncanny confidence.

As the castle loomed large in front of them, she dispatched one of her riders as a herald to inform the castle of their intentions.

CHAPTER 28

PUNITIVE STRIKE

Many things happened in Korelia after the war. Tending to the wounded was a top priority, followed by burial and mourning. On behalf of the lord, his retinue had dedicated several places as hospices in town to treat the wounded. Meanwhile, the castle staff was busy moving necessary goods, furniture, and themselves to the Eastern Mansion.

The reason was more than just to follow their lord around. It was because the castle's halls were being used for intensive care. The atmosphere was chaotic and gruesome, filled with echoes of painful cries, random screams, and sobs. Even with the help of Calub's stock of painkillers, there wasn't enough for everyone.

Thus, the lord took the younger staff with him to the Eastern Mansion. However, since the move was abrupt and unplanned, the mansion was still being cleaned and furnished. They occupied a different section from the one used by Sir Justin and Hugo, who had established their headquarters in the Billet complex to keep a close eye on the captured men and prevent any issues.

Following yesterday's battle, Three Hills and Korelia agreed to mend relations. Thus, they were technically at peace. The war had ended.

Despite the grand scale of the fire tactics that scorched the western plains, casualties were surprisingly limited. Those who died from the fire were already wounded from the battle or had been injured during the chaotic retreat.

The low casualties were by design. The Lord of Korelia's strategy was to incite panic and rout, not fire entrapment.

From the start, the main goal was to capture or destroy the encampment, particularly its supplies and baggage train. No army could survive without them and would be forced to accept a truce.

As luck would have it, most of the high-ranking members of the Three Hills survived the battle. Many of their nobles and famed Black Knights were captured alive. This favorable outcome undoubtedly paved the way for the two Houses to steadily improve relations.

In the midst of this, the arrival of Nicopolan mercenaries presented an unforeseen political twist.

Lansius

Sigmund stood in the hall of the Eastern Mansion, the sun still shining softly as he finished his report. "They wish to present you three Korimor knights, five South Hill knights, and six squires, as a token of goodwill."

Not surrendering but pledging allegiance?

Lansius contemplated while massaging his left arm. His fractured wrist was wrapped up in a wooden splint.

Thirty Nicopolan mercenaries and fifteen horses, small but not insignificant.

While he could attack these Nicopolan and take their horses, chances were, he could make better use of them. After all, information and knowledge were paramount.

And information from those who submitted tended to be more reliable, and since they were mercenaries, if Lansius captured them, nobody would pay their ransom.

Sitting at Lansius's side, Audrey calmly watched her future partner pondering the matter. Only when he snapped out of it did she comment, "If they intend to switch sides, there shouldn't be a problem."

Lansius felt slightly at ease with her words. He had no qualms about former opponents joining him; in fact, *The Art of War* suggested: *To capture the enemy's entire army is better than to destroy it; to take intact a regiment, a company, or a squad is better than to destroy them.*

Thankfully, it seemed that even in this world, switching sides after a war wasn't a big deal. "We need to be certain . . . Let's entice them with supplies and the promise of freedom so we can gauge their reaction. After all, they've already given us the knights and squires," Lansius remarked.

Sir Harold, sitting at the next table, chuckled upon hearing that. "Enticing mercenaries with supplies, I'd love to see that," he said, shaking his head in amusement.

Lansius grinned at his knight's comment. "It might be pointless, but I need to know just how much loyalty I can expect from them."

"The loyalty of the Nicopolan free company is to their profit," Sir Harold commented.

"Profit is something tangible and easy to measure. I can live with that. I doubt anyone here would stay if I couldn't pay for your upkeep."

Harold chuckled again. "It hurts my pride a little, but I guess that's the truth. But, my lord, don't lump me in with those Nicopolans."

"My apologies, I didn't mean that," said Lansius without hesitation.

Grinning at the lord's sincere reaction, the knight rose and bowed his head slightly. "Please, my lord, it's just me and my mouth. You don't have to."

Audrey just smiled, enjoying their banter.

Lansius knew Audrey's thoughts on Sir Harold. To her, Harold was a welcome addition to House Lansius, although she wasn't sure if he was going to stay.

Harold's knightly values were clear: to perfect his swordsmanship through training and battles. As such, he traveled from one conflict to another, seeking lords worthy of his service.

Audrey turned her attention to Sigmund, who had become an aide, as there were many still recovering from the battle. Audrey asked, "Sigmund, would that be all?"

Sigmund readily replied, "My lord, the deputy wanted to know whether to let them all in, which he suggested not to, or to just invite a few."

"Mm, the arrangement," Lansius murmured. Letting them all in would certainly pose an unnecessary risk. "Allow her in with an escort. The rest can camp outside the wall. Give them some of our spare tents."

"Arrange for some guards," suggested Audrey to Lansius. "I recommend Carla. She had little role in the previous battle."

Lansius nodded. He knew Carla had guarded Felicity and thus had not been credited much. "Yes, let's task her."

"Anything else?" Audrey asked Sigmund.

"Just one more thing, my lord: When do you plan to meet her?"

Audrey looked at Lansius, who decided, "Soon, but not today . . . What's her name again?"

"Lady Daniella. The herald informed me that the lady is the daughter of a nobleman in Nicopola."

Lansius rubbed his chin. "A nobleman's daughter turned mercenary?"

"There was a ballad written about a fierce woman mercenary," Sigmund said, almost too happy to answer.

Lansius was amused. "Can you play that ballad at supper time?" he asked while glancing at his future wife.

"Only if it ends well," she warned as their eyes met.

Sigmund smiled and bowed his head. "Most certainly, my lord and my lady," he said and departed from the hall to relay the messages to the marshal and deputy.

The hall returned to a temporary silence as they waited for lunch. Unlike during a campaign, members of the nobility typically only dined twice—at lunch and supper. They would have a little breakfast in their room, usually something left over from yesterday's meal.

Thus, during court sessions, an assortment of white bread, meat, and cheese was served on small platters, accompanied by a selection of fruits and beverages. Contrasting with the great hall, the mansion's hall was bathed in warm sunlight streaming in through its numerous windows, creating an enjoyable ambiance.

"What do you think about this Lady Daniella?" Lansius asked his knight while in between bites of a salty slice of meat with bread, Korelia's specialty.

Sir Harold took his drink before replying, "Well, she might have been a bastard, disowned, or disinherited. It happens all the time. Also, the Nicopolans have a tendency to try and live like nobles by forming so-called *free companies*."

Lansius recalled the opulent manor of Sabina Rustica. His thoughts then returned to the issue at hand—whether to accept or reject the Nicopolan allegiance. Eager to discuss this matter with his most trusted advisors, he asked, "Have Calub and his men returned?"

"They should be here around midday since they need to finish a patrol and pack up the yurts," answered Harold.

"Let me know when they arrive. I need to talk to him and Sir Callahan about this."

Without missing a beat, Sir Harold answered, "Certainly, my lord."

They were still keeping the news of Sir Callahan's death from Lansius. This was also why Cecile, Sir Callahan's oldest daughter, was missing from the lord's side. Fortunately, the lord didn't question her absence, as they were preoccupied with moving from the castle.

"My lord, you wanted to ask about Lord Jorge," Audrey reminded Lansius.

"Ah, that's right. Sir Harold, have you met with Lord Jorge's liaison officer?"

"Yes, I have. I assure you that he's pleased we provided enough supplies for them to camp out. He also expressed gratitude for returning some of their belongings."

"What belongings?" inquired Audrey.

"Nothing significant. Just blankets and spare clothes. I think we can treat them with that much for the sake of diplomacy," explained Lansius.

"I see . . . Well, it's good to know that the carts I captured are truly useful." Her voice was laced with sarcasm.

Lansius stifled a laugh. "A blessing in disguise," he muttered.

Audrey pouted slightly. "Yet you still cut my pay."

Lansius looked at her and gently said, "Rules are rules. Please don't do that again."

She sighed and smiled naughtily. "Only two carts for your dowry then."

"Eh, but I gave you three?" he argued.

"One is for my savings."

Lansius chuckled and applauded her. "That's smart. Good for you."

"Two baggage carts to marry a baron." Sir Harold chuckled. "The skald is going to write a ballad about this."

"Technically, I'm not yet a baron," Lansius quipped, and then to Audrey, he joked, "Please say three and that they were full of silver. Otherwise, you'll ruin my reputation."

However, Audrey was taking it seriously. "I told you, being a concubine is better. That way, I don't have to pay a dowry."

Sir Harold snorted, trying hard not to laugh. Their conversation was light, and the hall remained calm and serene. Beyond their banter, the only other sounds were the gentle wind and the chirping of birds from the garden outside. Slowly, the heavy memories of yesterday's battle were fading from their minds.

Lunch was served without much fanfare, as House Lansius's retinues were preoccupied with managing the aftermath of the war. Only Lord Lansius, Audrey, Sir Justin, Margo, and a small team of young staff and servants were present.

The affair felt intimate, almost private. Neither Felicity nor Hannei were present, both busy with their own business.

As they brought their own cook, the food tasted the same. The atmosphere remained pleasant, almost a bit dull, with only some light banter and discussion. After lunch was over, Dietrich, a cavalryman pressed into a temporary aide, entered.

His presence in the hall immediately sparked tension. The lord gestured for him to approach, and he stepped forward, reporting, "My lord, Batu's tribesman has arrived with a report."

"Bring him in." Lansius straightened his back in anticipation.

The tribesman, clad in looted armor, jogged to the scene. He admired the hall but quickly reported with a wide smile. "O Great Noyan. Overnight, we've caught over a thousand men! Right now we're sending them back to Korelia as you ordered."

Noyan?

The new title made Lansius chuckle albeit nervously. "I'm pleased with the result. But tell me, since when am I a Noyan?"

The tribesman flashed his teeth and answered with raw excitement, "My Noyan, you commanded at least several thousand people, including us. To us, you are our Noyan."

Lansius was elated. More than just an empty title, it was also a bond of honor and loyalty.

Complete victory . . .

He pondered for a moment before a realization dawned on him. Lansius saw an opportunity to advance his plans. In truth, the war wasn't over for him, and he couldn't help but consider the possibilities.

Meanwhile, Audrey drew the attention of Sir Harold.

The knight, ever perceptive, cleared his throat. "Pardon me, but what's a Noyan?"

"The leader of ten thousand people, our protector, our chief, our lord," the tribesman proudly announced.

Lansius could only shake his head at the title, while Audrey was smiling proudly.

Taking the opportunity while there was a lull, Sir Harold asked, "Is the hunt continuing?"

"Of course. There are still many stragglers to capture. But . . . what do you wish to do to them?" the tribesman asked curiously.

Sir Harold looked at Lansius eagerly.

He, too, probably wished to know. To him, aside from the nobles who could be ransomed, the rest probably just seemed like extra mouths to feed.

"Free labor," Lansius mused. "They have to earn their freedom back. I'll have them work on my building project."

The messenger chuckled and bowed his head slightly while putting his hand upon his heart. "O Great Noyan, may you and Korelia always be prosperous under the Lowlandia skies."

Lansius bowed his head a little as a sign of respect.

Audrey chimed in, "Please join us later for dinner."

"My lady, leader Batu ordered me to return. He needs all his warriors to herd the captured men."

"Then I shall send you away with baskets of food and drink," said Lansius.

"That'll be most welcome. Then, my Noyan, I shall take my leave."

"A moment," said Lansius. "What about the northern corridor? How is the condition over there?"

The tribesman happily replied, "Thanks to your great victory over the Nicopolans, the tribes there can live in peace."

Lansius nodded. The question seemed out of curiosity for the tribesmen's well-being, but he had a different idea in mind.

Is it overreaching? But they should be weak, and the path is open . . .

"Have you ever been to Korimor?" Lansius asked. The innocent question didn't raise suspicion. Only Audrey seemed to gaze sharply.

"Yes, my Noyan. I've seen its castle wall and city."

"With so many of them attacking Korelia, how many do you think are manning the castle?"

Now, people started to pay attention. Something was brewing. Even the tribesman felt it. "Likely, no more than a hundred warriors."

"How many days on horse to Korimor using the northern corridor?"

"Fast horses, four days. With baggage, six days. Carts and carriages around sixteen to twenty days."

Lansius pondered deeply, recalculating the state of his troops, their remaining supplies, and what would be needed for a swift campaign to Korimor. He also couldn't neglect the defense and supplies of Korelia.

The grain trade is yet to happen . . . Is this logistically feasible?

Lansius was reluctant to accelerate his plans for Korimor, which he had slated for next summer. Yet, he understood that in war, opportunity was king. Whoever failed to seize it was doomed to fail.

Since Baron Omin had struck first, Lansius now had a pretext for war. Nothing prevented him from launching a counterattack, and it would be considered legitimate.

This wasn't about greed; it was about survival. Two castles, and two baronies—this would make Korelia more resilient.

The two baronies might be separated by distance, but there was little outside challenge since Three Hills was there to shield it. Korimor's closest neighbors were Three Hills and Orniteia, the barony brought down by Midlandia last year.

"Opportunities multiply as they are seized," Lansius murmured to himself, reaching a decision. He turned to Sir Harold and asked, "If we were to launch an expeditionary force to Korimor, who do you think should lead it?"

The lord's question confirmed everyone's thoughts. The knight replied without hesitation, "The marshal is bedridden. Then it should be the deputy."

Lansius needed to make sure. "You won't take command?"

"I can assist, but I'm not familiar with commanding large numbers of men." Despite his station, Sir Harold was sensible enough to respect the hierarchy of command.

"Very well then. Since opportunity arises . . ." Lansius addressed the room, "Change of plan! Invite Lady Daniella for supper. Dietrich, please inform Hugo that I wish to see him now. Tribesman, I would ask you to sit and wait a little. We may have a race on our hands."

"A race, my Noyan?" he asked excitedly.

"Yes, either brother Batu finds Lord Omin first, or Hugo wins the Barony of Korimor. Each would be an equally extraordinary prize."

CHAPTER 29

SOLIDUS

With lunch concluded, Sir Harold excused himself to attend to security matters. There were numerous concerns to be addressed, as the Eastern Mansion was only lightly defended. So, despite the newfound peace, he regularly sent out patrols and kept his men on the lookout.

It was rather hard to keep his men alert. Their motivation had waned as the war was largely over, but Sir Harold, with his tall, upright posture and sharp fighter attitude, managed to keep them at their best. Even without his dashing armor, he was full of confidence.

Today, his requests for help had been answered. The marshal had sent fifteen select crossbowmen from Korelia Castle to bolster the mansion's security. The sight of them marching past the mansion gate brought relief to the knight. Without wasting time, he immediately briefed the newcomers on their assignments.

As for Lansius, after lunch, the staff urged their lord to retreat to his room. With the main chamber still under renovation after several years of neglect, Lansius used one of the guest rooms. Audrey slept in a nearby guestroom, and they spent the day in the adjoining hall.

With Cecile busy at the castle, only Margo was available as their page.

"How's Sterling?" Lansius asked Margo. The boy was looking prettier, and it was hard to discern his gender without looking at his attire. He would be a good candidate for spying duties if Lansius ever needed one.

"He's recovering, my lord," replied the page boy.

"Has his fever come down?" asked Audrey from her seat that overlooked a large glass window.

"Last time I heard, he has awakened. Lady Hannei has visited him."

"Ah," said Lansius while nodding. While he could order Hannei to heal his wrist, there were many lives at stake, and he trusted Hannei to do the right thing. "Drey, do you mind if I go inside? I'm going to write something."

Audrey shifted her gaze from the scenery outside the window to meet Lansius's eyes. "Please don't let my presence bother you, my lord," she added at the end since Margo was present.

Lansius entered his room and welcomed the large open window that let in the breeze to fight against the summer heat. He sat at the recently cleaned chair and took a stack of parchment from the dark, lacquered desk.

He took a deep breath and pondered for a while. On average, an annual barony income was around 300 gold coins. A barony was considered rich if it could gain 400 gold coins from the land. However, for Korelia, Lansius could only gain around 200 gold coins each year from taxes and harvest share.

Not all was in coins; a good percentage was in goods like grains, salted meat, local textiles, and domestic horses.

Above the barony were the viscountcies. Lord Robert's income from the White Lake Viscountcy had previously been 800 gold coins annually. However, since he lost Korelia, his income now stood at 600 gold coins.

From that 600, Lansius took another 300 as capitulation. Thus, Robert ended up with only 300. While it looked a lot less, it was still a baron's level of income. That income allowed Robert to slowly nurse back his House's strength and continue to rule his domain.

The gentle breeze greeted Lansius as he prepared the ink and the quill pen. While he didn't have his scrolls and records, he had memorized many of its numbers. So, he jotted them down to refresh his mind.

First was Lord Robert's past capitulation that became House Lansius's current wealth.

Income	In Gold
Robert's Baggage Train	1,400
Capitulation, a share of accumulated Robert's Wealth	2,100
Ransom payments from Knights/Squire families	800
Confiscated, looted items from war	600
A share of White Lake's annual tax	300
Korelia annual tax	200
Horse trading scheme with Midlandia	50
Sir Justin's horse smuggling	50
Total in Gold	5,500

| Total in Silver (1 Gold is 20 Silver) | 110,000 |
| Total in Copper (1 Silver is 12 Copper) | 1,320,000 |

Lansius finished the first parchment detailing his House's income from the past year. He set it aside to dry and began listing the current expenses on a second parchment.

He calculated the expenses for the six months since he had come into power. The largest expense was for the trench work, which he paid for in salt. Each worker received the equivalent of 5 copper per day for work that lasted effectively 90 days.

The combined cost of the trench work and the salt scheme was more than twice the upkeep of his army. However, he saw this as an investment and aid relief.

The second largest expense was the cost to maintain his military of 400 men-at-arms and crossbowmen. The standard rate for men-at-arms on a campaign was about 4 copper daily, including meals, while cavalrymen cost around 8 copper daily.

The previous year, Lansius and Sir Justin negotiated a standby rate that also included free lodgings and armament leases. This rate was half of the original campaign rate: 2 copper daily for each man-at-arms, including meals, and 4 copper daily for cavalrymen.

Considering that even master smiths, carpenters, and artisans only earned 4 copper daily, this was already a good living wage.

Expenses (Half a Year, 190 days, Standby rate)	In Copper
400 men-at-arms and crossbowmen. 2 copper daily	152,000
70 cavalrymen. 4 copper daily	53,200
15 squires, captains, lieutenant. avg. 5 copper daily	14,200
200 crossbow trigger mechanism. 20 copper	4,000
50 Arbalest. 6 silver (72 copper each)	3,600
40 Half Lance Armor. 3 gold (720 copper each)	28,800
Workshop 20 maesters. 4 copper daily	15,200
Trench Work, Salt investment 1,000 men. 5 copper	450,000
Total in Copper (1 Silver is 12 Copper)	721,050

With 1,320,000 copper in the coffers and 720,000 in expenses, Lansius's current wealth was around 600,000 copper or slightly less than 2,500 gold coins.

While 2,500 gold might seem like a lot, Lansius and his treasurer, Calub, weren't comfortable. The truth was, a small barony like Korelia could hardly afford hundreds of troops for the typical 40-day campaign.

In fact, the reason most campaigns only lasted around 40 or 60 days was mainly due to the financial burden.

Feeling the need for comparison, Lansius started to write on another parchment.

Normal campaign rate	40 days (in Copper)
200 men-at-arms on campaign 4 copper daily	32,000
20 cavalry on campaign 8 copper daily	6,400
Total in Copper	38,400
Total in Gold	160

Just like his previous calculations stored in the castle cabinet, a poor barony like Korelia, with an annual income of only 200 gold coins, could only afford two hundred men with twenty cavalry for 40 days. The total cost would be around 160 gold coins, not including other costs but factoring in food.

The costly nature of war led the nobility to draw from the populace to bolster their ranks. Compulsory military service or levied troops were basically free, with the nobility only required to feed them during the campaign.

Because of how inexpensive these levied troops were, they could outnumber the men-at-arms in any army by three to five times. However, as Lansius knew firsthand, there were serious issues with using them against well-trained and motivated soldiers.

Still, the high cost of war didn't prevent the nobility from mustering large armies, especially in times of emergency or continuous wars. The nobles could simply refuse or delay cash payments.

As Calub had said, in reality, no nobles paid in full. The usual scheme was to offer land grants for farming, tax exemptions for several years, promises of employment as servants or guardsmen, special permits for trade, and so on. As long as the baron remained in power, he could offer special privileges in lieu of payment.

Lansius wasn't unfamiliar with such tactics. After all, Cecile had been hired when Sir Callahan switched loyalties from Lord Robert.

However, Lansius drew the line at paying his soldiers. He didn't want any discontent among the men he had painstakingly trained. Many would say he spoiled his troops, but there would be a time when things were hard and he would need to drive them hard.

Nothing had prepared Lansius for his role, but he had come to accept his responsibility.

Lansius looked at the numbers again and mulled them over. He wished that someday he could sustain his army without having to dip into his savings.

Piqued by this idea, he decided to calculate the cost of maintaining his current army for a full year.

Annual Expenses for Current Military (standby)	In Copper
400 men-at-arms and crossbowmen. 2 copper daily	304,000
70 cavalrymen. 4 copper daily	106,400
15 squires, captains, lieutenant. avg. 5 copper daily	28,500
Total in Copper (1 Silver is 12 Copper)	438,900
Total in Gold	1,829

Lansius calculated that the military expenses for his current posture exceeded 1,800 gold coins annually.

This was before other costs like servants, guardsmen, cooks, gifts for guests, additional purchases, guild projects, etc. Meanwhile, Korelia's income was only 200 gold coins.

Seeing the absurd numbers, Lansius chuckled. He realized that he and Calub were rather mad to let this happen, but last year, they had only one shot at survival.

Driven by curiosity and a desire for a complete picture, Lansius carefully sharpened the quill pen and dipped it into the thick ink before writing down his House's annual income.

Annual Income	In Gold
A share of White Lake's annual tax	300
Korelia annual tax	200
Horse trading scheme with Midlandia	50
Sir Justin's horse smuggling	50
Total in Gold	600

Upon finishing, he compared the last two parchments and saw an income of 600 gold coins and expenses of 1,800 gold coins. He was clearly in the red.

And not just slightly—House Lansius's expenses were three times its current income.

Lansius sighed deeply, leaning back in his chair and looking up at the ceiling. His left shoulder felt a bit sore from the arm sling, so he rested his left wrist on the table.

With his shoulders relaxed, Lansius mulled over his idea of a standing army. The cost alone of maintaining a professional army year-round was ridiculously high. This was the reason such an arrangement did not become common in the medieval era—most feudal lords would simply disband their armies when they were no longer needed.

Even with his recent massive victory, Lansius was under no illusions about his future income. Though he could secure similar schemes with Three Hills and Korimor, he doubted he could maintain his current army solely from income.

But he understood that to limit his growth for financial reasons alone would be utterly foolish. He wasn't a clerk trying to do a profitable business; he was a warlord trying to fight his way out of the turmoil of the era.

Only might, backed by sound logistics, is what truly matters . . .

With the upcoming war in Arvena and the Imperium on the brink of collapse, things would turn a lot worse for decades before ever changing up for the better.

In the face of that, aside from food security, investing in troops and their loyalty seemed to be the correct choice.

This was where the ransom money and looted items played a role. They could amount to thousands and easily fill his coffers with gold and silver. Thus, House Lansius was still in a relatively good position for several years.

The issue was his Korelia building project.

Lansius wished to transform Korelia into a thriving city. He and Calub had read the records last winter and conducted experiments on the land. From what they gathered, the underdeveloped east side of Korelia held the potential for agricultural development.

Situated next to a river, the site was ideally suited for irrigation. Moreover, the area was prone to annual flooding in the spring following the harsh winter. The only issue was the lack of natural wind barriers. The steppe winds were fierce and strong, resulting in substantial water loss and significant temperature fluctuations between day and night.

They had observed firsthand that plants could initially thrive, but they would eventually wither and die due to the extreme wind conditions.

Therefore, quite ironically, what Korelia needed were walls and windbreak trees—not for defense, but for food production.

With one thousand forced workers at his disposal, Lansius planned to restart the stone quarry. This wall project would be costly, but it could provide Korelia with a permanent defensive structure and, potentially, swathes of fertile land.

Perhaps he could even use a section of the wall to construct a large tower as a new living space, as Korelia Castle was too limited.

Maybe even a windmill and watermill . . .

He reflected on history. The reason kings built castles was not merely for indulgence, but also to attract people from all social classes. The newcomers would sell their merchandise and offer their services to the workers, artisans, and smiths who labored there, as well as the growing noble class that moved to reside within the castle's vicinity.

Shops and stalls would spring up, offering food, clothing, and medicine. Drinking establishments, taverns, barber shops, tailors, bathhouses, theaters, entertainment venues, and various workshops would also emerge to meet the demands of the city.

Over time, these transient merchants and artisans would settle and become part of the city's population. Thus, what began as a castle-building project would transform into a thriving, bustling society.

Lansius wanted to emulate this tried-and-true method. He would likely have the funds after Lord Jorge's capitulation, but he needed to be prudent to avoid squandering it.

To feed and house another thousand men . . .

Regardless of whether they were forced workers, Lansius had to meet their basic needs. Grain would be an issue, and he considered exclusively buying wheat from Lord Robert and the Eastern Merchants for another year or two.

His trade balance might look ugly at first, but his pashmina shawl project would likely be profitable once the guild had supplied Korelia with spinning wheels. Additionally, as Noyan, Lansius could expect a share of horses each year, which would boost his horse-trading scheme.

Immersed in his work, Lansius delved into various calculations to ensure he wasn't overlooking any factors. Planning and data sheets brought reminders of his past life—how to plan ahead, make preparations, and devise contingency plans. Only now the stakes were the lives of so many.

Lansius stopped writing and put aside his quill pen. He was tired. Even after his victory, he still had a lot on his mind. First and foremost, he couldn't resist thinking about his decision to punish Korimor.

On one side, with Omin in prison, his military knowledge urged him to seize this golden opportunity for expansion. After surviving two major battles, soft-hearted as he was, even Lansius had become desensitized. However, the notion of attacking and conquering other people still brought him a moral dilemma.

"What a lame warlord I'll make," Lansius mused, finding irony in his predicament.

Of all the battles he had fought, none were driven by ambition, but rather a desire to save as many lives as possible. He recalled Lord Bengrieve's words describing him as "a selfless guardian."

Probably just a polite way of calling me a useless pacifist.

With a chuckle, he closed his eyes momentarily, only for another concern to surface.

Marriage . . .

He was about to marry Audrey. In itself, marriage wasn't concerning. However, for Lansius, it was more than just building a family. It would ultimately decide his fate, anchoring him permanently as one of the Lords of Lowlandia. This went against his wish for a simpler life, far from the burdens of leadership.

Despite his newfound status, Lansius still dreamed of sun-drenched meadows, the smell of baked bread in a village hearth, and the quiet joy of tending a humble garden. He yearned for an easy and carefree life, bloodless, and as normal as can be.

Ahh . . . to just sleep all day with books to read and hot food to eat.

If not for his strong sense of duty to those around him, Lansius might have packed his gear and left. Naturally, the responsibility for so many lives was not something one could easily become accustomed to. Thus, he questioned himself, striving to find some peace. After mulling it over for a while, he realized his thoughts were just running in circles. His indecision about attacking, his reluctance to accept responsibility, all boiled down to one single question. *Is everyone important to me?*

Like it or not, everyone was tied to him. In his quest to save them, they had become a part of his House. Audrey, in particular, became the embodiment of them all.

After this realization, his decision became clear. He couldn't bear to see her suffer anymore, and for that, he needed power and authority.

Korelia, Eastern Mansion

It was close to midday when the deputy arrived at the Eastern Mansion. He was hurried to the upper chamber where Lord Lansius and Sir Harold were standing, looking over an unfurled map of the province on the table. "My lord, you wish to see me?"

"Hugo, what do you know about Korimor Castle and the northern corridor?" asked Lansius as he gestured for him to come nearer.

Hugo looked surprised upon hearing it. "Korimor Castle? I heard its main keep and towers are bigger than Korelia," he replied while approaching the table.

"And the northern corridor?" reminded Sir Harold.

The deputy mulled for a moment, ignoring the hairs that stood on end on his arms. "It's a direct path to Korimor and even Midlandia, but it's easy to get lost there. Water is also scarce, and there are some rumors of banditry in the area."

"The banditry is by the Nicopolan raiders, the same ones we beat in the forest," Lansius explained. "Also, the nomad tribesmen know the route with fresh water even in summer."

"My lord, do you wish to attack Korimor?" Hugo asked, and Lansius could see the doubt written on his face.

Lansius remained stoic as he glanced at Hugo and spoke. "A good warlord expands."

The lord's words made Hugo swallow. His eyes couldn't hold a gaze against Lansius. Meanwhile, Sir Harold seemed to entertain the idea easily, as if it had occurred to him previously.

Lansius continued. "I'm neither a warmonger nor an opportunist by nature. Yet, I carry the weight of ten thousand souls on my shoulders . . . Hugo, we need every bit of leverage we can find. Because, at the end of the day, it's just us. So, are you with me?"

CHAPTER 30

ONE-EYED KNIGHT

Lord Lansius had made his intention clear to counterattack and seize Korimor, causing cold sweat to form on Hugo's back.

"My lord, I'm with you. Retaliating is only natural, but is this even possible in our current state?" asked the deputy.

Lansius looked him in the eye and asked, "Do you think we can't make it?"

"We don't even have two hundred men to spare. That's hardly enough for a siege." Hugo recalled the report on the troops they had left.

Out of four hundred core troops, one hundred and fifty were either dead, wounded, or too shaken to fight. To maintain order and keep hostages in Korelia, they needed at least another one hundred and fifty men. This meant there were only one hundred left for the campaign to take Korimor.

"Go on, let us know your full thoughts about this." Lansius encouraged his deputy to speak.

Hugo took a deep breath to calm himself down. "With fewer than two hundred, I even doubt that I could take even a small castle like Korelia. Korimor has better defenses. It survived siege attempts multiple times . . . Maybe if it's only a raid."

Ignoring his suggestion, Lansius asked, "So, you agreed that this is impossible?"

The lord's reaction gave Hugo pause; he mulled for a while before declaring, "Yes, it's impossible with just a small force."

Lord Lansius straightened his posture and gazed at Sir Harold, who simply nodded and said, "I've never heard of someone bringing fewer than three hundred men to siege a castle and winning."

"The rule is to bring three to five times the size of the garrison," added Hugo.

Lansius gave another look at the provincial map on the table. Its yellowing surface and fading ink couldn't hide its artful nature; however, it held little credible information. Just the general placements and borders of baronies, viscountcies—some even outdated.

"I've sent Audrey to meet with the surrendering Nicopolans. We'll have the defender numbers soon."

Hugo was surprised that Lansius was adamant about besieging Korimor. "My lord, even if they only have the smallest number of defenders, say a hundred, we need at least five hundred."

"Oh, we can't do that," Lansius dismissed. "We don't have the food to support five hundred in a siege."

The mention of food led Hugo to a conclusion. "You want to starve Korimor out?"

Lansius shook his head. "No, we likely have less food than them."

Hugo chuckled. None of this made sense. "Then, my lord, how do you plan to win?"

Lansius smiled. "I still have the nomad tribes' assistance."

"But they're still hunting for the remnants, and at most, they probably can provide only fifty horsemen."

"We also have reinforcements from Lord Robert," replied Lansius lightly.

Hugo was stunned. "Repurposing a relief force to a siege? Would they even consent to that?"

"Well, if they don't want to, then we'll make do with what we've got," the lord said with a shrug.

Hugo furrowed his brow. He knew Lansius had a plan, but he couldn't even guess a glimpse of it, which bothered him greatly. "Then, my lord, please enlighten me if you wish for me to lead the siege."

Lansius seemed amused. "Besieging a castle isn't all about the number of men and how much food you have."

His words sent Hugo and Sir Harold into deep thought.

Lansius continued. "We have the element of surprise. No one expects us in Korimor. We likely only need to be intimidating."

"Intimidating?" Hugo mulled over the words.

"Indeed. We don't need to assault the castle. We just need to appear large enough to intimidate," Lansius explained.

The lord's brief and enigmatic words hardly instilled confidence, but Hugo realized that was intentional. Lord Lansius had always acknowledged there was no guarantee that his plan was the best. Thus, he encouraged his retainers to think critically, that they might come up with a better strategy or pinpoint a weakness in his own.

The sound of hurried footsteps echoed from the stairs, and Margo, the page boy, entered. "My lord, I beg your pardon, but the guards report seeing cavalry to the east."

"Ha!" exclaimed Sir Harold, who then bolted toward the stairs.

"They're late," remarked Lansius, exhaling in relief.

White Lake Viscountcy

Lord Robert remembered how he used to watch a page boy named Michael with keen interest. Not having a son of his own, the Viscount grew fond of his cunning intellect and diligent attitude. This view was also shared by most of the White Lake nobility, who were charmed by the boy's perseverance, intellectual prowess, and his family's enviable standing. As he grew into a squire and then a knight, Michael continued to win the hearts of many influential men and women. However, his once-stellar reputation was no more.

Last year, as the marshal, he lost the war against Lansius's much smaller force. In the aftermath, he was captured and lost an eye. Despite having Lord Robert on his side, that alone couldn't save him from the wrath of the other members of the court.

Many noble families had lost their husbands, sons, or other relatives in the war. They blamed Michael, and Lord Robert was powerless to intervene at that time. Consequently, the ex-marshal was removed from the court and disgraced.

As such, the promise of betrothal to Robert's daughter was also called off. Many thought that was the end of him.

Since then, a year had passed.

While Lord Robert's influence and power had waned after losing the war, his House was still influential with a functioning administration. Lansius's generous capitulation terms allowed Robert to hold on to his seat of power.

The White Lake region had a yearly income of around 800 gold coins. As agreed upon his capitulation, Robert had agreed to send the requested goods and silver, equivalent to 500 gold coins, to Lansius.

That agreement still left him with a good 300 gold coins income, more than enough to live comfortably as a regional power. Moreover, of the 500 gold coins Lansius spent, Robert would recoup a sum from taxes and economic growth in his region. Thus, it wasn't hard for him to nurse his forces back.

Nearing the height of summer, a messenger arrived in White Lake, bearing news of impending war in Korelia.

As anyone could have guessed, Lansius's ascent as the Lord of Korelia didn't sit well with the nobles. It only worsened the delicate balance of power in Lowlandia.

Behind closed doors, many were arguing not to send help. If Korelia were defeated, then White Lake could break free. However, Lord Robert wasn't going to make the same mistake.

Many underestimated the Lord of Korelia simply because he didn't exude the confidence of a strong noble. Lansius's manner of speech and behavior showed little indication that he possessed the qualities of a leader. Yet, all of that didn't matter.

Robert had long understood that power came in many forms, and not every successful warlord was a charismatic leader. In fact, one of the most charismatic men in Lowlandia was Lord Jorge, who was the biggest fool in the region.

People who judged a man based solely on his physique and looks were due for a harsh reality check with Lansius. Although Robert wouldn't speak of this to anyone, Lansius reminded him of his younger self.

Despite all their failings as noblemen, both Robert and Lansius were skilled war commanders. In conflict-prone Lowlandia, that one skill alone was a desirable trait for a leader. That was why Lord Robert stubbornly prepared his men as reinforcements.

This time he chose to trust his gut and mustered two hundred men and forty cavalry, a respected force for a relief mission.

What was hard to find was a leader for the force. Almost no one would take the role. They all feared that Korelia would certainly be lost, and they would be implicated for leading a relief force.

While this might have looked like a setback, in reality, all of this played into Lord Robert's hands.

One-eyed Michael

Today, Michael met Astrid to say farewell. Their betrothal was no more, but Lord Robert allowed the meeting to take place. They met in a private garden to avoid prying eyes. Except for the usual lady-in-waiting and the old swordsman in the far corner, there was nobody else.

"Michael, what happened to your eye? Are you still in pain?"

Astrid rushed to her ex-fiancé as soon as she saw him entering the garden. His left eye was bandaged and covered with an eyepatch.

Standing there with a smile, Michael watched as the lithe figure approached, her graceful form draped in a flowing blue silken robe adorned with stylish silver embroidery. He replied, "It's alright, my lady. I lost an eye, but I gained a much more valuable experience."

"But . . . your eye, I should get someone to look after you!" she said anxiously.

"There's no need to bother, my lady," he reassured her. "Your humble knight just wanted to say goodbye."

Astrid cast her eyes downward. "Michael, I wish things could have ended differently for us."

"It was nobody's fault but mine. I blame nobody for my misfortune," he said lightly without burden. He had learned to accept his defeat. Gone was his bloated sense of entitlement.

For a time, there was nothing said between them. Michael looked longingly at Astrid. At a glance, she was a fair maiden with beautiful, long hazelnut hair, but her beauty couldn't hide the intellect that shone from her curious and proud eyes. It was this very thing that made Michael fall for her, but unfortunately, this was probably the last time he would see her.

"I heard you are leading the relief force . . . It's a long journey to Korelia. Can I get you anything, medicine or a fur coat?" she offered.

Michael thought about the offer and couldn't help but say what he truly wanted. "My lady, if I could regain my honor, would you still accept my hand?"

Astrid blushed at hearing that so unexpectedly. She glanced elsewhere to regain her composure.

The garden was lackluster this summer, the hyacinths and daffodils having already bloomed in spring. But there was a small row in the corner where a type of flower dared to defy the rest. The purplish-pink cyclamen flower was blooming boldly in the summer as if to give her encouragement.

"Sir Michael, don't take too long, or Mother will arrange another marriage."

He didn't flinch. It was only to be expected. "Another?"

"Yes, Lord Lansius had rejected my father's proposal," she said with a hint of relief.

"How outrageous! Surely there has been some mis—"

"Michael!" Astrid protested.

"P-pardon me, my lady." He just couldn't control himself upon hearing that the love of his life had been rejected by someone. It shocked him and made him vent without thinking.

Astrid shook her head a little. "You know, I heard that the baron already has two other noblewomen with him. Both are blonde, and one even has the bluest of eyes."

"High noble daughters?!" Michael couldn't believe his ears.

Astrid nodded, and Michael's jaw dropped faster than he could cover it with his hand.

I knew he was more than an ordinary noble, but I didn't realize just how big the difference is between us . . .

This also meant that Astrid and Michael could still happen. This realization bolstered Michael's spirit. "I will do my utmost, my lady. Please wait for good news from me."

"Michael, don't throw yourself into danger. I'm not worth your life," she warned, feeling bad that Michael needed to venture into a war just to be with her.

Michael bowed deeply and left. Within hours, he was leading the relief troops from White Lake. A few of his friends and longtime retinue were following him. Their fortunes were tied to him, just as Michael's was now tied to the fate of Korelia.

White Lake Relief Force

"Riders ahead," warned the scout who had just returned from the front.

"I see them," Michael replied after squinting. Approaching from the east, they had been fully armored since that morning, fearing that the Coalition might have subjugated the town of Korelia.

Their assumption seemed to be correct. Lansius was unlikely to send riders to intercept when his opponent was on the other side. Meaning, the riders approaching him were Lansius's opponents.

"Draw them in. I want to trap them between cavalry and infantry," Michael declared.

"Horsemen ready!" the lieutenant commanded.

Leaving their infantry to prepare their lines behind, Michael led the cavalry forward. He aimed only to steal a small skirmish victory while hopefully capturing a man or two for interrogation.

Forty cavalry in shining armor galloped through the grassy plains. Michael counted twelve horsemen in armor from the opposing force.

Upon closer inspection, however, their opponent was carrying a blue and bronze banner and rode calmly.

Intrigued by this, Michael slowed down his horse to a trot, and his cavalry followed.

"Blue and bronze chevron. Isn't that the Lord of Korelia's banner?" his lieutenant asked as they slowed down.

"It seems like it," Michael commented.

"Impressive, they still have the town under control. Lord Lansius must've pulled out some incredible defense," said another knight in his service.

"Let's meet up and ask. If they still have the town, then it'll be a blessing for our reinforcements." Michael spurred his horse forward.

After trotting a distance under the Korelia summer sun, they met up with the opposing side. A knight with an enviable jawline and a pair of sharp eyes raised his right palm and addressed them. "Hail, I am Harold, a knight of House Lansius. To whom am I speaking?"

Lifting his helmet visor, Michael replied, "I am Michael from White Lake; we're bringing reinforcements from Lord Robert."

"Ah, welcome to Korelia. Let us set up a place so you and your men can rest for today."

Harold's calm words, without any hint of urgency, aroused suspicion. "Rest? What about the siege?" Michael blurted out.

The tall knight chuckled and waved his hand dismissively. "Don't worry about it."

The tone made Michael uneasy. "What do you mean?"

"You're late by a day. The battle happened yesterday," the knight explained.

Thinking that the sun was still up and there was a chance of another battle, Michael said, "Then we must hurry."

Harold stared at Michael. "There's no need. Korelia has already won."

Michael's eyes opened wide while his knights looked at each other.

"The Lord of Korelia won the war?" asked Michael carefully.

"Indeed." Sir Harold laughed, pleased by the reaction. "We've won. Korelia is free; the siege has been lifted."

Harold's confirmation stunned Robert's knights. They couldn't believe what they had heard.

"Korelia won in just one day?" Michael asked again, this time fully amused by this absurdity.

"Against how many?" one of Michael's knights asked.

"Six thousand," answered Harold proudly.

Michael and his men were astounded. They shook their heads and chuckled, unable to believe what they had heard.

"Come, you'll see for yourself," invited Sir Harold as he turned his horse around and trotted with his escorts back toward the town.

"What should we do? Do we trust him?" asked his lieutenant, still harboring doubts.

"Get me a runner," Michael commanded. To prevent a possible elaborate trap aimed at his supply train, he sent a runner to warn his infantry.

"What do we do if Korelia is already freed?" his lieutenant asked as they went.

"Aside from joining the celebration and feast?" quipped Michael.

The man chuckled. "I'll be more than happy to entertain such a thought."

"If this is really true, then Lord Lansius is truly a frightening man . . ." Michael looked about for signs of trouble but found none. Instead, he saw shepherds and their flocks grazing lazily beside the northern riverbank.

Sensing no hostility at all, his lieutenant commented, "I see nothing suspicious. The shepherds acted calmly, and I see no glittering of swords or armor from anywhere."

"Then the Lord of Korelia is indeed a rising star," said Michael without hesitation. "To triumph over such numbers in a single day . . . I would be more than willing to pledge myself to his cause."

Little did he know that his support, stemming from a blend of respect and uncertainty about his future role after his current appointment, would be the final missing piece in the puzzle that would reshape the fate of Lowlandia.

CHAPTER 31

TWO PATHS

Eastern Mansion

One hundred troops, bolstered by the militia, were mobilized under Sir Justin's command. Sir Harold was to lead the column and greet the approaching relief force from White Lake. It was an unusual sight, as the siege had already been lifted, and Korelia had been freed.

Still, the townsfolk made merriment of it and greeted the forty knights like heroes for coming to their aid.

While the forty knights from White Lake entered Korelia, two hundred men, along with their supply carts and camp followers, headed north of town and set up camp near the river.

Inside the Eastern Mansion, with confirmation that the incoming army was indeed reinforcement, Lansius breathed a sigh of relief and adjusted the arm sling for his wrist.

The anticipation for the news gave Hugo time to think, yet he couldn't unravel how he was supposed to besiege Korimor with limited men and supplies.

"My lord," Hugo began. "Korimor isn't like Korelia. Maybe Korelia could be intimidated with just three hundred, but Korimor, even with just a paltry amount of defense, could comfortably fend off a larger number of invaders for months."

Lansius was content watching him speak, so Hugo continued. "We need more men, siege ladders, siege engines, and plentiful supplies if we plan to starve them out."

"Too bad they're burnt," Lansius commented about the siege engine, regretting the loss of good quality wood and timber that he could reuse. "But we don't need siege engines. They're slow and heavy."

Hugo's interest was piqued. "Slow, my lord?"

"Yes, we probably would lose the element of surprise if we marched with those siege engines. Even in parts, they are heavy."

Something didn't sound right, so Hugo argued, "But, even using the direct northern corridor, the men would still need to spend at least twenty days marching."

"That's too slow. I think we can do it in ten days."

"Ten days?" the deputy blurted out. "That means, a cavalry-only force?"

"Cavalry transport," Lansius corrected him.

Hugo rubbed his chin after hearing his lord's suggestion. While it was possible, it presented a dilemma on its own. "Does my lord think that the nomads would assist?"

Instead of answering, Lord Lansius gestured for his page boy to approach. Margo hurriedly presented himself in front of his master, who commanded, "Call the tribesman."

The tribesman came to the upper floor of the mansion. It wasn't as spacious as the hall below, but it was well-made and luxurious to his eyes. He saw the Lord of Korelia standing beside a table with a grand map on top of it.

Approaching with eyes on the ground, he bowed deeply and said, "My Noyan, how may I serve?"

Hugo's expression betrayed his surprise at the new title, but kept his mouth shut.

"Tribesman, I need to transport men to Korimor using the northern corridor. Is it possible?" asked Lansius without mincing words.

The tribesman, fully aware of this race that Lansius had proposed earlier, replied, "If they can ride, we can provide the horses. If they can't ride, we can borrow some of the tribes' wagons they used for yurts."

Lansius nodded happily, and the tribesman inquired, "How many men does my Noyan wish to move?"

"Two hundred," he revealed.

The tribesman paused for a moment before commenting, "It would be quite a task."

"Is it possible?" There was a slight concern in Lansius's voice.

"Certainly. It can be arranged," the nomad answered confidently.

Hugo asked, "With the hunt for remnants still ongoing, how could you provide more horsemen for this?"

The tribesman, still in his armor despite being indoors, grinned as he looked Hugo in the eye. "Not only our men but also our women and children expert riders."

And then he returned his gaze to Lord Lansius. "My Noyan, if you wish for this to happen quickly, then let me return before sundown."

"One more thing," said Lord Lansius. The tribesman bowed his head slightly, awaiting command.

The lord took a deep breath and said, "I need to talk about the tribes' future."

The tribesman didn't question and simply nodded deeply.

"How many wives does a tribesman usually have?" the lord asked.

"A prominent member usually has two or three."

"And how many children does your father have from his wives?"

"Five from my mother and three from my other mother," the tribesman replied without hesitation.

Lansius nodded.

"Listen well. If the number of nomadic tribes right now is over one thousand people, then in less than thirty years, you will probably reach ten times that number."

The nomad was pleased and declared, "Then you shall be the Noyan of twenty thousand souls."

Lansius laughed. Only after he took a deep breath did he find his composure. Rubbing his bandaged left wrist on his arm sling, he spoke, "What I'm trying to say is, you'll find a hard time finding pasture to graze."

This time, the tribesman was stunned with concern, his eyes widening momentarily.

"I heard some of your tribes ventured into Korimor's exterior because of the lack of grass west of Korelia. Is that true?"

"Indeed, such is true, my Noyan."

"It'll be ten times harder in twenty years," warned Lansius.

"It cannot be helped, My Noyan. Every family needs their goats and horses, and they need good grass to grow and produce milk."

"I understand. However, the number of folks will be so much that the grass around Korelia and Korimor alone won't be enough. Meaning you'll be moving closer to South Hill or Three Hills, which may cause problems. Worse, the tribes may even fight among themselves for water and grazing area."

The tribesman furrowed his brows before gaining inspiration and asked, "My Noyan, you are telling me this now. Does it mean you have an answer?"

The lord mulled momentarily, before replying, "I might have."

Bowing deeply, the tribesman asked, "Pray that you tell us, O Great One."

Lansius took a sharp breath. "Look at Korelia. The town is six thousand souls. Our people have a lot of shepherds and flocks, but we don't need to graze too far from town."

Furrowing his brow, the tribesman jumped to a conclusion. "Do you wish for us to learn to live in a city?"

"No, it would be taking you out of your roots. That wouldn't end well," Lord Lansius said with such clarity as if he had seen it happen before. "What I want is for the nomadic community to make small market posts."

"Market posts?" The tribesman was piqued.

"Indeed, between here and Midlandia, also here and Three Hills. They should be built within half a day's journey by cart."

The tribesman started to understand what this was all about.

"I want to build a safe route between Korelia and other cities. With a place to rest, men to provide protection, also food, clean water, and spare horses."

"So, my Noyan wished for the tribes to guard these market posts."

"Since this is my idea, I'll extend my protection to the family responsible for these market posts." Lord Lansius smiled. "The area surrounding the post should belong to the family for grazing. I'll also erect a small tower and assign men as lookouts and patrols."

The tribesman began to really like this idea, and his genuine smile returned.

"There's also another thing. Since merchants will come regularly, you can sell them many things, from cheese, meat, leather products, mare's wine, and even good horses. You should make a decent profit just by keeping the merchants happy and well-protected."

"It seems that my Noyan has thought this all through. I shall bring this matter to leader Batu and the elders," he declared passionately.

Lansius took a step closer and tapped the tribesman's shoulder firmly. "Please, convey my well wishes to them. Also, my gratitude for the horses and riders for two hundred men."

The tribesman bowed deeply and left with a face even brighter than when he came. He had such worthy news for his elders. Lord Lansius had been their Noyan for such a brief time, but he was already thinking far ahead into the future.

In the tribesman's eyes, Lansius was a leader unlike any other, someone to whom the nomads could fully pledge their fate.

Korelia

Audrey sat at the finest table inside the best inn in Korelia, sipping a cooled water to quench her thirst. She had been riding from the Eastern Mansion under the hot summer sun.

In front of her sat Lady Daniella, clad in her blue intricate surcoat that completely hid her Centuria steel cuirass. With the camp burnt and her horse lost in the woods, she had no spare clothes to wear.

In contrast, Audrey was not wearing armor but a black gothic dress. Behind her stood Carla, fully armed and ready.

Outside, the city celebrated the arrival of forty knights from White Lake. The merriment could be heard from inside the inn, which remained empty, as only one day had elapsed since the siege, and visitors from outside Korelia had yet to arrive.

Audrey put her silver goblet down, took a deep breath, and began. "So why the change of heart?"

Daniella bowed her head a little. "My lady," she addressed her host, as Carla had already informed her of Audrey's status as the future consort of the Lord of Korelia. "We are merely a free company in search of work. Unfortunately, we stood on opposing sides, but the battle has ended."

"Lord Lansius only made a pact with Lord Jorge," Audrey reminded her guest. "We have yet to capture Lord Omin. I believe you Nicopolans are paid by him."

"That is correct. However, we were contracted only to wage war on Korelia, and we have fulfilled our role."

Audrey snorted. As a squire she had a different view of loyalty. "So you won't even try to rescue your employer?"

"Regretfully, my employer has fled and left us with nothing. We're now forced to fend for ourselves."

Audrey looked to the side, aware that her gaze might cause discomfort. "I think all of this is pointless," she said. "I doubt Lord Lansius would want allies who would abandon him as soon as he lost a battle."

Daniella smiled. "I think this time it will be different."

"Why?" asked Audrey.

"Unlike Lord Jorge or Lord Omin, the Lord of Korelia is more promising. No mercenary would abandon such a good lord after just one or two setbacks."

Audrey smiled, knowing it to be true. Loyal or not, the mercenaries weren't foolish enough to squander a capable warlord. However, it was hard for her to trust Lady Daniella.

Like most people, Audrey was suspicious of Nicopolans, especially one who looked as smart and capable as Daniella. "Tell me, are you or your men involved in enslaving the tribesmen?"

Daniella's eyes widened. "I would kill my men if they ever did so."

"You honor your upbringing," Audrey complimented. "We shall ride together sometimes."

Daniella nodded politely. "It would be an honor, my lady."

Audrey almost rose but paused halfway, meeting the Nicopolan's gaze. Her instinct flared up, so she sat down again.

Carla looked at her questioningly, while Daniella remained unmoved.

"The lord wishes for me to ask you this: How many men defend Korimor Castle? How are their defenses and garrison? Also, tell us about their leader."

Daniella's eyes widened. She couldn't believe the implications of the question. Despite their miraculous victory, Korelia's forces were small and had suffered high numbers of wounded and dead. Thus, she hadn't expected swift reprisal.

Yet, clearly, Lord Lansius had entertained the idea, making Daniella realize just how completely the Korelians had turned the tables on the western lords.

Lansius

Inside his private chamber, the victor of this war, Lansius, sat comfortably on the bed. As he had expected, his retainers barred him from going outside. After Hugo and the tribesman had left the mansion, the servants brought Lansius a serving of warm broth with a duck egg and gruel.

It was okay, but he didn't like the pungent taste of the jumbo egg yolk. Nevertheless, his staff insisted it was good for bruises and bone healing.

With marriage planned for next week, Lansius wanted to be in good shape, so he consumed the broth, despite the bad aftertaste. He found himself wishing he could have simply fried the egg or salted it.

With Audrey gone to meet Daniella, the upper floor of the mansion was quiet. So quiet that Lansius could hear the ringing in his ears, a byproduct of training and taking too many hits on the helmet.

A small price to pay for victory . . .

All the tension from yesterday's battle had been eroded, although as he had experienced before, the horrors of war would linger for many months to come. He had seen flashes of men getting trampled beneath his destrier, but he was neither disturbed nor afraid.

He was simply mesmerized by how vivid the recollection was. Lansius shook his head; he didn't want to dwell on it. He drew a deep breath.

If only they knew that leaving people with nothing to do can actually hurt more than it helps.

He wished he had something to work on as a distraction. Otherwise, his brain would play those charging and trampling memories on repeat.

He drew another sigh, realizing he had yet to visit Sterling. Lansius missed the squire's company. The young squire possessed a good intellect and critical thinking that made him a valuable discussion partner.

Lansius considered calling Cecile, but he knew she had too much on her plate right now. Left with nothing else to do, he turned his attention to the parchments on the desk and rose from the bedside.

He approached the desk, pulled out the small wooden chair, and tried to get comfortable. With just one hand, he slowly put the stacks of parchment to the side. He wanted a fresh parchment for this one.

There was a plan he had yet to put on paper. His favorite quotes came to mind:

Knowledge isn't power; it's merely potential. Power comes from applying that knowledge. Wisdom comes from learning when and why to apply that knowledge.

Lansius had been pondering the situation in Lowlandia for a long time, ever since he had realized he was going to be independent in this land.

Great Lowlandia, with all its politics, blood feuds, and problems, was a province in a state of war. With the Imperium failing and chaos at the door, Lansius realized that a drastic measure was needed to rein in the province. A halfhearted attempt would backfire and lead to a bigger tragedy.

He saw only two options. The first historically occurred on the steppe plains near the Onon River, leading to the birth of the largest empire humankind had ever seen. Its method was effective yet inhumane.

History tells the story of Temujin of the Onon River, who, during his wars, ordered all men taller than the wheels of an oxcart to be killed. He spared only the women and young boys who wouldn't remember their fathers or uncles. In this way, Temujin—who would be remembered as Genghis Khan—ended the tribal blood feuds and paved the way for the unification of Mongolia.

Lansius wanted no part in such a method. So, he was left with another, less direct but equally drastic solution.

Thus, he sharpened his quill carefully, prepared his ink, and wrote several words:

征 *sei*
夷 *i*
大 *dai*
☒ *shō*
軍 *gun*

CHAPTER 32

BLOOMING

Sterling was recovering in the guest chamber inside the castle, one of the fortunate ones who survived the cold grip of death. The night before, many had succumbed to their injuries. Even among those who seemed to be recovering, a few had suddenly been overcome by fever and died.

He was lucky that the saint candidate had treated him; otherwise, the pain and swelling in his crushed leg would have been unbearable. The afflicted limb was now wrapped tightly, supported by wooden planks to keep it immobile.

Since this morning, Sterling had remained stable throughout the day. His fever had subsided, and he was restless, eager to do something. The physician, however, insisted that he rest.

Thus, he spent his day confined to bed, his only distractions being visits from comrades or castle staff. But as the sun dipped low on the horizon, people returned to their chores, leaving him alone.

The door to his chamber was intentionally left ajar to let in the fresh air and allow Sterling to call for help if needed. He was pleasantly surprised when a golden blonde girl entered. At first glance, she resembled Cecile, but her behavior quickly revealed that she was someone else.

"Who are you?" he asked.

The girl looked straight at him, her eyes narrowing as she examined his face. "Ah, you must be Sterling the squire." Her voice filled with recognition. "I'm Claire."

"Claire? Then you must be . . . I apologize. I'm so sorry for your loss."

Claire waved it off. "It's not your fault or anything. War is war. Father taught me to be ready."

Her words rejuvenated Sterling. He never thought that Sir Callahan's daughter would be this courageous. "I applaud your bravery."

"Your praise is misplaced." The fifteen-year-old girl approached Sterling and pointed at the darkened area around her eyes, explaining, "I already cried a lot before coming here."

"It's still amazing." He was genuinely impressed by her composure.

Claire giggled, showing one missing tooth.

"What happened with your tooth?"

"Oh, I tried to ride the old warhorse. She didn't like me and threw me off. Bad lady!" she said happily, with a grin.

Sterling nodded. Claire looked almost exactly like Cecile, just a tad shorter, but that was where the similarities ended. While the older sister was calm and in control, the younger sister was bubbly and full of smiles.

"I hope it'll grow better than the old one," she commented about her tooth. "Otherwise, it's going to ruin my already slim chance of a good marriage."

Sterling continued to nod at her story. He was enjoying her company.

"You know, without a father or mother, and being the second daughter with no estate, nobody is going to ask for me. Not that I care, but it still feels awful."

The squire chuckled, and Claire laughed too.

"I'm sure your sister will take care of you," Sterling reassured her.

"That I do not doubt. Actually, my father always said that if I were quiet, people might like me as much as they did my sister when she served as lady in waiting for Lady Astrid."

"No, stay true to yourself," Sterling disagreed, seemingly to Claire's surprise.

"But why? Don't men like quiet and obedient women?"

"Not at all. There are also many who like brave and outspoken women."

"I see." She nodded, with sparkles in her eyes. "What kind of men like a bratty and noisy girl like me then?"

He pondered for a moment. "Smart men who can match your intellect."

"Intellect?" She giggled. "I possess so little of it, unlike my sister."

Sterling pondered again and found the words. "Claire, you have your father's charisma."

"Charisma?" She blinked, her face turning serious like her sister.

"You have a charm and confidence that allows you to connect easily with people."

Claire listened intently; their gazes met, and it was Sterling who blushed as he realized just how pretty she looked with her golden eyes and long platinum-blonde hair.

He would never admit it, but he had a thing for blondes. With larger-than-life figures such as Felicity and Hannei around, the young squire was convinced that they were the golden fruit of this world.

Even amongst the staff and guards, there was never a lack of secret admirers—men who would gladly throw their lives away to protect them.

Oddly enough, while Sterling saw Cecile every day, he never felt anything toward her. He maybe even viewed her with some slight jealousy since the lord seemed to trust her better than him.

Watching Sterling turn quiet, Claire quickly used her palm to feel the man's forehead.

"It doesn't feel hot, but why are you turning red?" she asked, worried. "Are your legs in pain? Should I call for help?"

"No, no, I'm okay," Sterling assured her, his own heart beating fast.

Claire still looked worried, so he tried another approach. "I just told you that you have your father's charm, and I meant it. I barely know you, but I feel like I'm about to fall for you."

Most girls would laugh this off, dismissing it as a cheap and desperate line from a youngster. Even Sterling expected her to mock him. Yet, Claire smiled warmly.

"Gratitude for your kind words."

"You're not going to mock me?" he asked carefully.

"Why would I? You sound so sincere." Claire put her hand on Sterling's.

He smiled and hinted softly, "My feelings are genuine."

The girl looked happy, but this time there was some bitterness on her face. "You're the lord's confidant . . . With the lord being such a rising star, you too will rise high. I doubt you'll have a lack of honored ladies seeking marriage."

He furrowed his brows and protested, "That's not true."

She hid her hands behind her back and breathed deeply. "I only have my father's hair and maybe a horse as a dowry. You'll have a bad life if you're going to ask for my hand."

Sterling saw that behind Claire's bubbly behavior lay a maturity beyond her years. She was a girl with a strong heart, able to face her father's tragic demise, and had a level-headed view of life. Unlike those who sought honeyed words and the promise of an easy life, she didn't seem afraid of hardship.

"Claire, keep talking. The more you talk, the more I like you."

She was stunned. "Do you mean it?"

"I do. Tell me about the old warhorse, or about your father. I'm keen to learn about them."

This time, Claire blushed. "You don't have to. This is just because you feel sorry for my loss, right? Even he doesn't like to hear me babble; he just shrugs or shakes his head."

"No, I like listening to people." Sterling looked to the door, saw nobody, and whispered, "Lord Lansius rarely talks, and neither does your sister. It's easy to get bored."

"Ah, so the Lord of Korelia is also the quiet type." Claire covered her grinning mouth.

"He is," Sterling confirmed happily, and the two chuckled.

Afterward, there was an awkward silence until Claire broke the impasse. "I'll only be here for a number of days, but we should be friends."

Instead of answering, Sterling said gently, "Think about my offer. If you wish to know me better, then you can ask your sister."

Claire let out a sigh. "Life is so unfair . . . An hour ago, I was worried about so many things, including my future marriage. Then, I checked a random room on a whim and was suddenly proposed marriage."

She seemed to think on it for a while. For daughters of low nobility like Claire, marriage was largely decided by their parents. "But isn't this too fast?" she said eventually. "Or are you just playing with me?"

"Playing with you? Claire, your sister is the lord's cup-bearer. The same lord that all of Lowlandia feared. He'll kill me if I try something stupid."

"Mmm, but even thinking to take my hand is indeed stupid. How will you argue against this if they asked you?"

Stifling a laugh, Sterling said, "I'll just tell him that I'm merely following his lead."

"His lead? Oh, you mean, how Lord Lansius is to marry Captain Audrey?" Claire guessed.

Sterling looked smug. "I'm just emulating my lord's greatness."

Claire giggled, her eyes shifting to Sterling and his wounded leg. "It's not fun if only I talk. You should tell me about yourself. I want to know more about you," she stammered.

"Sure, sure, there's a chair over there. Please sit, and let me tell you about my life or my battles," said the squire energetically, forgetting about his pained leg.

Meanwhile, on the castle's upper floor . . .

"I can't find her," whispered Sigmund, who was temporarily overseeing the castle's security.

Nearby, the saint candidate was sleeping soundly, having healed many wounded throughout the night. Her clothes were stained with blood, and she likely lacked the stamina to clean herself, thus collapsed on a daybed. Now, Cecile was fanning her with giant duck feathers.

The cup-bearer wore a gray mourning robe and looked concerned, sad, and equally tired. Now, her sister was lost somewhere in the castle, adding more pressure to her mind.

"I'm so sorry. I should've guided her myself," Felis said, her brow furrowing in confusion as she wrapped the bloodstained apron. She had just finished administering care in the great hall's infirmary.

"Please don't be, my lady. I'm sure you're also busy," said Cecile gently.

"I'll keep looking for her," Sigmund reassured the ladies, and he left the Great Chamber.

Felis approached Cecile and patted her shoulder. "Don't worry. I'm sure she'll be fine, maybe just chatting with some staff."

Audrey, Eastern Mansion

Night fell, and Audrey returned to the mansion with half of her cavalry to bolster defenses. With the White Lake contingent camped north of the city, and Lord Jorge's Black Knights east of the forest, there was no lack of threats to Korelia.

Even within the city, in the billets, they had hundreds of captured knights and squires. With the passing of Sir Callahan, and Hugo preparing a campaign against Korimor, only Sir Justin and Calub were left to handle the situation.

As Lansius had commanded, they put enormous effort into avoiding problems. Handling captured men was a risky and delicate matter, especially when they were trained fighters.

Worse, Korelia was going to take in over a thousand captured men in the following days. The enormous number kept Lansius's staff on edge. Thus, out of concern, Audrey took her light cavalry to the Eastern Mansion as a precaution. Sir Harold welcomed the additional men, as he, too, felt tense because of the situation.

When she arrived on the second floor, Margo greeted her with a bow.

"How's the lord?" Audrey asked, slightly fatigued from all her dealings.

"My lord had an early supper and fell asleep when the weather turned cold," Margo replied.

Audrey nodded and looked around the private hall, whose small chandelier had been lit. "May I bother you to ask the kitchen to get me some gruel?"

"Certainly, my lady." Margo quickly left the hall, leaving Audrey alone.

She thought about the lack of security for Lansius and felt amused. With Sterling injured and Roger drawn to handle the matter of the army, the lord had no squire for himself.

Audrey slowly walked toward the master chamber and took a peek; she saw the lantern was lit safely and Lansius was soundly asleep. The window wasn't opened too wide, and everything seemed calm.

Satisfied, Audrey closed the door back and stood in front of it. She felt the sword's hilt on her waist, took a deep breath, and silently guarded the chamber.

She was still a squire at heart, and no amount of spoiling from Lansius or her new status as the lord's consort could change her. In Audrey's mind, Lansius would always be her charge, and she would gladly sacrifice herself for him.

Lansius

The Lord of Korelia had been sleeping since sundown and awakened a few hours after midnight. He was covered in sweat and threw his thin linen blanket aside.

His throat was parched, and he slowly got out of bed and walked toward the table.

He poured water from a silver pitcher into his cup and drank it down.

The cool water hit the spot. He took a deep breath and gazed around his room, enjoying the satisfying cool breeze that came from the window. Soon, he forgot the strange dreams that had been plaguing him.

He drank another cup and felt refreshed. Feeling the sweat on his face, he approached the stone basin on the corner and washed his face using the clean water from a copper basin.

Lansius felt so alive and sharp, and knew he likely wouldn't get sleepy until he saw the sunrise.

"You're awake?" a familiar voice called from the door's direction.

He saw her just outside the door. "Drey, why are you awake at this time?"

"May I come in?"

"Of course," said Lansius as he dried his face using a clean linen cloth.

"Are you hungry, do you need anything?" Audrey asked once she closed the door behind her.

"Eh?" he muttered and then remembered the unpleasant giant egg yolk. "Please, don't let them bring me that duck egg broth again. I've had it for lunch, after lunch, and supper."

Audrey giggled, hearing Lansius's complaint. "But it's good for you. You're getting livelier."

Her comment made him chuckle. "It's more because of a good sleep."

She responded only with a smile. Even under the dim light, her tanned skin looked gorgeous.

He remembered what time it was and furrowed his brow. "Drey, why are you not sleeping?"

"Um, we have nobody to stand guard, so I volunteered."

"You what?" Lansius asked, fully surprised.

"I'm still a squire, you know. I'm capable."

"I'm not questioning that. But you're . . ." Lansius hesitated, still finding it odd to call her wife. "I mean, I can't have my future wife stand guard for me."

"Well, I can't have Margo do it. He can't fight that well, and he needed sleep so he can perform his duties tomorrow."

Lansius chuckled at her pragmatism, hung the linen cloth to dry, and approached the brunette in black gothic dress. "Have you eaten?" he asked, wrapping his arms around her.

She smiled at his gentle approach but said softly, "Watch your left wrist."

"It's not as bad as yesterday, just itchy."

They finally embraced like a couple, feeling each other's warmth. It was long overdue.

"You smell nice," she commented.

"Must be the fresh hazel twig and clove toothpaste," he answered, caressing her hair.

Audrey tiptoed, and they shared several kisses until she giggled. "Lans, that's enough."

"A bit more?" asked Lansius passionately.

They ended up on the bed cuddling and enjoying each other's company. The only thing that barred them from going all in was the mourning period. They were fully aware that at sunrise they would need to attend the mass funeral.

Nobody spoke about it, but the thought always lingered in their heads. Thus, the couple simply lay together on the bed, finding comfort in idle chatter. She told him about her days, about Daniella, and how she had brought her cavalry to the mansion for added protection.

"Get some shut-eye. I can repay the favor and guard you," said Lansius.

She giggled at the thought. "No, I'll wait for Margo. He'll wake up in an hour, and then I can get some shut-eye."

"Then I'll have you for another hour."

"Hey, your wrist, be careful," she warned him as he maneuvered on top of her and kissed her passionately.

And then the door creaked open, followed by the sounds of female servants tumbling, groaning, giggling, and then running away from the scene.

"Oh, yeah, I didn't lock the door," said Audrey.

Lansius chuckled, got up from the bed, and went outside. He saw several maids still hurrying to escape. "Hey, be careful. Don't run, or you'll fall and bruise your knees," he warned gently.

"Excuse us, my lord, excuse us," the last one stammered, running away with a reddened face. Meanwhile, Margo stood bewildered, a blanket still draped over his shoulder.

"I swear Lady Audrey convinced me she'd take guard duty," the page boy reported.

"No, that's alright. She's with me," replied Lansius with a smile.

Margo looked around. "Where?"

"On the bed . . ." Lansius paused and regretted his choice of words. Margo's face now turned red.

"No, don't let your imagination go wild. She's sleepy, so I lent her the bed," explained Lansius.

"Ah," Margo muttered innocently.

"What seems to be the problem?" Audrey emerged from the chamber, exuding a threatening aura.

Margo stiffened his back and shook his head. "Nothing, my lady. Just some servants on fire watch getting—"

Lansius chuckled, dismissing the commotion with a wave of his hand. He knew the maids were easily frightened in new places and often patrolled in groups. "Let's not wake up the entire mansion," he said and then turned to Audrey. "You mentioned your cavalrymen are here?"

"Yes, stationed on the mansion's grounds," she replied.

"Good. Margo, get the guards on duty to wake Dietrich. I wish to see him."

"Why so early?" asked Audrey while Margo put his blanket away and walked to the stairs.

"Well, I'm awake, so better to work than to waste time. And with him around, he can guard me, so you can get some sleep."

"Ah," she nodded. "So, what are you working on?"

"Just some plans. I needed someone to ask about them."

"You can ask me," she pouted.

Lansius shrugged. "I can't think clearly with you around."

"Why is that?" She became curious.

"I see two big reasons."

She didn't get it at first until she followed Lansius's gaze to her bosom. She felt annoyed and crossed her arms, quipping, "It seems you're healthy enough to continue training."

"Nope, my wrist is broken, and I still need to do well on our honeymoon," he quipped back.

"My lord, you're already so lusty; you don't need a month of sweet mead," Audrey replied, smugly hinting at the customary honeyed aphrodisiac drink that was given to newlyweds for a month.

"Oh, ho, ho, spicy." He laughed at their silly banter. "Just the way I like it."

Audrey sighed but refocused her eyes and straightened her posture. "My lord, as your captain and future consort, I wished to learn of your plan." Her tone was polite but firm.

Lansius chuckled. "Since you asked so nicely . . . Tomorrow, after we visit the fields of glory, I'll attempt to bridge the divide between East and West."

Her eyes widened in disbelief. "To bridge? You're really aiming to unify the province!"

Lansius nodded, feeling the weight of responsibility settle heavily on his shoulders. "With Lord Jorge and the White Lake's commander in Korelia, we might manage to set Lowlandia on the right path. Pray that it happens, or else I fear that all this victory might be nothing but a bubble of happiness in the sea of tragedy."

CHAPTER 33

THE EMPIRE OF THE STEPPES

Lansius

The Lord of Korelia yawned and stretched out. He had just dictated a letter to Batu, officially informing him about the market post route and urging the nomadic tribes to produce more yurts. He also conveyed his wish to purchase or borrow more yurts to house the one thousand captured men intended to work in the stone quarry.

The yurts alone wouldn't be enough, but they would be a welcomed addition. Right now, all Korelia had was the shaft in the quarries that could be used as makeshift tunnel housing.

According to the staff, the shaft could house at least a hundred. For the unlucky rest, they probably had to resort to building mud houses or rammed-earth hovels. It would suffice for summer and fall, but just like their tents' counterpart, it would be inadequate for winter.

Without a good source of timber, Lansius felt stuck. He hadn't expected that housing a thousand would be so problematic.

Should I just tell them to sleep in the trenches and put some cover over their heads?

He pondered the problem but ultimately gave up on it for the moment. With two months left of summer, he felt he could return to solve this another time.

At least I have something as a last resort.

Outside, the sun was beginning to shine, coloring the dark, early-morning skies in glorious red.

"Umm, my lord," Dietrich asked from the desk, he just finished the letter. "I'm not a scribe, so my writing isn't good."

"Not too bad, better than Hugo but not as good as Calub," replied Lansius lightly as he read the finished letter. "This will do."

"You'll send it for real?" Dietrich sounded nervous.

"Yes, you'll send it personally to Batu, and read it yourself, so it should be fine. Also, bring the two biggest duck eggs we have as gifts."

Dietrich nodded, memorizing the command.

"That is all; you can leave now. The sun is rising soon."

"Yes, my lord." Dietrich began to put the writing tools on the shelf.

"Bring fresh wildflowers when you return," Lansius quipped.

The stalwart but comical man let out a chuckle, gave a polite bow, and left the chamber.

Now, Lansius was alone, readying his mind for the upcoming day.

To think, I'll negotiate the fate of Lowlandia after a mass funeral service . . .

The art of negotiation required him to be in prime psychological condition. While he could postpone, time was running out. This was the second day, and he needed to strike while the iron was hot.

Lansius knew he needed to shape this new balance of power, or else it would be filled with mistrust and prejudice. If such were to happen, then the tragedy of Lowlandia, a province in a perpetual warring state, would never end.

Thus, Lansius sat down, cross-legged, on the carpeted floor, and did something he had never done before. He sat still, emptied his mind, and meditated.

Time passed, yet the turmoil in his mind remained. He wasn't good at this, but now his thoughts were sharp. He could sense the points he needed to make and the arguments he should advance.

The door to his chamber opened, and Audrey walked in. She watched him on the floor and, instead of questioning, gave a sweet smile. "Morning, my lord."

Lansius jumped up to greet her.

Audrey extended her right hand toward Lansius. "Shall we have breakfast before the sun rises higher?"

This time, the somberness of her voice was evident. It was officially the start of the mourning day.

Lansius took her hand, and they walked together. After a light breakfast, it was time to pay their respects to the fallen in their last hour under the sun.

Audrey

Today was mourning day, the day they buried the dead and wept over them. After sunrise, they laid the brave militia and troops to rest. When the sun rose higher, they laid the men-at-arms and the knights to rest.

As people increased in status, they received better treatment, even in death. A wooden coffin was used, and a mound was raised.

Audrey watched when Calub broke the news of Sir Callahan's demise. Lansius, as expected, was distraught. He hadn't known Callahan had perished in battle. Everyone, even Audrey, had kept it from him.

The late Callahan was Lansius's mentor and trusted diplomat, and also the father of the cup-bearer. Thus, the loss was personal and tremendous.

Overcoming his grief, Lansius led the solemn procession and watched as his mentor's coffin was lowered to its final resting place.

The phrase "the last hour under the sun" was muttered by thousands who attended the mass funeral.

Beside Lansius, Cecile, covered in a gray cloak, tried to hold back her tears to no avail; she wept and cried her heart out. Surprisingly, Calub was there to comfort her.

Felicity was also present, wrapping her arms around Claire, Sir Callahan's younger daughter. She, too, wept with reddened eyes.

The marshal, Sir Justin, sat at the back. Despite his injured hip, he directed the whole proceedings with the assistance of Sir Harold, Hugo, and the other squires.

The Lord of Korelia observed the burial solemnly until a freshly made mound was raised. He then knelt in front of Sir Callahan's mound.

The headstone was yet to be engraved, so a simple wooden stake was placed. Lansius took summer wildflowers and a jug of good wine from Margo's wicker basket, sipped it, and poured the rest into the earth. Those around him followed his example.

Audrey took the wooden cup, sipped the wine, found it good, and poured it into the rows of mounds.

Resting beside Sir Callahan were two other knights, one cavalryman, one squire, over thirty men-at-arms, and seventy militia. Despite Lansius's miraculous victory, these men had paid the ultimate price.

Aside from this burial, there existed another mass burial, dug and prepared by captured non-nobles from the Coalition. Lansius had told Audrey that he wished to visit, but she persuaded him not to.

She didn't wish for him to shoulder the guilt. His retinues would shoulder it for him.

As the last drink to honor the passing was over, there was no prayer but only a mention of hope for the deceased to meet the Ancients and accompany them on their great hunt.

Looking at how Lansius carried himself, Audrey was no longer worried. The lord looked calm and only slightly saddened. It seemed that his battles had seasoned him; he was no longer the clueless clerk from Bellandia.

The sun was getting hotter, and as soon as the ceremony was over, at Sir Justin's behest, Audrey and Sir Harold spirited Lansius back to town. Despite

Lansius's surprisingly stable condition, they didn't want to risk him becoming lost in remorse.

The Lord of Korelia

Lansius still couldn't fully process the death of his tutor. His mind registered the loss, but his heart had yet to feel the pain. He didn't even feel angry at his people for hiding Sir Callahan's death from him, and this realization bothered him.

Have I become cold and heartless?

He questioned whether he had grown so accustomed to death that even someone as important as Sir Callahan meant little to him. Yet he found no answer, as there was so little time to process.

Lansius and his entourage rode back to Korelia. Just outside the town entrance, they were greeted by Roger. Behind the squire stood two knights in plain clothes, while another squire tended to their horses.

The lord reined in his palfrey horse, bringing it to a gentle stop, and the rest of his entourage followed.

Roger bowed his head, a generous smile on his face, and heralded, "My lord, the reinforcements from White Lake: Sir Michael and his lieutenant."

Lansius studied the one-eyed Michael, a man he had never met, despite having fought against him in last year's trenches. It was the same battle where Roger had nearly lost his life, saved only by Lansius's insistence on dragging him through the red, muddy trenches.

Meanwhile, Michael was prepared to hear scorn or censure. He had come late to Lord Lansius's defense. Thus, he bowed his head slightly, maintaining a straight but non-threatening posture as he waited for what would come next.

"Sir Michael." Lansius greeted him kindly and said, "Ride with me."

Sir Michael and his lieutenant complied, mounted their horses, and followed the lord northwest.

The Lord of Korelia brought his guests, along with Audrey, Sir Harold, and Hugo, to an abandoned village near the forest. There, he found a scenic spot and ordered a field command tent to be erected and food to be brought from the castle.

When everything was ready, Lansius sent Hugo to invite Lord Jorge to a meeting.

The Lord of Three Hills arrived with Sir Arius and Sir Morton, wearing brigandines instead of their plate armor. Due to the Mage Knight's presence, Sir Harold, Audrey, and Hugo stayed close to Lansius.

Despite some underlying tension, Lansius welcomed the two parties under the ivory tent, furnished with scissor-folding wooden chairs and tables. The table he prepared was U-shaped. Lansius sat at the center like a mediator while Lord

Jorge, Sir Arius, and Sir Morton were seated on the right, and Sir Michael and his lieutenant were seated on the left.

Before anything serious was discussed, Lansius had arranged for hearty meals from Korelia Castle to be brought out. Plates of food and seasonal fruits were soon distributed, and lunch commenced.

Just like Lansius, Lord Jorge had also attended a mass funeral service that morning, so emotions were running high. But the meals seemed to keep everyone at ease.

They closed the meal by sharing a few jugs of ale between them. It wasn't merry, but the atmosphere between ex-enemies and rivals was amicable and relaxed.

The lunch was over, and Sir Morton, who always exuded a subtly threatening air, addressed the host: "Lord Lansius, on behalf of my lord, please accept my gratitude for your hospitality. If there's nothing else, we don't want to overstay our welcome."

However, Lansius raised his hand to stop the sharp-looking captain. "Please, sit a while longer. Since the West and East have met here, I believe we could solve a problem or two."

Lord Jorge entertained the request and gave a nod of approval to his Mage Knight, who then relaxed his back and prepared to listen. Similarly, Sir Arius followed his cousin's instruction without a fuss.

Meanwhile, across the table, Sir Michael's eyes narrowed, caught by surprise by the mention of East and West.

"I apologize for my brashness," Lansius stated. "But I believe I might know how to solve Lowlandia's problems."

As he expected, the statement drew the attention of both parties and his own retinue.

He continued. "It's not hard. The question is, do we have the will to do it?"

His words piqued everyone's interest.

Feeling it to be cryptic, Sir Morton asked, "My lord, just what do you mean by that?"

The Lord of Korelia gazed at the Mage Knight. "I mean, I know how to stop the war in Lowlandia."

The tent fell into a stunned silence at the blunt answer. Only Lansius and Audrey kept their composure.

"Apologies, Lord Lansius, but please enlighten me," asked Jorge. "Do you have a way to bring peace to these war-blighted lands without killing half the barons, dividing their lands, and forcing their daughters to marry?"

"I do, in fact, have not one but two ways to bring peace to Lowlandia," Lansius revealed.

"Then by all means, my lord, please let us know." For the first time, the one-eyed knight, Sir Michael, found his words.

Lansius gazed at the one-eyed knight and explained, "As I said before, it's not hard . . . To solve the problem in Lowlandia, we simply need to house all the lords in one place."

A murmur of disbelief rippled through the tent, but Lansius raised his voice and pushed through, saying, "I will build noble rows, a grand bazaar, gardens, guild halls, and a city granary large enough to ward off years of bad harvest."

His plan dispelled some of the gravest doubts, signaling that these were more than mere empty words. The fact that Lansius had thought this through was enough to warrant serious consideration.

Lord Jorge shifted in his seat and asked, "Do you propose that simply by putting the barons together, we will reach this lofty goal?"

"The noble rows in my plan aren't just villas," remarked Lansius. He knew that the high nobles had areas designated as noble rows in the capital, where they could build their villas to stay while visiting.

Lord Jorge furrowed his brows. "Then what are they?"

"Permanent homes," Lansius revealed to a chorus of murmurs and head shaking.

Nevertheless, he continued. "I want all the barons' families to live in Korelia, and only the eldest son, younger brother, or cousin is to continue governing the land."

"Pardon me, my lord." A question rose from the left side. "You said about only allowing the eldest son, brother, or cousin to govern the lands? What about the barons themselves?" asked the one-eyed knight.

Lansius decided not to hide anything. "The barons may return every two years to handle internal affairs. They should arrive in the spring and leave before winter. However, their families must remain in Korelia."

Michael knitted his brow. "Why is such an arrangement needed for the family?"

"If their family remains in Korelia together with the other barons' families, then everybody can be sure that nobody is planning anything seditious behind our backs."

Michael was caught off guard by the frank answer, as were the others.

"The whole problem in Lowlandia is that nobody can trust their neighbors," Lansius explained. "Distrust breeds suspicion, just as jealousy breeds hatred. The race to arm ourselves will eventually lead to endless strife."

Tension emanated from the two parties.

"My lord and sirs, I assure you, this is the best way to solve the main issue," Lansius reiterated, his voice firm with conviction. After all, he was aware that a similar method had abruptly ended the conflict between powers in medieval

Japan. Despite the blatant hostage system, it proved effective. Within just one generation, the heirs of the daimyos became less attached to their original domains, thereby reducing the risk of rebellion in the countryside.

However, only doubt hung from the two sides.

Lord Jorge drew a heavy sigh and asked, "Lord Lansius, I truly admire your thoughts, but why do you put so much work into solving Lowlandia's problems? I mean you weren't even born here."

Lansius felt the stares from both sides. Their thoughts had been shaped by a world full of feuds and conflict. They knew that change was needed, but they were trapped in a mindset of conquer or be conquered. The only saving grace was that none that sat here had any connection with slavery. Three Hills and White Lake had no part in the raids conducted by the Nicopolans mercenaries, nor benefited from the slave economy, otherwise it would be hard for him to conduct negotiation without addressing the elephant in the room.

There was an uncomfortable air emanating from both sides, and all eyes were on Lansius, waiting for his next move.

CHAPTER 34

PARA BELLUM

Outside the tent, servants and a page boy loaded the dirty plates and trays to be returned to the castle. The wind breezed through, bringing relief from the hot summer sun. For them, despite being in mourning, today turned out to be a lovely day. However, inside the tent, the discussion concerning the fate of Lowlandia continued.

Facing stiff reactions, Lansius carefully reminded them, "This is why I told you all from the start: I know how to solve this problem, but the question is, do we have the will to do it?"

Like a tug of war, the discussion returned to where it started.

Right now, the two parties seemed neutral instead of disinterested in the idea. However, the idea that all the lords of Lowlandia needed to live in the same place and that place would be Korelia was quite preposterous, if not uncomfortably absurd.

White Lake's knight, Sir Michael, was especially worried about the nobles' reaction in Lord Robert's court. After all, they were the ones who banded together to oust and disgrace him last year. He didn't want himself or worse, Lord Robert, to lose favor.

Thus, while he had high hopes for Lord Lansius's idea, he thought it was simply too risky. Not to mention, for either Michael or Lord Robert, the idea offered little to no foreseeable gain.

Lord Jorge of Three Hills was in a similar situation. He showed openness but had yet to see any real advantage in Lansius's proposal. As a noble of his stature, he was the one who dictated peace or war. Thus, he seemed to have little to gain.

Meanwhile, Sir Morton had a different idea. The Mage Knight entertained the thought of peace. He had seen so much war and what it cost his brethren and the people around them.

For him, peace outweighed the discomfort of the barons. Still, he needed more than just promises or resolve before showing his support.

Lansius himself, without knowing either of the two parties personally and based only on the intel he had gathered, only counted their response as nothing more than feigned interest.

"My lords and sirs, this isn't hard," he tried again, from another angle. "Fighting a war is hard. Burying dead comrades is hard. Paying ransoms is hard."

Lansius gained some nods and continued. "Rebuilding a destroyed city or managing a famine from a bad harvest is difficult. But relocating the barons and their families to live in a newly constructed lavish complex, while it may be complex, is not hard."

Now, he received some contemplative looks, and he knew he needed to keep this momentum. "The people of Lowlandia are suffering. Harvests have steadily dwindled. The Imperium is facing a major crisis, and soon there may be more wars than we could ever imagine."

Lord Jorge shot his gaze at Lansius momentarily. He was curious about something but wasn't comfortable bringing the topic up.

Despite the lack of response, Lansius pressed on. "I believe we all share the same goal: to have a good life. Good houses for the men, fine mansions for the lords, and the means to keep our lands." He directed the last part at Lord Jorge, who nodded in agreement.

Turning to Sir Michael, Lansius followed up. "To marry, to have children, to enjoy a good harvest, to raise fine horses, to live happily. We share a common goal."

Lansius's pitch for a common goal seemed to be his most effective.

Feeling more confident, Lansius gazed at his guests and spoke plainly. "We can all live in peace, no more blood feud, no more rivalry. We're all young enough to start anew."

The air of doubt lessened, but there wasn't enough concrete benefit for either Three Hills or White Lake. Though the idea was promising, it failed to secure wholehearted support.

Sir Arius leaned forward. The dashing and lordly cousin of Jorge caught everyone's attention by asking, "Lord Lansius, your plan seems meticulous and promising, but I doubt the barons will enjoy living under someone else's roof."

Lansius mulled over the issues of freedom of movement, security, and even the ability to defend themselves. He then answered, "Any noble can have a grand compound in Korelia, as ornate and large as they desire, complete with enough guards to ensure security."

"Just how big will the security be?" Sir Arius asked again.

"I think we can agree on the number later, but say a hundred servants and a hundred guardsmen if they wish."

Sir Arius's expression indicated that he found the answer to be agreeable.

Finding his chance, Lansius further explained, "I have plans to maintain a ready force of a thousand men in Korelia. Four hundred from my own force, six hundred from all the nobles that join in."

Sir Arius kept his gaze, and Lansius continued. "With only four hundred, you don't have to fear that I can overpower the nobles. This new army will be a reaction force if something threatens us."

Lansius's elaborate plan and extraordinary confidence bothered Lord Jorge. When his cousin seemed satisfied, he cleared his throat and asked, "Lord Lansius, you seem so sure about this whole plan. Has this method ever been used?"

Lansius met the Lord of Three Hills's gaze and clarified, "Indeed, this method is known in my birthplace."

His answer led to murmurs.

"So it's true that you're not from this continent," Lord Jorge muttered. "So what happened to the nobles who followed this plan? Were they successful, and what do you call this . . . method?"

"It's called shogunate; it means a command tent." Lansius looked around the tent and added, "How befitting."

The comment managed to amuse Lord Jorge. "So, has this shogunate been successful?"

"In my birthplace, one of its aspects, the Sankin-kōtai, or the alternate attendance, has worked for hundreds of years, providing protection to its members without any immortal to lead them."

His last explanation seemed to garner more interest. "Protection?" Sir Michael asked, his one good eye looking sharp.

Lansius realized he hadn't touched on this one delicate issue. It was risky to offend them, but he needed everything in his arsenal to win this. "I assure you that this is not a one-sided hostage system."

The parties traded glances with each other.

"Entering the shogunate is protection," claimed Lansius. "The shogunate exists to serve your interests and protect your family and your House's legacy."

There was no real response, but their eyes were fixed on Lansius.

"All your lands, your inheritance, your will, and family succession, will gain protection."

"What kind of protection?" Sir Michael asked.

"Everything, including from coups," Lansius revealed. "The shogun, as the leader, will form a combined army to punish unlawful land grabs or illegal succession, and return the land in question to its rightful owner."

The look on the people's faces began to change once they realized there was an unforeseen huge benefit.

"With all the lords participating, we can guarantee that every realm is secure from coups. Any succession crisis will be dealt with by a joint force from all the members," he added.

The assurance led to profound changes in how Sir Michael and Lord Jorge viewed these issues. Now, they had something that benefited them, not just the promise of peace.

For the nobles, the issue of succession and inheritance was at the core of their problems. To them, their Houses were everything. Lansius's plan could potentially guarantee the survival of their Houses.

Lord Jorge met Michael's gaze and nodded at him. The knight politely nodded back in return.

"What do you think about this? I bet Lord Robert would be interested," asked Lord Jorge, studying Michael's face closely, looking for signs of doubt or approval.

"I'm not in a position to answer for my lord, but . . . this is promising," revealed Sir Michael, much to the others' delight.

Sir Arius smiled as Lord Jorge chuckled. Meanwhile, Lansius and his staff breathed a sigh of relief.

"Tell us more about this shogun and its alternate attendance," asked Lord Jorge, more interested than before.

Before Lansius could answer, Sir Morton leaned in, placing his lower arms on the table. "Apologies, my lord," he said, his words intended for Lord Jorge. Then to Lansius, he said, "My lord, even if you convince us, how will you convince the other barons? Are you going to force them out?"

Lansius wore a thin smile on his lips. "Aside from Korimor and South Hill, if they don't bother us, then we'll not bother them. Eventually, they'll see the benefit. Other than protection, every member who joins will enjoy a robust trade route."

"Robust trade route?" Sir Morton asked on behalf of the rest of them.

"Indeed. Thankfully, none of us are involved with the Nicopolan mercenaries who raid and enslave the nomadic peoples." He kept his tone level so as not to offend anyone.

For high nobles, being accused of slaving would be a dishonor. Thus they made an effort to distance themselves from it. Only people like Lord Omin dared to dabble in it, and even that only limited to turning a blind-eye on his mercenaries' raids.

Lansius continued. "I have forged a strong alliance with the nomadic people. I'll have them maintain protected resting spots, half a day's journey in horse-drawn carts between Midlandia and Korelia, and between Korelia and Three Hills. The resting spots will provide security, food, fresh water, lodging, and spare horses."

The additional trade benefit was a welcome addition. The two parties openly liked this idea.

"Moreover, when the two viscounts begin to build residences in Korelia, there will be a boom of trade. We'll need good timber and lacquer from Three Hills; grain, barley, and mortar from White Lake; as well as fine linen and artwork from Midlandia."

"You did speak about making a bazaar, so this is what you mean by that," Lord Jorge noted, unable to hide his excitement. Even he understood the amount of wealth gained from taxes and permits.

"Imagine rows of shops filled with peddlers selling wares, clothing, wool products, pottery, woodwork, medicine," Lansius enticed. "Korelia will become big. It has every potential to be so. It isn't a coincidence that Korelia has a large population despite being in almost constant war."

Lansius's latest statement again garnered everyone's interest.

"Most cities, even in Midlandia, only number four to five thousand. But Korelia has reached six thousand. Why? I believe it's because of the lack of plague in Korelia. The dry climate, the abundance of sun, and the lack of rodents due to abundant living space make it an ideal location. It'll serve as a great city."

"Strategic location, population, resilience to pestilence, and a seat of power," Sir Arius commented. As an educated man, he knew what these characteristics meant in city planning.

Indeed, even Tokyo began as Edo, a humble fishing village surrounded by marshland and lacking in fertile land. What it had was a power base, a thriving community, and the fact that its marshland made it easy to defend. While Korelia may not have Edo's sea access, its other qualities produce an almost similar effect.

"Also, a good place for breeding and trading horses," Sir Michael added happily.

Lansius was pleased with the reaction. Even Sir Harold beside him looked more relaxed; the tension in his jaw had lessened. Naturally, it was easier to trust someone united by a common goal than an ally who simply submitted.

Audrey seized the opportunity to pour Lansius a cup of water. He drank it straight down, his throat parched from all the talking.

Noticing this, the others also took the opportunity to pour themselves drinks, engaging in quiet discussion among themselves.

"So, will White Lake support this plan?" Lord Jorge asked, his eyes locked with Michael's, measuring the one-eyed knight's reaction.

Keeping his eye sharp, Michael responded, "I'll personally vouch for this plan to Lord Robert. While White Lake may be more beautiful, I'd rather sleep in the sand in peace than in a bed of roses amid war."

Lord Jorge smiled and licked his lips before declaring, "Then, Three Hills will be the first to pledge support." As a defeated lord, threatened from all sides, he was willing to give it a try. If it worked, he would benefit greatly from the trade and protection that could ensure his House's survival. If it didn't work, he already netted a good relationship with a powerful warlord.

Unaware of Jorge's true motives, Lansius was taken aback by the declaration until a gentle touch from Audrey on his right arm reminded him to respond.

"Then Three Hills can pick the best spot to build your estate," Lansius replied, ecstatically.

The Lord of Three Hills chuckled. "But first, let's pick a name. I doubt the High Council will agree to something like 'shogun.'"

"How about 'Lord Commander'?" suggested Sir Arius.

Lansius was about to answer when Hugo noticeably stared at him.

"My lord," Hugo hinted from his seat.

Lansius nodded to Hugo, aware of his hint, and then spoke. "The name can wait. Lord Jorge, it seems I'll need to ask for your consent regarding Korimor."

The words hung in the air. The tent fell into an uneasy silence as the men pondered Korimor and the aftermath of yesterday's battle.

Lord Jorge drew a deep breath, while the tent was battered by a strong wind. He then glanced at his cousin, who seemed prepared with a response. "We no longer have ties with the Lord of Korimor. He incited us to attack Korelia, looted our camp, and then got away with our baggage train."

"Then you'll have no qualms with me taking over Korimor?" asked Lansius again, to be certain.

It was an uneasy subject. Lord Omin was Lord Jorge's main enabler. All eyes were on Lord Jorge, who finally stated calmly albeit calculatedly, "Three Hills will remain neutral. It is within Lord Lansius's right to secure Korimor for Lord Omin's transgressions."

Another diplomatic victory for Lansius. While he didn't need to ask, it was better to do so to prevent friction with his new allies.

"Then what about South Hill?" Sir Arius threw a wild card.

Lansius had been thinking about South Hill. Unlike Korimor, the area was less developed and far from Midlandia. He wasn't interested, but he would be foolish not to punish them for their mistake.

"I'm going to send a messenger about our agreement to the Lord of South Hill. If he wishes to join, then I'll welcome him. If he rejects, then I'll wage war on him. His land will be split between our members," explained Lansius.

After the promising negotiation, Lansius and his entourage returned to the mansion. He had other matters to attend to. The most important was another meeting with Sir Michael.

Without wasting time, he invited the White Lake knight into the mansion's main hall. After they were seated, Lansius broached the subject of enlisting White Lake's relief force for Korimor.

The one-eyed knight looked surprised, took his time to think, and then declared, "I'll be honored to join in this campaign."

Hearing that, it was Lansius and his staff's turn to be surprised. They didn't expect the knight from White Lake to be so agreeable.

Lansius uncharacteristically asked, "Sir Michael, are you sure about this?"

Michael chuckled. "I'm ready to fight a great war to redeem myself, and my lord, you just gave me one."

Lansius couldn't help but grin. "I'll personally reward you with a tract of land in Korimor for your assistance."

"My lord, with all your plans for Korelia, I'd rather take a smaller piece of land in this city."

The response made Lansius chuckle. "A smaller piece of land in Korelia then. So, only one more thing to address."

Michael bowed his head a little. "Please guide me."

"Can I ask you to write a letter to Lord Robert? Tell him that Korelia wants to buy all the grain he can spare."

The one-eyed knight readily replied, "I'll return to my camp and send my fastest messenger to White Lake."

Happy with the result, Lansius invited Michael to supper, and the guest took his leave, heading back to his encampment.

Audrey, who had kept silent, now commented, "This is progressing smoothly."

Sir Harold chuckled, while Lansius and Hugo breathed sighs of relief.

"How's your wrist?" Audrey asked with concern.

"Not that bad," he reassured her.

"My lord, I must admit that you have crafted a really interesting plan to unite Lowlandia," praised Hugo.

Only now, after the meeting had concluded, Lanisus felt a wave of emotions welling up from inside. He had quelled them, but suddenly felt resentment toward his staff, who had kept Sir Callahan's death from him. Yet, he chose to be magnanimous. He wouldn't let his wounded pride ruin this sweet victory. "For peace." Lansius suddenly raised his cup.

The rest smiled and repeated, "For peace."

They drank their ales, and afterward, Hugo innocently mused, "We drank for peace, yet I must ask for my lord's guidance for war."

Si vis pacem, para bellum . . .

If you want peace, prepare for war.

Prepare for war, prepare for peace . . .

Lansius drew a deep breath, unconsciously moving his injured left hand with care. He had concerns about the plan, but he couldn't show them to his subordinates.

"May I know what is your plan to subdue Korimor Castle?" Hugo asked, looking expectantly at Lansius.

In front of Audrey, Harold, and Hugo, Lansius revealed, "Shock and awe."

CHAPTER 35

FALSE SAINT

Battle fatigue had finally caught up to Lansius. After the meeting with Sir Michael and Hugo concluded, he fell asleep on the daybed. However, it was not a peaceful rest: he found himself suddenly thrust back onto the battlefield in a dream.

The air was thick with the acrid scent of smoke, and distant shouts mingled with the crackling of flames. Blackened men ran and trampled over each other, desperate to escape the relentless advance of the fire. Fear and desperation contorted their faces as they fled, but the flames proved merciless, consuming everything in their path, even Lansius and his knights. Lansius jolted awake, heart pounding against his ribs, body covered in sweat.

"My lord?" Margo came to look after Lansius, and offered him a cup of water.

"It's nothing, just the heat, that's all," said Lansius, taking the water and drinking some. Despite his dismissive words, his hands were still shaking from the vividness of his dreams.

The water felt refreshing, and Lansius sat upright on the daybed. He looked out the window and saw the sun still shining bright. "Where is Audrey and the staff?"

"Lady Audrey is meeting with Lady Felicity, and Sir Harold is tending to his men and the patrols," reported the page.

"Ah, I see," Lansius murmured, taking a deep breath. He then slowly put on his arm sling, using it to support his bandaged wrist.

"Do I have a visitor today?" Lansius asked.

"Lady Hannei, Lady Daniella, and Sir Michael will join us for supper."

The last two were expected, but the first one wasn't. "Hannei will join us?"

"A messenger from the castle told me so, saying she will be returning to Midlandia tomorrow, so she wishes to see my lord today."

Lansius was surprised and pondered the reason. He rubbed his chin and relaxed his shoulders, saying, "Send a runner to the castle; say that I'll meet her at the mansion's garden when the sun is cooler."

"Yes, my lord."

While Margo left on his errand, Lansius, alone on the upper floor of the mansion, let out a deep sigh. The airy and orderly place felt so unfitting to his jumbled state of mind.

Currently, Audrey was learning about lady-in-waiting stuff from Felicity to prepare her for marriage. Meanwhile, Sterling was still confined in bed.

The cup-bearer, Cecile, was in mourning. Moreover, Calub had informed Lansius and Cecile about her late father's wishes.

Lansius had seen the younger daughter, Claire, at the mass funeral and felt saddened. He rested the back of his head on the daybed and just stared at the ceiling.

"Callahan, forgive me," he uttered, despite knowing that Callahan would likely wave it off and smile at him.

The thought lessened the pain, but the loss was still fresh.

He, of all people . . . one of the most capable people I know.

To Lansius, it was a terrible blow. And to think that he had just discussed matters casually with the Mage Knight who had done it was nothing short of absurd.

However, he knew that Callahan would have advised him to put on his facade. A conqueror must put his goals above his emotions.

The man had taught Lansius so much and even put himself in harm's way to protect him.

Lansius felt the sting in his eyes and whispered, "I'll do my best to take care of your daughters. I'll find suitable husbands for Claire and Cecile, if she doesn't accept Calub."

However, the image of Callahan in his mind seemed to frown. "I guess Calub is a good candidate for a husband." Lansius then chuckled at his own words.

The realization that he shared this burden with Calub made it easier.

Slowly, the feeling of guilt ebbed away. Interestingly, only afterward did he realize that Claire reminded him of Tanya. Lansius had never noticed it with Cecile, but somehow Claire's expression invoked memories of his little sister, and a wave of memories from Bellandia flooded his consciousness.

He missed his family and wondered how they fared now in Midlandia.

Lansius let out a sigh, hoping that Bengrieve would honor his part of the bargain and rescue them. Remembering his benefactor, he rose and took another cup of water from the table. With a letter to write, he strode to his room and sat down at his desk.

Taking his quill pen and ink, Lansius wrote a rough report about his victory. He inquired about the succession crisis in Midlandia and pleaded for information about his family's whereabouts. In addition, he crafted a more official letter pertaining to grain and horse trade between Midlandia and Korelia.

Lansius finished his letters and sealed them with wax.

When the day grew cooler near evening, he met Hannei in the garden.

The lord and his esteemed guest strolled through the garden, engaged in conversation. Although expansive and vibrant with greenery, the garden bore signs of neglect. The grass grew unevenly, and the shrubs sprouted haphazardly.

"Are you sure I can't convince you otherwise?" Lansius asked as they walked.

"Well, aside from the war, it's been fun here, but I just want to go home," Hannei said while looking at the medicinal flowers in the garden. "Besides, I'm also accompanying Sterling."

Lansius nodded. He had heard from Dietrich that the squire's injury was serious, although not life-threatening. Thus, Lansius had agreed for him to recuperate in the Healers Guild in Midlandia. "I really can't thank you enough . . . I hope he can recover fully."

"I feel the same way too. Rest assured, I count Sterling as my acquaintance," she replied as they reached the small gazebo.

"Hannei." His voice tensed up. "I'm worried about the situation in Midlandia."

She giggled as she sat on the wooden benches. "It's the battle of the nobles. I'm just nobody. I'll keep my head low and live in the shadows."

"But you're a mage, Hannei. People would—"

"A retired explorer, Lans. Grave digger they say. Nothing more," she cut in.

Lansius exhaled deeply but eventually nodded. He respected her stance and wouldn't push it further. He pulled an envelope from his pocket and gave it to her.

"What's this?"

"A letter for Lord Bengrieve," he explained. "Only give it to him if the situation is safe."

She accepted it and placed it in her travel purse. Then Lansius handed her thirty silver coins.

"Lans, you shouldn't have to."

"Please take it for snacks," he insisted.

"Merci, merci bien." Hannei put the coins in a different purse.

"So, what about Tia?" he asked. "Has her ankle made a full recovery?" He knew that Hannei had continued to care for the girl.

"Ah yes, there's a school in Midlandia that I want her to attend. Oh, I'll need your permission for that."

Tia and her deceased parents were subjects of Korelia, bound by law, and she needed permission to leave town. Lansius had heard about the school when he was in Toruna. It was one of the first non-noble schools in Imperium. Calub was one of its sponsors.

"The school for the commoners and landless gentry?" he asked.

"Yes, that one," Hannei replied excitedly.

She continued. "This world is changing, Lans . . . There are a lot more landless gentries now than when I came to this world ten years ago. Intellectuals, guild members with bright ideas, entrepreneurs; they're standing on their own without nobility or farmland to support them."

Seeing her so spirited, Lansius smiled. Calub and Hannei identified with this burgeoning new social class. The term "landless" was a mockery from the nobility, but they wore it proudly.

"Well, permission granted, but you might want to make a letter so I can wax stamp it," he said with a smile.

"Thank you." She smiled brightly. "Oh, I want to hug you, but I don't want people to misunderstand."

Lansius chuckled. "Let's not do that. I don't want to make Audrey jealous."

She giggled. "Good, be a responsible husband. Don't just treat a wife like a baby-making machine."

Lansius scoffed at the remark while Hannei grinned widely.

"Anyway, Lans, how's your amnesia? Are you still not remembering even your name?" she asked, looking at him warmly.

Her question stunned Lansius for a moment. "I actually stopped trying. Too much going on, you know," he admitted.

"I guess so, with the war and everything." Hannei nodded while dangling her feet freely.

"How about your name?" he asked.

"What about mine?" she asked, puzzled.

"Hannei, you haven't given me your real name," he reminded her.

The blonde giggled with flushed cheeks. "Say what? If you remember your real name, then we'll trade names. How about it?"

"I just remembered, my name is D'Artagnan," Lansius declared with a gentlemanly pose.

"No, you're not!" she snorted, trying but failing to stifle her laugh.

"No, seriously, that's my real name," he insisted, resisting laughter.

His antics made her laugh until she was gasping for breath.

The cool sunset breeze swept by them. Behind them, the mansion's many windows were beginning to be illuminated by chandeliers and fires.

"Oh, Lans . . . You seem okay. Audrey is worried about you. Earlier, she said you eat so little and don't get enough sleep."

"She's exaggerating things," he said, shaking his head. "I'm doing fine."

"Yeah, you look okay . . . Anyway, since you're about to wed, let me tell you a few things about the females of this world."

"What about them?" This piqued his interest.

As the wind breezed through, Hannei brushed her long hair from her face and said, "Do you know that women here only bleed once or twice each year?"

"Oh, now that you mention it, I did suspect something about it," Lansius recalled. When he lived on the road with Stefi, he'd never noticed her needing to take care of those things.

Hannei let out a small sigh. "It's quite enviable, really."

Lansius understood her plight. He supposed getting a period in a world without disposable sanitary products when you were used to them would be annoying.

"Anyway, if you want to have babies fast, you need to ask her about it so you'll know her fertility window," she advised.

"Umm, okay . . ." he muttered, realizing that the connection between period and pregnancy might not be well known in this era, especially among the younger generation.

This is starting to feel like a visit to the pregnancy doctor.

"Or you can just give her a good fuck all year round."

"Eww, this French girl is so vulgar," he exclaimed, making a show of looking grossed out.

Hannei burst into laughter and only managed to speak after taking several deep breaths. "Ah, one last thing," she said while still getting her breath back. "The pregnancy takes more time. I believe it's a whole year."

"Eh, not the usual nine months? Now, this is new . . ." Lansius pondered.

"Yup, it's because the humans in this world at one time in their history intermingled freely with the elves. And also, they're descendants of a shapeshifting dragon," she reminded him.

"Ah, the Ancients who begot the Grand Progenitor," he nodded, having read the lore.

"Yes, technically it's them, the half-god, half-dwarven who revitalized the failing elven bloodline. Humans are their offspring. You're familiar with the mythology?" she asked.

"Yes, I read the book," he said casually without sounding smug about having read the thick Imperium-sanctioned history book. However, he couldn't help but ponder why what she said was somewhat different from what he had read.

Half-god, half-dwarven . . . ?

"I'm pleased to know that you're well educated, my medieval baron," Hannei quipped.

Lansius wouldn't let her get away with that and quipped back, "I heard Tia reads the alphabet better than you?"

Her mouth was agape, and her eyes widened in surprise at Lansius's daring roast. "You black-haired imp, how dare you! I'm your senior here."

Lansius started to chuckle at her reaction.

"I can read, just not the common text," she said, still going at it, defending her wounded pride.

He held back his laugh until the mage laughed first. They shared a hearty, unrestrained laugh. Later, with cheeks reddened from laughter, they walked back to the mansion.

"So, when will you depart?" he asked.

"Tomorrow morning, I can't let the wounded wait any longer. Sorry for leaving while in mourning."

"That's ok. I'm sure everybody understands. We put priority on the living over the dead."

She exhaled deeply. "Look at you, Lans . . . So comfortably acting as lord, even about to get wed . . . Oh, so sorry that I can't come to your wedding."

"Well, it's not like you can help it," he said lightly.

She smiled and looked up at the sky, finding it poetic. "Here we are, two from planet Earth who have made ourselves comfortable in this different world."

"I hope our friends and families on Earth are doing fine," Lansius remarked.

Hannei obviously found it funny because she giggled after hearing it. She stopped and turned to face Lansius. "Remember to take care of Felis for me."

"Consider it done," he replied with confidence.

"But don't yield to temptation."

". . . excuse me?" Lansius protested in a high voice.

The French girl laughed with tears in her eyes and ran away from Lansius, her blonde hair shimmering in the golden sunset. Their chat today had been unusually amusing, a contrast to their previous encounters, which were filled with doom and gloom.

Time also changes all of us, eh?

Lansius smiled at the thought and slowly walked to the mansion where a feast was waiting.

Ten days after the victory in Korelia.

After a long journey through the northern corridor with the assistance of the nomads, the punitive force finally arrived at Korimor. Deputy Hugo and Sir Michael were leading fifty cavalrymen and a two-hundred-strong newly formed dragoon regiment, along with the nomadic horsemen.

"The castle sits on top of a hill, approachable from the northern side," Lady Daniella informed them from atop her horse. She was present as a guest and advisor.

Hugo nodded, contemplating where to make camp.

"Double the scouts, but try to look inconspicuous if possible," Michael ordered his lieutenant, who in turn ordered his riders to fan out.

Hugo wiped the dust from his face, where a thin mustache had begun to form, and gazed at the one-eyed knight. "We need to block the castle and city gate, so we must camp at the northern side."

"It's a big hill. We're going to be stretched thin," warned Michael. Unlike Korelia, Korimor Hill was taller and denser with trees.

"Well, the nomads' horses and numbers will hopefully make us appear bigger than we really are." That's what Hugo hoped.

"Then let's prepare for a siege," declared Michael.

"The old-fashioned way," quipped Hugo.

"Indeed," Michael agreed. His lieutenant quickly arranged for their men to dismount and prepare to assume formation. They planned to approach with loud noises, flashy colors, and a grand march right up to the enemy's front door.

With Lansius's plan in place, they felt confident about winning the siege. However, unbeknownst to them, they weren't the only ones making a move in Lowlandia.

CHAPTER 36

CHATEAU DE CASCASONNE

The cold breeze around dawn awoke Cecile from slumber. She tried to rub her eyes but felt that they were prickly to the touch. That didn't slow her down from her morning routine. She rose from her bed and approached the wooden table and basin, where she carefully washed her face with cold water.

Her roommates had awakened and lit another rushlight to illuminate their room. They took turns washing their faces and slowly changed into their work clothes.

Two were donning their brown-grayish russet robes and white head kerchiefs. Another was wearing a doublet with a belt and sword on her waist.

"Cecile, are you alright?" the one with the doublet asked.

"I'm fine, Carla. Just a bit sleepy, that's all," Cecile answered while finishing up with her attire.

"I see . . . Well then, please take care. Let us know if you need anything." Carla and two other girls left the room.

Cecile breathed deeply and prepared her mind for the day.

Today marked the tenth day after the war. A lot had happened over the past nine days. The biggest shock was the launch of a new campaign against Korimor. At least two hundred men, half from Korelia and half from White Lake, were participating.

The Korelians had never expected to even win the siege, so it was a seriously surprising development. For this campaign, they only picked those who were able to ride or, at the very least, stay upright in the saddle without falling.

Cecile heard that the nomads provided the horses and the horse guides, who could be boys as young as twelve years old. Each rider was provided with four or five horses as spares.

After the troops' departure, the lord himself continued to be in intense discussions with Lord Jorge about the future of their new alliances. It became the talk of the town, how the lord would spearhead a new hegemony in Lowlandia.

Messengers were also active. Many had been sent out bearing letters from the Lord of Korelia.

Cecile also heard about Sir Arius's hasty departure from Korelia on an errand, likely at Lord Lansius's behest.

Another recent development involved the rapid construction of a camp and a field kitchen to accommodate the thousand captured Coalition men. Under the guidance of Lord Lansius himself, dozens of yurts were erected, along with simple mud hovels, around a stone quarry.

Within the quarry, the old mine shaft was repaired, and general maintenance carried out by Korelia's newly formed Building Bureau, the Korelia Mason Guild. The architect behind the guild was none other than Lord Lansius himself. The guild served as an outlet for captured nobles who had education or experience in construction.

As it turned out, many nobles, including some Nicopolans, volunteered in exchange for a reduction in their ransom. The arrangement proved beneficial for both parties. Lord Lansius gained access to experienced talents, thereby reducing the time and resources required for various construction projects.

Meanwhile, the captured nobles found a sense of purpose, making them less likely to rebel.

With the new alliance being the talk of the town, even inside the billets, there was gradual acceptance from the captured nobles. Many had already sought forgiveness, begged for leniency, or expressed willingness to switch sides.

As for Cecile herself, the most personal change was the absence of her coworker, Sterling. The squire had gone with Lady Hannei to Midlandia to recuperate.

Sigh . . .

Cecile recalled when Claire admitted to her that Sterling had asked for her hand in marriage. Cecile was shocked but reluctantly agreed, as she could see it was not an irresponsible match since Sterling was on his way to becoming a knight.

However, as fate would have it, soon after, they were separated, for good or ill.

The younger sister now stayed at Cecile's quarters in the castle. Their estate was left running with the family's old helper at the helm.

While taking a new cloth to wipe the goblet, Cecile noticed the gray hooded robe that she had cleaned, dried, and folded. She tucked it away at the bottom of her wooden chest, wishing never to wear it again.

Two days ago, the mourning period had ended, and all the relevant castle staff, servants, and guardsmen had moved to Eastern Mansion to follow the lord, returning day-to-day life to a semblance of normalcy.

As for Cecile, Lord Lansius had given her a full month to mourn due to her circumstances, but she returned to work two days ago. The work kept her mind at ease, just as she had expected.

With her gear prepped and ready, she closed the door and headed to the cellar. Halfway there, she found Margo waiting with another servant.

Together, they descended the stairs and reached the mansion's cellar. The place was wide, but there were only several wooden barrels inside.

As the cup-bearer, Cecile took a sip from a barrel and checked whether the drink had deteriorated or tasted different. This part of the job was easy. Only rarely did she ever find a rancid or questionable taste.

The hard part was to safeguard the drinks for the lord at all times. She filled a jug of ale and a flask of wine. The flask was then kept in her shoulder bag along with a silver goblet. Meanwhile, the jug needed to be hand-carried because of the size.

For safety, the rule stated that the lord would only drink ale or wine from the cup-bearer. This was obviously to avoid poison, as it was hard to detect when mixed with liquor or alcohol. Throughout the day, a cup-bearer also monitored his/her health. If they suddenly felt sick or dizzy, then a poison expert would be summoned.

"Same as yesterday?" Margo asked with his patchy voice, a mark of adolescence. Yet, the boy still resembled a lass more than a lad.

"Yes, Margo, let's keep these two for the lord and guests. The other two should go for the rest," she instructed.

Margo and the servant filled their earthen jugs as directed by Cecile. After finishing with that, they locked the cellar and went their separate ways.

Cecile would wait for the lord to wake up. As the cup-bearer, she was also the lord's unofficial secretary. Almost all morning correspondence was done through her. Along with the drink, she was to entertain the lord with news, gossip, or other tidings in the realm.

This part of the job made the position powerful because she became privy to the lord's ears. Cecile could select what news and in what light they should be presented.

In relation to this, usually, some staff were constantly relaying information to her. But today, there was only one. It seemed that everybody was giving her time to mourn. However, it only made it harder. Without anything to focus on, the heart-wrenching pain returned as she sat idle.

Cecile was now orphaned and must assume the position of the head of her House. The thought made her unwell. Not only was she shouldering her little sister Claire and the estate, but also her own fate. Now, a marriage was looming, something she dreaded, as it would take her away from her family.

After Lord Lansius's victory, more suitors sent letters to Cecile. Without an uncle or older relative, it was awkward for her to handle her own marriage proposal. It wasn't the custom, but she felt fortunate. With her on the helm, nobody could dictate or force her into marriage.

As a knight's daughter, estate owner, and cup-bearer of a powerful lord, Cecile was currently the most desirable partner in Korelia. However, she felt that none of the suitors fit her situation.

Most suitors were second sons who wouldn't inherit anything. They aimed to wed Cecile to be financially independent. The ones with land were usually from far away, meaning she would need to move out, leaving her roots behind.

She didn't wish to leave her sister and abandon her father's estate that they had worked so hard to maintain.

Her only solace was a certain proposal brokered by Lady Felis: a marriage proposal on behalf of Master Calub. The man had shown affection and seemed to indicate the seriousness of his proposal.

Cecile sat still, but blood rushed to her cheeks when she remembered the way Calub had hugged her during the funeral, despite her unsightly appearance and the noise from crying her heart out.

Customs dictated that it was proper for only parents and siblings to hug each other in public. So, it was a surprising show of affection in public.

With mixed feelings, she exhaled deeply.

Calub had informed her about her father's last wish. She had thought deeply about it. To think that even on his dying breath, her father was worried about her broke her heart. Suddenly, her vision blurred.

She hurriedly wiped her tears with a piece of cloth. Nobody should see her like this again.

Cecile looked at the ceiling and tried to arrange her thoughts. Even from the start, the proposal started by her father was as good as being served on a silver platter. Calub was easily one of the most educated and courteous men in Korelia. He was also high in the lord's hierarchy, despite not being highborn.

What was more surprising was his request to marry into Cecile's family. Not the other way around.

Instead of using her father's words as a pretext, Calub had chosen to formally propose, with no less than Lady Felis backing him.

The alchemist even stated that he didn't mind the status as a male consort. He forfeited his rights to become the head of the household or to co-own the estate.

Cecile knew that no nobleman, not even a lesser one, would do this. Refusing the estate was refusing the income.

Thus, Calub's stance alleviated Cecile's biggest fear that her future husband would force her to split the income. Her estate wasn't rich enough that she could split the income and survive, especially when she needed to look after Claire.

What Calub had offered was such a gentlemanly act that naturally Cecile fell head over heels for him.

Moreover, unlike with other suitors, she had known Calub on a personal level. Both were Lansius's trusted confidants and had watched each other's backs and cared for each other's well-being.

A gust of air pulled Cecile back from her thoughts. A servant was opening the windows to let in more air. The sun shone through, and the corridor was getting warmer. Cecile rose from her seat, assumed an expression akin to a porcelain doll, and walked toward the lord's chamber.

After a flight of stairs, she passed two guards who nodded to acknowledge her.

Cecile nodded back to the guards and stopped in front of a sturdy door. She exhaled to clear her head and knocked on the door softly. All the staff knew the lord had trouble sleeping and would typically let him sleep longer.

Carefully, Cecile peeked through the gap in the door and saw the lord was still sleeping peacefully. She smiled and closed the door again.

Chateau de Cascasonne

Midlandia faced the summer with relative ease. There was no drought, and the farmlands were growing to their full potential. Everywhere in cities and towns, there was work or building to be done.

The Chateau de Cascasonne also underwent its annual maintenance during this time. Its curtain walls and towers were being cleaned of vine-climbing plants, and its vast gardens were cleared of unwanted shrubs and grasses.

These plants were a threat to the stone structure and also a fire hazard as they dried in the summer sun.

Inside the chateau, it was a world apart from the outside. Not just in the lavish decoration and furniture, but the inner part of the chateau was also kept cool either by mages or magic items, shielding the occupants from the summer heat.

Lord Bengrieve, the master of the chateau, had just returned after enjoying a morning ride through the woodlands. Aided by his pages and squires, he cleaned himself up and donned a comfortable black silk robe that draped over his toned, young physique before retreating to his study to work.

He was back to his old routine after having feigned an illness and retreated to his personal holdings. The seneschal simply didn't want to be bothered with the messy succession crisis.

Unlike other provinces, Midlandia was rather odd in that the holder of the title of earl was actually a figurehead and shared much of his power with Bengrieve's House. For generations, the House that controlled Cascasonne always became the seneschal and held greater military, economic, and political power than the actual lord.

Thus, despite the crisis, Bengrieve could stay away and still firmly hold power in Midlandia.

The master of the chateau faced the grand table and sat. The written reports were ready on the smooth elven wood surface. He glanced at the top one and read a report stating that Lord Arte had finished his business in the capital and was returning to Midlandia. Joining him was a carriage of the Imperium's officials and armed guards.

A waste of money.

The officials had been bribed to bestow peerage upon Lansius as a baron. Bengrieve had used the peerage as a grand prize, dangling it in front of Lansius so he would try to defend Korelia. But as it turned out, Lansius's position in Korelia had attracted too much attention.

Not even Bengrieve suspected that the West Lowlandia lords would decide to form a coalition against Lansius. It was an unexpected turn of events.

If it was only one lord's attack . . .

Against a coalition of three, and with only one year of preparation, there was little that Lansius could do.

Despite losing money, Bengrieve wasn't mad. To him, Lansius was a gamble, a curiosity to satisfy.

A general needed leadership skills, knowledge of strategy and tactics, and luck to win wars. Bengrieve was merely testing whether Lansius had luck on his side, and with three lords deciding to attack him, he was found lacking.

Bengrieve shifted his attention to another parchment on the table. It was a list of people who sought an audience. More names were being added to the bottom of that list, but he didn't feel like meeting any of them.

As a seneschal, he didn't hold court sessions, and as one on sick leave, he felt obliged to behave like one.

Despite not holding court sessions, there was no lack of people who sought an audience. They knew that Bengrieve held significant sway over Midlandia's policy.

To prevent wounding these important guests' pride without wasting his time, normally Bengrieve selected a few to entertain, but only at supper time. There, they would be preoccupied with the meal and strong ale, and he could distract them with music and dances.

However, with the succession issue in full swing, Bengrieve left the list as it was, signaling to his staff that he wished not to be bothered. He didn't want to entertain anyone but his own cohort.

And one of his cohorts was standing haughtily in the center of the chamber, looking at the ancient golem.

"Can this thing really fight against monsters?" Sir Stan mused, looking at the blue-painted metallic giant.

Bengrieve disregarded his bastard cousin's mutterings. Stan was often fascinated by the golem but never suggested anything about it. It was just his way of opening up a conversation after slipping through the door unannounced.

"What brings you here?" Bengrieve asked without looking up from his reading. He had one tome and several records to get through.

"My lord, there are tidings from Lowlandia," Stan reported smugly.

"You came this far just for that?" he asked, thinking it was about Lansius's defeat and retreat.

Stan just shrugged, but his smile didn't fade.

"So, where is Lady Audrey heading now? Orniteia or straight to Toruna?" asked Bengrieve.

The question only caused Stan to smile more widely, and he quipped, "So, the foreigner got you good too."

The host paused from reading his tome and glanced at his rude guest. "What do you mean by that?"

"A lot. Enough to make your blood boil," replied Stan.

"I doubt it." Bengrieve pondered for a moment but concluded, "There's no way Lansius is winning against the Western Lords Coalition."

Sir Stan grinned and revealed, "He already did. In just one day."

Bengrieve slowly rose from his seat, placing his hands on his grand-looking elven wood table as if to brace himself. His face and lips gave nothing away, but his hands clenched into fists.

"Would you like details?" Stan taunted him.

"That can wait." Bengrieve pulled back the sleeve on his left wrist, revealing a plain-looking bracelet with three small colored gems. He momentarily touched one of the rectangular gems. At first, nothing happened, but then a squire opened the door and entered, his eyes looking downward.

"Get in touch with the Hunter Guild," Bengrieve ordered.

The squire bowed deeply and left the room. He didn't need to ask which Hunter Guild representative to contact. Bengrieve only had business with the assassins.

CHAPTER 37

FORGOTTEN TOME

Audrey, Eastern Mansion

Two weeks after the battle, Lansius discovered he could exert force with his left wrist again. The physician was confident that the bone had mended, noting that the recovery was faster and better than they had hoped. Many, including Audrey, believed his quick recovery was due to the precious duck egg, a notion that humbled Lansius.

On the mansion's upper floor, Audrey watched as Lansius tested his recovered hand, practicing with an ornamental halberd.

The thin tunic Lansius wore revealed lingering bruises from the last battle, reminding Audrey of how he looked atop his horse when he proposed to her after the battle.

Feeling her cheeks flush, she pushed the memory aside; otherwise, her face would turn completely red. Although she usually didn't fret over small matters, the pressure of her upcoming marriage now felt very real.

Everyone she encountered, from servants and guards to peers and even supper guests, reminded her of how fortunate she was. And Audrey agreed with them.

Luck had led her to Lansius, an unassuming foreign man from Bellandia who had risen to fame by proving himself exceptional time and time again. His ability to command, lead his domain, and win wars even from disadvantaged positions seemed almost divine.

Thus, she understood that her time with Lansius was fleeting. As he continued to rise in power, he might engage in a politically advantageous marriage. Despite her status as his consort, Audrey knew she was merely low nobility.

Deep inside, Audrey was perplexed by Lansius's insistence on marrying her. She suspected it had something to do with his softhearted nature. After all, he did have a background as a teacher or scribe. However, reflecting on his accomplishments made her realize that no mere scribe could have achieved what Lansius had done. His strategic acumen in battle was almost surreal, as if he had been trained for war.

But how could one learn about this?

As a squire, Audrey had been taught how to fight, but few people were ever taught how to win wars. She had asked Lansius about this once, and he'd told her he learned it from books.

Heh, what an answer . . . But no matter. The origin of his abilities doesn't bother me.

The results were as clear as the sun. After the Battle of Korelia, even the usually arrogant knights openly admired him. His knack for strategy and leading battles was gaining recognition—such fearsome abilities housed in a man who was, in person, so gentle and caring.

And to think I am going to wed him.

The thought made her nervous, and the flashes of adult conversation between Felis and Hannei that entered her mind only made her more uncomfortable.

"Audrey?"

Lansius's voice startled her. Since Margo was out on an errand, they were alone on the upper floor. Lansius was scribbling something, while Audrey was peeling a costard fruit. "Y-yes?"

"Why are you looking at me that way?" Lansius squinted.

"Uh, oh . . . Nothing, I'm just wondering about . . . your hair, yeah," Audrey said, making up excuses.

"Huh, what about it?"

"Well, there are a few strands of gray." She had noticed them some time ago but never told him.

"Really?" He sounded mildly surprised.

"Yeah, let me pluck one for you—"

"No, no, let it be. I like gray better than this . . . black," he said, trying to pull a hair strand into his line of sight.

"Mm . . . I actually find black to be great," Audrey remarked.

His mouth was agape. "No way. You're jesting?"

Audrey stifled her chuckle while putting the knife down and arranging the sliced fruit on a platter. "No, it's the same color as my horse's mane, and I love it."

Lansius obviously thought differently because he suddenly moved closer, hugged her, and tickled her waist from behind.

"Euehh?!"

"Why are you comparing my hair to a horse's mane?" he protested.

Audrey burst into laughter, breaking free from his grip. As payback, she picked up a slice of costard from the table and shoved it into his mouth.

"A bit sour," he muttered, chewing.

"Well, everything has its season, my lord," Audrey replied.

"How was your meeting with Lady Felis?"

"Urgh," Audrey groaned.

"As I expected," he commented lightly, well aware that Audrey had little interest in learning the duties of a lady-in-waiting.

"It should be better next time. I'm going with Cecile."

"That's the spirit," Lansius commended.

Feeling a bit cheeky, Audrey said, "I'll suggest to Felis that you join the class. Your manners seem to lack polish lately, my lord."

Lansius groaned and changed the topic. "Anyway, speaking of Cecile, do you think she's really interested in Calub?"

"Of course. It's a good match. Cecile has status and land, while Calub has wealth and power."

"But what about love?" he asked cautiously, as if the word were fragile.

"Mm . . . that should be fine. She's pretty and blonde; he's educated, courteous, and in his prime. Many people have introduced their daughters to Calub, you know?"

"Really? But nobody offered me—"

Unconsciously, Audrey stared at him with a judging look. He looked startled and averted his gaze.

"Oh, sorry, I didn't mean to," she blurted out, quickly looking for an excuse. "You have two blondes wandering around the castle and sleeping in your bed. I doubt anyone would dare to compete."

"I wish people knew that you three have taken over my bed and exiled me to the dog house," he sighed.

"Dog house? Why do dogs need a house?" she asked.

He waved his hand. Sometimes Lansius used phrases that were completely foreign to her.

"Well, at least I have you . . ." he flirted, grinning.

"Yes, my lord, you have me. Just make sure to feed me properly," Audrey quipped.

"Roast meat for tonight, my dear?" His tone was so refined it made her snort with laughter.

The soon-to-be-wed couple savored each moment, aware that peace had become a luxury. They had yet to receive a report from the punitive force led by Hugo, Sir Michael, and Daniella to Korimor. Even with the speed granted by the newly formed dragoon regiment, the campaign could still end in disaster.

Moreover, Sir Harold had conveyed unsettling news gathered by Sir Justin. Utilizing his emerging black-market intelligence, the marshal reported that the border war was turning against the Imperium. The number of refugees was growing, and the threat of a massive famine loomed larger than ever.

The Imperium had never seemed so fragile, and the unrest could soon reach Korelia. No place was truly safe.

Midlandia

A hawk descended onto a perch atop a tower in the estuary, its majestic wings fully extended for a moment before it landed gracefully. The birdkeeper swiftly offered food and water to the majestic creature while removing a small tube from its leg. The tube contained a brief letter from the Hunters Guild.

As the sun dipped low, it cast a reddish hue on the chateau's curtain walls. For the inhabitants within, this signaled that the day's training and studying had come to an end. Now, it was time for supper.

For Bengrieve, supper was mainly a social event—a time to engage with his retainers and guests. Consequently, he ate sparingly, mainly partaking in simple snacks, fruits, and customary drinks.

Only as the evening deepened did Bengrieve have his dinner. Usually, he ate alone, disliking small talk and preferring the quietness of the night. Tonight, however, since Sir Stan was staying over, he invited him to join.

Besides Bengrieve's family, who were currently out of town, only a select few were privy to this occasion.

"I heard a hawk arrived this afternoon," Stan said, sipping his mead.

"It's from the guild. A representative will arrive tomorrow," Bengrieve replied.

Stan nodded, swirling his goblet to aerate his mead. "We should send support to Korelia," he said. "Otherwise, we may have a disgruntled agent on our hands."

Bengrieve chose not to respond, focusing instead on carving his roasted veal with a fennel and rosemary sauce, accompanied by green beans and brown bread. The meal was simple but hearty, reflecting the lessons his father and grandfather had instilled in him: how to eat, how to maintain his physique, and how to choose a noble spouse for more than just her lineage.

Unperturbed by Bengrieve's silence, his steward—an older-looking man in an impeccable wine-colored tunic—approached and interjected, "My lord, a messenger from my lady has arrived. She asks if you would like her to come to the chateau."

"What do you think?" Bengrieve inquired of the steward.

"While a child's education is paramount, I think a wife should be with her ailing husband."

"Very well, invite her and arrange a suitable escort. We wouldn't want anyone to take her hostage."

"Certainly. Shall I also arrange for assistance from the Hunters Guild?" the steward asked. He was well aware that nobody would dare to hurt her, but capturing her would not only tarnish his master's reputation but also destabilize the province.

"At your discretion," Bengrieve replied. The steward nodded and left the table.

Stan shifted topics. "What are your plans regarding the succession fiasco? Eclipse Castle is in an uproar." Eclipse Castle, more properly known as Lubina Castle, was the seat of power in Midlandia.

Bengrieve's face turned a bit sour. "Let them be. I care not who is the new lord."

"You sure?" Stan asked while lobbing roasted almonds into his mouth. "They may be powerless, but they can hinder your plan."

Bengrieve exhaled deeply. He had much to ponder, particularly concerning the likely demise of the emperor and the state of the Imperium. Secret letters from Lord Gottfried had even arrived, attempting to coax Midlandia into neutrality and promising beneficial support and coexistence when the Imperium fell.

As the crisis of the millennium loomed, Bengrieve's colleagues were undermining efforts with their petty rivalries. "It's painful to see people in power acting so foolishly."

"That's why you should take the lead," Stan suggested, while munching on a pudding.

The host clicked his tongue. He detested being paraded in front, losing his ability to observe from the sidelines. Behind the shadow of someone else, he could spot threats that would go unnoticed if he were bathed in the limelight.

"If you don't want to, then you need a new figurehead. They have no other son, bastard, or cousin," Stan commented, referring to how the easy life and decadence had destroyed the Earl House's bloodline.

Bengrieve pondered his options before saying, "I'll just accelerate my plan."

Stan grew serious. "I hope it's not the one that'll thrust me up."

"I trust no one else. Of course, this ideally occurs after several more merits. If only you had Lansius's achievements."

"Oi, oi," Stan protested but turned into a chuckle. "The man's a war genius. Me, I'm just too lazy of a bastard to be a puppet."

"But you're the correct bastard for my plan." Bengrieve delivered the joke with a flat face.

Stan chuckled dryly, and later added, "How about the Healers Guild?"

Bengrieve munched a rather large slice of veal, its center still red and juicy, and swallowed it. Without looking concerned, he answered, "I'm going to censure them for their involvement in the succession issue. That female is wrecking a high noble's household."

Stan was much more guarded. "Despite her looks, Saint Candidate Nay is quite popular and well connected."

"Bah! It's me who funded and directed the guild into this state; it's not for her to abuse." Bengrieve exhaled deeply to regain his composure. "In the end, everything is just a small hurdle. It'll only slow me down but won't stop me."

Stan sniggered. "Not even the Imperium?"

"Not even the Imperium," Bengrieve confirmed.

Stan had nothing else to say. Instead of finishing his malty mead, he opted for fresh water in a silver goblet and drank it down. Unlike in other places, the water at the chateau tasted sweet.

Soon after, the guest excused himself without finishing dinner and marched noisily down the corridor, likely flirting with the maids. Bengrieve didn't mind; if Stan took a concubine from his staff, he would be supportive. The fertility rate among the nobility was concerning enough that he even welcomed such an idea.

With his bastard cousin gone and dinner concluded, Bengrieve returned to his study.

A soft white glow from the transparent quartz lights filled the room. His indoor garden, separated by large glass windows, was lit by lanterns placed at its corners and around the gazebo.

Feeling satiated, he settled into his couch and picked up an old tome, *Elven Genealogy*, which he had been reading since yesterday. Although he had consulted another book on the subject, he felt compelled to cross-reference an older source for certainty.

Resuming from where he had left off, Bengrieve continued to read the forgotten tome.

Soon, the second watch passed, marked by patrols moving through the corridor. As usual, a squire entered the chamber and politely asked if the master needed anything. The staff's specialty was a fermented, dried, and roasted black cherry drink, but today he wasn't in the mood.

"Any word from outside?" he inquired, despite not wanting to hear any bad news.

"We've received no news from the capital or anything else of importance," the squire responded.

"That will be all," he said to the squire, who bowed and left.

His primary concerns were the latest developments from the western border wars, which had sapped the might of the Imperium, as well as the influx of refugees and the threat of famine. Equally significant were troop movements around the capital and any city lockdowns, as these could signal a move either against or in support of the throne.

Bengrieve could only assume that several high-ranking nobles also suspected the Ageless One was, in fact, an elf and likely dead due to old age. However, he understood that many would turn a blind-eye to maintain the status quo.

Yet with Lord Gottfried only a province away from the capital, the dynamics had shifted. The High Council and the House of the Imperium, represented by the Grand Bureaucracy, would be forced to reveal their hands. And when they clashed, Midlandia would be well-positioned to pick up the pieces.

No vassal east of the capital was content with two decades of continuous special taxes levied to fund the western border wars—especially when corruption ran high and many elites profited from the conflict.

The situation was frustrating, and many had sought ways to reduce, delay, or avoid these burdensome payments, though they dared not raise their voices. Behind closed doors, many eastern lords admitted they saw no future with the Imperium. They felt they were being milked for taxes with nothing in return but an aging, archaic bureaucracy that required bribes to function.

However, each was waiting for someone else to make the first move, to bear the blood cost. The rest would prefer to switch sides or declare independence when it was safe and convenient to do so. Thus, Bengrieve paid little heed to their expressions of support, knowing full well that they wanted Midlandia to shoulder the blame.

Bengrieve glanced at the silvery ornament on his right wrist, a gift from a mage as a pledge of loyalty. Noting the positions of the long and short hands, he muttered to himself, "Nine."

He continued reading. After dozens more pages, Bengrieve finally stumbled upon something intriguing. One of the yellowing, thick pages detailed the characteristics of a half-race from the Belopoeica commune that had gone extinct in the second millennium. Notable traits included humanlike facial features, non-prominent ears, and black hair.

"Another of the halves," Bengrieve muttered, concerned.

CHAPTER 38

FATES ENTWINED

Korelia Castle

As the aftermath of the war largely subsided, the Lord of Korelia resumed his court. For three days, the court and council focused on matters of war, hostages, the new masons' guild, accommodations for a thousand laborers, and new alliances. However, today Lansius would address a lighter matter vying for his attention.

Hand in hand, Cecile and Calub stood before Lansius, seeking his approval for their marriage. Rather than make an immediate decision, he invited them for a walk in the adjacent garden. Once they were out of prying eyes, he asked them to make their case.

Although Audrey was present, she remained neutral, not wishing to influence Lansius's judgment. Eventually, he invited Cecile aside for a private conversation.

Under the shade of a poplar tree, he inquired about her true feelings for the marriage, even assuring her that her late father's achievement was enough to secure the future of her House.

However, Cecile was adamant. The young woman's confident and mature answer did not surprise Lansius. He knew that people in this world often married and started families at a young age.

With no further reservations, Lansius led everyone back to the great hall and contentedly granted his approval. As tradition dictated, he formally blessed the new couple before closing the court. Thus, Calub and Cecile were officially engaged.

When the possibility of a double wedding was raised, the new couple politely declined. It was a courteous decision, as no one wanted to overshadow the lord's upcoming marriage.

After the court was over, in a secluded corridor, Calub shared his deepest fear with Cecile. "I hope you'll forgive me if our children aren't blond or fair-skinned, but dark-skinned like me."

His comment, after such a weighty court session, sent Cecile into a fit of giggles. Amid all the pressing matters, the skin or hair color of their future children was the least of her concerns.

A wise man once said that having a partner who could make you laugh was a good omen. That day, the halls of Korelia Castle were filled with laughter once again.

Lord Omin

Omin was in high spirits as the city of Three Hills loomed on the horizon. Despite his anxieties, Lansius had failed to give chase.

What a moron! That Lansius must've been getting his hands full with the prisoners and thoroughly captivated by the large ransom.

He snickered at the imaginary opponent. This had become Omin's favorite way to pass the time.

Although relentlessly pursued by the nomads, the Coalition's sheer numbers protected them from being tracked. Omin had sacrificed several of his valuable carts as a diversion, buying himself the time he needed to escape.

He openly mocked Lansius for using the nomads' assistance to chase them down. The nomads were, after all, composed of numerous tribes, many of which were undisciplined and too eager to collect trophies. Thus, Omin's ragged convoy managed to escape and reached the Three Hills.

The Nicopolan bodyguard rode ahead to announce Lord Omin's arrival. Unlike Korelia, Three Hills was a walled city. Despite the announcement, the soldiers at the gate asked Omin to wait.

Fifteen long minutes passed before a city official appeared above the gatehouse. "Under Lord Jorge's command, the city gates of Three Hills are to remain closed until his return. No exceptions," the official shouted.

Omin yelled back, "Please tell your lord that Baron Omin is here and wishes to meet him."

"Lord Jorge is not here. He's in Korelia," explained the official.

Confused, Omin said, "I'm not sure I follow. Explain yourself."

"We received a message two days ago stating that Lord Jorge is being welcomed in Korelia."

"T-that's Korelian trickery!" Omin exclaimed, a cold sweat forming on his back as he realized that Jorge might have been captured.

That incompetent idiot! He got the Black Knights and my Nicopolan cavalry and still got captured?

"We checked the writing and the signet stamp; they're authentic. Lord Omin, please leave. We can't open the gate."

Omin, now desperate, resorted to threats. "Open the gate, don't force my hand!"

His convoy looked on in disbelief. Even with the lucky stragglers who had joined them, their numbers barely reached a hundred. They were in no condition to do anything.

"Lord Omin, I urge you to reconsider," the city official replied indifferently.

"The Korimors are retreating in an orderly fashion; they'll arrive in three days," Omin countered, aiming to sound assertive.

However, his words had no impact. Troops atop the wall were already readying their crossbows.

"State your terms, then. Come down so we can discuss," Omin said, softening his tone.

However, another figure appeared atop the gatehouse, and everyone instantly recognized his face.

"Sir Arius," the Nicopolan bodyguard whispered. Omin, along with everyone else, was shocked to see him standing there.

"Lord Omin, please leave for now. I'm sure you have other matters to attend to," Sir Arius replied coldly.

Omin's shock quickly turned to rage. The fact that Sir Arius was there instead of Lord Jorge strongly suggested that a deal had been struck between him and Lord Lansius. Although Arius and his escort could travel light and use spare horses to overtake Omin's slow-moving, horse-drawn carriage, they would still have had to evade the nomads.

This seemed unlikely, unless Arius had been escorted by Lord Lansius's men and had taken a direct route to Three Hills.

Convinced his suspicions were correct, yet powerless to retaliate, Omin clenched his fists. The city walls were tall and thick; the ramparts were deep. He turned away.

Korelia Castle

A man in grand and beautiful black armor, hastily fitted in just five days by an armorer, entered the chamber. Today was a special day, and Lansius was flanked by his honored entourage in their best attire. The rich colors and their dashing attire exuded their charisma.

None other than the marshal himself, Sir Justin, had accompanied Lord Lansius in this procession. Alongside Margo, he had collected Lansius from the Eastern Mansion that morning and escorted him through the town, finally arriving at the castle in a grand procession.

Tens of knights served as the honor guards, while thousands of townsmen followed and gathered patiently outside the castle.

Inside the castle, the bridegroom was finally allowed to meet his would-be wife after several days of separation. The maids, in their best attire, escorted Lansius into a chamber where a lady in a fine ivory white dress was waiting.

The morning sun gently shone on the dress's silky surface, the small tiara, and the large golden ornaments, lending them a grand and majestic look.

Lansius was stunned. Audrey's face was aglow with sunlight, and her short hair flowed as if it were silk. She had never looked so beautiful. The stiffness in his face was mistakenly seen as nervousness, so the bride smiled, making the scene even more perfect.

"Well?" Audrey blushed and looked aside. Today, there was no pouting, just a genuine smile on her lips.

"May I take your hand, my lady?" asked Lansius, still bewitched.

Audrey nodded. "Certainly, my lord."

The couple, flanked by their smiling and grinning entourage, continued the procession held at the great hall.

In Lowlandia, it was local custom for noblemen to wear armor at their weddings. Lansius wore richly decorated black ceremonial armor, a gift from the Black Knights.

The bride's ensemble was a combination of heirlooms from three different knight families: the dress from one, the tiara from another, and the golden accessories from a third. Lady Felicity had generously financed the arrangements to ensure everything went smoothly.

There in the decorated halls, filled with flowers that emitted a gentle, pleasing fragrance, Lord Robert, who had just arrived two days ago, and Lord Jorge, who was supposed to officiate the marriage, stood side by side on the elevated platform.

Lansius had made a mistake in thinking that Lord Robert wouldn't trouble himself, but the old man was spirited. In reality, the two viscounts wouldn't let this honorable opportunity slip through their grasp, even going so far as to agree to officiate the marriage together. It was a situation never heard of before.

At the guest table sat representatives from Galdia and Salcesia, attending in place of their masters. Lansius had picked a later date for his marriage to accommodate possible guests, and his optimism paid off.

The marshal, already healed from his hip injury, walked with a perfect gait as honor guard for his charge. The couple ascended a finely carpeted, decorated dais where two viscounts awaited them, dressed in their regal attire.

Lord Lansius and Lady Audrey respectfully knelt, awaiting their blessings. The viscounts then offered their most eloquent words of well wishes, each trying to outdo the other.

Lord Jorge wished for the couple's pursuit of happiness and harmony, while Lord Robert hoped for luck, wealth, peace, and a multitude of children to guarantee easy succession. Overwhelmed by the flood of well wishes, the couple could only blush.

For the two viscounts, this moment was more than just ceremonial; it offered a chance to redefine their Houses' legacies, to redeem past defeats. From this day forward, if anyone dared question their honor by invoking past failures, they could proudly counter that they were the ones who blessed Lord Lansius's marriage.

Lansius's plans for Lowlandia made the event so enticing that representatives from the other two baronies also attended.

Looking back, this turn of events was shocking for all of Lowlandia. The transformation of a major siege into a sudden triumph, the marriage of the victor to a commoner, and whispers of a new alliance—it was all simply unbelievable.

The fact that Lansius didn't marry Lord Robert's daughter or Lord Jorge's cousins only added to the mystique surrounding him. Politically, it cemented his role as a mediator between East and West Lowlandia. Meanwhile, the commoners rooted for Lansius as their champion.

When the brief but lively ceremony was over, music was played, and the couple shared mead from a customary golden chalice to seal their marriage. The guests held their goblets and cheered to congratulate the lord and his consort.

Afterward, the newlyweds descended the dais and greeted the guests on their way to the carriage. All of their peers in the great hall watched the couple with joy and hope. Lady Felicity, who had been given the top seat alongside the two representatives, was the first to rise and clap her hands to celebrate the couple.

Following her lead, the row of knights, led by Sir Harold, Dietrich, and Carla, began to clap their hands. Next, Calub and Cecile greeted the couple; behind them were the senior castle staff, lieutenants, and the top men-at-arms of the army.

Snacks and more drinks were finally served to the guests while the newlyweds were escorted to the carriage for the grand parade around town.

Town of Korelia

An old man with a rounded belly and dressed in richly colored clothing jogged into the center of the town's plaza. His face was reddened from all the running, but he was happy.

Years had passed since the old man last represented Lord Jorge or any lord. He had fallen into poverty, but last week, Lord Jorge recognized him during a visit and recommended him to Lord Lansius as his herald for this special occasion.

"Hear ye, hear ye!" the man joyfully exclaimed in a loud, yet charismatic and clear voice.

His voice brought smiles to the faces of the old Korelians. The herald was a reminder of happier years long gone, and his return was seen as a good omen.

The herald continued. "The Viscount of Three Hills and the Viscount of White Lake have decreed that the marriage between Lansius, the Lord of Korelia, and Lady Audrey is officially recognized. As such, it cannot be challenged or annulled. In honor of this joyous occasion, today is hereby declared a holiday."

Some cheered at the declaration, but most held back, knowing the herald had more to say.

"The lord wishes for the people of Korelia to begin the festivities and participate in the merriment immediately. Three cheers for the newlyweds! May peace and prosperity bless their union, their domains, and all the good people of Korelia," the herald read aloud in the town's plaza.

Upon hearing this, the crowd cheered emotionally. Sporadic music and dances started around the town's plaza. Wildflowers adorned every street corner, either hung up or placed in vases. Townsfolk brought tables outside and began banquets with their neighbors.

The mood was joyous, especially when the newlyweds' carriage parade passed through. Parties erupted everywhere.

The wedding did not surprise anyone. Their lord was young and single, and two blondes had come to live in the castle.

But everyone had been ecstatic since Audrey was announced as the partner. The brunette was the town's champion. Her humble background and war exploits made her well-loved.

The townsfolk were also thrilled when Lord Jorge and Lord Robert agreed to officiate the marriage. Many of the older generations still remembered Lord Jorge's father fondly. The Coalition attack had tarnished that sentiment, but the repaired relationship was welcomed with open arms.

As for Lord Robert, his just rule in Korelia and his actions in eradicating corrupt practices had earned him the trust of the community before Lord Lansius's reign.

Today offered an opportunity to mend relations and forge stronger bonds anew. Now, for the first time, a Korelian could speak of hope for a peaceful future in the region without anyone correcting them for their naivety.

Lord Omin

At least I still got that bastard's baggage train.

Omin convinced himself that the venture wasn't a total loss. The amount of gold and precious trinkets was enough to rebuild his army. However, devoid of essential supplies from Three Hills, their situation grew increasingly dire.

Their only respite was the river that ran beside the city, where the convoy replenished their water supply. It was the first water source they had found in three days. With their thirst quenched but still hungry, the convoy trudged life-lessly toward Korimor.

In a desperate move, Omin ordered his men to scout for any nearby villages to raid for supplies. While they had carts filled with valuables, none were filled with consumables. Just yesterday, they had been forced to slaughter two horses for food.

The hot midday turned cooler, and they had yet to reach the place where they used to make camp. Suddenly, an unknown cavalry unit appeared on the horizon.

"My lord, it's the nomads," his bodyguard called out.

Omin couldn't believe what he saw. He had assumed the nomads wouldn't dare pursue them this close to Three Hills City. Panic rippled through his con-voy, plunging it into disarray.

With no other options, Omin quickly turned his horse and spurred it into a faster gallop.

I'm not going to be captured by this Lansius's dogs! I will never.

Omin chanted the mantra to himself, pushing his horse to its limits. Mean-while, the last of his escorts, many of whom hadn't even donned their armor, dispersed in the chaos.

He was reduced to only his bodyguard, having abandoned all others.

"Lord Lansius invites you all for a drink," taunted one of the riders in pursuit.

After a short but desperate chase, his bodyguard veered off, his horse too spent to continue. An arrow found its mark, striking the man's back and sending him tumbling to the ground.

"Not that one! Get him, get him!" the remaining raiders shouted, redirecting their chase toward Omin.

Omin urged his horse to even greater speeds, but abruptly, his world flipped upside down. He lost sight of the horizon, glimpsing only the blue sky before falling from his mount. He screamed as he crashed into the ground, tumbling multiple times and kicking up a cloud of orange dust.

Batu, the leader of the nomads, pulled back the reins of his horse and dismounted. Despite limping from a duel that took place four days earlier, he approached Omin. His band had dwindled to fewer than a hundred members, all of whom were exhausted and tasked with guarding their numerous captives. However, after Lord Lansius's remarkable victory, Batu was able to persuade other tribes to join them, bolstering their manpower.

Finding Baron Omin had proved challenging due to the size of the Coali-tion. Batu had encountered too many groups of stragglers across the Great Plains. That was why he had decided to gamble on a different approach, setting up an ambush between Three Hills and Korimor.

As it turned out, his keen insight had paid off. Batu unsheathed his sword and kicked Omin's body to flip him over. Recognizing the exquisite clothing and the golden signet ring, a broad smile spread across Batu's face.

"We've got him," Batu declared.

Upon hearing their leader's words, hundreds of riders erupted in cheers of victory.

CHAPTER 39

DANCING SHADOWS

Fleeting memories of conversations with Hannei about women's fertility came into Lansius's mind uninvited. He began to realize that her concerns likely stemmed from the fear that it might be difficult for them to have children. Unlike Hannei, whom Lansius suspected had been transported into this world, body and soul, his situation remained a mystery.

Is this my body, or am I inside someone else's body? But what are the chances that I ended up as a foreigner?

Everywhere he went, Lansius never saw a man with black hair. Black hair wasn't even mentioned in any documents. Sadly, Lansius couldn't even recall his origin, or whether this was truly his own hair color.

The crux of the matter was that Lansius and Audrey could belong to different species. Similar as they were, they might not be compatible.

Mmm . . . cold?!

Things started to fade, and Lansius awoke abruptly.

Was that a dream?

He was about to recall what the dream had been about when a sensation from his lower body drew his attention. It felt as if he had gone to sleep without a blanket or, more eerily, without pants. Fighting off the haziness, Lansius looked down.

The room was dim, lit only by a lantern on the table. Still, he could make out the silhouette of someone on top of him. Blinking, he recognized his newlywed wife. He was stunned by her actions. A single blanket draped over her shoulder serving as her only covering.

Audrey seemed to notice and spoke. "J-just lay still. Oh, and keep it erect."

Lansius was rendered speechless by the absurdity, at the same time captivated by her lithe, yet toned body. Then she got it right. "Oh," he moaned, his hand flying to his mouth a moment too late.

Audrey looked thrilled. "See, see, I can do it! I was just too tired last time," she said proudly, while wincing from pain.

So this is what it's all about . . .

"S-slowly," he warned her, not wanting her to get hurt.

Just a few hours ago, it had been their wedding night. After a feast that began at lunchtime and didn't conclude until dinner, both were exhausted. They had been so weary and nervous that they couldn't consummate their marriage.

Lansius hadn't given it much thought, but it seemed Audrey blamed herself and was trying to make amends.

As she began to move, awkward at first, the blanket slid away, illuminating her form under the dim light of the lantern. Her face flushed, and she closed her eyes but persisted.

"Easy . . . let's do it slowly," he guided her as she gently turned his world upside down.

"What time is it?" Lansius asked as they cuddled afterward.

"Not long after the fourth watch," Audrey replied, her eyelids feeling heavy and her mind so relaxed.

"Still far from dawn," said Lansius as he rose from the bed.

"Mm . . . Lans, where are you going?" Audrey asked from the bed.

"I'm thirsty. Aren't you?"

She shook her sleepy head. "Just a bit."

He walked over to a nearby table, poured himself a cup from a silver jug, and took a sip. "Why is it spicy?"

She stifled a laugh and answered, "That must be the spiced wine."

"Welp, we're out of water," he muttered after finding the other jugs empty.

"I think I emptied the last one before sleep," she answered while sitting up on the bed.

"Ah, okay, that's quite alright," he said while taking another sip of the spiced wine.

"Hey, want to go out and grab some water and snacks?" Audrey turned lively and started to dress. "There should be plenty in the main hall."

Lansius furrowed his brow. "Sneaking out? I'm not sure that's a good idea."

"Come on, Lans, it should be fun." She grinned and was about to take his hands, but halted after only a few steps.

"What's the matter?" he asked with concern.

"Mm, it stings . . ."

Realizing what she was getting at, he quickly apologized. "Sorry."

"Don't be, you dummy . . . Hey, Lans, I can call you dummy again, right?"

Lansius chuckled at her childlike request. "Well, I'm feeling rather generous tonight."

Audrey grinned happily like a little girl. "Oh, I almost forgot to fold the bed-sheet," she said rather urgently as if remembering something important.

"Why?" Lansius asked.

"It's a tradition. The bride keeps the bedsheet as proof that the marriage has been consummated," she explained without hesitation.

Lansius nodded and asked, "Did Felis teach you that?"

"Yep," she said, looking smug.

He couldn't help but erase her smugness with another kiss. They concluded their wedding night by sneaking around the mansion to quietly secure a jug of water, roast meat, and puddings. Oddly enough, this clandestine adventure felt rather enjoyable. They had the chance to observe the aftermath of the celebration.

The hall was filled with servants, staff, and even guests, all sleeping off their drunkenness. Lansius was pleased to see that everyone had enjoyed themselves.

Midlandia

On top of the green hills, three days away from the seat of power in Midlandia, there was a famous bathhouse. Since ages ago, its natural hot springs have been known to have healing properties. Two centuries ago, the Healers Guild bought the adjacent villa and opened their headquarters there.

People seeking treatment would come there as if on a pilgrimage. Several years ago, the late Sir Callahan had visited the place as an envoy from Korelia.

However, Hannei bypassed the famed location and ordered her carriage to go straight to Cascasonne. She knew of a friendly, unlicensed healer connected to Bengrieve.

Sterling, who was under her care, was recovering. But as Hannei had feared, his leg was causing him all sorts of pain. Magic could only boost the body's natu-ral recovery abilities. A wound that would normally take a day to heal could be hastened to just a few hours through magical intervention. However, it was pow-erless to correct the position of broken bones, which could grow haphazardly.

That was why Hannei needed a healer who typically was also a bone physi-cian and had enough knowledge about anesthesia.

Upon arriving at a small rustic villa that grew grapevines, Hannei met with several people before Sterling was admitted to their private hospice.

"Thank you for your kind help, my lady," said Sterling as he settled into his new bed.

"Don't mention it. Just understand that the treatment will tax both your mind and body. But don't lose hope," Hannei advised.

"Fight on!" little Tia also encouraged Sterling.

Their words made Sterling chuckle. "Will we meet again, my lady?" His sharp instincts told him that Hannei lived in a different social class and could easily disappear.

"I'll see what I can do. Just focus on your treatment," Hannei reassured him.

Sterling exhaled deeply and turned his gaze to the little girl. "Tia, take care of Lady Hannei for me."

The little girl grinned. "I'll be with Mistress Hannei unless she orders me not to."

The squire was pleased. Tia was the star of their journey; the entire way she had cooked, cleaned, and taken care of their needs without a single complaint.

With Sterling and several other men under the care of reliable hands, Hannei took the carriage to Chateau de Cascasonne. She had prepared for this journey, already changing into her usual brown servant's attire. She had also put on a brown wig before departing.

Tia was surprised by the change, and Hannei concocted a story to convince her to keep her hair and magical abilities a secret. The little girl seemed to take Hannei's explanation at face value and took it to heart.

Truthfully, Hannei had left her natural hair uncovered in Korelia because of Felis. She didn't want Felis to stand out alone, so she willingly made herself another target to confuse any potential attack or kidnappers.

Without Felis around, she was more comfortable with the wig to blend in with other people. Just like Lansius, she hated the spotlight.

Arriving at the chateau just before sundown, her carriage was stopped at the gatehouse. Hannei noticed the heightened security and found it unusual. Still, she merely attributed it to the ongoing succession crisis.

Like servants, Hannei and Tia approached the main courtyard on foot, under the watchful eyes of the guardsmen.

As they moved along and passed the inner curtain wall, something piqued Hannei's interest. Beside the garden, on a plot of land used to grow vegetables and herbs, a girl with golden blonde hair stood up.

Tia looked at Hannei with a questioning eye, but Hannei shrugged. She had never seen her before and decided to approach.

The bubbly and energetic girl noticed them and asked, "Are you two guests at the chateau?"

"I work here but have just returned from an errand," Hannei answered.

"Ah, nice to meet you. My name is Tanya; my mother and I arrived here several days ago," she introduced herself happily.

Hannei nodded and couldn't help but smile. She knew who they were and was pleased with their arrival. "Nice to meet you too. You can call me Hannei, I'm not a lady."

Hannei then glanced at Tia, gesturing that it was okay for her to speak.

"I'm Tia, nice to meet you," she said with a little bow.

Tanya was excited about the little girl. "I rarely see someone around my age."

"What are you planting here? Is this your garden?" Tia matched her energy.

Tanya giggled, watching Tia's curiosity.

"Do you or your mother need anything?" asked Hannei.

"We're pretty well-off here; maybe just some clothing for winter. But I heard the generous and benevolent lord is going to provide for us," Tanya said.

Hannei smiled at Tanya's cheerful nature. "I'm sure the lord of the chateau will take care of you."

Tanya tilted her head a little. "Although, I am quite curious. Why is he so keen to help us? It's not like we're worthy of his attention."

Tia nodded in agreement.

Hannei was pleased with Tanya's critical thinking. "Smart girl. Would you like to go to school? Tia is only a few years younger. It'll be fun to have friends at school."

"Friends, school? I'd love to," Tanya said ecstatically, while Tia's eyes beamed with joy.

Hannei kept smiling, but inside she was concerned for Tanya and her mother. Lord Bengrieve didn't usually do something like this. And certainly not without a good reason.

Bidding farewell to Tanya, Hannei and Tia proceeded to the main keep's entrance, where they found a staff member who recognized her. The man escorted them straight to the servants' quarters, where Hannei found a small waiting room.

There, she left Tia with her bags, promising that she wouldn't be long. Still under escort, Hannei then navigated the keep's long and winding passageways, passing additional guards stationed seemingly at every door.

She finally reached the corridor where Lord Bengrieve's study was located. Unlike anything she had ever seen in her years of service, the place was now a beehive of activity. Squires, messengers, and other staff waited in the corridors with reddened eyes and tired expressions. Cups of roasted cherry black drink that smelled like coffee were being refilled regularly. Incense was being burned to mask any smells.

Many saw Hannei and made gestures to acknowledge her presence. The steward noticed the gestures, found the newcomer, and approached. "Maester Hannei, this is most unfortunate timing."

"Master Steward, what happened?" Hannei quickly added, "I don't wish to bother. I'm only here to report."

"Many things happened while you were away," the old man replied with a fatherly smile. "Please wait in your quarters; I'm sure the lord will want to discuss something with you, but probably not tonight."

"Gratitude. Then I'll bother you no more." Hannei bowed her head to the old man who had done much to help her over the years.

She left the busy corridor and headed to her quarters at the far end of the complex. Despite her servant's attire, the maids knew perfectly well where Hannei stood in the hierarchy. They allowed her to enter the lavish compound in the chateau, a place reserved for high-ranking retainers.

Two days after Hannei's arrival, a summons arrived at her door. She prepared herself and told Tia to continue studying and to sleep if the meeting took too long.

Unescorted, Hannei entered one of the private chambers inside the chateau. The maids opened the door, revealing Bengrieve with reddened eyes and a tired expression.

As usual, Bengrieve was preoccupied with his dinner. It was the steward who gestured for Hannei to take her seat. She pulled up a chair at the far end of the table and sat quietly.

A maid poured spiced wine and brought some snacks. Hannei pretended to sip her wine but didn't actually swallow, fearing it to be laced with truth nectar. This was why she had hydrated sufficiently beforehand.

She waited patiently, rehearsing her reports in case Bengrieve asked for them.

"I hear you've brought a child. A servant or an adoption?" Bengrieve finally asked.

"I haven't thought that far ahead, my lord, but I intend to protect her and provide for her," Hannei answered.

Bengrieve nodded and took a sip of his water.

"When will you return Lansius's family?" Hannei asked. She suspected that Bengrieve was aware of her visit to the garden. To avoid arousing suspicion, she decided to be upfront.

"I have yet to find the brother," Bengrieve said plainly.

The lord turned silent, seemingly allowing Hannei to ask another question. She took the cue. "My lord, if you don't mind, what is the status of the succession crisis?"

"Ask the steward," Bengrieve replied. This small gesture allowed the steward to brief Hannei on the latest developments. "But you'll be disappointed," he warned.

Hannei squinted, trying to discern his meaning.

"It's not the succession. It's outside of Midlandia." Despite using a napkin to cover his mouth, Hannei noticed that her host was smirking, as if unable to contain his excitement. "We finally have the opportunity we've been waiting for."

His words struck Hannei. She understood that the last seams of the Imperium had finally frayed.

Korimor, Lowlandia

The arrival of the joint forces from Korelia and White Lake sent shock waves through Korimor. Panic ensued as the defenders barred the gates and manned their walls and towers. However, to their surprise, the joint forces did nothing more than set up camps and forage for firewood and timber for blockades.

For the next two days, the troops outside the walls refrained from setting up any siege engines or tunneling. They contented themselves with patrolling, keeping sentries, and observing the city from a safe distance.

The invaders didn't construct ladders or attempt other typical siege methods, unsettling the defenders. By the third day, not even a herald had approached the walls to announce the invading forces' intentions. The city finally raised a flag, signaling a request for parley.

Still, the joint forces made no response. Their camp showed little activity as if they were reluctant to even meet and make demands.

While the invaders' actions continued to baffle Korimor's defenders, the situation was well-received by the populace, who felt fortunate that there was no violence at their gates. They feared being drafted or expelled from the city to preserve provisions.

However, before midday on the fourth day, more troops arrived from the south, clearly a reinforcement for the joint forces. This turn of events disturbed the defenders' morale, pushing them to risk sending an envoy to the enemy's camp.

The discussion between the two parties had barely concluded when, from the west, an even larger group arrived—men and carts marching toward the city, outnumbering even the invading force. The flags were unlike any ever seen in Lowlandia.

CHAPTER 40

UNEXPECTED

Chateau de Cascasonne

Tanya, help me with the cabbage," Mother Arryn called from the kitchen.

"I'm still fixing my gardening basket," Tanya replied.

"It can wait. We can't have a house without fermented cabbage," her mother said sternly.

Tanya groaned, set aside her work, and headed to the kitchen. "If only they'd let us carry our stuff."

"Don't be ridiculous. It's good enough that your husband managed to get us out of Arvena," said Arryn, as she placed finely sliced fresh cabbage into small earthen jars.

"Oh, my poor husband, always disappearing after finding us a home," said Tanya dramatically.

Arryn chuckled. "What luck for you to find a man like that. Still, I'm surprised you even agreed."

Tanya grinned. "With a face and body like that and that much coin, who wouldn't?"

"That's why I'm skeptical. He's too good to be interested in a simple farm girl like you."

"Mother!" Tanya complained, to which her mother laughed.

Despite their talks, Arryn knew well why Tanya had agreed. While Marc had joined Lord Gottfried's military service, the family was still hard-pressed to pay special taxes to support the war. Their new overlord had let his men plunder if taxes weren't paid in full.

They would be in big debt, if not for a young traveling peddler who had just come to Bellandia. The man was looking for a wife and found Tanya attractive. Initially, Arryn disagreed because he intended to take Tanya out of the province, but the peddler convinced Arryn to move with him to Midlandia. He also didn't mind that the family couldn't afford a dowry.

Thus, they left a message for Marc with Connor, who was working as seasonal butcher for the army. They also left another message for Lansius, if he ever returned to Bellandia.

Lansius's story was a sad one. Tanya never mentioned the name anymore, as it was a painful reminder of the grim news that Riverstead had fallen and that Lansius had likely perished alongside the young lord.

After two months on the road, the family finally arrived in Midlandia. There, Tanya's husband owned a house, a small farm, and even had a helper. He left them a sum of money without even staying a single night, departing hastily with the claim that he needed to sell his wares in the next town.

They didn't see him again until several days ago, when he returned to pick them up in a hurry and whisk them away to this chateau, claiming he had bagged an important deal with a noble.

"I can't believe that your husband is affiliated with the master of this big chateau. And the lord even allowed us to live here," said Arryn as she poured brine water into the earthen jar.

"The lord of this chateau must've liked him enough," commented Tanya as she prepared another cabbage for the sauerkraut.

"If only you two were married for real," Arryn mused.

Tanya giggled. "But Mother, my marriage is real, at least on records."

"Well, married girl, time to learn to make good sauerkraut. Maybe then your husband will ask for your hand for real," Arryn teased.

"Mother!" Tanya complained, her cheeks reddening, much to her mother's delight.

Korimor Region

Hugo and Michael had blockaded Korimor Castle and the city, as instructed by Lord Lansius. The plan was simple, bordering on madness. They were to make no demands nor send envoys for discussion—only quietly occupy the area and block movements in and out of the city.

The troops were ordered merely to construct wooden fences, maintain their camps, organize patrols, and recuperate from the long journey. The nomads were allowed to graze far from camp and acted as eyes and ears around the area.

After three days of uncertainty, Korimor finally signaled for talks with the joint force. However, Hugo and Michael feigned disinterest. Lord Lansius had instructed them to simply wait for the envoys to come knocking.

The city was baffled by the invaders' continuous reluctance to negotiate or even make demands. Suspicion ran wild.

As if sensing the tension inside the city, Hugo and Michael sent a third of their troops southward under the cover of darkness. After several miles, the troops rested, ate breakfast at dawn, and then returned to their camp.

When they were within sight of Korimor, the troops marched with great fanfare. It was a ruse, devised by Lord Lansius. The camp welcomed the fake reinforcements with trumpets, cavalry escorts, and formal greetings.

To complete the trick, they even had their men move and rebuild their camps to make it appear as if the camp was expanding due to the newcomers pitching their tents.

The Korelians and the White Lake forces found the affair amusing, but the Korimor defenders fell for it. The city risked opening its gates, sending three envoys with gifts, hoping for an opportunity to meet.

Seizing the opportunity, Hugo and Michael prepared their act.

The camp's bustling activity helped maintain the illusion of a large army. It managed to impress the envoys as they were escorted into the command tent.

Wearing fresh, clean clothes, Hugo and Michael accepted the envoys, but instead of making demands, they acted more like guests trying to make acquaintances, rather than aggressors. Whenever the envoys sought demands or reasons for their presence, the deputy and the one-eyed knight showed reluctance to answer.

Finally, when it was clear that the conversation was going nowhere, Michael mentioned they were waiting for a transfer of power.

"Transfer of power?" asked one envoy in disbelief.

Michael nodded and let out a long, feigned sigh. "This is why we didn't want to explain. It's messy."

Another envoy stepped forward. "Please enlighten us."

Michael looked at Hugo, who nodded approvingly.

"Lord Lansius of Korelia has defeated and cornered Lord Omin. It's only a matter of time before he is brought here," the one-eyed knight revealed.

This simple answer shocked the envoys. They finally understood why the invading force had not bothered with demands or a siege.

Not all the envoys were convinced. The Nicopolan mercenary envoy shook his head and spoke openly. "Do you have evidence for this claim?"

His combative tone made the other envoys nervous.

"What kind of proof would you like?" Hugo asked disinterestedly.

"We have the trinkets," Michael reminded him.

Sighing as if troubled, Hugo gestured for his lieutenant to bring forward a large wooden box. Upon opening it, he pulled out an intricately embroidered pillow. "This was taken from Lord Omin's camp," he claimed.

The envoys were stunned. It seemed their lord's baggage had been captured.

They cautiously examined the box's contents. "Hey, be careful! This is my personal stash," Hugo warned, adding pressure to the envoys. "Not everything here is from your lord. We also have items from Lord Jorge's tents."

While they didn't recognize the silk, luxury items, or golden trinkets, they were convinced that such valuables were beyond the means of a mere deputy from Korelia. Thus, it was clear these items had been spoils taken from the Coalition lord's baggage train.

Only the Nicopolan envoy remained skeptical. "We have six thousand men and siege engines. How could you possibly defeat them?"

Instead of answering, Deputy Hugo and Sir Michael merely looked at each other. At that moment, Daniella entered the tent to the envoys' surprise.

Ignoring the envoys, she approached Hugo and Michael. "Deputy, sir, my men among the reinforcements are accounted for."

"Daniella, why are you with them?" demanded the Nicopolan envoy.

Daniella faced the mercenary squarely; he was one of the company leaders who had stayed behind. "What else can I do? I fulfilled my contract. Lord Omin was defeated and fled, leaving everyone to die."

"That's utter nonsense!" The envoy was in denial.

Daniella simply shook her head, looking at him with contempt. It turned into a staring contest, but she didn't back down. Eventually, the Nicopolan envoy lowered his gaze and fell silent. No amount of bickering would change the fact that their side had lost the war.

While the details could wait, Daniella's presence on the opponent's side was the strongest evidence that Lord Omin's defeat was real.

Daniella turned to the other two envoys. "Lord Lansius is a better leader. He has grand plans for Lowlandia and is generous to those who support him."

Distraught that even Lady Daniella had switched sides, the envoys finally relented. The House they represented had only a young boy as a possible heir, not even old enough to be a squire. Meanwhile, there were mercenaries whose loyalty was questionable but who would happily switch sides if offered better terms.

The fact that Lady Daniella was on the opposing side clearly indicated where the mercenaries' loyalty stood.

Behind closed doors, the House had confided their worst-case scenario to their envoys. Now, as an extension of the House's hands, the envoys began offering terms to Hugo and Sir Michael. Their goal was to negotiate before the captured Lord Omin was paraded in front of the city, which would embarrass their master and the House for eternity. Another reason was to prevent an internal struggle between loyalists who wanted to free their master and those who wanted to defend their holdings at the cost of everyone else.

To resist meant to allow internal strife to consume the city while also facing external threats. The envoys didn't want that and understood that most Lowlandians would simply choose to accept a new lord.

For the men-at-arms and commoners, Lord Omin and Lord Lansius were just another set of conquerors—the fourth to hold the city in less than ten years, from Jorge to his rebelling uncle, then to Omin who rebelled against his master, and now to Lord Lansius. In an internal struggle, they would not have the support of the populace, further risking conflict.

Therefore, the envoys hoped that negotiating now would yield better results, or at least some leniency in the terms.

After achieving a breakthrough, the envoys took their leave to discuss the matter with the reigning House and the rest of the city's defenders.

Hugo, Michael, and Daniella stood in front of their command tent, watching the three envoys ride their horses back to the city gates.

"Nice work," Michael congratulated Hugo.

"Couldn't have done it without you, sir," Hugo replied.

"Gentlemen," Daniella interrupted, "I've received reports from our nomad friends."

"Something happened?" Hugo inquired.

Daniella exhaled sharply. "Thousands are approaching the city from the west."

Hugo's smile faded. "Thousands? From the Three Hills area?"

"It's the route Nicopolans like me used to take when traveling from our home province," Daniella clarified.

Hugo studied her. "Are you implying they're Nicopolan mercenaries?"

Daniella met his gaze. "The nomads believe they're likely refugees."

"Seeking refuge in Lowlandia? But why?" Sir Michael interjected, puzzled.

"A great famine," Daniella replied, the words leaving a bad taste in her mouth.

Nicopola Province

For two years, bad harvests had plagued the Nicopola region. This was not uncommon, agriculture being dependent on the whims of sun, rain, and weather. However, the province faced a plethora of additional problems that exacerbated the situation.

Decades of high population growth, a continuous decline in fertile land due to the nobility expansion, and a large influx of refugees from the western wars had all pushed the province to its breaking point. The land and its people simply couldn't keep up with the increasing demands for food.

Now, they were on the brink of yet another bad harvest. The evidence was clear for all to see: even near the end of summer, the fields were already a lifeless brown with no hint of green. There was no hope for improvement, only the prospect of another season of harrowing famine and a deadly winter.

Panic set in, and people began raiding merchants and small communities for food supplies. Tensions boiled over among the three feuding factions: Nicopolan commoners, war refugees from West Centuria, and migrants from Sarmatia. Each blamed the others for the crisis.

Each group had endured unbearable pain and losses over the past two winters. This year, their patience had worn thin, and all sides were prepared for armed conflict. What began as isolated incidents of raiding soon escalated into widespread unrest. That summer, with everyone suspicious and hurting, the conflict entered a bloody new stage.

In unprecedented chaos since the founding of the Imperium, Nicopola was swept up in a massive armed conflict. Unguarded villages, manors, and weakly defended towns were sacked indiscriminately.

The noblemen tried to marshal their forces to contain the unrest but failed spectacularly. Unexpectedly, they lost the support of the middle class. As famine ravaged every social stratum, men-at-arms chose sides to protect their families and communities, rendering the nobles powerless.

Without sufficient manpower, the nobles retreated to their castles and ramparts, effectively becoming hostages in their own domains.

The crisis reached its peak, and the land was plundered clean. Within a month, not a single granary in Nicopola remained standing.

The high percentage of mercenaries among Nicopola's population made the conflict particularly deadly. Ironically, more food was lost to pillaging and arson than was gained.

Fall and winter were yet to come, but tens of thousands—primarily infants and the elderly—had already paid the ultimate price.

The Nicopolan crisis soon spilled over into neighboring provinces, many of which were already grappling with their own problems and committed to different fronts. Suddenly, the situation in the Imperium's heartland became dire.

Despite the urgency of the situation, no help arose. The Imperium failed to even send a detachment.

A grave mistake of such magnitude didn't go unnoticed. For those in power with keen insights, it was as good as a revelation. Three lords saw through the chaos and found the evidence they were seeking.

Lord Gottfried, ever ambitious, was the first to act. He mustered his forces and spread rumors that the emperor was ill and held hostage by the High Lords. This successfully sowed chaos among the populace and emboldened his followers in the north, who began to openly hail him as the King of Brigantes, the true name of the northern region.

Fearing turmoil in the capital, Lord Luis of Centuria began halting reinforcements to the western front. Although aware this could risk a total collapse against the nomadic incursion, he felt he had no other options.

Meanwhile, in Midlandia, Lord Bengrieve was clandestinely preparing his men for reasons that remained unclear.

While these lords pursued their agendas, their arrogance blinded them to the dagger at their jugular. Against all expectations, before the end of summer, massive groups of armed individuals emerged from Nicopola and invaded neighboring provinces. The crisis was in full swing and expanding exponentially.

The most devastating attack occurred in Elandia, sending its populace into panic. The region hadn't seen a strong harvest for nearly a decade, and the conflict now threatened to make them abandon their fields just months before harvest time. Famine seemed almost certain to befall a region already strained by hosting a sizable garrison against potential attack from Lord Gottfried's army in Arvena.

With Centuria occupied by fighting against the nomadic incursions, Elandia served as the last lifeline for the capital area. Its harvests and trade routes to Midlandia and Nicopola were vital for sustaining the capital. Losing Elandia—especially after the loss of Arvena—would lead to total isolation from the rest of the Imperium.

Armed groups also threatened to breach Midlandia's borders, prompting Lord Bengrieve to put his plans on hold and mobilize his private army to reinforce defenses in western Midlandia. Amid a succession crisis, this move risked weakening his grip over the region.

Korelia Castle

The news of the crisis in Nicopola and Elandia had yet to reach Korelia. There, the newlywed couple, still on their honeymoon, received a special visitor. Batu, the nomadic leader, had returned. Having heard about the lord's marriage, he came bearing lavish wedding gifts.

But first, another matter demanded attention. Sir Harold escorted a prisoner brought by Batu directly into the castle, where the Lord of Korelia was holding a special court session.

All parties had denied the prisoner's request for a bath and change of clothes. With little sympathy, Sir Harold pushed the man onto the cold floor, disregarding his high status. No one was in the mood for leniency; they knew this man was responsible for last year's spike in grain prices that had nearly starved them.

"My Noyan, I present to you the architect of the siege of Korelia," Batu announced proudly.

"So, this is the man who orchestrated our near starvation?" the lord inquired coldly.

Suddenly, a manic laugh echoed through the great hall, catching everyone by surprise. It came from the lady seated beside the lord.

Confused glances were exchanged among those in attendance. There seemed to be no immediate reason for her outburst.

Without care, the lady boldly approached the prisoner and locked eyes with him. The man abruptly looked away, shuddering uncontrollably.

"So, it really was you, cousin," she said, her voice dripping with contempt.

The hall fell into stunned silence.

CHAPTER 41

CITY OF KORELIA

Korelia Castle

The court of Korelia was abuzz with a shocking revelation: Lady Audrey declared the captured man to be her cousin. Anticipating denial, the Lord of Korelia approached the man. A tall knight promptly pinned Lord Omin to the floor.

Lord Lansius glanced at Lady Audrey, who nodded to indicate her seriousness. He then knelt and seized Omin by the chin. "We've never met before. I'm Lansius. Should I call you Omin, or brother-in-law?"

Omin shuddered uncontrollably, his mouth almost foaming at the implication of that word. The bane of his existence and his childhood heroine, united in matrimony. However, the tall knight shoved a waterskin into Omin's mouth and forced him to drink.

It wasn't even necessary; Sir Harold was simply telling the guest to behave.

Coughing and spitting out water after choking, Omin sat on the marble floor in sticky, dirty clothes, and feeling bloated from the water. He gave up. He couldn't suffer the humiliation anymore, and he was deathly afraid of being offered to the nomads as a slave. "Lord Lansius, what do you want with me?"

"First, is she your cousin?" Lansius asked.

"I have a cousin named Stephania," said Omin after some hesitation. "Indeed, the lady bears some resemblance to her."

Lansius seemed suspicious at how easily Omin admitted it. "But you've been separated for so long? Are you certain about this?"

"The eyes," Omin mumbled, then looked directly at Lansius. "You know it; she has the fell beast's eye."

Sir Harold heard the insult and was about to exact punishment, but Lansius signaled him to stop.

"I'll have my scribe prepare a letter of confession. Will you sign it?"

Omin was stunned. He knew it would seal off everything for which he had fought so hard. Yet, memories of how his father had taken everything from Stephania and her mother surged forth. He had done many cruel things, but there was some guilt still left in him. For him, Stephania was family and a childhood friend. Moreover, she was the only blood relative he had left.

Against all his suspicions, the former rising star of Lowlandia nodded. He saw himself fortunate to meet Stephania. Better her than Lansius, he thought. In her hand, his House might yet survive. "I haven't lost my signet ring. I'll write the letter myself if you agree to transfer my House to her intact, provide leniency for my House and myself, and absolve me of all accusations."

"You can't escape the law," warned Lansius.

"This is Lowlandia." Omin stifled a laugh before raising his voice. "You are the law."

Lansius exhaled sharply at Omin's remark that the victor could do anything he wanted in this lawless region. He stood up and looked at Audrey. "My lady, do you have anything to say to your cousin?"

"We'll chat about the good old times in Centuria after he's settled in the dungeon," she replied, eyeing Omin, who grew nervous. "Take care, cousin. And thank you for returning the House. I'll send some warm clothes later, just as Uncle gave me new warm clothes before he sold me as a servant."

The startling revelations continued to reverberate throughout the castle: Lord Omin was Lady Audrey's cousin. Furthermore, Omin had relinquished his House to Audrey to avoid being taken or confiscated by Lansius.

Lansius later learned the details of the events from Audrey. The story went that a decade earlier, young Audrey and her mother were evicted from their home following her father's untimely death. The instigator had been her uncle, Omin's father, who later sold the estate to purchase larger lands in faraway Lowlandia.

All this time, Audrey had been unaware that her House had left its roots and relocated, but now it was suddenly within her reach.

With Omin captured and facing punishment for his crimes, even without Omin's words, his House would naturally disinherit him to avoid political ramifications. Given Audrey's birthright and her position as the victor's consort, she was the obvious choice to become the new head of the House.

In a rare feat of justice, Audrey would reclaim everything Omin had achieved, including the entire fief of Korimor and the accompanying title. From that day on, she became the rightful claimant to the Barony of Korimor. Once merely the adopted daughter of a baronet, she was now a baroness in her own right.

City of Korelia

While the nobility kept the news of the crisis in Nicopola under wraps to prevent trouble, news of Lord Lansius's victory had spread like wildfire in Midlandia, attracting people of interest to travel to Korelia. Before, many had doubted Lord Lansius's reign, but now he had the most promising future in all of Lowlandia.

First, the grain merchants arrived, fulfilling their grain trade deal, followed by guilds from Midlandia offering their services. They had only been in Korelia for a few days, waiting for an opportunity to meet with Lord Lansius, when they learned of his grand alliance plan—a breakthrough that could transform Lowlandia into a powerhouse like Midlandia.

They were excited about the plans, and then they learned that Lord Lansius's consort had a claim over Korimor. The excitement reached a fever pitch. At this rate, they would do anything to fulfill the lord's whims so as not to be left behind in future projects.

Lord Lansius's first project was a dormitory for disabled veterans and an orphanage. A straightforward project, he wanted the building to be equipped with beds, chairs, plumbing, heating, and indoor washrooms. He also planned to provide the occupants with shoes, socks, and warm clothes.

He had allocated a sizable plot of land for them so they could grow vegetables. Deep down, Lord Lansius never forgot his experience as a farmer and a lowly scribe-soldier in Arvena. He wanted to give the unlucky ones a fighting chance. Lady Audrey was the patron for this project, due to her closeness to the veterans.

Next on his list was a public school. As he had expected, the guilds were quick to offer to build a branch of Midlandia's famous school for the landless. Lady Felicity wanted to become the patron and styled herself as the first headmaster.

Several other projects were slated for completion after the orphanage and school, including a bazaar, water mills, a guild hall, and a bathhouse.

In addition to these projects, Lord Lansius undertook two other major initiatives: the Korelia City Wall and the East Farmland. These were overseen by the Building Bureau, more commonly known as the Korelia Mason Guild.

The lord planned to expand the City of Korelia eastward while fortifying it with a wall and rows of windbreak trees. The aim was to prevent topsoil from eroding due to the harsh steppe winds. Included in his plans was a Grand Keep to serve as his new residence.

The lord chose to keep the project local, channeling resources from within his domain, but he also welcomed assistance from outside guilds. Guilds from across the Midlands eagerly offered timber, glass, marble, carpet, furniture, plumbing, and even decorative elements for the Grand Keep. However, the design was yet to be finalized.

By the end of summer, numerous proposals had been submitted and revised. Despite the rumors surrounding Lord Lansius, guildsmen found both the lord and lady to be agreeable and reasonable people.

Based on their informal meetings, what the Lord of Korelia wanted was a functional and cost-effective design for a castle. The lord particularly disliked ornamental pieces that served no function. While this would undoubtedly hurt the guilds' profit margins, it sparked great interest among the master masons.

Normally, most nobles desired a castle to showcase grandeur, wealth, prestige, or power. That usually meant grand archways, alabaster marble, and fine sculptures. Such features were generally the work of artisans, not master masons.

Master masons' passion was to create defensive structures. They found kinship with Lord Lansius, whose approach was more in line with their goals. Thus, the cooperation went smoothly. The master masons designed not only walls but also wells, cisterns, well-ventilated storage areas, and even some anti-tunneling measures inside the Grand Keep.

Rather than aiming for grandeur or breakthrough designs, they relied on tried-and-true plans that were robust and easy to maintain. When the blueprint was finally completed, everyone realized that the Lord of Korelia wasn't just building a keep to live in; he was constructing a fortress.

The Quarry

Excluding the knights and nobility, over one thousand four hundred men were captured. For security reasons, they were separated and assigned to different tasks. A hundred were tasked with building the dormitory, another hundred at the school, and another hundred served as field kitchen staff.

Based on recommendations from his Mason Guild, Lansius evenly divided the remaining men: five hundred were assigned to the quarry, while another five hundred joined the wall projects, which were primarily carried out by local laborers.

The last one hundred were the newly elected command staff and hospice facility workers.

From the start, Lord Lansius had instructed his men to use the ex-opponents' existing chain of command. They secured the captains' loyalty by offering them better treatment and a semblance of power.

The lieutenants enforced work and maintained productivity; Lansius had not set an overly high bar for production and gave them plenty of rest, especially those working in the harsh stone quarry.

The food was basic but edible: gruel, soups with hints of meat, and rye bread. More variation and rations were allocated to the quarry workers to offset their working conditions. They were also given ale every two days to keep them content.

The treatment they received actually exceeded their expectations. Most had feared being sold into slavery or being worked in the mines under brutal conditions, but here they were given humane treatment. Their only grievance was that they could not go home to help with the harvest or send word to their families, which saddened them greatly.

Another day passed in Korelia. That night, a commotion erupted in the quarry. Word spread that a lieutenant from South Hill had been killed in a quarrel with his men.

The lord's guards swarmed the camp, led by a high-ranking officer. An investigation was launched, impressing the men with its speed and thoroughness. After all, they were mere prisoners; usually, no one would bother.

By the time the sun was just above the treetops, a large entourage approached the quarry. The men were rounded up in formation and were shocked to see the blue and bronze chevron heraldry.

The Black Lord, a living legend, was there in person. The man who had defeated six thousand with only a few hundred. He was also the man who had survived a duel against a Mage Knight with merely a mark on his wrist.

Now, standing before them, he appeared visibly annoyed. The men quickly connected the dots, assuming his displeasure was related to the previous day's murder. Fear crept in as they remembered facing his wrath in past battles and the ensuing routs.

Filled with apprehension, many whispered among themselves, questioning their fate. "What kind of punishment awaits us? Flogging? Half rations? Sleeping in the open?" they speculated, too scared to look up as the lord approached to address them.

Yet, when he arrived, he remained silent. Instead, staff from the kitchen brought out ten fat sheep and slaughtered them right in front of the formation.

The red blood was collected in a bronze cauldron, evoking a scene from ancient sacrificial rites. The sight unsettled the men, including the lieutenants and captains.

Nobody could predict the enigmatic Lord of Korelia. Even the Lion of Lowlandia had failed to do so, as had Lord Omin—once considered a rising star—who now languished in the dungeon.

Now, the bane of Lowlandia took several steps forward, flanked by his guards.

"Behold, you are in the presence of the Lord of Korelia," announced his herald in a sweet voice that did little to ease the laborers' tension.

"At ease," said Lord Lansius calmly. It was their first time hearing his voice. He stood tall, clad in lordly attire, and his black hair was strikingly visible for all to see.

"Last night, a murder occurred here," he began, his expression stoic. "My condolences to the family of the deceased."

The crowd's eyes darted around, finding a young man who looked visibly distraught. Many also felt grateful for the unexpected warm, empathetic message.

"Our investigation has identified the culprits." The lord exhaled deeply and declared, "Let it be known that no crime will go unpunished here."

The guards brought forward two bound men.

"These men held a grudge against the victim for catching them asleep in a hidden part of the quarry," the lord continued.

Many shook their heads; such a motive for murder was seen as cruel and barbaric.

"Do you have anything to say?" Lord Lansius asked the culprits, who remained silent, too ashamed to face their comrades.

The lord faced the five hundred men standing in formation once more. "I know you're here against your will, but consider this your atonement for attacking Korelia."

No one dared to challenge the statement.

"However, I have treated you fairly. You may not realize it, but I've ordered ten sheep to be slaughtered every two days solely to feed you. True, the soup is bland, but that's because Korelia isn't a land of plenty. We don't have enough vegetables for everyone, and this year's harvest is likely to suffer due to the war."

The crowd murmured in surprise. Although they had found the food to be better than expected—superior, even, to what they had received while marching with the Coalition army—they hadn't realized the lengths to which Lord Lansius had gone to feed them.

"Hasn't it dawned on you that I've treated you as if you were my own army?" Lord Lansius asked, looking out over the crowd.

Again, murmurs of surprise rippled through the men, who exchanged glances as they considered the lord's words.

The lord briefly turned his attention to the two perpetrators, a look of disappointment crossing his face. Returning his gaze to the crowd, he said, "You've had it as good as you could get here. Many have advised me to send half of you to Feodosia to be sold into the Eastern Kingdoms. Is that what you want?"

The men shuddered. Tales of the abuses faced by slaves in the Eastern Kingdoms were well known.

"The older one will be sent to Feodosia; half of the proceeds will go to the family of the deceased. The younger one will be set to the Great Plains for the nomads to hunt," Lord Lansius decreed.

The guards dragged the perpetrators away. Their punishments had been meted out.

The crowd felt both pity and a sense of justice. However, they were left puzzled: Why hadn't both men been sold to Feodosia? And why was the younger one released into the Great Plains to be hunted by nomads?

Observing their puzzled expressions, Lansius threw out a wild card. "Make no mistake, you're not here because of me."

His words puzzled the crowd. Some were skeptical, thinking it was just sophistry.

"These guards are to protect my people, not to prevent you from running," Lansius challenged them.

The crowd immediately buzzed with murmurs.

"Do you remember who captured you and brought you here?" the lord asked, his tone ominous.

The crowd's suspicion changed into dread. Many shuddered or swallowed hard, remembering the nomads who had rounded them up.

"You're only here because you're under my protection, but it doesn't extend beyond Korelia. Beyond these walls, you belong to the nomads. Anyone who isn't here is at the mercy of the nomads, to do as they please. Now, imagine what they would do to you if you were seen as Nicopolans?"

The crowd went silent thinking about their plight. Many South Hill and Korimor people were once migrants from Nicopola and feared being misidentified as mercenaries.

The lord continued with a gentler voice. "I've promised my allied nomads that within three years, you will have made significant contributions to Korelia—from building markets and bathhouses to expanding farmlands and constructing city walls."

He paused to look at the crowd. "Those are the works that the nomads and I would appreciate. Fulfill these tasks, and I will grant you safe passage home."

A sense of loss clouded the faces of almost everyone in the crowd. As fearful as they were, three years seemed like a long time.

As if sensing their concerns, Lansius announced, "Starting next month and continuing through the fall and next summer, we'll hold monthly dice contests. Ten winners will be allowed to return home early."

This immediately piqued the interest of the men; their eyes widened, and conversations broke out among them.

"For the Korimors, after I acquire the castle. I'll send my official with records of your names to your hometowns or villages. That way, your families will know you're safe and can either wait for your return or visit you next year," he continued.

Many were moved by this offer. The hard work was something they were used to; it was the separation from their families that was unbearable.

"As for those from South Hill—bad luck! I've sent a messenger, but your lord is arrogant and unreasonable."

"Siege the city and force him out! We'd gladly help!" someone shouted, and many from South Hill cheered. They had little love for their current lord, whom they viewed as an untrustworthy usurper.

"Let's not get ahead of ourselves," Lansius warned, calming the crowd. "With your help, I'm sure we could take South Hill. But that would lead to more regions suffering from a bad harvest. And that would cause more people, including your families, to suffer. For now, focus on building Korelia. I'll deal with the Lord of South Hill when the time comes."

Lord Lansius's keen insight and benevolence that day only added to his growing reputation. He became the topic of conversation everywhere. Many were warming to the idea of having him as their lord, comparing him favorably to their leaders.

Lansius took a moment to rest between tasks and meetings. He had just addressed a murder case in the quarry—the first fatal case among the forced laborers. While he could have let the case slide into obscurity, he feared that morale would plummet, which could be dangerous to everyone involved.

Thus, he seized the opportunity and tackled the issue head-on. Adopting the role of a politician, Lansius used cunning words to move the captured men as he wished. It wasn't the question of correct or wrong. It was the issue that there would be anarchy and blood if he couldn't inspire them.

What he wanted to say, but couldn't convey, was: they were creating a path to a united Lowlandia by surrendering three years of their freedom.

Like it or not, peace wouldn't be achieved without a price. Everybody had to pay the price, and Lansius and his troops had paid their due.

On a lighter note, Lansius was also occupied with numerous projects, including the challenging Duck Breeding Project in the forest. He believed the forest would serve as a natural habitat for the ducks.

Historical records showed that the native ducks had originally been found in forested areas and were later bred in meadows, much like horses, but with only marginal success. So, he aimed to return them to their natural environment. Strategic fences, shelters, and designated feeding grounds were constructed to keep the ostrich-sized ducks in place.

The shelters also ensured that the breeders had a secure back door to easily gather eggs. It would still require courage, but it should be doable. Preliminary reports were promising; it seemed the forest was providing enough food that supplemental feeding was less necessary.

Knocks on the door interrupted Lansius as he rested on his cushioned bench.

Margo, the page boy, opened the door a crack and nodded at the whispered words.

"What is it, Margo?" asked Lansius.

"An urgent missive from Deputy Hugo."

Lansius stood up, alarmed. "What does it say?"

Margo took the missive from the messenger outside and handed it to Lansius.

He didn't recognize the handwriting, but it was neat, likely belonging to Sir Michael or Lady Daniella.

We have captured Korimor but are now facing three thousand armed refugees from Nicopola, possibly more. Reports indicate that a severe famine has occurred in the Nicopola region, and the thousands who have arrived seem intent on plundering the Korimor countryside.

We are currently in a standoff, as they fear our nomads, not realizing that our nomadic group consists only of children and the elderly. We request reinforcements and further instructions. Lady Daniella is attempting to broker peace.

Lansius was stunned but quickly moved to the table where he kept a large map of the Imperium.

"Arvena, Nicopola . . . not good," he muttered to himself. "If this has spread into Lowlandia, then Elandia is doomed, and along with it, the capital."

CHAPTER 42

LULL BEFORE THE STORM

Felicity

Lady Felis, still occupying the master chamber in the castle, was disassembling a new crossbow. Her desk was cluttered with tools, various cords, and spare parts for the trigger.

She wanted a more comfortable grip, and Hannei had given her the idea for a pistol grip. The only problem lay in modifying the trigger, so she experimented to create some parts with the help of a smith.

Today, the parts arrived, and she was about to reassemble the trigger when she felt a warm feeling reaching out to her.

Felis immediately touched her necklace and felt a warm sensation in her mind. She rushed to her bag and spilled its contents onto the bed. Rummaging through the items, she found the bracelet she was looking for.

It was a precious find from her days exploring the dwarven ruins. As far as she knew, there was only one in existence. She put it on, and a burst of emotion surged forth.

"Love, are you safe? Where are you?" the voice from the other end whispered as their minds began to intertwine.

My lord, how I've missed you. Does this mean you're back in Midlandia? I'm in Korelia; I'm safe. They're treating me well here.

"I'm so glad to hear that. Yes, love, I've returned. It's a shame I couldn't bring this wonderful item to the capital, but the place was as dangerous as we suspected."

I'm thrilled to feel your thoughts again. How was the journey?

"Rough. The road was incredibly dangerous, even with our armed escorts. Signs of trouble were everywhere. Anci even claimed he saw fell beasts lurking near the camp several times."

The Elandia forest is ancient. He could be speaking the truth.

"I believe him. Oh, before I forget, the mission is a success. I secured support and funds to retake Arvena."

That's most fortunate, my lord. Congratulations!

"Naturally. How's life there? I heard Lansius won a big victory. I was worried for you when I learned he was up against three lords."

Felis felt a wave of raw emotion from Arte.

Don't worry, he kept me safe. Korelia troops won big.

"So the rumor was true after all . . . It's good to know that Bengrieve's money wasn't wasted. Mm, to think that my squire has grown powerful now."

Yes, the unassuming man turned out to be special.

"I'm rather envious of him. But in a good way."

Of course, my lord. There's also something else; we just found out that Audrey is a cousin to one of Lowlandia's barons.

"Audrey? Isn't she the woman squire Lansius is looking for?"

She's the one! They've just gotten married. As it turns out, her House had relocated to Lowlandia and achieved incredible success. But since they lost the war to Lansius, all their possessions are now up for grabs.

"Married? And to think he'd choose such an outlier, a shield-maiden nonetheless. But, what a turn of luck!"

Indeed. Now they could potentially claim the barony.

Flashes of emotion emitted from Arte, almost akin to a hearty laugh. "So many surprises in Lowlandia. How fortunate those two are!"

Don't you also want to marry someone like her with a barony at her hand?

"No, love, you're perfect. I doubt she's as open-minded as you. Not even the ladies in the capital are as bold and daring."

Felis blushed and her emotion carried to Arte.

"Besides, I'd definitely lose support if I married a baroness with a history of being a shield-maiden. What is Lansius thinking? Is he always this bold, or is this normal in Lowlandia?"

Lansius is always bold. He's a beast in sheep's clothing. But really, even in Lowlandia, I've never seen another shield-maiden. I have seen a Nicopolan captain, but she's a noblewoman turned mercenary.

"It must be great to have that degree of freedom. Throwing caution to the wind like it's nothing. I suppose he can afford it, especially after a series of big victories."

Nobody is against the marriage. People seem to be fully supportive.

"Fascinating. Do you think he's planning something by marrying her?"

Felis chuckled. *How could I fathom someone like him? They call him the bane of Lowlandia.*

"A fitting name . . . Oh, don't tell Lansius, but officials from the capital should arrive in about three weeks. They're resting in Midlandia right now. But I guess he doesn't need them as much anymore."

Which is perfect. He can save himself from having to offer bribes.

"Hah! Indeed, the officials will likely ask for bribes."

Felis smiled and decided to ask. *Will you also send your carriage for me, my lord?*

"Of course, it's best if we're together. You wouldn't like to hear it but aside from Midlandia's succession issue, there are all sorts of problems brewing."

I'm aware. Even so far in Korelia, I heard all kinds of unsettling rumors . . .

"Love, there's much I want to tell you, but the item's power is fleeting."

Indeed, I feel the voice getting farther and weaker. Felis felt the voice in her mind fading as the magical item's power waned.

"Till the next opportunity, love."

You too, my lord.

Flushed with emotion, Felis removed her finger from the bracelet. Alongside mere thoughts, they also shared glimpses of their deepest desires, as minds are wild and uncontrollable by nature.

Felis couldn't wait to be with Arte again, the man who was unafraid of her wild side and lifelong secrets.

Lansius

As night fell, instead of burning midnight candles, Lansius decided to adjourn the war council. He felt there was no need to exhaust his retinues over things beyond their capabilities.

In the case of Korimor, there was simply no easy way out. Thus, although the need to reinforce Hugo was pressing, Lansius chose to remain calm and only planned for a small advance party.

He was keenly aware that Korelia was already filled with captured men and understood the risks of sending out another hundred or so troops to Korimor.

Moreover, he needed to warn Lord Jorge and Lord Robert. While still contemplating his plans for Korimor, the powerful duo of Korelia retired to their bedchamber.

Lansius locked the door while Audrey went behind a folding screen to change her clothes. She still hadn't selected a chambermaid to assist her. Fortunately, she didn't fancy a fine gown, so dressing wasn't a big deal.

Since Audrey didn't know much about gowns, it was Felis who had helped her find attire for formal occasions. However, most couldn't fit her properly, as she was too athletic compared to a regular woman.

With no reputable tailor in town, they had ordered several new dresses from

White Lake. Lansius was eager to see her in well-fitted attire, believing that hand-me-downs didn't do her justice.

Lansius placed a fresh log into the fireplace and then changed clothes. According to custom, while the lower classes often slept in their daily clothes, some in the upper class chose to sleep naked, enjoying the luxury of privacy and the comfort of good blankets.

However, having grown up as a squire, Audrey was more comfortable wearing simple clothes to sleep. Moreover, due to old habits from their time on the road, the couple kept gambesons, swords, and crossbows nearby.

After changing into his simple shirt, Lansius went to the corner of his room where a stone washbasin with drainage was located. He took a freshly cut young twig from a clay platter and chewed one end. The bite easily produced a bristled tip, which he used as a toothbrush.

The twig felt refreshingly gingery, mixed with a paste of powdered clover and salt. After a quick gargle, he was done. Next, he washed his face using clean water from the copper basin.

Finished with cleaning up, he stretched out in bed. It was probably not even eight p.m., but he felt sleepy. Ever since getting married, he had come to cherish their private hours together. Only during these times could they simply be a normal couple.

He often contemplated how much he had been through to reach this point in life. Looking back, he realized there were many moments where he could have failed, or taken a wrong turn and ended up dead.

However, there was no shudder or fear from it.

Life is funny; it keeps knocking me down but also elevates me to greater heights.

His own thoughts gave him pause. "My lady," he asked, "why didn't you tell me about Omin?"

"What about . . . Lans, stop calling me that when we're alone," Audrey complained from behind the lacquered folding screen.

Lansius chuckled. He had teased her enough after the surprising reveal two days ago. "But really, you're the baroness now. I'm just an impostor. You should rule, and I'll be the consort. What do you think?"

Only groans came from behind the folding screen. Then Audrey appeared, wearing a deep blue linen nightgown, her face flushed and irritated. She walked briskly toward the bed and pouted in front of Lansius. "Let's keep things as they were. Nothing has changed except my title."

"Yes, my lady."

She jumped into the bed and tickled him, causing Lansius to burst into laughter. "Okay, okay, I'm sorry, ackk!"

Lansius, half-laughing and half-gasping for air, asked again, "So, Omin . . . ?"

"What about him?" she retorted moodily.

"Don't you find his name a bit unique or suspicious?"

Audrey sighed. "I thought it was merely coincidental. Sometimes, identical names can happen, right?"

"Omin? What part of that name is normal?" he complained.

"I thought it was common." She shrugged, got out of bed, and went to brush her teeth.

"Drey, since you're a baroness, could you knight several men for me?"

She turned her head around quickly and asked, "Eh, I can do that?"

"Of course, you can," Lansius smiled. "Transferring power internally within the House doesn't require the Imperium's consent. So you're a full-fledged baroness now."

"Then I should be the first," she exclaimed excitedly.

"First to do what?" Lansius knitted his brows.

"To knight myself!"

Watching her innocent face, Lansius burst out laughing, leaving Audrey red-faced and frowning.

"Drey, you're already a baroness."

Realizing her foolishness, Audrey pouted.

"Come here," he beckoned with open arms.

Feigning anger to hide her embarrassment, Audrey turned away to finish brushing her teeth and then wash her face.

Once she was done, Lansius said, "You know, we've come a long way from pitching tents by the roadside."

"Mm, yeah . . . I still can't believe we live in a mansion like this," Audrey said, looking around at the painted ceilings and the bright, colorful tapestries.

"A lot still needs to be fixed, though," said Lansius. The place looked old but was still better than most rooms in the castle.

"I'm looking forward to seeing an even better room than this," she said with a small grin, then climbed into bed beside him.

Lansius took a deep breath, looking at Audrey beside him. How he wished their conversations could always be like this—just a normal couple. "Drey," he said, his tone becoming serious.

"Hush," she interrupted. "I know . . . Let's just sleep like this and forget about the lord stuff for now. It can wait."

Lansius smiled and hugged her tightly. "This is why I can't be happy with anyone but you."

Audrey bit her lip, clearly pleased with the compliment.

"You know . . . I couldn't say no if you needed to enter into a political marriage," she said softly after a moment.

"As if I could. I'm merely the consort to the baroness," Lansius reassured her, treasuring the moment.

The answer earned him a solid kiss.

"Margo is still up," Lansius warned.

"He's old enough to be a squire," Audrey replied, crawling on top of him. "Besides, I already told him to retire to the staff's quarters."

"What did you tell him?" asked Lansius.

"That I'm perfectly able to guard you," she said and giggled. Hearing that, with a swift but gentle motion, Lansius rolled, taking her with him as he shifted their positions. And so, the two attempted to fulfill the ultimate duty of nobility—to produce an heir.

Nicopola

As summer drew to a close, the clashes across the region became ever present. Driven by hysteria and starvation, people began attacking even those within their own factions.

Livestock and wildlife had been wiped out; even insects and birds had become scarce. After sundown, Nicopola fell into an eerie silence, broken only by the wind. As food sources dwindled, people resorted to eating tree bark and other desperate means for sustenance.

Half-eaten corpses littered the side roads and back alleys. In hidden markets, what was grimly referred to as *gray flesh* was being bartered as food.

Unable to endure the hardships in Nicopola any longer, tens of thousands set out for neighboring provinces. This second wave came fully armed, well aware that they would not be welcomed and expecting heavy resistance.

Their desperation was so dire that many also risked venturing into the conflict-prone region of Lowlandia. Now, thousands were converging toward the Korimor region and its almost-ready to harvest fields. Their goal was not just to find food. Knowing that Nicopola would remain conflict-ridden for years to come, they came to settle and occupy.

Sir Harold

In record-breaking time, the preparations for reinforcement were completed. Normally, mobilizing a barony would take weeks—sending bannermen to invite knights, recruiting from towns and villages, and contracting men-at-arms.

The speedy preparation was due to the high readiness of the Korelia troops, who lived in billets within the city or in nearby villages. Additionally, the lord had ordered only a small advance guard, further expediting the process.

Tonight, Sir Harold was preparing his gear. He was to lead the advance guard to Korimor. Alongside him, his squire prepared their winter gear and other personal supplies, as Lord Lansius had instructed them to be ready for winter in Korimor.

"Squire," Sir Harold called when they were halfway through their preparations.

The shy squire looked up. "Yes, sir, is there anything else?" he stuttered.

"You don't have to accompany me on this campaign. It's risky."

"B-but what would I do without you, sir?"

Sir Harold smiled. "Your father gave me a warhorse, so I accepted you as my squire. You've followed me long enough. Your training is complete. Take the horse back and return to your father."

"That's not necessary, sir. I will follow," the squire said, bowing his head.

"Don't be blinded by greed. This is Lowlandia; you'll be closer to death than to knighthood. Return to Midlandia and start a life."

"I will follow. You can take another, more capable squire, but I'll still follow," the squire proclaimed, a sense of pride in his voice. Even though he was timid, he enjoyed the camaraderie of Harold's war-crazed warband. He had found a sense of brotherhood, unlike anything he had ever felt before.

The tall knight smiled at his squire's bravado and stubbornness. The timid young man displayed a level of guts and loyalty sometimes absent even in knights. In silence, they carried on with their preparations, fully aware that battle was likely on the menu.

At dawn the next morning, the advance guard—consisting of fifteen knights and an equal number of squires—was seen off by the lord and lady at the city gate. Then, guided by a nomadic tribesman, Sir Harold's small warband and the pack animals headed northwest without much fanfare. All were volunteers, and all looked somber.

CHAPTER 43

PERICULUM IN MORA

Despite the looming military crisis, construction projects in Korelia continued to thrive. Sir Justin, as the lord's highest-ranking staff member, and Calub oversaw a workforce comprising five hundred Korelians and fifteen hundred others. They managed not only labor allocation but also the various raw material supplies, many of which were brought in from outside the city.

To sustain this extra workforce, they needed more than just a field kitchen. As a precaution against plague, they set up a barber shop for basic hygiene and medical care. This was followed by a clothing repair shop and a permanent blacksmith on-site to maintain working tools. Guildsmen also played a part, supplying ropes, pulleys, and other basic amenities.

Korelia had never seen an operation of this scale before. Extensive digging was carried out to lay the foundation for the city wall, a delicate operation overseen by the experienced master mason. Meanwhile, in the Eastern Farming Project, the land survey for the windbreak trees had been concluded with a complete map. They moved forward with the next step: selecting the correct trees for Korelia.

Lord Lansius wanted a diverse range of trees for windbreaks, not just poplars. These trees would be planted in rows to shield the topsoil from the harsh winds of the steppe. Calub consulted the relevant guilds, who supported such a method, as they had seen it in their records.

Hearing of their interest, the Alchemist Guild offered to provide specialized fertilizers and growth-boosting concoctions. Naturally, Lord Lansius and Calub were interested.

Calub personally found it amusing that his guild's research on the beast-eating mandragora plant could be repurposed for something beneficial. If all went well, the windbreak trees would help retain enough topsoil to sustain taller and fuller grass, turning the field into a meadow suitable for grazing.

The manure from the livestock would fertilize the soil. Furthermore, before winter, they planned to direct laborers to make minor modifications to the landscape, enabling the field to retain snow during the winter.

As an experiment and to foster growth, Calub and his team had relocated suitable younger trees from the forest to the eastern farm area. Great care was given to them, recognizing that these trees were crucial to Korelia's future.

The general design called for rows of windbreak trees on both the eastern and western sides of the new farming zone. They also planned to plant multiple rows of elms, poplars, and shrubs to protect from the now infamous dry summer Southwind.

Lord Lansius and his staff hoped that, in the long run, these windbreaks would either make the land suitable for agriculture or transform it into good pasture for horse breeding. Either outcome would prove beneficial to Korelia and its people.

Small Council

Yesterday, Lansius had consulted his council to discuss Hugo's request, but aside from writing one letter and deploying Sir Harold as an advanced guard, they did nothing else. For certain, nobody wanted to send more troops to Korimor. It was simply too risky for Korelia.

While Sir Harold only commanded fifteen knights and fifteen squires, Lansius entrusted a mission to them.

Korimor had turned from being served on a silver plate into a pit hole of ambition. Lansius had pulled his chair to sit against the window. He needed time to think.

While Lansius was deep in thought, Audrey was engrossed in a book recommended by Felis. Though she appeared frustrated, she continued reading. Beside her, Cecile, the new chamberlain, was reading scrolls from various sources laid out on the table.

While it was more common for the nobles to accept verbal reports, Lansius chose to put his correspondence into letters, especially for dealings and negotiations. That way he had written documents as proof.

After her appointment, Cecile was taking over some of Calub's role as he was overworked with the urgent Eastern Farming Project.

As for her older role, Margo had stepped up to become the cup-bearer. Cecile had thought to recommend Claire to take the job, but Claire had ideas of her own. Right now, Claire was accompanying Lady Felicity as a lady in waiting.

An earth-scented breeze blew inside the chamber. The changing of seasons made Lansius exhale deeply.

Time is running out.

"Drey," he called.

Audrey glanced at him. "Yes?"

"I think I should go . . ." he replied ominously.

She let out a long sigh. "Can't the marshal do it?"

Lansius stared unfocused before answering, "As much as I respect Sir Justin, this requires my presence. Besides, he has his job cut out for him. Looking after Korelia is a major thing in itself."

Audrey rose and approached Lansius, lowering herself to meet his gaze before pleading, "I say we abandon Korimor. Even if it's supposedly mine, it's not worth risking another pitched battle."

Lansius nodded. He knew she was speaking the truth. Even if the whole castle and town were raided, the walls and defensive structure weren't going anywhere. They could simply wait for the Nicopolans to move away after eating up all the food and then reclaim the city. However, he had other concerns.

"I'm worried about the refugees," revealed Lansius.

Audrey squinted her eyes. "The Nicopolans? My lord, they're not your people."

"I know, but they're also not our enemies. There must be something I could do." Frustration filled his voice.

Audrey exhaled deeply. "I also wish they could be saved. But is it going to happen?"

"My lord, lady, if I may," Cecile interrupted. "You can save select people. You need manpower to guard your realm, also educated men to help you as you'll likely have two baronies to manage. I also heard that Nicopolans are excellent farmers and adept at their crafts."

Lansius found it wise and quoted, "A wise man once said, the enemy of my enemy is my friend."

"The problem is, we can't save the rest. And how would they react?" asked Audrey.

"They'll continue to plunder every village and town they can find," Lansius speculated. "And after Korimor, they will either take the long journey to cross the Great Plains into more prosperous Midlandia, or continue to Three Hills."

"Many will die," Cecile commented with a sense of regret. "Lowlandians didn't have that much to begin with. The Nicopolans will attack people who barely have enough to survive winter."

Lansius's shoulders slumped while his neck muscles tensed from all the worrying and thinking. Nothing in his modern education prepared him to face such a dilemma. Worse, he believed that this wasn't the whole picture.

"Their deaths are in their own hands, not yours," said Audrey all of a sudden.

Her comment stunned him for a bit, and he felt the need to reveal the other side of the equation, "I'm actually more worried about Umberland."

Audrey looked puzzled and glanced at Cecile, who took the initiative to stand up and lay out an incomplete map of Lowlandia, along with two books to prevent the yellowing map from rolling back up.

Audrey returned to the table and studied the map.

"This is Umberland, situated between Nicopola, Elandia, and Three Hills," explained Cecile.

"They're mountainous terrain. The lord of the heights they called him. It was almost impassable to get there from Elandia. One book mentioned deep ravines and gorges. However, it had a well-known mountain route to Nicopola." Lansius's nerdiness wowed the other two.

"Why can't I get that kind of information from the books I've read?" Audrey complained.

"There are many kinds of books," replied Lansius warmly.

"My lord, so what about Umberland?" asked Cecile.

"If thousands of Nicopolans have reached Korimor, it means that Umberland is finished," said Lansius gravely.

There was growing nervousness in Cecile's face, but Lansius continued. "This is probably why Umberland didn't join the Coalition in the first place. They read the writing on the wall and refrained from moving their men out of fear of trouble from Nicopola."

"They were wise to do so," commented Audrey.

"Umberland is why I need to go to Korimor and see the situation for myself. I can't do it from Korelia," said Lansius.

Audrey was confused. "But why? What do you want to do with them?"

"They're akin to the Western Gates of Lowlandia. If they remain open, then we'll see a greater flow of men from Nicopola. Maybe even in tens of thousands."

The explanation made Cecile nervous. That amount would dwarf the population of several cities in Lowlandia. It might be enough to destroy the new balance of power, Lansius had tried so hard to achieve.

"We can't inform the hungry Nicopolans that there's no food in Lowlandia. They wouldn't believe us, so we must close the gates." He looked at Audrey. "For this to happen, I need to secure Korimor before harvest."

Sir Morton

The Mage Knight was increasingly pleased with the progress made on the Grand Alliance. Meetings had taken place between the Lord of Korelia and the Lord of White Lake to formalize the concept. Now, despite their recent loss, there was assurance that Lord Jorge could pass his inherited lands on to his House without fear of external threats.

Morton remained optimistic that the elusive peace in Lowlandia was finally within reach despite learning about the new issues involving Nicopolan refugees in Korimor.

A few days earlier, the Mage Knight had requested an audience with the Lord of Korelia. Although he preferred to wait for a better time, he felt that time was running short and he might not get another chance. He also feared arousing suspicion if he kept this information to himself.

Fortunately, the day before his departure, an escort arrived to take him to the castle. His master, Lord Jorge, had not only granted permission for the meeting but also expressed enthusiasm about both the issue and the prospective bargain.

Morton, donned in a doublet sourced from donated supplies, rode through the scorched field where the Coalition army had been defeated.

Upon arriving at the castle's courtyard, he realized it was his first time setting foot there. Unlike Lord Jorge's older retinue, he had only joined the lord's service less than a decade ago. His eyes swept over the castle, where his lord had been born.

"Sir Morton, welcome to the castle. My lord and lady are expecting you," said a man with a melodious voice.

"Gratitude," Morton replied as he dismounted. Handing his horse to a stable boy, he followed the escort inside. As requested, he was led to the Great Chamber for some privacy. Although he noticed several armed guards, he paid no heed. It was common for a Mage Knight like himself to be viewed as a threat.

Lansius

Still thinking about the aftermath of the council meeting and what to prepare for his departure to Korimor, Lansius noticed Sigmund enter the Great Chamber, followed by Morton.

"My lord, my lady," Sigmund addressed his master. "Sir Morton seeks an audience."

"Please, come in," Lansius said, staying seated. He had approved this meeting because he was likely departing for Korimor the day after tomorrow.

Morton stepped forward. "My lord, my lady, please accept my gratitude for this audience."

"Sir Morton, it's good to see you. Would you like a seat and some refreshments?"

"Please don't let my presence bother you, my lord. I've only come to deliver good news."

"Good news?" Audrey perked up. After the council meeting and what Lansius had revealed, she was desperate for some good words.

"It's so fitting that you're the one who asked that, my lady. The good news concerns you."

Audrey furrowed her brow and looked at Lansius, who said, "Do share this good news, Sir Morton."

Instead of speaking, Morton produced a letter from his small bag. Sigmund, who was nearby, took it and handed it to Lord Lansius.

"This matter might best be discussed in the utmost privacy," Morton suggested.

Breaking the wax seal, Lansius read the brief contents, his eyes widening. Without a word, he passed the letter to Audrey, who had a similar reaction.

Enough distance separated them from their guest for a whispered conversation, so Lansius leaned toward Audrey. "Does this make sense to you?"

"Lans, I can protect myself. You should leave. If he means ill, the others can charge in while I defend myself," she whispered back.

"No, I'll stay. It's not as if I'm unarmed." He met her gaze and added, "If he attacks me, you can flank him."

Audrey nodded. They had discussed this beforehand. Sir Justin, Roger, and Carla, along with select knights, were fully armed and waiting in the corridor. Although Lansius personally trusted Lord Jorge, he wasn't foolish enough not to take precautions against a Mage Knight.

"Very well. Sigmund, leave us," Lansius commanded, his voice stern enough that Sigmund didn't question him.

Sigmund led the remaining guards away but left the door ajar.

"May I approach?" Sir Morton inquired.

Audrey gestured for him to come closer. Morton advanced cautiously and then knelt, possibly to demonstrate he meant no harm.

"Is this true?" Lansius asked regarding the content of the letter.

"I have no reason to lie." The Mage Knight smiled, his expression contrasting with the threatening air around him. "Apart from you, my lady, during the banquet held outside the city wall to celebrate your marriage, I also noticed your cup-bearer and her younger sister. Both possess the gifts."

This revelation left Lansius stunned.

The rarest gift of them all. The gift of magic.

It was something even he did not possess.

"For three candidates to be found in a faraway town in Lowlandia—that's not an insignificant boon. Perhaps it's a blessing from the Ancients."

Audrey shifted in her seat. "I have a mage friend in Midlandia. She said I don't have the gift of magic."

Sir Morton furrowed his brows. "My lady, that's impossible. You exude a faint but unmistakable energy. I've seen it clearly since we first met in that tent outside the forest. Plus, you have the hunter's eyes."

"Explain what 'the eyes' mean. People seem to refer to it by many names," Lansius interrupted.

Morton pondered for a bit, trying to come up with a condensed answer. "People say that a good hunter acquires the eyes through hard training, but it's the other way around. Good hunters are born with the eyes. Without them, one couldn't survive the gaze of a fell beast."

Audrey trembled at the revelation.

Morton continued. "While they would blatantly refute this, mage and hunter skills are overlapped. We draw from the same power but manifested differently."

"Does every hunter have eyes like mine?"

"Only the top ones, those who are assigned to hunt fell beasts."

"But the one I met said otherwise. He implied it's just a skill," said Audrey, frustrated.

Sir Morton scoffed. "They would never divulge their secret. This information is my gift to you," he said with pride. "Now you know the secret. My lady, you're born a hunter and mage."

Audrey mumbled something inaudible and looked upset over something.

Lansius was wary but asked, "Does this mean she can wield magic?"

"For my lady's case, becoming a fully fledged mage may be out of reach. However, there should be a way for her to learn an ability or two. I won't be the one to teach her, but if you permit me, I'll write to my guild. They'll likely be interested and can send someone more discreet."

Lansius took a deep breath and looked at Audrey. The news, coming just a day before they were leaving Korelia, had stunned them both. Sir Stan and Hannei had always said Audrey's abilities were nothing more than the hunter's skill. Now it seemed she was more than that. This made them question their trust in Lord Bengrieve, Sir Stan, Hannei, and maybe even Calub.

Is this the reason Bengrieve saved and treated her so well? But for a man like him, who probably has a dozen mages or so, why is Audrey so special?

Sensing his attention, Audrey snapped out of her thoughts, took a deep breath, and relaxed her stance.

Then Lansius recalled something and shifted his gaze back to Morton. "You said *for her case?*"

"Unfortunately, your cup-bearer's gift has faded. It's likely that she never had much to begin with. Training her would be impossible. But her sister is another matter." Morton paused to gauge the lord's response.

Seeing no reaction, he continued. "I'd like to take her as my apprentice and keep it discreet. I'll even marry her if need be, to avoid gossip. I shall return her a mage within several years. In exchange, I ask that you forgo the ransom for several Black Knights close to me."

Audrey bit her lip, while Lansius felt torn, not over the ransom, but for another, graver reason. "Sir Morton, I'm honored by the offer, but there are several problems . . . the largest being that their father was one of the knights you killed."

CHAPTER 44

THE WHISPERS IN THE WIND

Audrey

After the meeting with Sir Morton, Audrey finally understood why Isolte, her Knight Master, had chosen her—a scrawny little servant from the outskirts of Elandia. She had assumed it was because she was born Centurian.

Located where the old capital of the first Imperium used to be, Centuria was worlds apart from the eastern part of the Imperium. Its people considered themselves more cultured than the rest of the human realm. The Centurians were reserved in attitude, never expressed disapproval directly, and were considered more courteous.

Little Stephania was anything but that. So, for her first year with Isolte, she held back from being herself. She tried to become the perfect Centurian girl: reserved, diligent, and unquestioning. Until one day, Isolte told her she was too stuck up.

Hearing that, Stefi dropped her facade, surprising Isolte with her brash and daring attitude. It was a fond memory that still warmed her heart. However, she now understood that Isolte had chosen her solely for her inborn power.

She had thought their special relationship, her hard work, and trust had led Isolte to make her an esquire. But now, knowing that Isolte could see her *gifts*, their relationship felt superficial and hollow.

"Talk to me, Drey," Lansius said as Margo closed the door, leaving them alone in the small hall next to their bedchamber.

"It's Isolte," Audrey replied, sitting on the daybed. "I thought she chose me not for something I was born with."

Lansius sat beside her. "But your eyes are part of you."

"I didn't want them. I hate them. Every kid hated me. My uncle hated me. And the various masters I've served never let me work in the main house, only in the barn," she said bitterly.

"Drey, that doesn't make what your Knight Master did for you any less valuable. She simply never had the opportunity to explain her reasons."

Audrey took a deep breath and rose, walking to the window to let the breeze calm her. After a moment, she glanced at Lansius. "You're right. It's foolish to linger on or blame her for this. She met an untimely end. That's all."

Her eyes narrowed as another thought crossed her mind. "But what about Hannei, or that hunter Sir Stan invited?"

Her question led Lansius to massage his temples. The loss of trust was clearly bothering him.

"There are always layers of secrecy in Toruna," Lansius replied after a while.

Audrey sighed, anger and frustration welling inside. "Too bad we can't confront them," she muttered.

"We don't need to," Lansius responded. "It's fortunate that Sir Morton exercised such caution. We can keep this matter under wraps. They have their secrets. Now we have ours."

Lansius – Small Council Chamber

"No, I'm coming and that's final," said Audrey, placing her hands on the table.

"Somebody needs to lead Korelia," Lansius argued as calmly as he could.

Audrey looked at the other three council members and insisted, "Sir Justin, Calub, or Cecile can handle that."

The trio shifted uncomfortably in their seats. Trying to keep the atmosphere from growing more tense, Lansius spoke in a half-pleading tone. "They're not the lord of the castle. But you are the baroness."

"I'm sure the marshal holds high enough a rank," Audrey retorted.

Sir Justin shook his head. "I'd rather handle the war business. Though I may not possess your war acumen, my lord, I believe I'm competent enough to execute whatever plan you may have."

Lansius drew a sharp breath. "The problem is, there's no plan. I must go and see for myself. At best, I've only got a diversion. Besides, Korelia is at even greater risk. I need capable people here, and you three are the best I've got to prevent riots."

Lansius noted how the weight of responsibility made the three slump in their seats.

Calub cleared his throat. "Sir Justin, I believe you have something to say about your mercenary friend?"

"Oh, right," Sir Justin said, his enthusiasm returning. "My lord, I was thinking of inviting more of my Arvenian allies into Korelia. Men-at-arms and cavalry."

"As long as they're loyal. But won't that put us in competition with Lord Arte?"

Sir Justin paused for a moment before answering. "My lord, not all Arvenians wish to return to Arvena. Given the current situation, many are looking to start anew, even in far-off places like Lowlandia." Breaking a smile, he added, "Many are inspired by you, who made a name for yourself."

Lansius was rather stunned. "Inspired by me?"

"That is correct. You're a rising star, and everyone wants to align themselves with you," Sir Justin replied, his tone proud, as if he were an older brother to Lansius.

Calub added, "I believe this is also why Lord Jorge and Lord Robert are competing to gain your trust, as are the guildsmen I've worked with. Even Tribesman Batu understands that."

Nodding, Lansius slowly realized how his rising fame was starting to make a difference.

"That's why you can't afford to lose, my lord," warned Cecile cautiously. "A loss would undo all of this. Please reconsider your strategy for Korimor."

"She's right," Audrey pointed out. "In the end, Nicopola and Umberland are not your responsibility."

Lansius sat there in silence, reevaluating his choices. Only afterward did he lean back in his chair and say, "There's no other way. I fear that more Nicopolans will move through Umberland, and while Korelia may remain safe, the entire east of Lowlandia might destabilize. It'll invite new power and ruin our chance of peace."

His words put his top retinue in check, but the baroness wasn't backing down. "So be it," she said firmly. "Cecile, please tell Dietrich to prepare the light cavalry."

Cecile, without hesitation, rose and headed for the door.

Lansius opened his mouth to speak, but Audrey cut him off. "You promised."

Fighting off his guilt, Lansius tried to reason, "Please, be reas—"

Audrey cut him off again. "Also, I'm pregnant."

"What—WHAT?" Lansius shot up from his seat, his knee hitting the table. The pain was only eclipsed by his shock.

Even Cecile stopped at the door and turned around, her expression one of surprise. Lansius glanced at her, and she quickly shook her head, signaling she had not been aware of this.

Calub and Sir Justin sat awkwardly, exchanging glances. Normally they would offer congratulations, but the situation was far from normal.

"I don't want to raise my child alone," Audrey said nervously with cheeks flushed.

"But how? You haven't even had your period this year," Lansius asked, wincing from the pain but still in disbelief.

"Tsk—" Audrey clicked her tongue again.

Cecile snorted, Calub coughed awkwardly, and Sir Justin turned to look out the window, suppressing a laugh.

Eh?

Lansius looked back at Audrey, who was avoiding his gaze and whistling nervously.

"Youuu!" he growled after realizing the lie. Instead of blowing up, he felt drained and sank back into his padded chair.

I give up . . .

There was nothing that could restrain Audrey from exercising her authority in Korelia. As a baroness and captain, she could easily assemble her forces and follow him to Korimor. "Fine, if you're that stubborn, you can come," he relented.

"Alright!" Audrey slapped the table as if sealing a deal.

Lansius rubbed his temples and said, "Promise me never to do that again."

"I promise," Audrey softened, grinning broadly. "The next time you hear it, it will be real."

The mood in the chamber improved drastically, and Calub seized the opportunity to excuse himself. "If you'll excuse me, my lord, lady, and sir, I need to double-check the supplies for the campaign."

"Gratitude, for the efforts," Lansius responded.

Calub looked at Lansius with a hint of worry but said nothing. Turning to Cecile, his fiancée, he offered a warm smile. "You should stay. I'll pass the word to Dietrich."

"Gratitude. Wear your hat out there; it's hot," Cecile replied, holding the door open for him.

"Will do," said Calub, exiting the chamber.

Turning back to business, Lansius continued, "Cecile, since I'll be away, could you write a letter for me?"

"Yes, my lord." Cecile retrieved a quill pen, ink, and parchment.

Lansius had promoted Cecile to chamberlain due to her growing competence and his trust in her. Like her father, she had a knack for reading people, catching subtle gestures and unspoken cues.

Although Calub never officially held the position of chamberlain, Cecile was taking over the bulk of his job. What remained was the treasurer role. The transition had been smooth, possibly due to their abilities or their close relationship.

While it wasn't good practice to employ husband and wife, Lansius was so out of talent that he had no other option. Only now did he understand why nepotism was so prevalent in medieval times.

When Cecile was ready with the ink, quill pen, and parchment, Lansius dictated a letter to a guild in Midlandia, outlining his purchase order for the first two prototypes of spinning wheels.

Despite the crisis, he couldn't abandon his project. Developing, improving, and maturing a design requires a significant amount of time. When peace ever arrived, he wanted this to be ready.

Soon, the letter was completed. Lansius promptly placed his hands on the table and addressed the room. "May I have your attention," he began. "Tomorrow, after meeting with the two lords, I will lead the remaining cavalry to Korimor. I'll rendezvous with Sir Harold to try to secure the area. Stay vigilant for trouble, both external and internal."

Lansius looked at each of them and saw nods of agreement. "Sir Justin, while I'm away, your priority is to maintain peace among the captured men and the forced laborers. To ease your burden, I'll take a dozen of them who have shown a willingness to switch sides."

He then turned to Cecile, adopting a more solemn tone. "If food becomes an issue—as we're unlikely to have a good harvest—feel free to order more grain. Lastly, please look after Lady Felicity."

After concluding the council meeting, Lansius noticed Audrey conversing with Cecile and Calub. He realized she wasn't usually this obstinate.

Is it a wife's intuition?

He felt the urge to intensify his preparations. Korimor could be far worse than he had imagined.

As Lansius had expected, his plan to lead a small reinforcement to Korimor came as no surprise. Furthermore, the two lords had been in Korelia for an extended period and were quite ready to return home.

Soon, Lansius received word that the two lords had decided to return the following day, likely to avoid the appearance of trying to occupy Korelia in his absence.

What he hadn't expected was a request from Lord Jorge. The Lord of Three Hills expressed his desire to tour the castle before departing from Korelia, and Lansius was happy to oblige.

He instructed Cecile to gather the old staff, many of whom still held fond memories of Lord Jorge and his family. With time running short, he then sent a rider to invite Lord Jorge to visit.

Accompanied by several horsemen, Lord Jorge rode to the castle. Upon arrival, only one knight, one squire, and a servant followed him inside. "It is very gracious of you to let me walk around the castle," the dashing guest in full regalia remarked.

"Please, the castle is yours, my lord," Lansius replied as they strolled through the century-old corridors.

"Don't address me like that. I consider myself your peer," Jorge said, clearly amused.

"I can't do that, my lord. I'm merely a vagabond borrowing your castle," quipped Lansius.

Jorge chuckled at the jest and paused at an old stone column. "The castle feels larger in my memory. Now, even the corridors seem narrow, and the courtyard small," he commented nostalgically.

Lansius could only nod in agreement.

"You would do well to enlarge this castle or perhaps build a bigger one," Jorge suggested.

"I have plans to build a keep on the east side," Lansius revealed. "When it's finished, perhaps I should return this one to its rightful master."

Jorge grinned at the offer. "This castle used to be my cradle, so I have some fond memories, but I won't let my whimsical wish cause trouble." Grabbing Lansius by the hand, he led him through the castle in a role reversal. With help from the old staff, they even found some hidden keepsakes from Jorge's childhood.

Lansius felt a camaraderie with Jorge. Both were young leaders, burdened with immense responsibilities, striving to bring order and prosperity to their respective realms. There were matters only they, as lords of men, could discuss.

In this regard, Jorge treated Lansius as if he were a cousin, and Lansius hoped that this could serve as a solid foundation for their alliance.

As they were winding down in the Great Chamber, a messenger arrived, escorted by Sigmund. The messenger handed over a sealed letter in a cylindrical wood container.

A squire in Lord Jorge's entourage accepted the letter and handed it to him.

"What's this?" Jorge inquired, reading the letter from Three Hills and quickly dismissing it. "Ah, this nonsense again."

"May I know what the tidings are?" Lansius asked.

"It's silly, bordering on seditious," said Jorge. "It's unbelievable how even my family in the capital is spouting unfounded rumors from the streets."

Lansius listened seriously, and Jorge took notice.

"It's not worth your time, but if you're interested . . ." He offered the letter to Lansius.

Lansius took the coarse paper and read the first part: *The Ageless One is dead*, followed by other events that supposedly served as evidence. Some of the details were more convincing than Hannei's last warning. He folded the letter and gave it back to Jorge. "It's disturbing if true . . ."

"Indeed, but there might be some truth to it," Jorge's tone changed, now certain that Lansius was already aware of the issue.

"How so?" asked Lansius.

"In his previous letter, my nephew mentioned some unsettling changes in the capital. Ranking people went missing without a trace. Some even spoke of assassins."

"It seems we're living in dangerous times." Lansius sighed at the grim news.

"Even for Lowlandians like me, this is starting to reek of the end of the Imperium," said Jorge with a hint of frustration in his voice.

Lansius leaned back in his seat. "We don't have the power to intervene in the conflict. Not even Midlandia is that powerful. However, we can make Lowlandia a haven for our people."

Jorge nodded and raised his goblet without saying anything. Lansius followed, and both drank their goblets in silence.

"When will you depart?" Jorge asked.

"Tomorrow, as soon as my preparations are done."

Jorge mulled and promised, "After I've reached Three Hills, I'll send my men to Umberland to see the situation. I'll also post a messenger to link up with you in Korimor. While my troops are exhausted, I could still muster several hundred men-at-arms if you wish to use them."

"Gratitude, but don't let your guard down. Keep Sir Morton close at all times," Lansius advised.

Jorge nodded, and the two lords continued their conversation. As the sun began to wane, Jorge declined the invitation for supper in the castle, preferring the company of his men.

As Jorge rode back to his camp with his entourage, Lansius couldn't help but think about the weight of the rumors that had possibly spread to Elandia and Tiberia. Now, with threats at the border, feuding nobles, famine, and the death of the emperor, the continuation of the Imperium seemed unlikely.

Lansius shuddered as the red sunset cast its glow over the entire western plains of Korelia. His entourage formed around him, shielding their lord and champion who would leave them the next day.

Without Lansius, many were worried about the fate of Korelia. So much was at stake, and pessimism grew, worries that the glory days were already fleeting and an age of strife was returning.

CHAPTER 45

TARRACAN MAN

The day had yet to grow hot when a formation of men assembled just outside Korelia. Lord Jorge led the formation, flanked by a modest number of cavalry. The horses had been either ransomed or loaned from Korelia, all backed by Lord Jorge's guarantee.

Lord Robert was also present, leading his smaller cavalry at some distance. The sight was impressive if not grand. The last time these forces had assembled here, they had been enemies. Now, they were allies.

"My lords, the success of our grand plan rests with your return in spring," Lansius said as they met in front of their armies.

"I shall return," Robert declared firmly. "Even if I have to drag my wife with me, I will be back next spring."

"Same as the Lion. I'll bring my family here—no dragging necessary," Jorge added, matching Robert's enthusiasm.

Both chuckled at their shared jest.

"I'll arrange for the city inns to accommodate your families," Lansius offered, grateful for their support. "I'll even look into renovating the castle and the Eastern Mansion in case the inns aren't sufficient."

Robert nodded, pleased with the offered hospitality. "Lord Lansius, I don't have anyone to spare but a few knights, but you may take Sir Michael and his men under your command."

"Gratitude, for your support," replied Lansius.

"Well, then," Robert said, addressing the two younger men. "Until we meet again next year. May fortune favor you both."

"And may good health and fortune accompany you as well, Lord Robert," Lansius returned.

"Stay strong, Old Lion. This alliance needs to happen," urged Jorge.

"Aye, I have no plans to die just yet. In fact, I feel rejuvenated," the older lord quipped, delighting the other two. He then summoned his escort and mounted his horse. "If Korelia faces trouble, send word to White Lake. I'll organize a relief somehow."

"Your concern is much appreciated, Lord Robert." Lansius bowed his head a little.

Without another word but a smile, Robert and his cavalry rode toward the City of Korelia, intending to pass through its main streets, cross the bridge, and move through the developing eastern region before heading east toward their own territory.

"I should make haste," Jorge told Lansius.

"Indeed, the sun grows hotter."

Jorge signaled his squire, who in turn called the coachman. The carriage, a gift promised by Lansius, approached.

"Lord Lansius, I'll hold up my end of the bargain for Umberland. And remember, you can count on Three Hills if you ever need a place for refuge."

"I will keep that in mind," Lansius assured him.

Jorge entered the carriage, and his entourage assumed their positions. "Please send my regards to the Baroness of Korimor," he said with a polite smile. The carriage then departed, and Jorge rejoined his army, marching westward through the Great Plains.

The Three Hills forces had recovered many of their men by staying in Korelia and flying their banner high. A large number of captured men from Three Hills had also been freed, although their weapons and armor were confiscated.

Evading capture, more than a dozen knights and squires from South Hill bent the knee to Lord Jorge, bolstering his ranks. Now, at least a thousand men marched under his banner.

While the number was substantial, unfortunately, only two dozen had their horses, and Jorge needed them as escorts. Meanwhile, Lansius required speed and couldn't afford to take slow-moving footmen with him to Korimor, especially with the harvest season closing in fast. Thus, despite the potential aid available, Lansius couldn't utilize it.

The sky had clouded over when Lansius and his escorts returned to the castle to finalize their preparations.

As the sky began its vibrant descent into hues of orange and pink, Lansius stood at the edge of the castle battlements, his eyes set upon the vast expanse of the Great Plains of Lowlandia. The wind blew in from the west, due to the sudden temperature change, but he remained quiet, his mind focused on the impending journey and battle that lay ahead.

Beside him, his wife Audrey leaned against the stone wall, her gaze firmly fixed on the fading beauty of the sun.

"That's our guide," she commented, just before the guards on the lookout made a small commotion while pointing to the west.

Lansius didn't respond but watched as ten horsemen leading fifty horses approached Korelia. Tapping the stone wall and feeling its sturdiness despite its age, Lansius drew a deep breath. "Shall we go then?" he asked her, offering his arm.

Audrey smiled, took his arm, and squeezed it gently. The two descended, and their staff flocked toward them. Solemnity, fear, and nervousness were evident on their faces, but Lansius stood firm and unburdened.

"If only you would let me ride in a carriage to Korimor," said Felis to Lansius, staring with her deep blue eyes.

Lansius smiled at his trusted blonde friend, whose uncanny luck had likely played a role in his success. "Unfortunately, haste is necessary this time. Please take care, Lady Felis."

She nodded, then whispered, "Be good to your wife, or I'll send Hannei to ruin your life."

Lansius coughed at the unexpected threat, while Audrey sported a nervous smirk.

Next, Lansius met with Sir Justin and Calub. "I'll send word when I'm able, and we'll reconvene in the fall or spring."

"I'll also send reports periodically, but be warned—I've never commanded a city before," said the marshal.

"Governed," corrected Calub, and the three chuckled. One by one, they clasped hands, offering Lansius good wishes and some advice for the journey ahead. Similarly, Felis and Cecile embraced Audrey with sisterly affection.

Outside, the city's people gathered to catch a glimpse of their departing leaders. As the sun dipped lower, Korelia seemed to lose a part of its brilliance, mirroring the departure of its twin stars as they prepared to embark on a perilous journey.

The lord and lady, accompanied by Dietrich, Sigmund, Carla, the captive Omin, and a small contingent of thirty cavalrymen and squires, set out from Korelia. Despite the risks of bringing Omin, his presence was necessary to ensure a smooth transfer of power and to minimize resistance from his House.

Lansius needed Korimor's submission before they could redirect their efforts against the threat from the Nicopolans.

To cover the greatest distance, they chose to travel at night, hoping to double the range without fear of the summer sun. They were prepared to eat lightly and rest during the heat of the day. Each rider, carrying only the essentials in saddlebags, brought along five spare horses. They rotated these horses regularly to maintain their stamina throughout the long journey.

The lanterns the guides carried would be their guidance, and the stars in the sky their only illumination.

Nicopolan Armed Group

Sergio the Tarracan visited the tent where he had secured a cage from a slaver compound he had pillaged. Inside the small cage sat a lady in gray, ragged clothes—a disguise. As Sergio entered, she opened her eyes, giving him a look that seemed both to judge him and remonstrate against his presence.

This woman had nearly incited fighting among the Nicopolan group Sergio had brought from Nicopola. Fortunately, one of Sergio's lieutenants caught wind of her schemes.

"Lady Daniella," Sergio addressed her while she stared at him. "You'll be pleased to know that the group you've been talking to are rotting in the sun as we speak. A human body can only endure so much."

"It's a shame, but many more will take their place. Next time, we won't be caught," Daniella retorted fearlessly, despite clearly being parched. She had been given only a bowl of watered-down gruel once a day.

Sergio chuckled at her audacity and knelt. "I've heard you haven't begged for food, but I think in a few days, you will . . ." His words trailed off as he rose with a taunting smile, unobscured by facial hair.

As he was about to leave, she warned him, "Your plan in Korimor will not work. You'll only lead everyone to their deaths."

Sergio turned around and raised his voice. "Foolish woman! I have led them through the raging Central Nicopola, across the steep mountain paths of Umberland, and into this fertile land, all the while ensuring everyone had enough to eat. Who else can do that?"

"Obviously, any brigand with an army of hungry men could! You simply took food away from towns and villages along your path and left them with nothing to eat. What's so surprising about that?" she said, venting her anger.

"High words from mercenaries like you!" he exclaimed. "I challenge any man or woman, nobles even, to do better than me. But where are they?" He spread his tanned arms wide in a gesture of challenge. "None are here. Why? A noble wouldn't waste time on thousands of hungry peasants, just like your new lord. He'll bide his time until we depart. But we won't!"

"You don't even understand the logistics of feeding this many people," she retorted sharply. "Your faith is misplaced; there's not enough food in Korimor, even if you harvest everything."

"You'll learn that I'm not only as competent but also more benevolent than any noble. In time, you'll come to respect my authority over these Nicopolans and even try to convince your friends in that castle to leave the city."

Daniella offered no response, and Sergio left in frustration.

He was barely ten feet away from the tent when his men approached him. One whispered, "Sergio, it's getting harder to raid for food. By tomorrow, we'll have nothing for the refugees."

"Take the usual amount from our stockpile and mix some gray meat with horse meat for tomorrow's soup, but do it out of sight," Sergio replied. He needed the refugees to pressure the city into surrendering.

"But what about us?" another asked. "We haven't had bread for days, just watery gruel. Can't we take more from the stockpile?"

"Patience, men," Sergio said, placing his hand on the man's shoulder. "Haven't you smelled the sweet fragrance of the bakery from the city in the morning? We shall have them soon enough."

Sergio noticed the doubt lingering on his men's faces, so he added, "Kill the thought that there's a better solution. Korimor is our best bet. Three Hills will be well-defended. Korelia and South Hill are too distant, and they don't have a good harvest."

His men began to nod.

"Let's stick to the plan and hold for another month so we can let the refugees harvest the farm for us. I'm sure whoever is inside won't be able to hold out much longer, especially once they see us harvesting. Then we can move in, secure the city and the castle for the winter, and assume our roles as overlords. Don't you want to become a squire or a knight?"

Sergio's words began to inspire his men.

"Don't you want a land of your own and laborers to call you master? I can give you all of that if you have the courage to hold out. Things will improve after the harvest." As usual, Sergio's charisma and persuasion won them over.

Sergio had always dreamed of joining a mercenary company. Unable to join due to multiple rejections based on his background, he aimed to start his own free company instead and succeeded amid the outbreak of the Nicopolan crisis. While for many these were times of great sadness and tragedy, for Sergio it was a time of opportunity.

Korimor would be the crowning jewel of his achievements. Convinced that all he needed was to wait for the harvest season, he was sure the crops from the fields around Korimor would be enough for his men. When that time came, the city would probably give up, since they couldn't last without the harvest.

When that happened, Sergio planned to offer them a fair deal, one he intended to honor until a sufficient number of his men and refugees had entered the town. While he had no qualms with the Korimor people, when he had to reduce the number of mouths to feed, he would certainly favor his followers.

Sergio planned to push the Korimor people to attack another barony for food and shelter. Even if they failed, it wouldn't matter to him. Moreover, it would even assert his power as Lowlandia's newest powerhouse.

Michael

After finishing with his administrative duties, the one-eyed knight sat on the battlement. Despite the heat, he insisted on sitting there, a wicker hat his only protection against the sun. He was there to signal his small reaction force should he spot any signs of an escape attempt by Daniella and her group.

Michael kept blaming himself for letting her infiltrate the Nicopolans with just a handful of her men. Now she was captured, and he had no means of rescuing her.

The enemy was more cunning and able than they appeared. The Nicopolans held their ground despite several harassing attacks from Hugo and Michael's cavalry. The Nicopolan strategy relied on concealing their troops behind refugees and using the elderly and children to impede any attacks on their formation.

The Korelian small cavalry was both exhausted and horrified, forced to trample and kill innocents before even engaging the enemy's main force. Worse, by now they couldn't risk another attack, as the Nicopolan numbers had swelled. Initially numbering three thousand, their ranks had grown to an estimated six or seven thousand.

Now, their cavalry, bolstered by the nomads, was sufficient only to deter the Nicopolans from attacking the rest of the nearby settlements, which had become an increasingly reliable source of food and medicine.

"The odds are not looking good at all," he mumbled to himself.

Today the sun had almost set, and things seemed eerily peaceful. There was no turmoil in the enemy camp, no ruckus—meaning no escape attempt from Daniella.

Michael sighed. It had been a week since her capture. He knew Daniella was alive; the enemy kept pestering them for a meeting. A meeting they couldn't entertain, for the Nicopolan demands required the Korelian forces to abandon the city.

Such demands filled the Korimor people with suspicion. Even inside the city walls, the situation remained precarious.

Food rationing had soured everyone's mood. The populace was lethargic, anxious about the fate of their harvest, now in the hands of the Nicopolans. Harvest time was just a month away, and if plundered, many would perish in the upcoming winter.

As a precaution against internal strife, Hugo and Michael had barricaded many entrances to the castle, leaving only the main gate open. They prepared for the possibility of fighting enemies from without and within and had stockpiled all their supplies within the castle.

Michael knew that despite their surrender, the Korimor people had little trust in them. The only thing binding them together now was a common enemy and the belief that the Korelians were the lesser of two evils.

Fortunately, both sides feared the nomads who still roamed freely outside, leading to a stalemate. The Nicopolans couldn't lay siege, fearing a rear attack by the nomads if they committed.

The Korimor people, along with the Korelian force, were trapped inside, unable to face the massive force outside. Meanwhile, the nomads, mainly composed of children and the elderly, could do little but keep their distance.

The rhythmic footsteps on the stones prompted Michael to turn his head.

"Anything new, Sir Michael?" inquired Hugo the deputy who, from the looks of it, had just been eating, as evidenced by the fat smudges on his thin mustache and lips, along with an aroma of ale.

"Only several public floggings over something. Couldn't make out the details; too distant," Michael replied.

"I see . . ." Hugo remarked, gazing into the distance at the enemy's camp. "Should we send a scout to investigate?"

"Already done. They'll be back after dark, though I doubt they'll learn anything useful."

Hugo nodded and commented, "These Nicopolans . . . It's remarkable how they manage to maintain order with so many untrained people."

"Their trust in that Tarracan Man is enviable," Michael mused.

"The one who feeds his followers with bread as sweet as nectar and honey," Hugo recited, echoing stories from captured men from earlier skirmishes. "Sir Michael, what is your take on such a man?"

"If that is true, then he is indeed a living legend and ought to be enshrined. Perhaps it would be best to confine him in a tower so he can continue producing that remarkable bread in peace, ensuring all of Lowlandia does not go hungry this winter."

Michael's jest elicited a chuckle from Hugo, though it too quickly faded. The atmosphere was too sour, too heavy, even for veterans like them.

As Hugo's gaze returned to the sweeping plains, Michael stood. "It's time to rotate the cavalry."

"Take a drink or two and some rest. I'll keep an eye out for Lady Daniella," offered Hugo.

"Gratitude, deputy."

"No need, I share the blame for allowing her . . ." Hints of bitterness were apparent in Hugo's voice.

Taking a deep breath, Michael headed toward the gatehouse, where he found cool shade and a squire who readily offered him a drink. He was about to descend the circular stone stairwell when Hugo's shout from the battlements halted him.

The one-eyed knight hurried back and saw Hugo pointing southward. Others hastened to the battlements for a better view.

Michael followed Hugo's gaze and beheld a towering cloud of dust rising from the south. "From the south?" he whispered to himself, more a statement than a question. An experienced cavalryman from White Lake, like him, knew such a cloud was raised by hundreds, perhaps thousands of horsemen.

The swirling dust continued to obscure the finer details, yet the vastness of the disturbance unmistakably heralded the coming of a massive cavalry force.

Excitement rippled through the ranks as men beckoned their comrades to witness the sight. Along Korimor's southern wall, eyes were fixed on the emerging spectacle.

"Look, our nomads have noticed and are reacting," a squire blurted out excitedly.

The advancing force appeared as a mirage beneath the blazing sun.

Michael continued to ponder. He had no clue who in Lowlandia could muster such power, or why they were in Korimor at this time. Meanwhile, among the Korelians, speculation pointed to one name alone.

"It's only been ten days since I sent the letter. This is impossible," Hugo said, shaking his head.

Michael shared his skepticism, but as if to mock their doubts, the unmistakable blue and bronze banner appeared proudly on the horizon. Its bold and striking colors finally cut through the dust clouds as the galloping horsemen trod upon the green pasture of Korimor.

"The lord's personal banner!" erupted from many throats at once, cheering wildly in recognition. The cheers grew louder as hundreds, if not a thousand, horsemen appeared out of the swirling dust, their warhorses thundering across the landscape.

Confirming it with his own eye, Michael clenched his fist and pounded the wall in a burst of excitement, a large grin spreading across his lips. Meanwhile, Hugo and his men shouted the nomad's war cries, jubilant beyond measure.

Almost instantaneously, news of the reinforcements spread like wildfire, galvanizing every member of the Korelian force and drawing the gaze of all within the city.

Initially, people thought the Korelians had gone mad, but soon the excitement caught on, spreading rapidly. Before long, everyone in Korimor heard of what was happening outside the walls. Faster than anyone could have predicted and ever unpredictable, the Lord of Korelia had arrived.

ABOUT THE AUTHOR

Hanne is the author of the Horizon of War isekai series, originally released on Royal Road. An avid reader and writer, her "realistic" fantasy stories feature historical details with military-grade accuracy (i.e., gambesons, poleaxes, logistics, and all the intricacies of the feudal nobility).

DISCOVER
STORIES UNBOUND

PodiumAudio.com